# MULBERRY BEND: AISLING'S STORY

## LADIES OF MISCHIEF #3

### KAREN DEAN BENSON

Dear Judy,
I hope you enjoy
Aisling's Story
❤

Karen Dean
Benson

MULBERRY BEND: AISLING'S STORY
Copyright © 2016-2018 by Karen Dean Benson

ISBN: 978-1-68046-374-3

Published by Satin Romance
An Imprint of Melange Books, LLC
White Bear Lake, MN 55110
www.satinromance.com

Published in the United States of America.

Cover Design by Mad Cat Designs www.madcatdesigns.net

*To my brothers, Michael, Patrick and Brian; and our father, Earl Eugene (Mickey) Benson, I dedicate Mulberry Bend.*

*This story is hardly a brush stroke on the canvas of Irish immigration. Our father's reticence to talk about our Irish ancestry, kept us from knowledge of a rich heritage. We did discover that several generations previously our ancestors were O'Bannon, not Benson. And, our father did sing to us when we were little, he paraphrased the lyrics from McNamara's Band.*

*Oh, me name is Mickey Benson, I'm the leader of the band,*
*Me sons are Michael, Patrick, and Brian*
*Me daughter's Karen Ann.*
*The concert of the horns and fifes surely make for jiggin'*
*Come along little legs with your kickin' and leapin'.*

# ACKNOWLEDGMENTS

Dear friends, family, and critique partners, Karen Auriti, Judy Dickinson, Mary Margaret Ellis, Ruth Hartwig, Eileen Jackson, Doris Lemcke, Ginny Zimmer, and Sarah Zulewski. Your willingness to read and patience to listen assists in creating this world. I also owe a debt of gratitude to a great circle of friends who lent their ear as I hashed out this or that.

Nancy Schumacher, Caroline Andrus, and Shelley Schmidt, at Melange Books continue to make my dreams happen.

My brother Brian, Corporal Benson of the 4th Michigan Reenactment Infantry of the Civil War (Company I), provided me with historical perspective gained from his years of reenacting.

Aisling and I are grateful. Thank you, thank you, thank you, and God Bless! As always, dearest Charlie hugs and love.

The cover is significant in that Bow Bridge is the first cast-iron bridge in Central Park (and the second oldest in America). The bridge was built between 1859-1862.

Bow Bridge, named for its graceful shape, is reminiscent of the bow of an archer or violinist. This handsomely designed bridge spans the lake, linking Cherry Hill with the woodland of the Ramble. I could not imagine a more romantic setting for Aisling and Kegan to stroll.

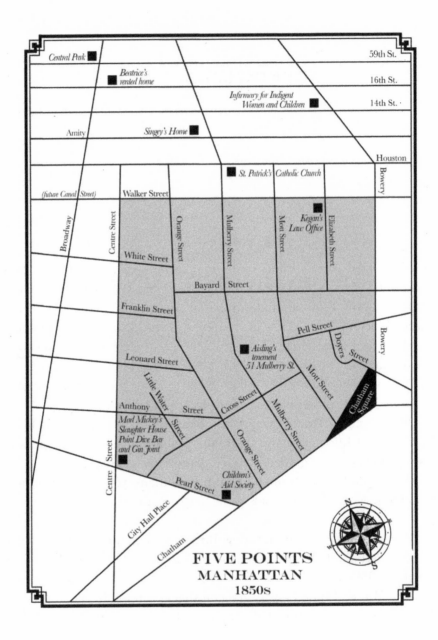

FIVE POINTS
MANHATTAN
1850s

# PART I

**June 1863 - October 1863**

# CHAPTER 1

**June 1863**
**Smythe Farm**
**Gettysburg, Pennsylvania**

*A*lan bent over the pitchfork laden with straw, carried it to the horse stall and scattered it about the floor. The roan, familiar with the worker, nickered, received a pat on the nose, and small talk. A fresh pail of water and oats to replenish the leather pouch completed the mare's needs.

Alan moved to the next stall and bent to chores, better than listening to the belligerent voices drifting from the loft where Mr. Smythe goaded, "A right upper. Faster. Harder."

A squeamish feeling grew at the thud of fist to flesh. "That's my boy. Watch his left." Mr. Smythe's two sons, Hector and Earl, in their late teens, worked the farm with their father, who boasted of money to earn with the skill of boxing. Men wore leather gloves and beat at each other until one fell to the floor, a bloody-pulp loser after the count of ten. The man standing earned the purse.

Grit and dust floated down as the sons beat on each other while circling the slatted floor above. Grunts and cuss words tangled with

3

beams of sunlight drifting through slim openings. Alan hated violence provoked by the father. How much longer before Mr. Smythe included his foster child in the game?

Mr. Smythe ended the fight. "Enough now. Save some for baling. Earl, you got the better of him again. You'll make my fortune, son."

Hector did not use the ladder; he jumped to the floor of the barn. Earl descended the steps with his dad following. Alan scooped up another load of straw, dropping it over the next stall. Ducking under the rope across the opening, Alan intended to become invisible until they left for the fields. Patting the bay's withers, he spread the bundle about the small space. A prickling sensation alerted him to the presence of another.

Hector's size took up the opening to the stall, hairy arms crossed his chest, large for eighteen, a full-grown man. A trickle of blood seeped down the side of his cheek from his forehead. His legs planted wide; a cold, flinty darkness sparked in his eyes. Alan knew the dangerous, brooding look. Every time Mr. Smythe forced such behavior on his two sons, Hector smoldered with anger.

He growled, "You about done?"

Alan shrugged.

"Follow me." Already the sign of swelling and redness spread across his cheek. Alan heard the father congratulate the younger brother, though Hector's balled fists were blood spattered with retaliation proving he got in a few punches.

Alan sensed the resentment and wrath and balked. "I've got chores. You know your da when I don't finish," he said, fists shoved defiantly under armpits.

Towering over the youth, Hector's open palm rammed against Alan's arms. Alan, stumbling backward, spread his arms wide gaining balance. Hector, shoved Alan in the chest, against the stall.

Unnatural silence hung in the moment. Shock registered on Hector's face as he glared at his open palm then at Alan's chest.

Every fiber of Alan's body was suddenly on alert. Stunned, wordlessly gaping at each other, Hector's lips moved, his startled voice rasped, "Yer a girlie." He thrust his palm once again on the little chest.

"I'll be damned six ways to hell, you got little ones, but you got 'em all righty."

Aisling couldn't find her voice. Her knees buckled, the wall supported her, kept her from escape, too. Hector's hawk eyes brightened appearing monstrous as blood trickled down his cheek.

She froze with the realization her disguise was over. He flexed his fists, jaw clenched, eyelids lowered over his keen assessment of the younger, smaller person. "Drop yer pants."

Her heart hammered. She opened her mouth to scream. His palm cupped her lower face in a death grip.

His other palm squeezed against the bib of her dungarees and the small mound of flesh beneath. "Little nibs, but they'll do." His brow touched hers. Spittle from his lips flicked over her face when he added, "You'll let me, or I'll tell." She squirmed, kicking his shins.

Mr. Smythe's voice boomed from the other end of the barn. "Hector. Where'd you get to?"

Aisling kneed Hector between the legs. His mouth popped as wide as his eyeballs bugged. It cost him not to yell. Groaning, his hold on her slackened, he could not ignore the summons from his da. Ham-like paws clasped his nether parts. He threw her a murderous glare. "We do this later, girlie. My da won't take kindly to your lie these past years. I'll tell him you been givin' me what I want all along. You ain't got no say on my land." His shoulder banged against the stall as he lumbered to his pa's summons.

She sank to the ground, a wild ringing in her ears. Gulping air, she could not quit shaking. Her mind sped over the tenuous hold on normalcy to the mess of her life. She had no control over her circumstance beyond the moment. Each day awaking on a pallet hidden behind a draped sheet at the end of the hallway, she faced her shadowy world. The length of cotton that shielded her privacy flapped at whim, like her life.

*A*isling O'Quinn was one of the orphan train children from a tenement in Five Points, Manhattan. Unlike the hordes of children who lived on the streets of the slum, she lived with her *máthair*. At a young age, she began dressing as a boy to walk the streets looking for work. A matron from the Children's Aid Society caught her shoving an apple in her pocket and demanded Aisling take her to her parents.

With the thief clutched firmly in hand, the matron confronted her *máthair* who was too weak to lift her head off the cot. Her voice so frail, she whispered, "Take my child to your sanctuary for two months, 'till I'm on my feet."

When the matron asked her name, Aisling spoke up. "Alan, ma'am. Alan O'Quinn." Her *máthair* was too weak to argue the point. What started out as blarney became fact. Lads had a way, lassies did not.

Arriving at the orphanage, a gang of others about her same size pressed against the walls, filling the corridor. There was an awful din of crying and shouting, arms clutching bundles. The sight mirrored what she must resemble only a hundred times more.

Women herded them into double lines, led them outside to a wagon ordering all to sit on the floor and make room for the rest. Aisling considered this an adventure; snuggled close to others most of whom were of somber nature. A second wagonload followed. She counted fifty-nine in her load. So many needing to be fed and bedded at night. Her *máthair* wanted this and she went willingly, though she would miss familiar folk on the streets. Her dearest *máthair*, all alone, could hardly use the pot by herself, let alone chew food. Aisling knew her parent's love and that comforted her knowing her *máthair* would eventually come for her.

Her *athair* had faded to a dim memory. A robust man, his brains were bashed by cudgels in a workers' strike at the meat packing plant when she was seven. Five brothers succumbed on the ship that brought them from Dublin to a new life, as her parents would say. A sudden fever grabbed the boys while crossing the great ocean. Blessed with a vial of holy water and shrouded, their bodies slid down a plank into the cold, black water; one by one, day after day, until all were gone. Half the immigrants on the boat gave way on that crossing from the motherland.

Shortly thereafter, before the ship arrived in America, her *máthair* birthed Aisling. Her name meant vision or dream in the Irish tongue. That is the love they had for their only daughter, and only child.

Aisling, jostled amongst the children in the wagon and wished she had not begun as a lad with the Children's Aid Society now that she would not be on the street seeking work. The wagons jolted to a stop; adults lowered the gate, helping them off. She lined up with the rest, clutching her bundle, wondering why they boarded a ferry to get to the orphanage. She'd never been on a ferry. Her nose twitched with the earthy scent of wet boats moored on the Hudson River, pungent ripe fish, coupled with the noise of bargemen shouting. The bustle was industrious taking all her curious attention.

A man, holding a list, checked each name as the next child stepped onto the first step. Some of the orphans ahead of her cried and balked. Glancing at the line behind, Aisling stepped aside. One of the matrons grabbed her arm. "Where do you think you're headed, laddie?"

"I'm not getting on the boat." She jerked her arm out of the woman's grip.

"You most certainly are." The matron clutched her jacket, pulling her close. "The papers all signed. You're going to a better life."

She yanked herself out of the grasp. "My *máthair* said two months."

"She put you in our care, didn't she? What is your name? I'll check." She loosened her hold and some of Aisling's fear quieted. By this time, her place in line reached the man with the list.

"Do you have Alan on your list, sir," the matron asked.

His finger slid down the page then stopped. "O'Quinn?"

Aisling nodded.

"Step lively, son. We've a long line behind ye." The woman grabbed hold of Aisling's arm hoisting her up, then moved her along the aisle; together they sat on a bench. Her clutch firm, there would be no escaping. Aisling's grew mulish. Once across the Hudson River, the ferry ride ended. In a double line, they walked to a train and boarded to places unknown. The days passed much like the one before, like the snap of fingers, she became one of the orphan train children headed to places away from New York City. Silt from the engine drifted in the windows as dreams of her *máthair* and their one-room home dissolved into thin air.

Depot after depot, the orphans paraded in a line on the platforms until all families had taken the orphan they wanted. She lasted to the end, sullen, grieving all the way to Gettysburg, Pennsylvania.

At each train station, their numbers dwindled as strangers paraded up and down the boardwalk looking them over. Like shopping for bread or fruit, they squeezed to see how fresh and plump. The matron, and a man from the Children's Aid Society, warned they should smile and look the families in the eye, especially the mothers and fathers. Be quick with yes sir, yes missus. Aisling refused to conform; her heart belonged with her *máthair*. She was not adoptable; she already had a family. The O'Quinn's from Fingal, Ireland, and Five Points, even though just she and her *máthair* were all that remained.

Stubbornness brought her to the end of the line with six girls in dresses and no one interested in fostering her. Her sullen demeanor grew. She refused to yes sir and no sir to the folks expecting to take her. She assumed the leftovers would return to New York City. She intended to be a leftover.

A husband, wife, young daughter, and two sons slipped their mocking gaze over her. It was clear the dad thought her small for a lad, the instant his hard gaze flicked over her. He wanted a boy, hopefully bigger. Fists clenched, she hung her head and whispered prayers to the Blessed Mother. Down to the nub of the whole, giving children to strangers, and pickings slim, she hoped they'd pass her by. Her sense of pride played games, however. Pretending to be what she was not might get her chosen. Would her sin against God thwart her?

His heavy step thumped to the end of the platform, then slowly back up the line. Please, please take one of the hopeful girls desperate for a family, she prayed. His sons kept pace, the mother and daughter lagged. The burly man, mud on his boots, dungarees with filthy bottoms, walked past all the children. Then he retraced his steps, grabbing her upper arm, squeezing. "Thin," he said over his shoulder to his wife. The young daughter, big hazel eyes, stared at her gold copper hair sticking out from the cap. "Probably eat more than the work I'd get out of him," the father groused.

The matron from the Aid Society smiled. Aisling knew the drill, heard it in every train depot between Gettysburg and Dowagiac, Michigan where it all began. "You will have to sign a contract stipulating he's schooled on a regular basis. There will be periodic checks to see how you all fare. There is a trial period. If he doesn't suit, he can be returned."

The man nodded. "Dregs of the pot, I'm thinkin'. Nothin' but riff raff left. My sense tells me to wait for the next train." There was a long pause while his sons argued for an extra pair of hands for the farm. "I'll teach him to clean the stalls, feed the horses," chimed the tallest of the two sons.

He sighed. "I'll take him." His somber, beady scan swept the length of her. "What's your name, boy?"

Aisling O'Quinn on the tip of her tongue, she sensed the truth might free her. The matron spoke up. "Alan O'Quinn."

"Plain as can be a lazy Irish clod. Looks like a girl, don't he?" he said with disgust, a snarly grin outlined blackened teeth.

---

*N*ow exposed for what she was, and unable to defend herself against the brutish Hector, her breathing quieted, the ringing in her ears eased. She glanced about the stall; the only sounds were the horses shuffling and snorting. Hector most likely followed his father to the pasture where the day's chores waited.

Aisling closed her eyes and leaned against the wall, her legs spread out in front of her. She ached for her *máthair* and squeezed back tears of desperation. The memory of her beloved on the cot, shivering with fever came unbidden sometimes. Foolishly, in the beginning, her naivety allowed her to think her *máthair* would come for her.

A recurring dream of Five Points seemed the only plausible, obtainable possibility. She had nowhere else to go, did not even know another family well enough to seek refuge in the Gettysburg area. Mrs. Smythe never behaved as a mother to her own daughter. Why would she care about Aisling, whom she knew as a boy? There were no neighbors with whom to seek refuge. There was a teacher she liked, but hardly knew. The Smythes were not churchgoers.

Taking a deep breath, she hoped to quell the nausea then pushed up along the wall, weak-kneed. Her queasy stomach settled. She could not stay here. There was no safety, no trust in Mr. Smythe to protect her. He never once took a personal interest in her labors or at the table when they all ate together; as if she was a ghost, an invisible thing that sat in the chair, did as told. Unless her work was unsatisfactory, then she best beware.

Once was all it took to understand her place on the farm. Only once, when she failed in her duty and it never happened again. She shook off the misery of that time and glanced about the barn. Through the open sliders, she could almost make out the men toiling in the field.

A long time ago, she discovered Hector burying an object like a jar. He would put something in it that clinked. He hadn't known she spied him from a stall. On shaky legs, she scrambled to the corner where he dug. In little time, a jar, half-full of coins and a pocketknife unearthed. She sank her hand into the jar grabbing a fistful of coin and the knife, wrapped them in a cloth, tied it, and shoved it in her pocket then replaced the jar, quick as a squirrel hiding acorns.

At the dinner table that night, she listened to the conversation between father and sons, but avoided looking any of them in the eye. Hector argued with his da about joining the Unionists, but his father refused, the argument one of labor for the farm. Hector's hard glare bored into her. It sent shivers down her spine. He held power over her with his knowledge. In a moment, he could change her life. She could scarce breathe or eat in his dark, sneaky presence.

That night she had no trouble staying awake. An owl hooted; the half-lit moon cast its creamy gauze across the yard.

Thankful they'd given her the end of a hallway to sleep on a pallet, she didn't have to walk on creaky stair treads. She carried her boots and slowly walked the floorboards past the Smythe's bedroom, inch-by-inch.

Mr. Smythe mumbled, she prayed it was in his sleep, but then she heard his feet drop to the floor. He dragged the pot from under the bed. As his steady stream splattered into it, she opened the door and slipped out. She hid in the shadow of the house, waiting. A wind stirred the branches. Moonbeams drifted in and out of a passing cloud, stars twinkled. No one stirred in the house.

Clarity came to her in the night air. Slipping into her boots, she headed off in the direction of town. Alone in the night but for animals in the woody copse, she knew enough about wildlife in the last three years to know they wouldn't hunt the road, they stay to the forest. She walked most of the night, eventually coming to the outskirts of town. With no idea where the teacher lived, she couldn't show up at school. It would be the first place the Smythes would search.

Her stomach growled. Already, hearty meals were a memory. She nestled under a low-branched tree behind the school to wait the rest of the night. A plan would come to her in the morning.

In the dark, stars overhead, she recalled life in the tenement. All that she knew about family and home she learned within those four walls, up four flights. She remembered the three of them in the evenings, her *athair* stoking a pipe, her *máthair* opening the only window so the smoke would curl out. If wintertime, they endured the pungent scent. They didn't have a grate to keep warm, but her parents talked about the years they lived in Ireland. It wasn't hard to imagine a big stone firewall glowing red and orange with dried-bog turf cut into peat-logs. Once in a great while her parents would talk about their boys. Aisling asked their names—and repeated the sounds after her *athair*, whose deep voice filled with pride and reverence as he spoke, "Alsandair, Conlaodh, Donn, Flann, Liam."

During the years with the Smythes, Aisling recited the names of the dead that made up her family, *Athiar*, Alsandair, Conlaodh, Donn, Flann, Liam." Never her *máthair's* name would she add to the singsong litany, because she was alive and waiting for Aisling.

About the time her *athair* died, their life began to change. Her *máthair* worked in a laundry in the afternoons, schooling Aisling in the early mornings. Her *athair's* wit and joy-filled laugh sorely missed at those times, as was the scent of his pipe smoke. Neighbors shared meals and concern, Aisling remembered the evenings as the hardest, her *máthair* sitting at the table in whispered conversation with a friend or two as Aisling drifted off to sleep with the comforting sound. There were bits of food, and neighbors to sit with. When her *máthair* began working ten-hour shifts, she took Aisling with her, and things began to change. A year into their routine, her *máthair* inquired about a school for children from the tenements, but Aisling threw a fit. She insisted her *máthair* teach her everything she needed to know.

Then a new fear entered Aisling's heart when she was about ten. Times when her *máthair* didn't feel well enough to go to the laundry. Those times Aisling ventured out alone seeking work that might pay in food. She began dressing as a lad for safety's sake. It was on one of these ventures she got caught stealing and was taken from her *máthair's* bedside by a matron of the Children's Aid Society.

With the night forest around her, memories of life in the Irish tenement floated about; and guilt came unbidden. She remembered her parents hugging and singing songs from their childhood, trying to teach Aisling the Irish. Her tongue would try; they teased her efforts, enjoying the sounds, giggling as they listened. The dear love they all shared was real. What would the matron say to her *máthair* when she came looking for her daughter? The agreement with the Children's Aid Society was not for keeps; just two months until her *máthair* regained her health.

Her heart clutched with the unbidden shame. She'd been a thief; wrenched from her *máthair* because of it.

# CHAPTER 2

*A*isling waited in the high growth down the road from the little
school. The red building was the only place she could be like
her old self. She loved reading and writing. Miss Haslett praised her
ability with script, said she formed perfectly legible letters. Aisling
yearned for praise and wrote slow to form the words the way Miss
Haslett taught.

The dong of the school bell drew the students off the playground.
Unless the growling in her stomach gave her away, she was safe. Would
Mr. Smythe search for her at school? She had to quit in late April
because of the spring planting. However, Miss Haslett kept the school
open year-round for those who could attend. There were many times
she envied Giselle going off in the morning. At the dinner table most
evenings, Aisling listened intently to the stories Giselle told of Miss
Haslett and her lessons.

Aisling must have nodded off because the sound of laughing voices
jarred her from sleep. Students poured out the door, down the four steps,
onto the road, scattering to their homes clutching books they
would read.

Drawing the bundle of coin from her pocket, she untied it, spreading
out the contents. Stacking the twelve one-penny coppers, three five-cent

coins, three dimes, one quarter, and one Indian-head dollar, a sigh of relief swept over her. This was a small fortune. She would be able to pay for the train to New York City. Carefully placing the coins in the center of the cotton, she knotted it securely then shoved the small bundle in her overalls, the knife in another. Reflexively, she patted both bulges against her thighs where she stashed the funds. Her heart could not squeeze out enough relief that she'd caught him burying his treasure. It crossed her mind that he would wonder who had found the coins. She hoped he blamed her. She planned to be long gone by then.

Later Miss Haslett, satchel in hand, and the familiar, large-brimmed hat secure on her head, closed the door, and walked past Aisling's hiding spot. She waited until her teacher was almost out of view then followed at a distance. They walked like this for nearly a half hour toward the edge of town. Bird song filled the air; a few puffy clouds dotted the sky. Soon big elms towered over a white washed home, a shed out back painted to match. Aisling stayed in the bushes until nightfall when Miss Haslett lit a lamp in the front room. She rocked in a chair, head bent. Maybe she was reading. Aisling's heart ached for her *máthair* picturing her in the evenings, after they ate. Her loving smile, the way she brushed her daughter's hair remarking on the curls that coiled about her fingers. The happy times before her *athair* died.

Aisling crept around the perimeter of the home then out back around the shed. The door easily swung open revealing burlap bags in a pile, a rake, a broom, and a wagon. Hunger assailed her, and weariness overtook her. She sank onto the cloth bags falling instantly asleep.

---

*W*hen she woke, it took her a minute to remember. A shimmer of light crept along the bottom of the door of the shed. Oddly, a sense of safety came over her; she opened the door. Pink daylight across the horizon edged out the moon, low in the sky.

Twin magnets of hunger and thirst drove her from the shed. Shortly thereafter, Miss Haslett walked, in her prim step, down the lane in the direction of the school.

Aisling peeked around the front of the house. Yellow flowers budded alongside the little path to the front door. She went around back and found the door locked then noted a nearby window open a crack. She took her boots off and climbed in the window, landing in a bedroom then headed toward the kitchen. She began a search of the cupboards. Pushing aside checkered drapes in front of shelving revealed a bowl of onions, glass jars of crackers, applesauce, and tomatoes.

A white box on little legs in the corner she knew to be an icebox. The Smythes did not have one; they kept their extra food in the cellar. Some of the tenements in Five Points had iceboxes. Opening the door, she saw a pitcher of milk. She carried it with both hands to the table, found a glass, and drank. Her second glass finished, she brought the jar of crackers to the table and tried to hold back from finishing the entire batch. She drank another glass of milk. Cool and slick on her throat, it reminded her of her *máthair* when she would climb the stairs with a small bucket of milk taken from a cow at the market.

Aisling cleaned the cup, surprised to note the level of milk in the pitcher down by half as she placed it in the icebox. She hoped Miss Haslett would not notice. Swiping up crumbs, she licked her palm. Glancing about the neat, tiny room, she satisfied herself there would be no trace of her presence.

Curiosity made her peek around the corner of the kitchen into the living area. Aisling warmed to the dainty, perfectly suited space. A settee adorned with knitted doilies on the headrest and arms, a table with a lamp. This is where Miss Haslett tatted at night, her needles clicking in her clean fingers. Aisling glanced at her own hands wiping them against the denim of her bibs. A picture of an older couple displayed on the mantel flanked by two candleholders. Miss Haslett had a likeness to her parents. She was kindly giving Aisling reason to hope she had a nice life with her parents.

Suddenly overcome with her own imperfections and shortcomings, she retreated from the room, and out the window, to the shed.

Dozing, she mused the day away, waiting for darkness alit with moonlight, and then walked into town. When she attended school, she was driven in by Hector or Earl, unless on rare occasions, Mr. Smythe had business and drove her himself. There was never any leisure to explore. A silhouette of the school's bell tower against the night sky lured her toward the end of Chester Street. Piano music with laughter filtered through the night air.

She tried the door of the school, but found it locked. Not surprised, she looked for a window she could reach that would open but was unsuccessful.

Aisling sat on the back steps, out of the way of any light and considered her plight. It had to be near midnight with the moon directly above. She remembered that train depots post schedules on the door, so she headed to the station, keeping to the shadows. A ray of well-being lightened her mood.

At least two miles later, she found the train schedule posted on the window, but it was on the dark side of the depot. There was no way she could read it. In disgust, she kicked the wall. A man's voice yelled, "Come back tomorrow. I ain't gettin outta bed at this hour."

She spun on her heel, running as fast as her legs would carry her, staying to the shadows. Stopping to catch her breath, she found herself in front of the general store. A place the Smythes shopped on a regular basis. Sweat trickled down her armpits. Her mouth was dry.

Her ears began to ring as dread flushed through her. Fighting nausea entwined with body-shaking fear, she again worked to catch her breath, slowly calming herself with the knowledge that no one was about. The only sounds came from a piano and merry making from a place of entertainment in the next block, where ten or more horses stood at the railing.

Her imagination rambled over her time with the Smythes, including her deep resentment toward the Children's Aid Society, because they did not have authority over her; she knew her sickly parent had not signed over the right to give her away.

Her sullen reverie broke with the sound of shuffling feet. She flattened against the shadows of the store. Men in uniform marched down Main Street, rifles slung over their shoulders. Dear Mother of God, were they searching for her?

It took a long time, staying to the dark, evading bands of men with rifles, before she got back to the shed. Once there she fell onto the pile of burlap bags into a troubled sleep.

The next morning, Aisling stretched and yawned, her stomach

growled with hunger. She cracked the door to the shed noting the raised window on the back of the house. She guessed it was about eight from the position of the sun in the sky. Miss Haslett would be at school. A quiet morning, no bird song in the air, a little overcast as if it might rain. She crept low toward the home, took her boots off, left them on the ground, and climbed in the window heading for the kitchen, anticipating a cool glass of milk and more crackers.

"Good morning, Mr. O'Quinn. I have been expecting you. Perhaps we could have breakfast together."

# CHAPTER 3

*A*isling stopped dead in her stocking feet. Her gaze slithered about the room half expecting Mr. Smythe. Her breath stuck in her throat in shock at seeing her teacher sitting at the kitchen table, making a list with pencil and paper, her glasses almost slipping off the tip of her nose.

"You better take a breath, or you'll collapse. You needn't worry. We are alone."

She gasped. "How did you know? Does Mr. Smythe know?" Her attention snapped to a broadbill on the kitchen table, *WANTED* in big bold letters across the top, her likeness drawn below. *Runaway—promised reward* blazed across the bottom.

Miss Haslett took off her glasses, neatly folding them on top of her pad. "It is not hard to figure out when someone eats your food. But when your foster parent brought this by late last night, I concluded you must be sleeping in my shed."

Aisling dug her shaking hands into the pockets of her overalls. "I'm sorry, I couldn't help myself."

"Oh, I'd say you helped yourself plenty." Miss Haslett's pretty, blue eyes lit with merriment. Aisling could have cried with relief in that moment. "Sit." She pointed to the only other chair in the kitchen. "Tell

18

me what's happened that you feel it necessary to run away. You could have come to me with a problem, Alan. It is one of the situations where teachers can help."

Aisling could not tell Miss Haslett what Hector tried to do. Her safety relied on hiding beneath the clothes of a boy. Cautiously, she took one-step backward, then another.

"I can't force you to stay. I do think a nice breakfast would work wonders for a conversation about your situation. How do bacon and eggs sound with some toast? I've even squeezed oranges." She stood up, reaching for an apron on a hook.

Aisling's stomach weakened the desire to flee. "Men with rifles marched through town last night?"

The lines on Miss Haslett's face became apparent with an obviously serious thought. "You think the Smythes sent them for you?" She pulled out a cast iron skillet and put it on the stove, then began slicing a slab of bacon into strips.

Aisling's mouth watered. "When you say that, it makes me feel stupid."

Miss Haslett looked up, her pretty face awash in sadness. "I wish it were easily explained, however, the rumors in Gettysburg are alarming. Apparently, the Confederate Army is expected. We could become a military battleground."

She sank to the chair. Her mind raced about the facts. She glanced at her teacher. "That's why Unionists are here?"

Her teacher set the knife on the cutting board then wiped her hands on the apron. "Alan, right now my biggest concern is you. I am trying to understand what has happened that you would run away from the farm. Granted the Smythes are a callous lot, but they have provided you with a roof, clothing, they allow you to come to school."

Aisling palmed her hands then squeezed them between her knees. Her head hung down. "My *máthair* only wanted me gone two months till she got better. The matron put me on the train against what she said."

Miss Haslett softly placed her hands on Aisling's shoulders. "I am so sorry, Alan. You could have told me this a long time ago. There is surely something to rectify your situation. You're from New York City, right?"

"Five Points." No one had asked her where her home was in three years. "We had a room with a stove and two beds. Up four flights."

Miss Haslett patted her shoulder then stirred the sizzling bacon that filled the air with smoky goodness. If she squeezed shut her eyes, she might think her *máthair* stood at the coal burner, flipping the strips, fat crackling, singing an Irish tune. Happy with her lot and her daughter, she would share some whimsical anecdote about the women in the laundry making Aisling ache with laughter the singular way her *máthair* told stories with what she called her Irish lilt.

Now she realized the devastation of their poverty. These walls were not black with soot; slops did not fall past the window from the tenement above. She grieved for what was, the fear she lived with the past three years, and now the unspoken quiver of anxiety over her *máthair's* health.

"There is the Aid Society man who makes his rounds every three months with foster children. He checks the records I take each day and was more than satisfied with your attendance, and the high grades you earned."

Aisling considered Mr. Smythe's perseverance regarding her presence at the school. His motivation was not her learning; it was the labor on his farm. He would not risk losing her. She had no doubt he sent the soldiers to find her. A creepy sensation prickled the skin on her arms. She stood so quickly the chair fell backward. "You sent a message to him thinking food will keep me here?"

She swerved on stocking feet, but Miss Haslett was quicker. "I did not." She held fast to Aisling's arms. "Look at me." Their eyes locked. Miss Haslett's were ablaze with fury. "I had already sensed something before you quit to help with planting. Until you trust me, there is nothing I can do for you."

With her hands firm on Aisling's arms, she forced her to sit in the other chair, grabbed the fallen one to its upright position. "Tell me what I can do to help you, Alan. I know you're hurting, but I don't know how to make it better."

Several wagons rumbled down the one-track lane in front of Miss Haslett's abode. There appeared to be more traffic than usual. The sounds drowned out by the drama in the kitchen were now obvious in the silence. Aisling would not tell the nice teacher why she ran away, the threats from Hector, what he planned to do to her.

To shed her disguise, was to be unsafe. The security of her hidden identity would assist in her arrival at Five Points. It was obvious Hector had not told his da, because the poster wanted a youth, not a maid.

A ragged breath came with her words. "I don't know about trust. I only know my *máthair* needs me, badly."

Miss Haslett ran her hand over the top of Aisling's hair, patting the curls. She sat opposite then placed her hands in her lap. "How long since you've been gone?"

"I was twelve when they took me."

"Hmm. Another day won't hurt, will it?" Her eyebrow raised in question.

A knock on the front door brought Aisling out of her chair. She clamped her response shut then threw her teacher a mean glare.

"Stand behind the kitchen door. Don't make a sound."

Aisling did as told.

A pall of apprehension hung in the air, a quick glance about that all appeared normal; Miss Haslett opened the front door. "May I help you?"

"Union Cavalry, ma'am. General Meade has asked all citizens to find shelter away from Gettysburg, ma'am. Will you need assistance to make that happen?"

"No, thank you. I have an offer from my nearest neighbor. I plan to leave noon tomorrow. Can you tell me if the Southern Army has advanced on Adams County?"

"Yes, ma'am. Information is they are encamped and preparing for battle."

The teacher shut the front door. Aisling stepped out from behind the kitchen. "The Rebs are coming?"

"We've been informed. Gettysburg sits between the two armies. Ten roads radiating from the center of town. More than likely those roads will be the battleground for the encounter." She picked up a fork and bent over the stove. "Bacon is over ready. I hope you like it crisp."

Aisling grinned. She could not help herself. "I'll like it the way you make it, ma'am."

They ate in silence. Aisling helped with clean up. Miss Haslett hung the damp dishrag over a rack. "Alan, you heard the soldier. We need to plan for you. But you will have to trust me in this."

Aisling nodded and tucked her hands beneath her armpits.

"Mr. Smythe should be too concerned with his farm to press any kind of hunting party for you. However, we cannot stay here; the danger is too great. There will be room for you in my wagon. My suggestion would be to travel with me, perhaps disguised to hide your hair. I plan to stay with a family near York."

Aisling unfolded her arms shoving them in pockets. Her fingers gripped the ball of coin, and the pocketknife. She hesitated to reveal her plan lest the teacher try to restrain her. Surely, there would be a train depot in York, or at least tracks she could follow with rails heading east towards New York City and her beloved Five Points.

---

*T*he wagon was half-full of Miss Haslett's two suitcases and a few articles of sentimental value. Aisling helped load blankets, pillows, some food, and a small barrel of water. Extra provisions were included in case they had to spend more than one night on the road.

All Aisling owned were the clothes on her back. Miss Haslett gave her a jacket and a clean shirt, clothes her brother left when he visited last year. She would be leaving Miss Haslett at some point on the journey, never to see her again, and decided not to mention her plans. "You think of everything. I've taken advantage of your goodwill."

"Nonsense. How does one plan an escape during wartime? I'm glad for the companionship, and the assistance. Don't underrate yourself."

They sat on the buckboard bench. Miss Haslett smiled a glint of mischief in her eye. "Ready?"

Aisling pursed her lips and nodded. A thrilling sense welled. She was going home. Her years on a farm were her past, not her future. She glanced at the remarkable woman next to her, the woman who unwittingly came to her rescue. "Where did you learn to be a teacher?"

"We lived in Philadelphia. I graduated from Western University of

Pennsylvania. They allowed me to attend because my father was a professor."

What a wonderful life. Upper schooling, a father encouraging her. "I want to live in a home with books."

Miss Haslett laughed. "You surprise me. I don't recall you ever taking a book home."

"Mr. Smythe didn't allow lamps for reading or knitting. If you could see by fire, it was okay."

"You didn't want to read by fire?"

"Hector and Earl made fun of reading."

Miss Haslett rolled her blue eyes. "Did Giselle read?"

"She knits with her mom most nights."

"What did you do in your extra time?" She slapped at the reins encouraging the mare to move along the dusty road toward Main Street. The overcast day promised to be muggy.

"Helped with chores, sometimes I went to my pallet to be with my memories." She shrugged. "Most times I'd go to the barn, talk to the horses. There was always something to set right in the barn."

"How would you like to drive us the rest of the way out of town?"

Her face must have lit up like a lantern because Miss Haslett handed her the reins. Firm but gentle at the same time, her hands gripped the leather strips; she clucked, and the mare never broke stride. "Thanks." She did not want to tell her this was a first, that she had never driven a wagon. In her mind, she had. Each time she rode to and from school, she calculated the ease of it in the hands of the Smythe men.

"I brought a felt hat of my father's. You need to wear it when we stop in town. I think it will hide most of your hair. The brim is large. Mr. Smythe doesn't suit me as a man with much patriotism, but we don't want to take any chances, do we?"

"Not me. I am never going back. He's a mean man."

Miss Haslett glanced sideways, questioning. Aisling continued, "He makes his sons fight. He says there is money in boxing and he wants them to learn. I know he favors Earl over Hector. I could hear it plain when he spoke. Every morning my job was to clean the stalls, water, and feed. I heard him order them to fight."

"Did he want to train you to box?"

Aisling glanced at her. "I...I was afraid he would. Hector always bled, split lip, black eyes. My size, I'd probably get killed."

A laugh bubbled out of Miss Haslett. "You aren't big for a fifteen-year-old boy. It is my experience boys do not usually get their growth as early as girls do. You will begin to sprout up in the next year or so."

As they rode into town near the crossroads, two brigades of infantry paraded in the center of the main street. If the seriousness of the soldier's presence didn't mean war and killing, it would be thrilling to watch.

Miss Haslett directed Aisling to pull over and tether the wagon on a side road. She put a hat on Aisling's head, down low over her ears, tucked in a few straggles of copper gold, and off they walked to Main Street. She liked that her teacher fussed over her. It made her more than excited for her *máthair*.

After a week of rumor mills, the truth stared Gettysburg's two thousand occupants in the face. Citizens waving pieces of cloth and makeshift flags joyously received nearly three thousand troopers. Men, women, and children elbowed their way to the crowded walkways vying for space. General Buford established his headquarters at the Eagle Hotel, and his soldiers stepped smartly to a drum roll past the steps where he saluted them. He looked magnificent in his dark blue uniform studded with gold buttons, and pristine white gloves. He was dazzling and important.

Her sense of belonging to the moment was powerful. A Union Army fighting against Confederates, even though she did not exactly understand the reason. Maybe Miss Haslett would explain it to her on their ride to York. The last time she felt like she belonged to anything or anyone was the morning she foraged food for her *máthair* and did the only thing possible by filching an apple from a cart. Well, she would do it again if warranted. Family takes care of each other.

"Gotcha, girlie." A hand clamped on her arm, dragging her backward. She stumbled over her boots trying to stay upright. Hector! Sainted Mother. She swung her arm upward and screamed. He flicked the hat off her head and it twirled to the ground, crushed by his filthy boot.

He dragged her from the crowd, everyone's attention on the

marching and General Buford. Hector shoved the two of them in a small opening between two buildings and then pushed her ahead of him down the alley. "Get goin'."

She took off on a run. Smaller than he, she maneuvered quickly in the tight space, rounding a corner, she ran smack into a grocer hauling garbage to a barrel. Hiding behind him, she begged, "Help me, please."

Hector stopped at the end of the alley and glanced quickly about, spying the grocer and Aisling hiding behind. "So, this is where you got to. Games over, come on, *Alan*," he said with a sneer of contempt.

"He's going to hurt me, help. Please." She clung to the grocer's waist.

The man put his hands behind and hauled her before him. "What's this you say?"

"Don't let him take me," she cried.

"He's my kid brother. Our da is leaving and he doesn't want to go."

The grocer's keen eye swept from Hector to her. "I'd likely think you lie. There's no family resemblance, Get on out of here." Hector did not budge an inch. "Go on, or I'll get one of them soldiers to do the job for me."

Hector took a step backward and glared an evil eye at her, causing her skin to shrivel. However, the grocer's assistance reminded her she had a backbone, and she straightened and glared at him, chin in the air.

Miss Haslett rounded the corner of the alley at that moment. "There you are, Alan. I've looked everywhere." The felt hat in hand, she brushed at the grime, punching out the bowl to its former shape.

A big grin on his round face, the grocer said, "Miss Haslett, good day to you."

"And you, Mr. Gottlieb. Chatting with my pupil as if you haven't a care in the world. We need to get on with our day. Sorry for the rush."

She held out her hand for Aisling to follow and took notice of Hector. "Well, well, I'm surprised to see you this morning, Hector. No sparring with your brother today?"

He rubbed his jaw, clearly surprised at the question. He took a step backward, shaking his head.

Mr. Gottlieb said, "And don't you be bothering those littler than you. You are nothing but a bully. Get on your way."

Hector glowered. Aisling held her breath, waiting for him to leave the alley. He took his time backing off. His piercing burn on her was like a promise, he would still get her. He was hateful. Evil filled his soul. He'd been bred to it by his da.

Miss Haslett advised they stay in town an hour and wander about should Hector trail them. She did not want him to know the direction they traveled.

Finally, rid of him, they left Gettysburg traveling northeast. With a degree of certainty, Miss Haslett believed Hector had given up the search. Perhaps Mr. Gottlieb's threat of soldiers worked. Other wagons and carriages on the road to York brimmed with families. Aisling found it difficult to think Hector would be in one of them. His da would not give him this much time away from the farm. At least she hoped she was right.

Because they got such a late start, they spent the night with other travelers at the edge of a clearing, sleeping under the wagon. It was a balmy night, stars bright. Miss Haslett took off her hat and jacket and neatly set them on her suitcase, then slept in her clothes.

Aisling placed the felt hat in the wagon alongside Miss Haslett's, and lay down on her blanket, snuggling with a pillow. She was content this night, stars above twinkling; the soft breathing of her teacher near enough to hear.

From somewhere far, far away, Aisling recalled a lullaby her *máthair* sang many a night when her *athair* worked late. *Sleep, baby dear, sleep without fear. Shularoo, la roo, la, shularoo la, shularoo la rye, sleep baby dear, sleep without fear.*

Far too grown for her *máthair* to cradle her now, the memory warmed her and made her love her parent more, if that was possible. The night sky held a star her *máthair* might be looking at this very moment. Would she wonder where her daughter was and when she would arrive? "Soon, *máthair* my love."

---

## *July 1, 1863*

*B*efore dawn, Aisling heard sounds of rousing from the other travelers. She took a moment to collect herself, grateful for how rested she felt, perhaps the first time since taken from her tenement on Mulberry Street.

Miss Haslett was on her back, arm flung to the side, breathing softly. Aisling threw the cover off, stretched, rolled from beneath the wagon, and stood. The mare snorted, wanting her oats no doubt. Aisling took the reins and led her to the pond nearby. She held the bag of feed and once the mare satisfied herself, Aisling returned to the wagon.

Miss Haslett was up, jacket and hat where they belonged, and smiling. "You haven't wasted a moment, Alan. A handy lad to have on one's travels."

"I think it'll be a bright day with the looks of the east." She began harnessing the mare. Miss Haslett folded and loaded the blankets and pillows. Along with the other wagons, they were well on their way by the time the sun rose.

The clop of horses, rattle of wagons, and someone playing a mouth organ were the hum of the road for the most part. A volley of faint shots rang in the air. The sound would stop, then another volley. An unmistakable cannon roar shook the ground, reminding them why they were on the run. Miss Haslett took over the reins for a while and with a free hand, patted Aisling on the arm asking if she was all right.

Aisling asked, "What made the war start. Do you know?"

"It has been on for two years. A perfect example of two different mindsets fighting to uphold their individual ideals." Her lips pursed in a grimace as she snapped the reins and clucked to the mare. Taking a deep breath, she continued, "This war is brutal and wasteful, all over a southerner's right to own, buy, and sell human beings."

Aisling's mind twirled. However, money had not changed hands that she knew of anyway. Isn't that what happened to her? "That's a terrible way to treat others. I feel it goes against God's will."

Miss Haslett's gaze slid over Aisling's face, a look of sadness clouded her features. "The south uses dark-skinned Africans as slave labor. Nevertheless, that is not to say white-skinned people are not forced to slavery, too. I'm sorry your circumstance didn't come to my attention as soon as it began."

Aisling nodded. "Me too. Though, it is ended now. I'm grateful for your understanding, Miss Haslett. Very grateful."

Silence grew between them, as both were lost in contemplation. The rhythm of the mare's gait, and the clinks and creaks of the three wagons a comfort in the early day, a misty fog fading with the sun's heat.

"You make the south's slaving sound plain and simple. I'm thinking there is a lot more to it than that."

"And you would be right." Miss Haslett said. "Not all northerners share the same opinion. Some make their living from cotton, and without slave labor, they will lose a lot of their profit. The south will probably not recover from the economic upheaval of its entire way of life should slavery end."

"Why is the color of skin what determines who is to be slave or master?"

"You ask a provocative question. Historically, from the beginning of recorded time, there has been slavery. Asians have castes that determine the lowest of their culture. In some cultures, it is religion. Unfortunately, in our south, it was the color of skin."

"Where I come from it was being Irish. I remember my *máthair* and *athair* going back and forth over it. Seems Irish are thought shiftless."

"I could hardly subscribe to that impression knowing you, Alan. I know how hard you have worked for the Smythes. You've always been among the brightest of my pupils." She glanced over at her. "Perhaps the idea comes from the overcrowded conditions in Manhattan that all immigrants were forced to endure, not just the Irish."

Aisling considered her opinion, the squalor, the lack of opportunity, the sickness from hunger. "When I get back home, I intend to change our life, my *máthair's* and mine."

Miss Haslett sighed. "I'll be sorry when that day comes, but will you promise me something?"

If there were a way to repay her teacher for this kindness, she would climb mountains to do so. "Yes, ma'am. Anything."

"Continue with your schooling. Do not stop until you have satisfied that inquisitive mind of yours. Promise me."

"Oh, that will be easy enough, to be sure. You can ask far more of me than such a simple thing." Somehow, this conversation lightened her mood. No one had asked of her anything of importance in years. It made her feel like a real person, as if she mattered.

"There is the difference, Alan. Not all think it easy and simple to continue learning."

The first wagon in line came to an abrupt stop. Miss Haslett reined in the mare. One of the men in that wagon jumped down and ran into the woods. A man in the second wagon did the same. Aisling jumped down. "I'll see what's up." She ran after the two men before Miss Haslett could stop her.

There were four soldiers, all dressed in blue jackets. Two stood behind bushes holding rifles, two others lounged against a tree and appeared seriously wounded. Blood stained clothes wound about his head and mid-section, and the arm of the other.

One of the men from their wagon train asked, "Have you news from Gettysburg?"

"Yes. Not good. General Buford is dead. Early this morning. The confederates are gaining. They've taken over the town."

Aisling knelt to inspect the wounded, asking if they needed water. Both nodded in reply, and she ran back to the wagon.

"Buford's dead. The Confederates have taken over Gettysburg." She gushed to her teacher. "And the men need water."

"Dear God." Miss Haslett scrambled down off the wagon and dug in her bag for tin cups. Aisling dipped them in the barrel and scrambled back to the woods. The men drained the tins. She ran back to the wagon refilling the cups and returned to the thirsty soldiers.

By this time, wives joined their husbands along with Miss Haslett. Together the group decided to give the men room in their wagons and get the two wounded to York.

Once again, the three wagons headed northeast toward safety, away from the horror of Gettysburg fallen to the enemy, a black cloud rising behind them giving truth to it.

# CHAPTER 4

*T*he two soldiers not wounded jumped in Miss Haslett's wagon. Infantry Privates Jake and Conner hailed from upper New York. Both men declared they were escorting the wounded to a hospital and were gladdened to know York was the destination of the three wagons.

Aisling overheard snippets of their conversation leading her to believe they were deserters rather than escorts. The party stopped alongside the road for lunch. It was in this setting Private Conner walked with her to the creek to water the mare.

She asked, "Will you return to Gettysburg once your friends are with the doctor?"

He removed his stiff wool cap and swiped at his forehead. She realized he was young, maybe her age even though he had growth on his face. "Right now, I'm not sure what we plan." He scrutinized her. "How come you're not in uniform?"

"I've been living with a family who kept their own sons from signing up. It didn't occur to me they'd treat me any different."

"She kept you from it?" He nodded toward Miss Haslett then placed the cap back on his head, the top half of his face in shadow.

"She's my teacher. My *máthair* is ill. I'm needed back home."

"Home is York? You'll see her today, then."

She drew the toe of her boot in the sand at the creek's edge and firmed a decision. "Miss Haslett, I've not told her yet. I plan to leave once we get to York. She has friends there. I'm going on to Manhattan, Five Points. That's my destination." She quit shuffling the toe of her boot in the dirt and glanced at him. "I haven't exactly told her this, yet. She'd try to stop me, and I need to get home."

The bottom half of his jaw curved upward. "How will you get there?"

"Buy a seat on the railroad."

"If you partner up with Jake and me, you won't have to spend your coin."

She glanced at him. He clearly figured her to be a male, which brought a measure of comfort. She asked, "You're deserters?"

"We're going to lose the war. We lost the battle already. Men dying all over the land back there. Jake and I are all our families have. We owe it to them to stay alive. We don't see us as deserting so much as surviving." His features crumbled into sadness. He swiped his hand across his brow and pinched his nose. "It was a fearful thing to be a part of." His hand quivered as he drew it from his face. "I don't want to die because the south means to keep slaves."

"You're so certain they'll win?" The mare lifted her head and stepped away from the creek. Aisling held to the reins and clucked. She began the short walk up the path to the others and Conner walked alongside.

"I saw it. Lee launched an all-out offensive right through the streets of Gettysburg from the north to the south, blues dropping by the dozens, hundreds. Right and left of me, dying, bleeding." He drew in a deep breath, and his hand shook like a leaf in the wind. His knees almost buckled, but he grabbed a low hanging branch and stopped walking.

She waited with him and tried to picture Miss Haslett's little house and the school. Probably gone by now. The Smythe's farm, the horses she so carefully tended and fed. What would become of them? "What about your wounded friends?"

"They can't travel. Gary is probably not even going to make it. We'll do the decent thing and stay until medical help takes over. Then hop a train. One thing for certain, we ain't going back."

---

*T*he wagons arrived in York at nightfall. The medical doctor's office and home were in the same building and situated at the end of Main Street. The doc came out and assessed the carnage in the wagons. He asked the men to carry the two badly wounded soldiers into his Infirmary.

Miss Haslett and Aisling stayed with them and said their goodbyes to the other families, who needed to get their children settled and wagons unloaded. They sat in chairs outside the examining room waiting for Doc Ellington to evaluate the extent of the injuries.

Miss Haslett said, "I didn't want to ask in front of Privates Jake and Conner. Do you know their plans? Will they return to Gettysburg?"

She shrugged. "Conner talked about the battle. General Lee is winning the war. He does not see victory for the Unionists. Dead are everywhere, all over town."

"Those poor boys. I suspect they are not much older than you are. Are you all right talking to Private Conner?"

She shrugged. Miss Haslett was a decent woman, a great teacher, and the kindest person she knew besides her *máthair*. She hated evasiveness with this woman, but an alternative didn't present itself.

Miss Haslett slid her arm around Aisling's shoulder. "I know what you're planning, Alan. I cannot stop you, and I think it would be unfair of me to try to do so. But you're young with so much potential and I want to guard that if I can."

"Conner is a year older than me." Her voice sounded whiny.

Miss Haslett patted her shoulder and took her arm away. "That's why I can't stop you. I understand times are different for youth of today." Her fingers folded together, as if she decided. "There's an obligation to the Children's Aid Society I can't overlook. They accepted responsibility to find you a family in Gettysburg."

So close to solving her problem of travel to Manhattan, she could not let this opportunity slip away. "How about if we don't talk about this anymore?"

"Ah, see how clever you are?" Miss Haslett stood and shook the wrinkles from her skirt, her gaze cast downward. The carpet woven with green ferns, had a black background. A large round mahogany table centered in the middle. In a soft voice, she said, "If I am to ever have a child, I'd want him to be exactly like you, Alan, diplomatic, ingenious, a lover of reading, and kind almost to a fault."

Conner and Jake stumbled out of the surgery, wiping away tears. Jake cried, "Gary didn't make it. Too much blood gone." He put an arm against the wall and leaned his head on it. "Mike will recover. But the doc has to cut off..." he choked on his words, "... his arm."

Conner slumped into a chair next to Aisling. "It is the worst."

The doctor came out rubbing his hands on a towel. Fresh blood stained his apron. He spoke to Miss Haslett. "Arrangements will have to be made with the funeral director. I haven't the time. I need to perform surgery on the other young man before his situation worsens. I will put him up in the Infirmary. Probably a month or more until his wound heals. I think I can save the upper portion."

Distraught with grief, Conner and Jake couldn't talk. Miss Haslett spoke up. "Alan, you and Conner rouse Mr. Patterson. He is the funeral director. His home is three or four blocks down on the left. I'll stay here with Jake."

Aisling and Conner returned with news Mr. Patterson would provide two shovels and a small plot in the corner of the cemetery. He also gave them a shroud to cover the body. They would transport Gary's remains in the wagon and Conner and Jake were to dig the grave.

Four hours later brought the dawn of another day. Thursday, July 2. Drifters came to York, soldiers in blue, Unionists. The news was ominous. The Union's defensive position south of town received fragmented attacks from the Confederates. Union forces held Culp's Hill, but the Confederate forces drove back the Unionists from Peach Orchard, Wheatfield, Valley of Death, and Devil's Den with a staggering number of casualties. General Lee enjoyed two days of triumph, his army invincible and undefeatable.

Gettysburg's rolling hills and farmland now lay covered in the blood of thousands of Unionist dead. The outlook was grim at best.

# CHAPTER 5

*J*ake, Conner, Aisling, and Miss Haslett lined the parlor of the doc's sitting area. On and off, they grabbed snippets of sleep when it became impossible to stay awake, the backs of their heads supported against the wall. How Doc Ellington managed to stay alert and perform his duties was beyond comprehension. He commandeered both Jake and Conner to assist him when he sawed through the bone of Mike's lower arm just below the elbow.

Daylight came through the upper portion of the windows not shielded by curtains. A maid who arrived a few minutes earlier, served them coffee and biscuits. Until this minute, none of them realized they had gone without supper last night.

Aisling knew Miss Haslett needed to get to her friend's home; they would be worried about her. She was not surprised when her teacher suggested a plan. Conner and Jake wrapped Gary's remains in the shroud Mr. Patterson sold them and carried him to the wagon.

The two young men said goodbye to Mike, who for the most part had not roused from his amputation yet. The doc assured them this was usual under the circumstances. Conner dug deep into his pocket and handed the doctor several coins and his heartfelt thanks.

Gary's body was loaded in the wagon. The two men sat in the back,

Miss Haslett and Aisling on the bench, and they drove almost a mile to the home of her friends.

Miss Haslett's brow arched questioningly at Aisling.

"If it is all right, I'll go to the cemetery with them."

Miss Haslett handed the reins to Aisling, then leaned over and planted a kiss on her brow. "I trust you to do the right thing, Alan."

"Yes, ma'am." Her teacher climbed down from the bench and waved goodbye as they moved toward the end of town where the sad business would take place. Miss Haslett looked tired. She had a right to be. Neither she nor her teacher expected to sit in a doctor's office all night with deserters.

Aisling was anxious to leave but could not intrude on Conner's sadness. She needed to wait until he was ready. She understood burying his friend hurt. The devastation in both men hung like a black cloud obscuring all else. A moment of clarity overcame her as she realized this was not all about her quest to return home. Conner and Jake lost one dear friend. Soon, they would part. By now, Miss Haslett probably lost her school and home. Aisling still had her *máthair* and her home tucked safely in Five Points.

Arriving at the cemetery, Conner and Jake began the grizzly work of digging. She tethered the mare and walked among the few wooden crosses and gravestones. It occurred to her, once the battle in Gettysburg was finished, this cemetery would most likely grow and double in size, if the reports were believable. From the news of Gettysburg's devastation so far, she had no reason to suspect otherwise.

Her brothers buried at sea; and, sadly, she was too young to know where her *athair* lay buried. She did remember marking his grave with two rocks she and her *máthair* found in the woods near the cemetery. The rocks signified wife and daughter standing guard, keeping watch. When she arrived at their home, her *máthair* would take her to his gravesite.

The two men wiped their brows and headed to the wagon. They each held to an end of the shroud carrying it to the grave. She left them to their bereavement of Gary. Even from a distance, sadness overwhelmed her. A darkness deep inside, the excitement of going home replaced by Conner's and Jake's loss.

Drawn from her introspection by a loud argument, she glanced at them, shovels in hand replacing the earth. Their voices carried in the stillness of the early day. A disagreement of great proportion ensued.

"...parents...jail...money...trains..."

It was not too hard to figure out their concerns. More than likely, she would be on her own by nightfall.

Conner offered to drive the wagon back to the home where they left Miss Haslett. Aisling knocked on the front door, and a young girl opened it. "You're here for Abigail, aren't you?"

"Well, if that's Miss Haslett's Christian name, then yes. May I speak with her?" Of course, she would have a given name, why am I surprised.

When Abigail came to the door and stepped outside, Aisling realized how much the name suited her, feminine and courteous. Miss Haslett's voice held concern. "You look all done in. A hard task burying the dead." She nodded to the two young men who stood outside the gate. They acknowledged her with a hat off and a nod.

Aisling lowered her voice. "Conner and Jake argued at the cemetery. It is difficult for them for sure."

Miss Haslett folded her hands in front of her and eyed Aisling in silence.

"I owe you everything. You've helped me get this far and I'll always be grateful to you."

"...but you have to go home."

"I do." A deep breath of gratitude for her understanding escaped Aisling's lips.

"You promised me you would continue your education when you get settled. I'm holding you to it, Alan." She took a step forward, and then stopped as if changing her mind.

Aisling asked, "Would it be all right if I write to you from time to time?"

"That is a wonderful idea." Miss Haslett's face brightened with a smile. "I'll look forward to hearing about your progress."

On impulse, she wrapped her arms about Miss Haslett and squeezed hard. "Bless you, Abigail." She wanted to use her given name; it made her feel close, like a friend.

Overcome with emotion, the teacher swiped at her cheeks. "You know better than to address your elders with familiarity. Now you'd better get on, or I'll think of a reason to not let you go."

Aisling's heart swelled as she walked toward her future. Miss Haslett would always be a friend. She stood on the walk until Aisling glanced back before rounding the corner and walked out of sight. Not before parting from her *máthair* had anyone treated her so kindly, almost with...love. She did know about love and missed it with every fiber of her being. Conner and Jake smiled as if they settled their disagreement. They would get her to the place where love waited.

---

*T*his was the third day of train travel. They had hopped from the Camden Ambroy branch in New Jersey to the New Jersey train. With luck, Aisling would be in Manhattan tomorrow night.

Conner and Jake planned to take the New Jersey to the Patterson into northern New York. The click of the rails was soothing. Aisling lay on a bale of hay, her body rocked with the motion. Someone slid the side door open a foot. The men in the car grouped around hay bales playing cards, a game causing raucous laughter that split the cool evening breeze with vigor. Ten men and boys occupied the car. Conner told her the longest leg of travel for her was going to be from Philadelphia to the New Jersey shore. She would catch a ferry to Manhattan and walk the rest of the way to Mulberry Street. She remembered the ferry ride from almost four years earlier.

Travel was unbelievably easy. She figured her smaller size allowed the rest of the men to ignore her. Conner kept an eye on her always. Jake chided him from time to time, good-natured teasing. Jake and she were the same age, though she was smaller by far. Conner had taken it upon himself to look after both, her especially.

The mournful sound of the whistle split the night air. Someone shouted *going over the Delaware*. The wheels made a different sound as they crossed the wooden bridge, clickety-clack, clickety-clack. On her back, she crossed a leg over her knee and chewed on a long piece of straw. Her body gently rocked with the sway.

Soon she would be sixteen and had been away nearly four years.

Christmases' at the Smythe's were sparse, but excitement was always in the air just the same. That is what sifted through her memory arriving at the door to her home, a Christmas kind of elation even though it was July. A tra-la-la that her *máthair* would sing with her lilt; Aisling expected no less.

The lonesome sound of the whistle blew again, and several of the men jumped up from the bale, playing cards scattered to the floor, and rushed to the sliding door. The train braked, and they hung on with the jerk of the stop. Aisling rolled off the bale and jumped up.

She looked for Conner in the dusk of the evening; he appeared from the dark corner of the car. Jake said, "It wouldn't be us, would it?"

Conner shushed him. "How can that be, Jake? Think on it and put your head straight."

"But..."

"No buts. Half the men here are like us, don'tcha know that. We're all trying to leave it behind." He shoved Jake onto the bale off which Aisling had rolled.

She laughed. "Comfy isn't it."

He glared at her. She said, "You'll be home soon. In time all this will fade."

His jaw jutted. "What makes you think you know me?" He jumped up off the bale, fists clenched. "Let's have at it."

She stood her ground. The light was fading fast, the train at a standstill. Everyone's attention on the foggy ground outside the slider. "I didn't mean anything bad. I don't know how to fight. You'll punch me, but I won't punch back, and then you'll feel worse than you already do."

He stepped within an inch of her. "What makes you so sure?"

"Because I'm as scared as you about what's ahead. You don't know what I am returning to, just like I don't what you're running from. What I do know is we are both unsure and worried. You have a family who will rejoice. I can only hope I have the same thing."

He continued to glare, but his fists opened, his chin lowered. Through pursed lips, he said, "You yap like a girl," and spun on his heel to the other end of the car.

The whistle blew three short blasts. Within a few minutes the cars jerked, the wheels moved, and they were on their way again. Speculation flew about what had happened, but no one knew. The card game resumed. Conner threw her a slanted smile and nodded in the direction of his friend with a wink.

Tomorrow.

---

*C*onner jumped down off the boxcar and held out his hand to assist Aisling as she landed on all fours, stood, and wiped at her knees. "I'd of helped," he said.

"No need." She glanced at him, tucking her copper gold curls under her cap. "You better load up; you don't know how long it is here for."

He glanced back at the slider on the car. Two of the older men relieved themselves out the open door. He quickly said, "Sorry."

Her shoulders shrugged in nonchalant recognition. "So what." Something was amiss with him. He hovered. "You're on to upper New York then, you and Jake. Your families will be heartened, will they not?"

It was midday, no sounds of approaching trains. No one about. This was the end of the line for the New Jersey rails. The scent of the Hudson River and the cool breeze assailed her. Home was across the river. Eager to get aboard a ferry, she glanced at Conner edgy as ever. Her gaze locked with his, she remained quiet, waiting. Her thoughts fully shifted to what lay ahead, not behind.

He mulled something, consternation clearly on his face, and she continued to wait. He had been kind to her. Even in his grief and burying his friend, he had been polite. Unusually so considering the weight of the war and his desertion.

"I know, Alan. I know it is not your true name. Someday I want to come back and find you, but I need your real name."

She was about to protest but decided against it. "What makes you think it is not?"

His gaze swept out above her, to the puffy clouds. "You'll hate me if I'm wrong, but I think you're not a boy." He winced and crossed his arms defensively.

Something inside her rejoiced, then quickly doused with fear. She masqueraded so long now, what was giving her away? "I don't hate you, but you're wrong. Is it my hair getting long?" Reflexively, her fingers tucked strands away.

Grim faced he said, "It is not your looks a'tall. It is something in your manner. Jake made me think so back when he said you yap like a girl. I've got sisters and I know what he meant. I've pondered it ever since, and he's right." He uncrossed his arms, shoved his hands into pockets, stood there sad faced and tired looking. "I'd not say so in front of him. I know you want to get home and it is safer to travel like a lad."

She said, "Now I know why you hovered about, watching. You figured me incapable of seeing to my own welfare." Warmth spread through her. He affirmed caring for her. Different from the way Hector confirmed her gender.

"If I get to Manhattan, how will I look you up?"

"By O'Quinn. We're from Five Points. It is where I lived when the Society people took me away. It is where I'm headed now."

He placed his hand on her lower arm, squeezing. "Then that's where I'll start when the time comes, Miss O'Quinn." His face broke into a smile that lit up his sad, gray eyes.

"I'm not saying you're right, Conner. I'm not saying that at all."

The whistle blew. He withdrew his hand and flung himself onto the floor of the boxcar legs dangling a moment until he scrambled in, and then stood. "You'll see me again, O'Quinn."

"It'll be a bright day for both of us." She did not wait for the train to move, slung her little bundle over her shoulder, and headed into her own future. The tune to *Where Do Fairies Hide* came to her. *Music in the air, fairy wings upon the earth, and mischief everywhere.*

Conner flattered her with his guessing, no doubt about that. She was near enough to being a girl again anyway, as soon as she found her *máthair* and they set their lives on a path for the future. She had promised Miss Haslett she would get in school and hoped she would be able to keep her word.

She had almost all the money she stole from Hector and paid the one-cent fee to the pilot of the Cunard steamer. It was two cents round trip, and no way did she need to pay for that. The seven-minute ride allowed her time to scrutinize the skyline of Manhattan, where the tops of buildings jagged the blue sky. To her right was Staten Island. When she glanced over her shoulder, she saw the blue hills of New Jersey. She had ridden the ferry with the orphans, but because of her bewilderment then, none of it was familiar now.

The ferry approached a forest of masts and spires, and beyond the domes and houses interspersed with trees, the sun broke through a smattering of clouds. It was a sign; she would be stepping on her land in minutes. She hummed the tune again. *This fairy would never have to hide again, and her wings would land her on the soil of her home.*

Walking the boat's plank to the pebbled ground, she kept herself from kissing the land. Her throat tightened. Tears threatened. She punched the air with a fist. Travelers brushed past her as she glanced about, almost knocking the bag out of her hand. She shifted it to her other hand and swiped at her brow, surprised at the relief that came over her as the world bustled about. The smell of peanuts roasting on a vendor's cart reminded her she hadn't eaten since yesterday.

Irregular streets lined with rows of warehouses and stores, many of brick, stone, and a few of white marble confused her sense of direction. She walked to the corner of Barclay and Greenwich and took a deep breath. The pungent scent of briny water, horse droppings, the familiar clip-clop of carriages, and idle conversations as people milled about brought clarity; she was home—after almost four years.

In some respects, she might be grateful to Hector for giving rise to fear and safety. Who knows how old she would have been before arriving at this moment if he had not shoved her. She leaned against a brick building witnessing the animation of a world lost to her far too long. It took her breath away, the senselessness of her absence; as if she emerged from abduction, not protected as the Aid Society professed.

Loud, abrasive sounds came from a street north of where she stood. Drawn to the commotion she found herself on Washington Street, where there were mobs of men, some carried guns, others cudgels that could bash brains. She proceeded to a shopkeeper standing outside his business wiping hands on an apron. "Sir, what is happening?"

His gaze slid from her boots to the hat on her head. "You dumb fool. Did you not sign for the draft yet? Otherwise you'd better git on outta town."

"What draft, for what?" She stepped closer. The mob's noise deafening and she wanted to hear what he said.

"Where you been boy, in a cave? This is the second day of the draft. Men don't wanna leave their families." Pulling a watch from his pocket, he said, "You got here in time to read the list of names. Start time was 10:30 a.m." He nodded at the mob. "They's angry and restless."

A fire engine, *Black Joke Engine Co. No. 33*, came through the street scattering everyone. The shopkeeper said, "Their chief's conscription two days ago got them all stirred up. Fightin' a war to save blacks. They don't get the sense of it. Blacks—and Irish— should go first."

She had applauded herself, that her timing to leave Gettysburg was perfect with the battle between the North and the South. Yet, this was far more dangerous to contemplate, and it was taking place on the streets of her home. She nodded to the shopkeeper and cautiously made her way toward Pearl and Cross—the southern portion of Five Points, the corner near their tenement 51 Mulberry Street, where her *máthair* waited.

As if innocent, or deaf to the riot several streets over, a vendor selling flowers beckoned her. She crossed over Broadway and bought an arrangement of blues and yellows of which she did not know the names, but the colors were bright, and they smelled wonderful. Her *máthair* would be so surprised. The vendor wanted an Indian Head. Giddy at the future that lay ahead, she gave her two.

Even with the bitter scent of smoke, Aisling immersed in the moment. A recurring dream these past years included her standing on this corner of Cross and Mulberry glancing up the street to the bend where her home was, up on the left, 51 Mulberry Street, a six-story tenement. She didn't recall the dreary facade or the stench in the streets and was glad of the sweet smell of the bouquet. Several lads and a woman sat on the front stoop, and smudged faces scrutinized her boldly. It was summer time, and the children were barefoot even with such filth about.

Chiding herself that she had not bathed in almost a week nor enjoyed a change of clothing, she smiled and skirted around them the few steps to the front door.

With each step up the four flights, she encountered soiled rags, rats scurrying at her intrusion, empty bottles, and heaps of garbage. The putrid odor and foul emanations gagged her. How did her *máthair* survive this? Already sickly when she gave her daughter over to the matron, who helped her? Who carted her water up the four flights from the hydrant at the corner? Who emptied her pot?

Aisling stood for a moment on the fourth-floor landing. The sudden realization of how utterly poor they had been overwhelmed her. Two doors, theirs on the left, Bartley's on the right. Other memories flooded back, and she reached for the knob to her home. Locked up, she knocked. No one answered. She pounded. No one responded. She chided herself of course. Her *máthair* would be at the laundry. She knocked on the Bartley's' door and heard steps and an exchange of words.

"Waddya want?" shouted through the door.

"I'm Aisling O'Quinn. My *máthair* lives across the hall."

"No one lives there."

"Since when, do you know?"

"Mebbye three years now."

"Are you the Bartleys?"

"Don't know any Bartleys."

The fear that she squelched for so long burst forth in her heart. The blackened door, shut and no doubt locked against her, became a foreboding. "Do you know the name of the family below you?"

"Yer askin' too many things. Get on yer way now." Hollow footsteps shuffled off.

She had not allowed herself to think the worst and would not give in to it now. She was not her parents' child to cave so easily, at least until she knew better, one way or another.

She sucked in her bottom lip and dug her teeth in until it hurt, bringing her back to the moment at hand. A bit of a problem presented itself. If she went to the Aid Society, they would probably already have learned she was a runaway. She decided to ask after her *máthair* at the laundry and bounded down the steps two at a time.

The urchins had not moved, but the woman stood on the walk, hands on hips. "Did ye get yer answers, what ye came for?"

Aisling's brow wrinkled with confusion. "Do you know me?"

"Not ye, but yer crown of hair. Yer ma spoke of ye."

Her mouth gaped. "What do you know of her, where is she?"

"Last I knew, taken by the Little Sisters of the Poor to St. Patrick's."

Aisling's relief was palpable. She was safe, fed no doubt, cared for with loving hands. "I can't thank you enough."

"How long ye been gone?"

"Almost four years."

"Do ye recall the Cathedral is up on Mulberry?"

She remembered all right. Every Saturday weekly confession, each Sunday Holy Communion and Mass until her *máthair* was too weak, and then she'd go off on her own for her weekly duty to St. Pats. Six or seven blocks north. The exact detail escaped her.

"I'll be off, then. Thank you again, Mrs..."

"Mathers, dearie."

"Thank you, Mrs. Mathers."

"You skirt that mob. Go up Chatham. It will take you away from their mischief."

With renewed vigor, she took off in the direction of the church clutching the blue and yellow bouquet.

# CHAPTER 6

*S*t. Patrick's Cathedral took up the whole corner of Mulberry. She climbed the two steps and reached for the door. The cool interior gave her relief from the heat of the afternoon. There was a strong scent of beeswax candles in the air. She had not been inside a church since the matron caught her stealing.

She slid into a mahogany pew, set the bouquet on the seat and, kneeling, made the sign of the cross. Bowing her head, she whispered a Hail Mary then an Our Father. It occurred to her to include an Act of Contrition. She was so close to answers, had waited all these years, and now, almost home.

Taking a deep breath, her chin rose over her prayerful fingertips, and from where she knelt, she slowly scanned the fourteen depictions of the Stations of the Cross placed at intervals on the walls. The beautiful altar railing and the marble floor caused her to speculate whether her *máthair* had been well enough to enjoy Mass since the Little Sisters of the Poor brought her here. She dearly hoped so.

She landed on Manhattan's soil in the middle of a riot, went first to her tenement, and now here. The sound of a scraping chair, a door opening and closing, caused her to glance at the back of church. A priest she did not recognize approached from the confessional.

"Seeking safety from the riots?"

Obediently she stood. He glimpsed the bouquet on the pew. "Not really. I've been away, I returned to find my *máthair*. A woman outside our tenement told me the Little Sisters of the Poor brought her here." Aisling suddenly realized something important and grabbed the hat off her head. Only women wore hats in church. "Sorry, I forgot I was wearing it." Stupidity, plain and simple. Something had given her away to Hector and Conner. She needed to be on guard, especially with a priest. He might not help her if he knew she was a liar.

"No worry, lad. I am Father O'Mara. If you tell me your name, I might be able to help you."

"Alan O'Quinn, Father. My *máthair's* name is Agnes O'Quinn." In it now, lies and all.

"Come with me, we'll find some refreshments for you while I look through our records."

Almost as if it had ears, her stomach growled. Father O'Mara glanced at her with an arched brow and smiled. "Sorry, Father. I didn't plan it." She hadn't eaten since late yesterday with Conner and Jake still on board the New Jersey train. Conner shared his jerky and crackers with her.

He said, "There is some unrest on the streets now. You didn't come through the wharf section, I hope."

"I took the ferry. A shop keeper alerted me, and I kept eastward on the streets." She grabbed up the bouquet from the pew. Father O'Mara led her to his office, a nice little parlor at one end. Windows glistened with the sun cheering the room. A woman answered his pull on the bell rope. "Bring us refreshments please, Signey. Make them hearty if you will. I've quite an appetite."

He motioned her to sit then went to his desk. "How long ago would your mother have come to our mission? Do you know?"

She considered the time involved. "I was put on a train June 1860."

His head of pure white hair snapped upward, he scrutinized her. "You're one of the orphan train children." More a statement than a question.

"No." A flush of heat rose out of her collar. She stood, grabbed her hat and the bouquet. Father was quicker; he stood in front of the closed door deliberately blocking her exit.

"I have no intention of hurting you, Mr. O'Quinn. I'm a man of the cloth, please remember that."

"Yes, sir...Father." She stepped back, placed the bedraggled bunch of flowers on the table at hand, and twisted her hat with nervous fingers.

"Why don't we begin at the beginning? It appears you might have quite a story to tell, and I've got the whole of the afternoon to listen." He gestured to the chair she sprang out of and sat in the nearest to it, putting his elbows on the chair arms in a relaxing manner. "I'm ready when you are."

She glanced at the closed door, at the hat in her hand, at the flowers whose petals had begun dropping, then back to Father O'Mara. A flush of heat rose to her cheeks, and she could feel the discomfort. She gauged his dedication to the Children's Aid Society and his position as a Catholic Priest. He would return her, no doubt. She was so close to finding her dearest parent, so near to the truth of her whereabouts. How could she not take a leap of faith? How could she not believe in the goodness of this Priest, though she knew him not?

She warred another moment as he patiently waited for her to make up her mind. Her gaze slowly lifted to lock with his. "You'll have to make me a promise, Father."

He laughed aloud with what sounded like delight. "A true Irishman if ever I've met one, even as young as you are. You'll bargain with me."

"That you will not inform the Children's Aid Society about me."

"I need to know how old you are."

"My birth date is April 2. I will be sixteen on the next then. Old enough to take care of myself."

His gaze left hers and wandered to the window at the end of the parlor as he considered this. His fingers drummed the end of the chair arms. "Were you born in America?"

"On a ship from Dublin in 1848. My parents lost my older siblings to the fever, in the crossing. My *aither* died in a meat packing strike, leaving my *máthair* and then she sickened, and the matron took me with a promise to keep me until she got on her feet. But the matron put me on a train instead."

"By what fortune were you allowed to return not yet sixteen?" His brows rose up his forehead with the question.

Her smile slanted, she tried to hide it, ready as she was to trust him, and willingly took the chair opposite, putting her hat over the knee of her overalls. "I'll admit to leaving in such a hurry I was unable to say goodbye."

"They didn't try to find you?"

"I wouldn't say that exactly. Posters were put up with my likeness, but a war between the Unionists and the Confederates in the town sort of covered any tracks I might have left."

Father O'Mara scrutinized her a long minute, perhaps trying to decide if she spoke the truth or not. What she said would have to stand; she did not intend to change her story, even if it was not all the truth.

The servant opened the door and pushed a cart laden with delightful aromas that caused her stomach to growl so loud, Father O'Mara's face broke into a solid grin, even his eyes twinkled.

Aisling tried to eat with a measure of dignity, but her hunger got the better of manners. She licked her fingers of icing laced with cinnamon and reached for an apple.

Father wiped his mouth with a napkin and took up his tea. "Here is my proposal, Mr. O'Quinn. We have a vacant room upstairs in the rectory where you can stay. I will give you a daily list of jobs around the churchyard as the weather allows. Otherwise there is plenty needs be done within. You will take your meals with Signey in the kitchen as she takes hers. She leaves after dishes are done and is back the next morning in time to make breakfast."

Aisling said, "You have not agreed to the promise yet, Father."

"So, I haven't, have I?" He set the cup on the tray.

"Here's the problem, Mr. O'Quinn. You are not of age yet. However, if I can find your *máthair*, all is well. I will set myself to that task. Until then, I will say nothing to anyone about your situation, other than I am housing an Irishman until his circumstances change. Is that agreeable to you?"

Aisling's heart soared. She wanted to hug him with overwhelming gratitude and sing and twirl about the carpeting. "Thank you, Father. I will try not to disappoint you."

He grunted at that, but the smile still lit his features. "Signey will show you where to bathe. She will also direct you to a room in the cellar where we keep donations of clothing. See if anything fits and give your self a change or two. You'll need one for the wash with garden work."

He went to his desk and placed paper and pen on a clear space. "Can you read and write?"

"I've been schooled since six years of age."

"Then write your name and your parents' name on this and where they came from in Ireland. The date, if you know when that was, and add the number of your tenement, too." He tapped the paper. "It will help me in my search."

She went to the desk, sat in the chair and picked up the pen. Father said, "I'll leave you to it. When you finish, go to the kitchen and Signey will show you to your room."

"Thank you, Father."

It had been awhile since she held a pen. Not since the last time she was in school, four or more months ago. She dipped the pen in the ink and began with her parents' names. It didn't take her long to complete the task. Leaving the paper to dry, she scooped up the bouquet and went in search of the kitchen.

Signey, elbow deep in flour, had a pot on the oven simmering with the aroma of chicken. "There you are. Have a seat and I'll finish up then turn you about the place. Your name is Alan O'Quinn then?"

Aisling nodded. "Sure smells good in here. How long have you worked for Father O'Mara?"

"More than twenty years. Too long, some days, not enough others." She slapped the dough roughly, mounded it on the plank table, and laid a damp towel over the top. "That'll do for now." She wiped her arms and hands clean. "Come with me, I'll show you the bins, where to bathe, and your room. From the looks of you, you're more than ready."

Aisling said, "I intended these for my *máthair*." She held out the flowers. "But it seems she's not to be found so easily and they need water."

"They do indeed." She took the offering, pulled a vase from the cupboard, and pumped water into it. "At least a day or two more left to enjoy." She set them in the middle of the table.

50

Aisling wordlessly gave thanks to the Saints for her good fortune. To top it all off, she would be reunited with her *máthair* soon. She followed Signey down the steep stairs to the cellar. A light came through a window, enough to allow Signey to put a match to a lantern. "Let's dig around in here and find some clothing to fit."

Signey held up a pair of knee breeches and asked, "Are you beyond wearing these?"

Aisling wanted to say she was beyond anything to do with boy's clothing, but instead she said, "I prefer trouser bottoms." Having said that, she found a pair and held them up; the length was right, and she set them aside.

Signey asked about spatter dashes made of stout wool.

"Set them aside, they're good for a cold winter's day for sure." She promptly found a middy blouse, a jacket and a wool sweater, and another middy blouse, folded them and made a pile on the table.

"You'll need another pair of work pants like you've got on, too, I'm thinking." Signey dug into another trunk. "And here we are." Signey held them up to Aisling. "A good size," adding them to the pile.

"I've been knitting socks for the poor box. I'll bring several pairs when I come in the morning." She folded articles that wouldn't do and replaced them.

Aisling surveyed the room. Gowns in a multitude of colors made her want to touch them, feel the softness. She stayed her hand; Signey might think the gesture odd. The sooner Father O'Mara found her *máthair*, the sooner she would be in proper outfits.

At any rate, she scooped up the pile set aside. "I'm fortunate to have the loan of articles that fit, and are clean. It has been awhile with all the traveling."

"That's what Father said. Come, I'll show you to your room and the tub. I put some water on to boil before we came down."

"I appreciate your kindness, Signey. Maybe you'll have something needs be done in the kitchen once I've washed and changed."

Signey shifted a wistful eye on Aisling. "You'll wish you hadn't offered, Mr. O'Quinn."

*F*ather O'Mara leafed through the stacks on his desk. His gaze fell on the paper he had given Alan. The script flowed in perfectly formed letters. He would have questioned the identity of the writer, but the script held the answers he needed to find Mr. O'Quinn's mother. He was not sure he would ever read a more legible, neatly written page. To think a lad wrote it. More like what a lass would have done, and perhaps not even then.

He planned to get to work on the search for the mother first thing after morning Mass. The dates and names should give him a good start.

*K*egan Galliger rapped on the open door to his office. "Afternoon, Father." He held up a brace of documents. "I needed to I'd drop these off as long as I'm in the neighborhood."

Kegan, fresh out of law school, was the son of William Galliger who was a wealthy second-generation Irishman. His mother died a few years ago, and his father remarried a younger woman. The senior Galliger was among the leaders in raising funds for reforming the foster child system of New York City. Kegan, as a new lawyer trying to make a name for himself, offered to assist Father O'Mara with St. Patrick's legal documents. Kegan also had a streak of benevolence in him. The apple didn't fall far from the tree in the Galliger household. St. Patrick benefitted from his advice and common sense.

Father asked, "Were you able to find the documentation on creating the Archdiocese?"

"It is all exactly where you suggested I look. I plan on filing the Vatican documents this afternoon."

"What about making copies, and filing those in another building? That would surely secure their future."

Kegan sat down, crossed one leg over the other, and steepled his fingers. "I intend to do that very thing. However, I am swamped at Trent and Johnson, and copying every document will take a vast amount of time. Can you hire someone?"

"I'd worry about the translation. You know the tone and the legal intent of the documents."

"What if I work with the transcriber? It would double the effort and cut in half the amount of time involved." He grinned. "It has merit; even you have to agree, Father."

The Priest glanced at the paper written in the lad's script. "Will this do?"

Kegan glanced at the uniformity. "I should say so. As usual, you are way ahead of me."

At that moment, Alan walked into the office, arms full of clothing. "I wanted to say thanks, Father."

The Priest moved away from the chair, revealing Kegan's presence.

"Excuse me, I didn't mean to intrude." The lad started to back out when Father stopped him.

"No, no, no. Come in. As of this moment, I've taken you off garden duty and am putting you in charge of writing."

Alan took a step into the center of the room and peered over the stack in his arms. "Am I being promoted, and I haven't even begun?"

"You won't think so." Kegan stood. "Is this the author of the script?"

"Kegan Galliger, meet your new assistant, Alan O'Quinn."

The two nodded to each other. Father said, "Mr. O'Quinn, you'll be working directly with Mr. Galliger on transcribing some documents for us. I'll leave it for him to set up a time that is convenient as he works during most days."

After the lad left, Father asked, "Have the streets quieted?"

"A crowd of five hundred or so outside the Provost Marshall's office, demand an end to the draft. The *Tribune* is part of the protest. They support it."

"A sad business, as both sides have a valid argument."

Kegan said, "Politicians are squabbling about how to contain the rioting."

Father added, "The Archbishop might be hesitant to jump into the fray."

"In this town, politics and religion are closely aligned."

"It'll be the downfall of us all if it continues." Father waved the paper in hand before placing it on the desk. "At least the Archbishop will be pleased to know the Vatican documents will be taken care of properly." Then he added, "This is only Monday. We'll pray it dies down by mid-week."

---

*A*isling hummed her way up the stairs to the first bedroom on the right. With an eastern view, she would catch the sunrise each day. Her life shifted right side up almost in the wink of an eye.

This was the first time ever she had a room of her own, a door to close, a window to look out, and a bed with sheets, blanket, and a pillow. She neatly placed the clothing into the dresser, opening each of the three drawers. A waft of cedar, fresh and clean, tickled her nose.

A cross on the wall above the headboard reminded her of God's goodness. She knelt making the sign of the cross and gave thanks. This surely meant finding her *máthair* was the next best thing to happen.

# CHAPTER 7

Friday, July 17, the *Tribune's* banner headline read, *New York City Draft Riots*. When the new military draft lottery got underway, mobs opposed the federally mandated conscription. Aisling knew this is what she encountered with her first step on Manhattan's soil. The mobs' demonstrations morphed into violent uprisings against the city's elite, exposing the deep racial, economic, and social divisions that underlined New York City's environment during the Civil War.

Cocooned within the confines of the rectory, Aisling heard bits and snatches between Father, Signey, and Kegan. Buildings caught on fire, *Tribune* workers faced off mobs with heavy gunfire, and blacks targeted. Violence spread like wildfire, until the Mayor formally requested the War Department send Federal troops. On the third day, the largely Irish Catholic mob dispersed when Archbishop Hughes delivered an appeal for peace. By mid-day, the first of more than four thousand Federal troops arrived, fresh from the horrors of Gettysburg.

Aisling looked at her ink stained fingers. She had come a long way but couldn't deny that her circumstance with the Smythes continued to haunt her. Hector was a result of his father's bullying, pitting one son against another. A shiver coiled its way along the skin on her arms at the memory of what he'd said to her that morning in the horse stall, what he'd intended to do to her.

She forced herself to think in the present. When Father asked her to write down about her parents, she was elated to sit at a desk and write with a pen on paper. Her *máthair* would say, *better watch what you wish for, you might get it.* A grin curved her cheeks.

Mr. Kegan Galliger explained to Aisling the necessity of copying all the documents from when Pope Pius IX created the Archdiocese of New York in 1850, and John Hughes had been elevated to the status of Archbishop. Manhattan consisted of mostly wood-constructed buildings. With the sad occurrence of so many burning to the ground, it became necessary to take precautions to protect the documentation of such an historic event.

Aisling, with her perfect hand, was glad to do her part to help preserve them. She rubbed her fingers and stretched them, then bent to her task. She worked on the second floor of the Cathedral down the hall from Father O'Mara's office. A large mahogany table surrounded by twelve chairs occupied the center of the room; plenty of windows along the south wall afforded good light. Mr. Galliger encouraged her to get up, stretch, and go for a walk now and then.

When she arrived this morning, he placed a box of papers on the table and spread out the items for copying. "You're quick with your writing, Alan. It was a good day when Father O'Mara met you."

Her mind raced to the moment of that encounter in the back of church, filthy, hungry, bewildered, trying to find her *máthair*. "I'd say it was a good day for me, for certain."

He pulled out a chair and sat across the table, casually placing both arms atop, fingers intertwined. His fingernails were clean, hands strong, a black onyx ring encased in gold on his right ring finger with a scroll that she could not decipher. Manly, handsome, friendly, she shifted her gaze. What if he could read her mind—she would die.

"Father's manner can be gruff; you have to know how to handle him." Kegan pulled his fob chain out of his waistcoat and checked the time.

Her contemplation drifted to him, handsome face, clean-shaven, black wavy hair almost to his collar, and eyes the color of robins' eggs, sparkling with humor. Comfortable with him, more like a contemporary than the bedraggled youth she looked like. What should she feel masked as a lad? She could hide what was on the outside, but inside she had a problem. With her hand, she brushed down the copper-gold mass of curls, but without means to contain them, she no doubt looked unkempt.

As if he knew what she was thinking, his gaze went to her hair, flustering her. A drop of ink splattered to the table and she let go the pen and reached for a cloth. "Oh, I've made a mess."

"Nothing to worry about." He pulled a handkerchief from his pocket, leaned across the table and wiped at the ink. "There, right as rain."

With wonder, she looked at him. "My *athair* used to say that."

He pressed the cloth into her ink-stained hand. "Keep this in case there are more drips." The warm skin of his fingers and the firmness pressing into her hand sent waves of something up her arm. Distracted, she nodded dumbly, and stared at the ruined handkerchief, his initials embroidered in the corner. "It is beyond saving."

"Now you have a rag to use in the future." His fingertips patted the back of her hand sending shivers up her arm. She drew her hand to her lap and lowered her eyes.

He sat back in his chair, drawing his arms to his lap. "Father O'Mara didn't mention if you have family in Manhattan."

"My *máthair*, Father's trying to find her for me. She's been ill. The Little Sisters of the Poor brought her to St. Patrick's."

"He's a good heart. If anyone can find the underlying cause of a problem, it will be him. You're in good hands, Alan." He smiled and added, "Cleaner than yours to be sure, but as capable."

Her fingers twisted about the cloth in her lap, and a smile spread across her face. "You're jesting with me."

"It is a relief to know you can tell the difference. I do want us to get along, and we've hours and hours of work ahead. I can't be here for all of it. The law office I work for wouldn't allow it."

She understood and pulled a sheet from her stack. "Here are some words I'm not sure I've copied correctly."

It was a long list of Latin phrases. He read aloud, "Q.E.D., a shortened version of *quod erat demonstrandum* basically means *which was to be demonstrated.* Viz. is a short version of *namely, or that is to say.*" He scanned the rest of her notations. "You're extremely precise. I'm not sure I would have drawn attention to this when I was your age."

Her brow wrinkled at that. Her age? How young did he think she was, eight, ten?

He handed the list back, saying, "Translate exactly as is, but continue to inquire."

"Yes, sir." She bent her attention to the task, finishing any conversation between them. His chair scraped the floor.

"Tomorrow then, Alan. Thank you for the fine transcription." He patted her shoulder as he passed on his way out of the boardroom.

That evening Aisling sat across from Signey at dinner. She made short work of the delicious pot roast pie smothered in gravy.

The housekeeper said, "I enjoy watching you eat. I like a healthy appetite in a lad. Reminds me of my brothers. Couldn't get enough. Ever."

Aisling said, "It was always me with my parents. Except when I lived with a family. Two boys and a girl."

Signey's sharp gaze focused on her; a kindly face with wrinkles that spread out from her inspection. She was a robust woman, different from her *máthair*, and Mrs. Smythe, both of whom were frail or sickly. "You're a great cook."

Signey laughed. "And you'd know about preparing meals?"

"I know about eating them for sure," she said before another spoonful went in her mouth.

"Has Father made any progress in finding your mother?"

"None so far. The Little Sisters of the Poor placed women in several different locations, and he is checking each one. I'd like to go with him and make sure he's not overlooking something, but the transcribing takes all my extra time."

"You don't have to work in the garden, you know. Father doesn't expect you to do both."

"I like both. And, if Kegan doesn't think I'm falling behind, I'll continue."

"Kegan is it?"

"He calls me Alan," she said as a fork full of mashed potatoes smothered in beef gravy entered her mouth.

"No reason." Her fingers tapped the table. "There's to be a festival at the Episcopal Church this Saturday. The women do fine embroidery and display it beautifully. I go every year. I don't expect you'd be interested in going with me?"

Aisling grinned. "Why not?" she said as she scooped the spoon across the last morsel of gravy.

"Being a lad and all."

"I...I would like to walk on the streets. I miss the crowds. And I can carry your packages."

"Of that, I'll be glad. I do forget you lived on a farm. When I was your age, I lived in the outreaches of Scotland. Urban areas do have their intoxications."

"I don't know anything about needlework."

"And why would you? I'd expect you to know more about horses and such."

Her eyes rolled. "I cleaned stalls since twelve. I know plenty about horses." Giving voice to the truth, nevertheless, she needed to remember who she was supposed to be.

Signey pursed her lips. "Hmm."

"You don't believe me?"

"Oh, it is not that. What are you, fifteen, sixteen?"

"I'll be sixteen April second. What are you thinking?" A loaded question, maybe she did not want to know what the housekeeper was thinking behind her wrinkled brow and all-knowing blue eyes.

"Not much. I've not been a mother, but you are proficient in an odd assortment of ways, transcribing, gardening, horses." Her fingers continued to tap the table.

"Don't forget eating," Aisling said as she put the last morsel of roast in her mouth.

That brought a guffaw from the housekeeper. "Right you are. I'll wash up and be on my way. Tomorrow is another day, and Father has a meeting with local charities here in the hall. I'll have baking to do early on to be ready."

"Sampling, that's another thing I'm handy at." Aisling picked up her utensils and plate and carried them to the sink.

Signey was off with a last remark, "Keep Saturday free then."

That night after scrubbing the ink off her fingers, she snuggled beneath clean sheets and sighed. With the scent of fresh air on her pillow, her life was better than she had ever dreamed. The decision to leave the farm was necessary considering Hector's discovery; however, it had been frightening to venture out on her own. Someone watched over her, for sure. Someone up in Heaven showed her the path to St. Patrick's and Father O'Mara.

And, Kegan Galliger.

He was the nicest looking man she had ever laid eyes on. His kindness made her heart soar. It made her not want to be a lad, which was impossible. However, it set her mind to wandering over possibilities that roiled with bewilderment and the unknown. She threw back the blanket and dropped her feet to the floor.

Like the men who gambled on the train, she would take a chance. She heard them say things like, *a pig in a poke, a leap in the dark*. In shirt and pants, barefoot, lest she make undue noise, she felt her way down into the kitchen, took up a match where Signey kept them, and went to the cellar.

She lit a candle and carried it to the table stacked with women's wear, which were mostly dark colors and drabs. She drew a gray off the pile, shook it out, and held it to her shoulders. It was long enough but twice the size of her waist. The next was brown with a dirty hem, and she put it back. Another brown, three-quarter sleeves with a tiny bit of lace appealed to her. She held it up, the length was right, even the width.

Holding it against her, she twirled and gasped with delight. This is what it would be like to be lass, a woman perhaps. A hand went to her hair, the springy curls wrapping her fingers. She covered her face with her hand feeling the smile spread across her mouth. Was she pretty? She took a deep breath. Would Kegan think she was pretty?

Suddenly frightened and insecure in a way she never considered, a dark cloud came over her. Still hugging the gown, she dropped to her knees on the dirt floor of the cellar and broke out in sobs.

Where was her *máthair*? She so desperately wanted her, wanted the feel of her arms about her, and wanted her soft lilt filling the air with a lyric. She wanted to be the lass her parents gave birth to on the ship after they lost all their sons.

With grief overwhelming her over the loss of a past she could never reclaim, her heart rent with pain. She drifted to the dirt floor, her wet cheek resting against the rough muslin of a poorhouse gown with a bit of lace on the cuff.

When she woke, the candle had snuffed itself out and a tiny bit of pink dawn sifted through the small window high on the wall. It took a moment or two to regain her whereabouts. When she did, she scrambled off the floor and the gown still clutched in her hands. Overcome with desolation, she let go of it as if it were on fire and it heaped to the dirt floor. She covered her face with her hands in despair.

The only motivation to move was the probability the rectory would begin to stir. Signey would push her key in the lock at the kitchen door and catch her creeping back to her room, dirty hands, in her lad's underclothing.

She grabbed at the gown, shook it and replaced it with the others, and ran up the cellar stairs. Scurrying to her room, she shut the door, and glanced in the small mirror over the washbowl. What had she dreamed to accomplish last night? Was it a weakness in her?

A promise to do whatever she needed to keep this position strengthened her resolve. She would forego any such weakness again; at least until Father found her *máthair*, and they rebuilt the life taken from them.

# CHAPTER 8

The days passed in a blur of transcribing and sometimes in the late afternoon, gardening before supper with Signey. Aisling saw little of Father O'Mara who was involved with the dedication ceremony for the Paulist Fathers. Recruited to organize along with the Mayor, together they involved the Irish Brigade unit from New York City, whose ranks filled with many parishioners of St. Patrick's.

Saturday was enlightening following Signey through the Episcopal bazaar. Everyone knew her, though Aisling figured most were not Catholic. Signey tried to interest her in needlework, but she passed. Sitting and sewing, even though a lass, held little interest for her. Signey's purchases of raspberry and blueberry jam were Father's favorites. She also bought a potholder made from someone's old dress. Some boys played kick-ball, and Signey encouraged her to join, but she declined.

They stopped with several of Signey's friends and talk focused on the news reported in the *Tribune* of Gettysburg's triumph of the Unionists. Aisling jammed her hands in her pockets and leaned against a tree as they discussed it. Miss Haslett came to mind. She needed to write and ask about the town, and more importantly, if the school and her home remained after the fighting.

Reflecting on her teacher, she must also tell her she was not a lad. It was necessary and important that Miss Haslett know her true name. She trusted her teacher would not give away her secret.

Signey trimmed Aisling's hair last night. It had gotten long enough to put in a braid. Signey considered a youth's hair should rub the collar and no longer. Aisling was not going to disagree. Signey also pointed out that she had grown an inch or more since coming to the parish and unashamedly put the credit where it belonged, on hearty meals. She ordered Aisling to rummage through the poor boxes in search of longer pants.

Aisling had avoided the cellar since the night of her emotional outburst and reluctantly descended the stairs, lamp in hand, forcing herself to face her behavior. More than likely, she was the last to be down here, and placing the lamp, she allowed her gaze to fall on the brown muslin with the bit of lace. There it lay on the top of the heap, a symbol of her great grief and childish dreams.

She dug in the trunk where first she found pants and middy blouses. Holding up a pair of trousers to her waist, she noted how truly short her current pair had become. She changed and placed the short pair in the trunk for someone else to benefit. Her body was rounding out on top, and lately she had taken to wearing two shirts at a time. Pulling a vest from the trunk, she slipped it over top of the middies. With the cooler weather of autumn, she would not be overdressed.

Another change in her body startled the daylights out of her three months ago, shortly after coming to live at the rectory, a part of becoming a woman. When it began, she was able to hide clues by dumping the rags in the outhouse. Oddly enough, almost four years of sleeping on a pallet at the farm between the bedroom doors of Mrs. Smythe and Giselle, she picked up enough from their conversations to understand what might happen to her someday.

Taking her breakfast dishes to the sink, she thanked Signey for the oatmeal.

The housekeeper said, "I think Father's got his hands full today. And Mr. Galliger arrived earlier than usual, so you best be on your way, now."

"Are you baking those nice raisin and walnut cookies today?" Aisling eyed bowls heaping with the ingredients on the counter.

"So, now is it, you've become a beggar like that man of the cloth, have you? If I ever get some peace in this kitchen, I might find time."

Aisling left laughter behind as she scurried through the door.

Seated at the table in the boardroom, Kegan's attention was on reading material, and he looked up as she entered. "Good morning." A smile lit his face. "You've scripted this perfectly. I would be so far behind if it wasn't for you, Alan."

"It his taught me a lot about the making of a parish."

"Perhaps you'll make a decision to become a Priest yourself?"

Her mouth almost dropped open at the absurdity. "Ah, well...er, maybe."

"From what I know, vocations come in many forms and out of nowhere. Not all devoted get the calling in early childhood."

Not trusting her voice, she nodded in agreement and sat down, pulling her work to the space in front of her.

Diligently transcribing a document from Pope Pius IX, Aisling tried to keep her mind on the task; but Kegan's reference to the priesthood nagged at her. She set the pen in its holder, folded her hands, and said, "So, what you've decided about me is that my living here in the rectory, under the benevolence of Father O'Mara, means he's expecting a *quid pro quo*. And you have had this discussion with him?" Her eyebrow rose in question as she challenged.

"Sharp you are, Alan. And no, we've not discussed you, or the priesthood, or the fact you dress out of the poor box in the cellar."

She gasped. Her hand flew to her chest. "How do you know that?"

"You're wearing a vest I outgrew years ago. I remember it because my aunt made it for me out of her dead husbands evening coat. Personally, that idea caused me to have an aversion to wearing it and I am grateful it is finally getting the respect it deserves."

She didn't know whether to laugh or cry. Indignation had her glaring at him, but the feigned mockery so plain on his face made her succumb to delight. "Shame on you. It came from your aunt. *I'll* wear it with pride and always say a prayer for your uncle when I do so."

His blue eyes glowed with mischief. Black lashes, the envy of any girl, opened wide. What was he thinking? Silence settled over the table, except for what went on in her raging confusion.

Finally, he said, "He earned a place in Heaven after forty-five years of marriage to my aunt. But I'm sure he will appreciate your prayers nonetheless."

He must have a grand family, full of love and memories. "Do you have brothers or sisters?"

"No. Nevertheless, it's more than made up for with cousins. A dozen of them. At least I can escape when I want. How about you? Any siblings?"

"My parents lost five sons because of a fever that raged through the ship when we crossed in 1848."

"But you survived." His dark brows drew together with concern. "There is a reason for this. You have a mission."

"I was born toward the end of the sail, after the fever had done its worst. I was told half the passengers died on the crossing."

"I would argue there is an explanation for you to have survived. Something that you will do or be in life. You are, after all, the son that lived are you not?"

Of course, he knew her as a son who survived. He would be shocked to find out she was the daughter and the last of the O'Quinn's. Not a son who would have been preferable, no doubt. She gathered her wits and smartly sassed, "A Priest you mean, a son to honor their faith?"

"No. I'm thinking not. The more I get to know you, the more I am considering a reformer of sorts. A challenger of ideas. How much schooling have you?"

"Consistently up until last April."

"Well, a good start on any path you might decide. But don't give up your education."

Her fingers flipped over the corner of papers piled in front of her. She glanced across the table at him. "You are the second person to say that to me."

"Who is it that knows you better than I?" His eyes widened with the question, a touch of mockery in them perhaps. She could not decide.

"A wonderful teacher. My last to be exact."

"Here in Manhattan, then? Maybe I know him."

"It is a she. And she taught in Gettysburg."

His mouth widened. "You were in Gettysburg in June—July? Dear

God, Alan, a good thing you got out. Have you read the papers? Thousands died."

Aisling suddenly became interested in the stack under her hand. She snatched up the bundle and began filing through it. "I almost forgot, I've gardening to finish before supper and so I'd better get this transcribing done." She threw him a weak smile. "Can't chat all day. I'm not a lawyer like you."

A look of contempt, or maybe confusion flickered in his brooding glance; he took up the pile he'd previously looked at, nodded in agreement, and began reading. She wished she knew what he was thinking.

Father came into the kitchen after supper and thanked Signey for the delicious Irish stew and dumplings, his favorite. He glanced about the shelving and she asked, "Can I help you find something, Father?"

"Where have you hidden the cookies? I caught whiffs in my office. I know they're here." He glanced in the pantry, shuffling jars of put-up vegetables.

Aisling got up from the table before Signey answered him. "I'll show you, but she'll only find a new place once I do." She parted the curtains that hung over the pots and pans and revealed a large glass jar filled to the brim with delights.

"A glass of milk would be an answer to prayer." He glanced at Signey over the rim of his glasses.

He set the jar on the table and pulled up a chair. "You know better than to deny me when I'm forced to endure the aroma of your raisin and walnut specials!"

Signey said, "But it does get you into the kitchen now and then, doesn't it? Like mice, both of you."

Aisling's contentment was such she forgot to ask Father if he had any information about her *máthair*. It was not until later, snuggled in bed, that she realized she had not.

Rain, thunder, and lightning lashed the streets of Manhattan for two days. Signey groused about leaving the rectory for home during the storm, but there was no alternative. Her cat would never forgive her. Lucy was an orange and white shorthair with a meow that could wake the dead, according to Signey.

First in the kitchen this morning, Aisling grew concerned. The housekeeper had not arrived. This hub of the rectory did not come alive without her direction, waving her spoons and pans. Aisling waited for Mass to end before alerting Father.

She knocked on his office door and entered. "Signey's not come in yet. Should I do something?"

He was reading a note just delivered and waved it at her. "Her cat's gone missing and she's afraid to leave without it in the house."

He glanced over the rim of his glasses. "Can you make coffee?"

"I'll try." It shouldn't be too hard. She watched Signey make it numerous times.

"Good then. The Mayor will be here within the hour. If you know where Signey hid them, bring a plate of cookies, too."

Twenty minutes later, back in the kitchen, Aisling reentered the kitchen from delivering a tray of coffee and cookies when the housekeeper blustered through the back door like the storm itself, dripping with rain.

"That cat is good for nothing. Caused me more trouble than she's worth." She shook out her raincoat and hung it on a hook, placed her boots beneath, and sat in a chair to put on shoes and tie them.

Aisling said, "The real problem with your lateness will be if I've made coffee that harms Father and the Mayor. I'm sure I'll hear about it in due time."

Signey looped an apron over her head and tied it at her waist. "They'll not notice. You've not heard their chatter, like hens."

Aisling gathered up dishes and put them in the sink, shook her head. "I'm off to the boardroom."

"Before you go, tell me how you get along with Mr. Galliger. I have heard he is a nitpicker. A perfectionist."

Aisling shrugged. "I haven't seen it. He teases a lot. Seems pleased with my efforts."

"That makes me ease up." She placed cups and saucers in the sink. "Alan, I've been thinking. Could your mother...well, is there the possibility that your mother didn't recover from her illness?"

Aisling clenched her jaw. Fear of that very idea kept her from speaking.

"Father O'Mara has not found any leads. I'm trying to work it out in my own head, that's all."

Aisling warred in her heart with the same unanswered questions. The housekeeper crossed the kitchen and hugged her. "You aren't alone, Alan. This is all our cause, you know. To find your mother or find out what happened to her. We've become of a family of sorts, and you need to know that above all else."

Aisling wanted to sink into her embrace. The changes in her body, more than anything, would not allow closer contact. Young women had no rights, could not make decisions affecting their futures. Her strength came from parading as a youth. She bit back tears of frustration and squelched the fear of the unknown. What if her dear *máthair* is not found? What if Aisling must remain a youth and grow to a man, then live her life as such?

A sob caught in her throat. She bit her lip to keep it from bubbling forth and backed away from Signey, almost tipping over a chair. "I've got to transcribe. I'm late." She ran from the kitchen.

Misery followed her along the halls. She wanted to take refuge in her room and bury her head under the pillow.

Father O'Mara came from his office at that moment. "Alan, the coffee? Was it your first effort?"

Leave it to this dear priest to swing her musing in another direction. "Well, you are none the worse for it."

"I'm a guinea pig, now, is that it?" He laughed. "I also wanted to mention that the Little Sisters of the Poor have kept excellent records on their placements."

"That is good to know. I'm grateful for all you are doing to help me, Father."

He took note of the open door to the boardroom and followed her into the room. "Good morning, Kegan."

"And to you, Father." Kegan stood when the priest entered.

"Sit, sit. I don't want to stop progress. All's going well I presume?" He dug in a pocket of his cassock, drew out a handkerchief, and began cleaning his eyeglasses.

"Alan is stuck with the most work. He is an excellent transcriber. Lucky for us you found him so willing." Both men grinned at her.

Heat rose up her neck onto her cheeks. A mass of confusion, she would have preferred a bed and pillow. Deep into pity from her earlier thoughts, she tried to swallow.

Father slipped on his glasses, tucking the ends behind his ears. "Well, I won't detain you." He stepped to the hallway leaving the door open.

Aisling reached for the tools of her occupation. The ink jar, the stand with the pen, and the next stack to transcribe. She needed to put her mind to her work, bury feelings that wanted to crawl into her heart.

"To work it is then," said Kegan. "You're a dedicated lad." He resumed reading yesterday's finished document.

The harder she concentrated on her task, the more her attention centered on her parent. A tear stained the sheet she worked on, then another. She swiped an arm across her nose and pinched her eyes.

Kegan pushed back his chair and came around the table. "What can I do?" He placed his hand on her shoulder and leaned over. Aisling sniffled and wiped her cheek with her shirtsleeve.

His fingers tightened on her shoulder, his voice filled with concern. "Are you ill?"

She shook her head, not trusting herself to talk. She didn't feel ill, more like bereft. What if Signey's suggestion was indeed fact? What if her *máthair* was dead? She couldn't make herself say the words; it might make them come true.

One hand on her shoulder, Kegan placed the other on her arm as it rested on the table. "Alan, should I call Father O'Mara?"

She looked up into his deep blue eyes, the identical color as her own. His sincerity overwhelmed her. Her hand covered his on her shoulder. Tears spilled down her cheeks. "I'm so sad."

*F*ather O'Mara stood in the hallway witnessing a tenderness he suspected. Struck by Kegan's obvious concern for Alan, he noted the solicitous attempt to calm in the face of...well, Alan said it, *I'm so sad.*

He needed to prod the Little Sisters of the Poor to try harder. The poor lad lived in limbo yet had adapted to life in the Rectory with nary a ripple. The devastation on Kegan's face as Alan looked up at him took the priest's breath. He saw a longing so heart wrenching, it almost made *him* teary eyed.

He quietly backed away and returned to his office. What he intended to inquire about struck him as unimportant now.

Troubling innermost ruminations came to him at odd moments through the evening. One second, he wanted to knock on Alan's door. The next he wanted to pay another visit to the Mother Abbot and discover the flaw in her record keeping that she could not find a simple woman, widowed, with a son taken from her, who lived on the fourth floor of the tenement on Mulberry. How much more direction would an organization need to give him answers? He even had a proper date, June 1860.

He was not much of a drinking man, but he opened a cabinet in his office, poured himself a small whiskey, and sat in front of the fire as he rummaged through the day. Kegan was a young man with high moral ambitions. Donating his understanding of the law to St. Patrick's was an honorable endeavor. The young man had goodness in him, too. Alan adored him; he saw it this afternoon in the way Alan's eyes lifted in despair as if Kegan had a rope to toss a drowning person.

The vision of it wrenched him. Alan appeared so vulnerable, alone, and small, not robust like a lad ought who to work the garden vigorously. In a whisper, Alan had said *I'm so sad.* The words haunted him.

# CHAPTER 9

The rain continued to beat against Aisling's bedroom window. It soothed her. The constant patter reminded her of early years lying abed and her *máthair* a few feet away at the stove stirring porridge, her *aither* already gone to the meat packing plant.

She threw the covers back; splashed water on her face; drew on trousers, two middies, Kegan's vest, socks and shoes, wetted and combed back her hair, and went down to breakfast.

Signey was humming when she entered the kitchen. Two places already set. "Get yourself a cup of milk. I'll be done with this in a minute." She stirred a pot of oatmeal. Aisling liked the connection to her *máthair*. She hoped today would not be so emotional, wanted it to be a productive, happy day.

Scraping the chair back, she sat. The housekeeper joined her, and together they whispered the breakfast thanks and began eating. Between mouthfuls, Signey hummed. A quirky smile curved the side of her mouth.

Aisling asked, "Your cat sent you off in a good mood?"

"I've other things besides my cat to warm my heart."

"Ah. Should I inquire?"

"No need. Nothing to be shared now. Which reminds me, Father has asked us to his office when we're done with breakfast."

"Oh, oh. What's up?" Aisling set her spoon down.

Signey shrugged.

Finished, they washed the few dishes and walked the hallway to the business side of the Rectory. Father was behind his desk and stood when they walked in. "Take a seat please."

They obediently sat.

Father said, "Alan, tell me your real name, the name you were given when you were baptized."

All her breath whooshed out, and she shot up out of her seat. Father commanded. "Sit, girl, for I am positive you are of the fairer gender."

Aisling obeyed. Her wide-eyed gaze swept from him to Signey, who was grinning from ear to ear.

"Well?" Father said.

"I...I..." She could hardly say her name, could not form the sounds her *máthair* voiced in her soft Irish. "A..."

"Spit it out," he commanded.

"Aisling." She cast a cautious glance at them. "My given name is Aisling O'Quinn."

Her head buzzed. She'd not said it aloud in so many years; as if foreign, like she talked of someone else. "Aisling, it is." She nodded, "Aisling." A small smile came to her at the sound.

Father stretched out his hand. "I'm pleased to meet you, Aisling O'Quinn." She put her hand in his and he shook it. All the while Signey sat next to her humming. Or, was it the birds outside in the elms?

Her hands folded prayer like in her lap. "How did you guess?"

His impish expression and squinting eyes reflected an inner self-satisfaction. "It might be my deductive instinctual powers that made me look at you and listen to you more closely than I did a few months ago, in the beginning."

Signey admonished, "Or, it might have been that you aren't exactly masculine acting or sounding."

Aisling glanced from one to the other. "You aren't angry I lied to you?"

Signey nodded to Father as if giving him permission to speak, which inspired Aisling. They must have decided together that she wasn't a lad; two angels who cared about her.

Father pulled up a chair to form a little circle with Aisling and Signey. "We suspect it was safer for you to dress as a lad. Tell us when it began?"

"I think when I was tenish, when my *máthair* couldn't go to work sometimes. For a while there was a little money to buy food, and it was safer to go out that way and get it."

"Will you trust us with the truth of the train?"

Her future was already in their hands, and she had no reason not to trust either of them. "I was caught stealing food by a matron of the Children's Aid Society. She made me take her to our tenement. My *máthair* was bedridden, sickly from the lye in the laundry. She gave her permission to the matron to take me. She swore to come get me in two months' time. The matron promised, and we left."

Signey asked, "That was the last time you saw your mother?"

She nodded and looked at her hands twisting in her lap. Her beloved *máthair* shivering on the cot, a weak smile played on her thin lips, though it hadn't reached her sad eyes that were filled with heartache at all the losses she'd endured. In this moment of memory, Aisling considered her *máthair's* pure heart. She truly believed her daughter would be cared for at the orphanage.

Father's inquiry came next. "How did you end up on the train?"

"I don't honestly know. There was confusion in the hallway at the orphanage, lots of others about my age and size. We were put on wagons, taken to the ferries, and then put on trains. When I realized we were leaving Manhattan, I tried to escape, and the matron hung on to me 'till we got to the trains and sat on the benches."

Father and Signey remained silent. Aisling added, "We were told how to yes sir, yes ma'am, and look them in the eye when the people who wanted children looked us over. They are foster families. I had it in my mind that if I did not behave in a civilized manner, at the end of the line, when I was left, they would take me back to my *máthair* glad to be rid of me."

"And...?" Signey asked. The concern in her voice matched the wrinkles on her forehead. She no longer hummed, and the twinkle in her blue eyes was gone.

"I ended up with a family who wanted a boy to work the farm. They had two older boys and wanted to teach another. I learned how to care for their horses, and they signed a paper agreeing to school me."

She took a deep breath, with all the remembering. "I fooled the matron posing as a lad. There were several girls, and me at the end of the line before this family took me. The farmer's angry eyes—he wanted a boy to work for him and did not think I was big enough. I prayed he would pass me up. The matron gave my name, Alan O'Quinn. I still thought he'd let me go when he said he'd wait for the next train, but his sons made a case for another pair of hands to work the stalls. He pulled me out of the line and said he would sign the necessary papers. I accepted it as what was meant to be."

"You were with the family for three years?" Signey's voice fell low with something, disbelief.

Aisling gulped air, tried to calm. What Signey, and Father, would conclude of her was vital. She glanced into each pair of eyes darkened with something she could not decipher. "I won't lie to either of you— not ever again. Please believe me."

At some point in her explanation, Father had gotten off his chair and stood against the wall, arms folded in front of him. He had not taken his eyes off her. His head shook, then he came to her, pulled her up, and hugged her. "We are giving you freedom to be who you are and tell us of the misery, Aisling. There is love in this room, and heartfelt concern for you. You are safe here." He let her sit back in her chair, and he leaned with his back against the wall.

Signey swiped at her cheeks. "So, tell of the three years."

"Closer to four, actually." The memory of those years a dark cloud of apprehension that never left her. What she said was, "It wasn't a bad time. They allowed me schooling until planting time each year. I slept on a pallet on the floor at the end of the hall between the parents and their daughter."

Signey leaned over and rubbed her hand. "How did it come about that you left?"

She considered long and hard before answering. "One of the sons..."

taking a deep breath as she recalled the violent scene in the stall, she said, "He confronted me..."

Father grunted his arms unfolded. "Did he hurt you?"

She could not look him in the eye and kept her attention on her twisting fingers. "I think he wanted to but at that moment his da called for him. And I ran away that night when they slept."

Signey grabbed her, hugged her, hard. "Dear Mother of God. What you've been through and such a sweet thing you are."

Father walked to his desk, shaking his head. "You are a strong, determined young woman. I would suggest even a pioneer of the foster children who ride the trains. You took matters into your own hands when you realized you weren't safe."

Signey sat back in her chair, holding Aisling's hand, squeezing. "I knew there was something about you that didn't fit quite right. I never imagined you a girl until Father met me in the kitchen early this morning before Mass."

That made sense to her. Her fingers twined with Signey's.

Signey continued, "But Father has an announcement to make." She continued to squeeze Aisling's hand and glanced at him standing behind his desk, as if again, giving him permission to proceed.

Clearing his throat, he said, "I'm going to miss you, Aisling. However, it is time you become the person God meant you to be. Signey and I believe it is best if you live with her and learn to become the young lady you've kept hidden all these years."

Her mouth dropped open. Of all things, freedom to become a young woman was not one of them. She lived with a fear he would call the Children's Aid Society and return her. Tears stung her eyes. She sat quietly yet filling with a wonder, she had never known. Her charade at an end, tears of relief brimmed, and she lost control.

Signey gushed with enthusiasm. "We'll not make a fuss. In a few days' time, I will enroll you in St. Patrick's school for young ladies under your real name. It is uppermost in our minds to protect you and not draw a comparison to the lad Alan O'Quinn."

With the back of her hands, Aisling swiped at the rivulets on her cheeks. Her breath quivered. "What of my transcribing? What will Kegan think of me?"

"Ah." Father exclaimed. "We've got that figured, too. Signey will take the documents back and forth. You will work on them in your new home. I do not think we need to involve Kegan in your transformation. I will say you've gone off, which is not exactly a fabrication."

"Will you still search for my *máthair?*"

He nodded, his lips pursed. "The draft riots have kept me from it. Now that all is somewhat back to normal on the streets, I made an appointment with the Mother Abbot the end of the week. However, Aisling, you must not expect this to be a fairy tale ending. We can hope and pray. However, it is important to be pragmatic in light of your mother's fragility and illness when you were separated."

She knew the truth of what he said and could not control the yearning in her heart. The softness of her *máthair's* Gaelic, how she would push back the curls on her face, the fuss she made over cleanliness.

Aisling recalled toward the end of their time together when she got into the cot with her tiny *máthair,* hardly bigger than Aisling herself, and wrap her arms about her fragile parent, trying to keep her warm even in the heat of the summer, was saddest of all.

Was it possible she was the angel in Heaven watching over her now? Aisling squeezed her eyes shut, hoping to chase away her fears. She needed her *máthair* even if it meant that fourth floor tenement in Five Points, and she promised to wear lads clothing the rest of her life if it would make it so.

---

*A*fter they ate, and dishes done, Aisling packed up her few belongings and went home with Signey They walked north on Mulberry, passed Bleeker and strode left on Amity. Signey motioned at a neat little whitewashed, wood home with a black knocker below the window on the front door. White lacy curtains hung over the window. She saw a necessary house in the back near a shed, bordered by large privets. They walked up the neat stone path to the porch.

Signey opened the door and an orange-white cat greeted them with a low growl. As she lit a lamp, the cat rubbed up against Signey's skirts and purred.

The cat's yellow eyes settled curiously on the intruder, back arched, tail in the air, and it scampered down the hall.

Signey laughed. "You've invaded her home and she's letting you know you aren't welcome."

Aisling had never lived with a cat, they were not allowed in the farmhouse. Barn cats didn't make pets; they kept rats under control, which kept maggots and lice under control. She shook the memory away, chastising herself for the disagreeable replection.

Signey took her hat off and laid it on the table in the hall. "Let me show you to your room. A coverlet is over the mattress to keep the dust off. Linens are in the cupboard in the hall." Aisling followed her, tracing the exact path of the cat.

Signey lit a lamp on the dresser up to maximum glow. "A smidge dusty, no one sleeps here. But now it is yours." The cat plunked in the middle of the bed, leg extended in the air as she cleaned herself.

Aisling laughed. "Well she knows something's up. She's either telling me this is where I'll sleep, or she's claiming the space for herself." She glanced about the small chamber. Printed-paper embellished the walls with ivy and yellow roses. The bed was made of white iron wrought into a curved design on the head and footboards. A rocker with green cushions graced one corner; a high dresser with five drawers, and braided rugs on both sides of the bed completed the room.

Signey said, "I'll put the kettle on."

Aisling set her bundle on the chair and shooed the cat off the coverlet, gathering it up. She opened the door to the front porch and shook out the dust. Emotionally drained since this morning, she tended to the necessities of the moment, glad for the rote duties, and made up the bed with sheets from the cupboard.

Signey's voice trailed from the kitchen as she talked to Lucy, probably replenishing her food and water dishes. A keen sense of emptiness crushed down on her; once again, she loosened the hold on her past. Tenuous though it was, it was her history, one of the threads of herself. Her mosaic past made her yearn for two parents, with one roof, and meals at the same table morning, noon, and night. Siblings to share would be like icing on the cake in her dreams.

Father O'Mara's pulpit voice overrode her musing; *count your blessings.* Her life changed again; transformed one more time. Her brain needed to catch up. Her prayers tonight would include a certainty. Father O'Mara and Signey were guardian angels, and she would thank God for them and her *máthair.*

Today had been her last transcribing session with Kegan, awkward to say the least. Knowing she would never see him again, not giving a proper goodbye was awkward. Nevertheless, if she told him, with his inquisitive nature, he would want to know her past, and Father insisted she keep it to herself. Father said he would give a plausible explanation for her leaving, and she trusted him.

Earlier today she had listened to Kegan describe a charity event he attended the previous evening with his parents. She read and wrote all the while, listening to the events in his life that separated them in so many ways. She would miss his camaraderie. He treated her with respect. Made her aware she possessed gifts, allowed her to feel good about herself. If they were true friends, maybe her lies would not rend their relationship, though she knew better. Kegan, a principled man, a lawyer; she, a liar, if it did not hurt so, she would laugh at the absurdity.

Finished making the bed, she put her few belongings into the drawer, and followed the sound of Signey's voice who sat at the table, the cat in her lap receiving an ear rub.

Tired, Aisling wanted to say something to this loving woman, but the only thing that came to mind was incredulity. "I can't believe within the space of so many hours, I've become a girl to you, and changed where I'll live for now." Her gaze swept the neat little kitchen, its sink, the windows, planked floor, and the table with two chairs. Her gaze came full circle. "I don't know how to thank you. I have nothing to give that will match the gratefulness I feel."

Signey's cheeks flushed with her smile. "My dear, having you here is enough for me. Knowing you are safe and have a roof over your head." Her brows rose impishly. "My roof." She shooed the cat off her lap and went to the counter. "Consider how grateful I am you are not a lad. It is thrilling. I would have taken you in even then, but that you are a young woman means the world to me. So, don't dribble on about how to thank me. Because you're already doing it."

"Seems I've spent my life in trousers and boots."

Signey wiped up crumbs on the counter and glanced over her shoulder. "You'll have a struggle with corsets, not that you need one, but proper young ladies wear them."

"I do want to be a proper young lady." The pitiful scene in the cellar came to her. Never in a thousand days would she have believed her life would change into the truth.

Signey left the sink, stood in front of her, and placed warm palms on the sides of her face. "And I will help you as best as I can. I cannot replace your mother, but I certainly can be the next best thing. An aunt perhaps?"

Aisling's cheeks widened with a grin. The warmth of *Aunt* Signey's hands brought a sense of security to a frail past and an unknown future.

Signey straightened the counter again. "Father has given me two days off. He even opened his purse. Once the moths flew out, he found a bit of money at the bottom. We're going shopping, my girl."

The next morning, after washing breakfast dishes, they went up Broadway several blocks to a general store where already-made dresses were on display. From the skin out, Aisling needed clothing. She'd never worn a chemise, stockings, or drawers.

Carriages clacked over the cobbled street, the scent of fresh manure added urgency to the bustling activity. Awnings hung over window fronts as women in capes and men with walking sticks rushed past. Everyone bustled with reason to be about. She enjoyed the earnestness. Most especially school and dressed properly as a young woman, thrilled her beyond dreams. Her *máthair* would be over the moon. She cast a sideways glance at Signey as they bustled up Broadway.

Signey chatted of nothing else but A. T. Stewart's Department Store as if it was a cultural experience. Manhattan's first large dry goods retail store. Cloth, ribbons, thread, bed linens, glassware, toys, jewelry, even furniture were all part of Stewart's. Signey's animated voice declared that one could peruse the entire establishment without the obligation to purchase anything.

It didn't take long for Aisling to realize why Signey revered Stewart's

Department Store. Two men attired in black from head to toe opened the front doors, allowing the women to step into the first-floor main section. They passed glass topped counters gleaming and twinkling with bottles and jars. Crystal chandeliers glistened overhead. Aisling inhaled the sweetest scents in the entire world.

Clerks, hair coiled atop their heads, crisp white blouses and black skirts, milled about, perhaps waiting to assist. Aisling whispered to Signey. "I've not dreamed of a place like this my whole life." She glanced at her shabby, poor-box attire, lad's work clothing. She was as out of place as a mouse in the kitchen. "I should go." Beneath lowered lids, she cast a look about the women at counters feeling their ridicule.

"Absolutely not. We'll march up this staircase where they keep the women's department. Wait till you see the delights up there."

"It is the sight of me I'm concerned about."

"Nonsense. We're here to fix the situation. Now you follow me." Signey squared her shoulders and placed her gloved hand on the mahogany banister. Aisling kept her eyes on the back of Signey's dress and obediently followed her up the steps to the women's department.

Two cotton chemises, three pair of stockings, one wool and two cotton, a boned corset, four pair of drawers, a pair of leather shoes, three shirts, and a hoop later, Signey and Aisling were directed to a parlor where they sat, exhausted.

A woman, most probably the head clerk, approached them. "Would you care for tea?" Her dark eyes flicked over Signey, then centered on Aisling.

Signey said, "That would be welcome. My niece and I are exhausted and still have more to do."

The woman's eyes widened at the word *niece* and she looked closer at Aisling. "Ah, may I be of some assistance beyond the tea, then?"

"We will need to purchase a day gown or two."

Tea served, Signey and Aisling reached for the refreshment. The head clerk walked off and spoke to two young ladies who disappeared behind some curtains.

When she came back into the showroom, she clapped her hands. Almost immediately a wonderful display of gowns appeared. Shop girls carried them into the room, spread across their arms, skirts trailing the floor. These were serviceable day dresses with long sleeves and high necks made of cotton, fine wool, and silk.

Aisling's eyes grew larger and wider with each display. Totally awkward in her clunky boots and trousers, and overwhelmed with the need for all the underclothing, she glanced at Signey, who had been eyeing her.

"Well, my dear, I think you should pick at the least two daily garments, and I would really encourage you to choose three."

The first shop girl spoke up. "With your copper hair, miss, blues, and greens are best."

The second shop girl suggested. "You're a nice height, medium tall, and slender. Vertical stripes would do fine on your figure."

Overwhelmed, Aisling couldn't think. "I can't." She pleaded with Signey. "You must select for me."

"All right then. I want my niece to leave here completely dressed in her new things." Signey tapped her chin. "Which one will fit her without necessary alterations? That will be my first choice."

A shop clerk came forward with a sage-colored gown, puffy over sleeves, and a darker green ribbon at the waist, with matching braid around the neck and down the front. "Miss, if you would stand, we can hold this up for a quick assessment."

She stood, and the clerk held it to her shoulders. Signey gasped at the sight. Her eyes watered. The reaction caused Aisling to step away from the clerk. "What's wrong?"

"Oh, my dear, everything is right. It is perfect. Go into the back room with the clerks and have them dress you. Quickly. My heart can't wait for the vision."

Signey indicated the parcels they already accumulated. "Take what you need."

The floor manager remarked to Signey, "Your niece is a lucky young lady."

Aisling flashed a huge grin. "My aunt is tired of the way I dress." She winked at Signey, and then followed the shop girls who gathered up their purchases and off the three young women went to the dressing parlor.

Behind a screen in the dressing room, Aisling took off her boy's clothes letting them drop piece-by-piece in a pile on the floor. The life she lived shed like the skin of a snake as the boots, socks, trousers, and two middies plopped atop each other. The vest, Kegan's uncle's vest, she folded and put aside.

The clerk handed drawers, a pair of stockings, and the chemise over the top of the screen. "You'll need these, miss. Tell me when you are ready, and I'll help with your foundation garment."

Clerk Joan came around the screen with an off-white corset and the hoop. "You won't need your waist pulled in by this." She wrapped the corset about Aisling's midsection. "You're nicely slender." She giggled. "You can't imagine some of them we get in here, strangled by the corset, but the dress must fit at any cost to comfort."

"If I don't need it, why must I wear it?" Aisling's hand swept over the cotton fabric that held the boned strips in place.

"It gives a trim line for close-fitting bodices allowing them to sit smoothly. Once we put on your day gown, you'll appreciate the sense of it then."

The wonder of dressing as a young lady drowned Aisling in silence. What if it were her *máthair* outside in the sitting room waiting? She quickly swiped at wetness forming in the corner of her eye.

Joan pulled gently on the laces that crisscrossed in the back of the corset. "You're a striking young woman, miss. I'd think you're plenty pleased to be showing yourself off as the beauty you are."

Irony came to mind, but the clerk meant well. Not used to compliments, Aisling had no reference to accept such and desired to be alone right now to perhaps savor it, but mostly to make sense of it.

Unmindful of Aisling's inner turmoil, the clerk chatted on. "You've kept your hair short. Will you allow it to grow now?"

Did she mean now that I am a *lady?* Aisling closed her eyes a moment. The clerk would have no idea of Aisling's history. Surely, she means well. Chastising herself, she said, "I believe I will, yes. Do you have any suggestions with my transformation?"

"Oh?" The clerk, finished with lacing, walked around Aisling, facing her. "I didn't mean anything bad, miss. I think you striking." She picked up the hoop skirt, flapping it to open. "There's many young ladies will envy you to be sure. I can tell you are timid about your looks. Young ladies come every day; you are definitely a cut above what I've serviced." Her voice lowered to a whisper. "I shouldn't show partiality."

"It is safe with me." Aisling's laughter floated in the air. "And I thank you for shaking away my nerves."

Joan placed the hoop on the floor. "Step inside the middle and I'll pull it up."

As she followed the direction, Aisling said, "Men have it easier that's for sure."

The shop girl drew the hoop up and looped the laces about Aisling's waist. "I've brothers. They haven't an idea in their skulls to what's necessary for women, not one idea."

Finished with securing the hoop, she said, "Now, we'll finish you off with the sage. A more perfect color for you, I can't imagine." She unbuttoned the bodice, top of the skirt, and dropped it over Aisling's head.

Light wool floated downward. Aisling slipped her arms into the sleeves and Joan began buttoning the back. Aisling slid her hands over the front, along the waist and skirt. "It is so soft."

Joan walked around the finished product, tweaking the skirt where it draped. "It is a lovely fit, miss. Ankles are not supposed to show, and it hangs just right. You'll have to remember to hold the skirt up a tiny bit when you need to navigate puddles and such."

"So much to learn. My aunt intends teaching me. She's quite eager for this change."

"Seems a loving woman. You're fortunate."

Aisling pursed her lips. She certainly was that.

"Time for you to look in the mirror, miss. It is on the other side of the screen."

Her skirts swished as she moved. The hoop swung slightly, a strange sensation as it hung from her waist. The leather shoes were comfortable, not as clunky as were the boots. She'd taken note of Signey's stride when they walked up Broadway to Stewarts and tried in earnest to keep to a lady-like pace.

Her mouth gaped, and she slapped a hand to cover the shock as she took in her image in the mirror. A curly mop of copper, pale skin dotted with a few freckles, and then the most gorgeous gown she had ever set eyes on. The little white collar and the sleeves of the blouse were a contrast, otherwise she was completely covered in the softest of greens like spring buds before they unfurl.

What would she become wearing such elegance? The sudden picture cast her into an unknown future that held the possibility of greatness, of schooling beyond the normal, of learning sciences and medicines. Her breath caught up with her brain, and she said to Joan. "Thank you for this...this..."

"The cinder-maid change, like the fairy tale?" The clerk grinned from ear to ear.

Aisling hugged her. "Yes, oh yes."

In the sitting parlor, Signey tapped her foot in anticipation. An hour had easily passed. She finished her second cup of tea when a clerk entered the room with their purchases. In her wake, Aisling glided into the room, ladylike.

Signey rose. "Even better than I imagined." The ferns on her bonnet waved in the air as she nodded. "Aren't you going to be Lucy's meow when we get home?"

Aisling couldn't stop grinning.

Signey added, "I knew this color was perfect for you, but I wanted you to choose the next two gowns and knew you'd have a better idea once you were dressed."

The head clerk clapped her hands. Joan and two other clerks entered with day dresses over their arms. Aisling and Signey chose together, a mauve and cream plaid, and a blue stripe that matched her eyes. A three-quarter dark-brown coat, gloves, and a bonnet were not optional. According to Signey, they were necessities and became the final purchases before leaving Stewarts. Father's purse was nearly empty.

Hunger dictated the shoppers find a place to enjoy lunch and talk about the morning's adventure. They walked two blocks before encountering the Gramercy Tea Room on Broadway. Aisling practiced walking without causing the hoop to sway. She had craved this for some time now, in public as a young lady. She fit the image she'd dreamed.

# CHAPTER 10

There were a dozen tables in the tearoom covered with white linen and small pots of flowers in the center. Signey chose a table in the front of the large window overlooking Broadway, the street jammed with carriages, utility vans, and people.

Though the draft riots ended in late July, it wasn't unusual for military men to be about. Even though the draft rioting in the meatpacking district had quieted, soldiers from Gettysburg still roamed the streets. The fear had been that rioting would spread to the rest of Manhattan. Buildings had been burned, coloreds beaten, a horrid testimony to the ravages of war.

Aisling guessed the Unionists on the streets wearing uniforms must be on leave, perhaps honorably discharged, or perhaps still on active duty. They walked with authority much as she had observed on Main Street in Gettysburg the day before the now famous battle.

Waiting for their order she glanced at Signey, eyeing her brown felt hat with a fern wrapped about the brim. Her delight in the activities of this day caused weariness now. "You probably would like to be home with your feet on a stool and Lucy in your lap."

"I'm happy to be right here, right now, with you." Signey unfolded the linen napkin and placed it on her lap. "Father's going to be full of questions. He has taken a deep interest in you, a caring one. He is a lovely priest, but I've not seen this side of him. You're in capable hands."

Aisling let her gaze wander out the window to the streets. "I never dreamed I would sit in a tea room, gowned as I am." A wind was rising. A man ran after his top hat as it landed in a puddle. He captured it with the tip of his cane then drew it toward the edge and gingerly tiptoed around the water to retrieve the sodden mess.

"I don't think it is too soon to enroll you in school. Now that you are dressed proper, we could present ourselves to the principal tomorrow," Signey said.

Aisling tore her attention from the streets. "I'm more than ready."

A server delivered their order, small sandwiches with *pâté maison*, and little scones filled with raspberry, and green tea. Signey's cooking expertise showed with the delicacies she ordered. "More than ready, are you?" She reached for a tasty liver sandwich. "I suspect you were born ready to learn. That's what I think."

Aisling picked up a knife and fork to cut her sandwich in half. "Tomorrow it is."

They ate in silence having acquired quite an appetite. Aisling touched the bonnet on her head. The purchase happened so fast, she hardly recalled the style. She knew it was brown, shaped as if a little pot lined with mauve ruffles that matched the tie under her chin. Her fingers lightly skimmed the scalloped edging. Perhaps it looked as if she waved because several uniformed soldiers passing the window waved back. One of them winked at her.

Within a split instant before lowering her gaze, she caught the unmistakable image of Hector Smythe wearing a Unionist uniform. Startled to the point of shock, she dared not sneak another glance and lowered her head. He might be just as unnerved and ogle her bold-faced. Out of the corner of her eye, she saw the soldiers move on. Her breath loosened. She hadn't realized she held it in her astonishment. Then she doubted what she saw remembering his father had angrily refused him to enlist.

Her hand shook, and she lowered it to her lap. She wanted to run back to Signey's home and hide. Her best course of action was to act normal. He may not have recognized her. She took a deep breath and glanced over her shoulder. The sidewalk was empty.

Thank God.

"You look as if you've seen..."

"A ghost? I think I have."

"Who?" Signey practically choked. "Who do you know?"

"One of the sons where I lived."

"Not the one who..."

Aisling nodded lips tight with inner panic.

Astounded, Signey said, "He couldn't possibly recognize you. *If* it was him."

"You're probably right. My hair is covered. Yes, I believe you are right." He had guessed she was a girl before she ran away and that increased her fear. He would expect her to look like a girl, not like Alan. She dabbed her lips with the napkin, really wanting to drape it over her face.

Signey suggested they leave, and her jitters caused her to stand so quickly she almost knocked over the chair. "A horrid end to a grand day."

"Dwell on your gowns or your new shoes." Signey paid with the few coins left in Father's purse. She laughed. "Now, there's a reason for moths to fly out."

Aisling lifted five of the wrapped packages. "Did he expect all of it would be spent?"

"Don't you worry about that. Stern though he appears, he has a heart of gold with a real sincerity in your welfare. He asked if you could live with me even before I had a chance to offer. He intends no question about your background." She gathered the four other packages stacked on an empty chair and cast a serious look at Aisling. "As a man of the cloth should be in this day and age of society's alarming lack of propriety. All brought on by the war, is what I think."

Aisling and Signey armed with packages, maneuvered the sidewalk. Pedestrian traffic lessened as they walked onto Amity. Aisling asked, "Is Father ashamed of my family?"

"Indeed not. He thinks you are a miracle. It is not a shame to be poor, he, if anyone, knows that. Your circumstances came about with your father's death, and your mother's fading health. That you persevered in the face of your parent's misfortune, elevates you, it does not cast shadows on you."

Aisling shifted the boxes a little, making it easier to navigate. "What concerns him about me, then?"

"The Children's Aid Society keeps records. They have since they began fostering children a few years ago, sometime about 1853 if I recall. The family you lived with may contact them to say you have run away. In that case, they may investigate."

Aisling's voice surprised even herself when she said, "They will look for a lad, Alan O'Quinn. And O'Quinn is almost as popular in New York as Smith."

"That's my girl." Signey gave her a sideway glance. "Spunky."

What Aisling kept to herself was the panic thinking of Hector. Was that him? Would he investigate her disappearance with the Aid Society? Would Mr. Smythe have sent him to New York to find her? She recalled Hector pleading with his father to allow him to enlist. If it was Hector and not some look-alike, he must have run off and enlisted without his father's consent. He was in Gettysburg the day of the parade, one day before the battle. Prayers whispered on her lips as they walked toward home.

They arrived to find a neighbor leaving the front porch; Lucy curled up in the woman's arms.

"Miss Blackwell." At Signey's greeting, the woman, dressed from head to foot in black, looked up. "I was returning your cat."

Signey dashed up the walk. "How did she get out? We've been gone all day."

"I came home after a luncheon, and there she was cleaning herself on the front step. I've enjoyed her company but am going out again and hoped you were home."

Signey set her bundles on the stoop, took the cat from her, and introduced Aisling. "My neighbor, Emily Blackwell. This is my niece, Aisling O'Quinn, come to live with me. She'll enroll in school tomorrow."

Miss Blackwell's face lit with curiosity. "What are your interests, Miss O'Quinn?"

"Science, medicine. I'll have to be tested to know where they'll place me." She glanced at Signey then back at the stern looking woman, hair pulled back in a tight bun, a no-nonsense hat perched squarely on her head.

"A noble profession for a young woman."

Aisling expected to be patronized. Miss Blackwell's response was a surprise.

Signey said, "Miss Blackwell and her sister Elizabeth operate the New York Infirmary for Indigent Women and Children."

Aisling brightened. "Do you accept aides? Someone like me in between my studies?"

Miss Blackwell gave her a hard stare. "It wouldn't be glamorous, nor would pay be involved."

"I'm used to hard work, and if it benefits the poor, all the better."

"Spoken like a charitable young woman, Miss O'Quinn." Her quizzing grey gaze honed on Signey. "Get her settled in school. Then bring her to me once she knows her schedule. Encouraging the sciences and medicine with young women is a particular interest of mine." Her pale brows rose on her high forehead and she gave Aisling a nod. With a twirl of her cape, she was off, black skirts swishing about sensible black shoes.

Later, after washing supper dishes, Aisling put away her new clothing, some tucked in the drawers of her dresser, and the gowns on hangers, in her pretty room. For a moment, she cradled Kegan's vest thinking of him working alone in the boardroom. Did he miss her? Alan? Beginning life as a young lady, something she only dreamed of, caused her to forgo working with a kind, generous, wonderful man. A man whose eyes danced with merriment as they worked, whose glib tongue teased, who spoke to her as an equal, though she discovered he was much older, seven years to be exact.

Reverently, she tucked the vest in the bottom drawer for safekeeping, then joined Signey and Lucy, who purred up a storm, in the parlor. Signey lit a fire in the grate and rocked in her favorite chair.

"I think you impressed Emily, and that isn't an easy accomplishment. She and her sister are extraordinary. I'm sure you wouldn't know, but her sister is the first woman to earn a medical degree in the state of New York, in all of the states, matter of fact."

"They are medical doctors, then?" she replied with awe in her voice.

Signey nodded. "Encountered a lot of discrimination to get there. From what I know, a heap of prejudice cloaked Elizabeth's admittance to medical school. When the male students rose up in indignation, she asked the president of the student body to take a vote. Much to everyone's surprise, Elizabeth's included, the students voted her in."

"Is Emily also a doctor?"

"Yes, earned hers in England or Scotland, I don't recall exactly where. They've run a clinic for years and moved into a new building over near Stuyvesant Square last year or so. If she accepts you, that's most likely where you'll go when not in school."

Lucy jumped off Signey's lap, wandered over to Aisling, and sat on her haunches directly in front of her, yellow eyes staring.

"She's waiting for an invitation to sit on your lap."

"So, I'm accepted, am I?" She made kissy sounds with her lips, patting the cushion beside her. Lucy lifted her paw, licked it, and sauntered off toward the kitchen.

Both women chuckled. Signey said, "I think this house is filled with head-strong women."

The knocker on the front door banged. Aisling gasped. She obviously had not rid herself of panic at seeing Hector.

Signey took note of her reaction. "I'm guessing it is Father. He is wondering what we have been about. As curious as Lucy."

Sure enough, Father's voice filled the hall when Signey opened the door. He entered the parlor full of smiles and took off his glasses that steamed with the warmth of the fire. "Do I see a vision of loveliness?" He pulled a kerchief from his cassock pocket and wiped the fog from his eyewear.

Aisling warned, "Your purse is empty, I know that much." She stood up to welcome him.

Placing the glasses over his eyes, he stared at her, releasing an "Oh my," he murmured, his palms together as if praying. "I came here to determine how Alan fares. It is apparent the chrysalis surrounding him has cracked open, and now a lovely copper butterfly." He looked over the rim of his glasses. "You do know there is such a thing?"

She shook her head. Filled with love for this dear priest, she couldn't help but give him a hug. "Not quite as you imagine, I'm sure, but certainly my gender now. Not that cloddish lad."

Signey came into the room with a tray of tea and cookies. "If you'll sit, Father, we'll tell you how we spent the day, and your purse."

Without mentioning the undergarment selection, Aisling and Signey delighted in filling him in on their excursion at Stewarts. Aisling wanted Father to understand the difficulty for a lad in trousers suddenly thrust into a hoop. The topic too awkward to discuss with him, how the garment swayed, the measured steps and ladylike maneuvering, but he listened with rapt attention.

Retrieving his kerchief, he wiped the sides of his eyes. "I never imagined. Thank the Lord I was born into the male gender."

Signey said, "Aisling thinks she may have spied the Smythe son on the streets today."

Aisling spoke up. "He wore Unionist military. He was in the company of others like him."

"Did he notice you?"

"I'm not sure. I do not think so, because when I glanced back at the street, he was gone. I believe he would have approached me had he known."

"The streets continue to fill with men in uniform. Hundreds roam the city waiting for the call to action. Let's hope you were mistaken."

Signey added, "Once you're attending school, you won't have time to dwell on him."

Aisling placed her cup and saucer on the tray. She glanced at Father. "We are going to school tomorrow. I can't wait."

Signey said, "Aisling met Emily Blackwell today."

"Now, there's a woman who doesn't let friction get in the way of the future."

Signey proudly mentioned, "Aisling asked if she could be of service at the Infirmary."

Father, about to bite into his cookie, stared at Aisling, his brows high on his forehead as if in wonder. "Is this so?"

"I've wanted to help when I could, but I've never been in a position. Nursing has been with me since my *máthair* became ill. It popped out of me to ask if I could be of assistance."

"Popped out?" He reached for another chocolate delight. "What was her response?"

"She asked me to contact her when I've got my school schedule fixed."

Signey added, "We'll know more when they test her for the grade she should be in."

He glanced at Aisling. "My guess is you'll be somewhere near the finish of what they offer."

"I didn't receive full years of education in Gettysburg. I missed out on a lot."

"Kegan extolled your knowledge, your innate understanding. He could not say enough about you. He's sorry you've moved on." Father pointed toward a package Signey placed on the foyer table when he arrived. "That's the last of the transcribing that needs be done. I do not think there is a rush. Tomorrow will be a busy day for you."

Aisling asked about Kegan. "Was he curious who would finish up?"

"I didn't give him a chance to inquire. Of course, he will recognize the script. I can evade any questioning with non-specifics. The least known until you are eighteen, the better for all concerned."

When she suddenly rose from the divan and walked to the window, she felt their concern. Aisling's mind roiled with uncertainty; was it gowned as a young lady for the first time in her life, or the opportunities afforded her? Not quite certain why, but she wanted stewardship—craved obligation and duty. She had slept as if a dog on the floor had lived behind a piece of cloth separating her from whatever came her way. She craved substance to make herself feel worthy.

Facing both angels, she said, "I will give back the goodness you've shown me. I don't know exactly how, but I will, and my first endeavor will be to apply myself in school. I hope to make you proud. You've been the kindest, most loving people I've ever known." She paused a moment, then added, "Save my *máthair*, of course."

Silence filled the parlor after her speech. No one moved for the longest moment. Lucy purred from Signey's lap, the fire crackled as it warmed the parlor.

Father cleared his throat, wide-eyed he glanced at Signey. "Did she declare her intention to become a teacher?"

Signey informed, "I heard doctor."

# CHAPTER 11

*M*uch to Aisling's surprise, after a week filled with testing in school, she passed all exams; and, with Signey's help, arranged for entrance into nursing school. Aisling felt as if she floated on air when she reached the kitchen at the rectory. Signey was elbowing her way past the kitchen door, headed toward Father's office with a tray of tea and cookies. "Follow me. We will talk in Father's office. He is in a frazzle over the Bishop's latest demands. I think your schooling progress will lighten his mood."

The three settled around the small table holding the tray, Father was quite pleased to hear of Aisling's latest accomplishments. He reached for another cookie when Signey warned, "Too many will give you indigestion."

"Well then." He frowned, put it back on the tray, and took a deep sigh.

Aisling didn't think her news, passing the entrance and exit exams, lightened his mood. "I hear the Bishop has you organizing his latest fund raiser?"

"Yes, well, he's a very busy man himself. However, I think he forgets running a parish isn't a walk in the garden."

Signey slapped her knee. "I've never heard you speak so before. Something's got you agitated, but I'm thinking it is not the Bishop, is it?"

The look of surprise on his face caused Aisling to laugh. "She knows your up and downs."

He said, "Time for me to get another housekeeper. I've no secrets."

Signey countered. "I'm not worried, there aren't any who'd take the job, believe me."

He sipped his tea and set the saucer on the tray. "There is another matter that weighs heavy on my heart. I'll get to the point of my feelings then." He faced Aisling. "There is only one way to tell you this, my dear." He placed his palms together. "I've met with Mother Abbot. And my news is not what you want to hear." His serious gaze locked with hers.

Her eyes keenly on him, he withdrew several papers from the breast pocket in his robe and began to read. "An Agnes O'Quinn from the bend in Fifty-One Mulberry Street was taken to the Infirmary in delicate health June 30, 1860. She took her last breath September 21. Mother Abbot wants you to know she was at peace and your name was on her lips."

He paused to allow Aisling time to reconcile. After a few minutes, her voice shaky, she said, "Please go on."

Father lifted the papers and continued. "Your mother was able to supply background information. She was born in Fingal, married Gradleigh O'Quinn who was born in Mallow. They married in 1834 at St. Brigid's in Fingal. They had five sons, born between 1836 and 1844, at the time they sailed to New York in early spring 1848."

He repeatedly glanced at Aisling as he read from the document. Tears wetted her cheeks. Signey reached over and squeezed her hand. He added, "The rest you surely know. You were born on April 2, 1848, aboard the *Constitution* out of Dublin to New York. I've read the manifest and it confirms your birth, and the deaths of their sons." He slowly folded the sheets of paper and creased the edges with his fingers.

Father placed the papers on the table. "Your mother's gravesite is in St. James's cemetery. Your father was a highly regarded member of the Hibernian Society, and as such, family members have plots in the consecrated ground. They are buried side by side with markers, but no stone."

The weight of it all crushed down on her. The futility of their lives—seven family members—dead. It was difficult to summon thankfulness for the early years with them. She needed it to be forever. Though a lifetime would not have been enough, what value should she place on twelve years?

Her heart had clung to the hope her dearest *máthair* lived. Aisling bent over her lap wrapping arms about herself. Sorrow filled her throat, pained her heart. She had so hoped there would be grown-up time with her. Time to share accomplishments, and a life better than the one they had lived.

The name Aisling meant vision or dream. Her *máthair* said so. All she had from her time with them was the name. Blurry eyes opened. Salt tears stained the sage of her brand-new, store bought dress. She looked at her cupped hands as they unfurled in her lap. Empty hands, empty heart. She glanced at Signey who wiped her own eyes and Father who pulled a kerchief from his cassock and blew his nose.

Otherwise, silence fell to the requiem of the late afternoon.

# PART II

**Two Years Later
April 24, 1865**

# CHAPTER 12

## Manhattan, New York

*F*ather escorted Signey and Aisling to City Hall where Mr. Lincoln's coffin was borne up a circular staircase under the rotunda. At noon, there was a private viewing by invitation only before the public viewing at one o'clock. Horrendously sad and unbelievable after all Lincoln accomplished with his dedication to the country as president, and then shot to death.

Signey wiped tears as she and Aisling stood behind Father. He touched the open casket and bowed his head in prayer, then stepped back allowing Signey and Aisling to approach together. Had she been spared viewing her parents like this? Her *athair's* wooden box had been nailed shut. She was young enough and had tried to understand why he was in a box; her *máthair's* burial happened just about the time she was settling in with the Smythe family.

She put her arm about Signey, who could not hold her sadness in any longer. Then Father led them down the stairs to the large room below. Tomorrow Mr. Lincoln's coffin was to be in a fourteen-foot funeral carriage and drawn by sixteen horses wearing black blankets. The viewing proceedings would wind through Union Square, eventually heading to Albany before returning to his burial site. A rumor whispered about was that Mr. Lincoln's young son, Todd, who died two years earlier, was exhumed. He was to be reburied alongside his father when they reached the destination in Springfield, Illinois.

Since the beginning of the New Year, Aisling's life was spinning out of control. She finished her first year in nursing school and was almost halfway through her second. Two months had passed since the assassination of the president. Aisling left the Infirmary early and walked south on Second. The civil war continued to rage on. The *Tribune* called it the ripping apart of the United States. Her only real connection with the war had been listening to Conner and Jake talk of the bloodshed in Gettysburg as their boxcar rattled along the tracks heading to the New Jersey shore. The same railroad that brought Mr. Lincoln's funeral bier to New Jersey, then on a ferry to Manhattan; almost exactly the way she came home.

She put so much behind her these past two years. Shed fears of bumping into Hector after she convinced herself she saw him in a Unionist uniform; enrolled in nursing school; put to rest thoughts of her beloved *máthair*. However, she'd not quite gotten over Kegan. He came into her thoughts at the oddest moments causing her a wistfulness she didn't know how to handle.

Bustling south on Second, she needed to drop off books at home before going on to Mulberry and St. Patrick's. The further from the Infirmary she walked, the more carriage, and pedestrian congestion she met, mostly shoppers. It was early afternoon; workers would not be on the streets this early.

Entering through the kitchen door, a muffled scream, and the crash of a jar sent her running to the pantry. Signey stood on a short ladder, pickles, and glass splattered across the wooden planks of the floor. A strong vinegar odor assaulted Aisling's nose. "Am I too late to offer an extra pair of hands?"

"Drat." Signey held her hand out to Aisling and descended the ladder. "I've a tray ready for Father. Would you be a good girl and carry it over for me? He wanted pickles with the sandwiches, but there lies the last of them." She sidestepped the mess on the floor and went in the direction of a pail and mop.

"You take it, I'll clean up." Aisling said.

Signey's head shook. "You take it up. He was asking about your work at the hospital. You can answer his questions while you are at it. You haven't been around, you know." Her voice trailed off as she stuck her head in the closet.

Aisling left with the tray. Father was at his desk, glasses slipped down his nose. He appeared in deep concentration. When he looked up, a big smile greeted her. "I've been missing you."

"I've brought tea if you have time to get caught up." She set the tray on a small table between the two chairs in his office. As he approached, they hugged and sat.

"I'll pour while you try to wipe the ink off your fingers."

He followed orders, and then reached for his cup. "Has Miss Blackwell promoted you yet? I've been expecting news any day."

"Your expectations are greater than the reality. Remember Father, not everyone believes in me as you do."

He rejoined, "What happened with the mother who delivered twins? Do I recall recognition you received for quick action with one of the infants? Breathing in his mouth brought him to life. She doesn't think that remarkable?"

Aisling closed her eyes and shook her head. What was she going to do with him? He assumed she would conquer the world some day. "Anyone would have done the same. It is common procedure."

"You've worked for Miss Blackwell almost two years. It is time for recognition."

She leaned over and patted his arm. "It will come. I'm doing well as an assistant's assistant."

"I think I'll pay her a visit and take your graduation documents from school to show her how you tested beyond what St. Patrick's could offer when you first enrolled so long ago."

She drew the teacup from her lips. "Promise me you'll do no such thing. I would die of embarrassment."

A knock sounded on the door, which stood ajar. Father said, "Come in."

Kegan Galliger strode into the office. He nodded at her but spoke to

Father. "On my way out of the office, this came over the telegraph." He handed Father the sheet.

Aisling's heart hammered in her chest as Father read, "The war ended June 22, with the last shot." He glanced at the two younger people eagerly attentive. "Thank God above. Our nation has suffered unbearably. Whole families severed by death and politics. President Lincoln must be rejoicing from Heaven."

Kegan smiled. "Perhaps our nation can begin to heal now." His glance shifted to her. He clearly did not recognize her.

Aisling fidgeted under his stare and lowered her gaze. She tried to think of the soldiers walking the streets of Manhattan, hundreds of them. Every day widowed women and fatherless children used the Infirmary, families torn apart without means because of the war. She wondered what would happen to the Unionists now that the war ended. She tried to rid herself of the idea concentrating on the larger one that remained.

Kegan absolutely did not recognize her. In this instant, that fact alone saddened her greatly.

"Aisling?" Father's concern jolted her.

She stared at her hands, a tightness wrapping about her chest, and tried to cover her emotions. Kegan, had taken a chair, close enough she could touch him. "I'm thinking of the widows and fatherless children who come to the Infirmary."

Kegan said, "I hope our government will step up with pensions. Right now it is a slide rule according to disability." He held a stack of documents on his lap.

She cast a side-glance at him. He was obviously here with church business to attend.

"I just realized I failed to introduce you both. Excuse me." Father said, "Kegan, this is Aisling O'Quinn. She works with Miss Blackwell at the Infirmary and attends nursing school. Aisling, this is Kegan Galliger, a lawyer who donates his expertise to St. Patrick's."

Aisling could not rid herself of the shock that he didn't know her. She nodded, at a loss for words.

Kegan said, "O'Quinn? Any relation to Alan O'Quinn, a young lad?"

She forced a normal breath and shook her head. She felt his blue gaze practically glued to her hair. Of course, he'd remember Alan's copper gold curls.

Forcing herself to look at him, he asked, "Irish, right?"

She nodded again, like a wooden puppet, and glanced at Father whose brows rose high. He appeared just as surprised as she that Kegan showed no recognition at all.

Oblivious to her identity, Kegan continued. "So was he. O'Quinn is common enough in Manhattan." He added, "I'm not acquainted with the Blackwell's, though the Infirmary is known throughout the city for all the good and care it does. In what capacity are you employed, if I may inquire?"

Father broke in, "She's in her second year of nurse training, and if all goes well, intends to pursue a medical degree after she graduates next May."

One of Kegan's dark brows rose. His intense blue eyes again scrutinized her, as if noticing her anew. He rose from the chair and placed the documents on the desk, as he leaned against the piece of furniture, he said, "Congratulations, Miss O'Quinn. Most women your age prefer to marry and start a family."

Her emotions were calming to a comfortable balance. The shock of seeing him calming, she found her voice. "You must be a modern man to have the ability to envision a woman beyond the kitchen and without a dust mop in hand."

He guffawed. "By golly, Father. You've made friends with a Bohemian feminist. Who would have considered a man of the sod, and a priest to boot, would encourage a young woman to such lofty expectations?" His arms crossed as he moved away from the desk.

Father winked at Aisling. "I've nothing to do with her dreams. She's been this way since the first day I met her, a mind of her own."

The heat of embarrassment crawled up Aisling's neck. "Bohemian feminist is it? I will have you know Bethany Crawley and Junemarie Sibbens, whom I am sure you have read about for their philanthropic endeavors, regularly donate hours each week at the Infirmary. I'm sure there's no time to scrub a sink."

Kegan's eyes twinkled. "And you mention them because...?"

Now she'd stepped into it. Even her ears burned with frustration. "Though they are wives of prominent New Yorkers, they're forced to use pseudonyms to publish. The press consistently maligns their articles as *Bohemian*. A phrase only an uninformed man would use." Her chin rose, and her eyes glared with satisfaction.

"Ah." Kegan, arms still crossed against his chest, rolled on the ball of his shoes, merriment clear on his features. "Labeling them as Bohemian keeps them from running a household, is that it?" He was full into his delight on the subject.

Frustrated, she took a deep breath, "Why must a woman be labeled as anything other than a woman?"

His glinting eyes darkened. He bit the side of his lip. He used to do that when Alan questioned him. "I enjoy an inquiring mind. When a woman takes to the newspaper to further her cause, it is an unnatural ploy. Then, not to use her real name? Come now, Miss O'Quinn, surely you recognize their lack of integrity if they need to hide behind a sobriquet."

Holding in the gasp that threatened to escape, she spoke slowly, "It is clear you are the one uninformed." She stood, smoothing out her skirts. "I'm expected back at the Infirmary by four thirty. They are short staffed right now." She cast Kegan what she hoped was a dismissing glance and pecked Father on the cheek. She practically tripped over her own shoes leaving the office.

Stopping in the kitchen, she announced, "The war is over."

Signey's hand flew to her heart. "No. When?"

"A week ago. Father read from a telegraph message."

"'Tis a shame Mr. Lincoln isn't here to witness it. Thank the Lord above."

Aisling said, "I'll be late tonight. Emily asked me to fill in for one of the nursing staff."

"Might it not be a good idea to sleep at the Infirmary rather than walking home in the dark?"

"I'll be fine. The lamps will be lit."

Signey looked closer at Aisling, "Are you bothered? Was Father grumpy? I know he's had a lot on his mind lately."

"No. It is not that." She drew her cape over her shoulders. "Kegan is with him right now. Walked in after two years and didn't recognize me."

"Well, isn't that what we want? For you to be such a lady, no one would notice the lad. Who finally and fully is gone. I'd say that's grand. Show's you've done a remarkable transport with yourself and your life."

Rain pinged against the window above the sink. Aisling pulled the hood over her hair. If she did not, the curls would tighten like a sponge. "You're right, of course. But, still..."

"Count your blessings girl. Now get on before you're late."

She hugged Signey and went off in a flurry of concern regarding Kegan and his total disregard for the child she had been. How could a man be so blind? A smart man at that.

# CHAPTER 13

$\mathcal{A}$ woman in a dark cape, hood over her head, scurried around the corner of Mulberry onto Second. Hector stood back in the shadow of a doorway out of reach of the mist grown to rain.

Copper gold curls tumbling out of the hood caught his attention. He followed the woman east on Second. His tongue moved the toothpick from one side of his mouth to the other. He pulled the cap lower, drew up the collar on his jacket, jammed his fists into pockets, and walked against the buildings, keeping less than a block from the caped figure.

When it was clear the war was ending, Hector shed the Unionist uniform and searched for means to earn a living. He was no longer that forlorn son, battered by a younger brother, and at the will of a man who, he was to discover, wasn't his father. No matter what Smythe thought of him, he was no longer that pathetic bastard.

He followed her as she hurried north on Bowery, then right on 14th and scurried up the steps into the Infirmary for Indigent Women and Children. His wartime cunning to lure and capture came into play. He stepped into the doorway of a building across the street and watched as the woman shook off her hood after stepping into the entrance. Her brilliant hair set her apart from any woman he'd ever known. The blood raced through his veins as he eyed his prey.

He bit down on the toothpick. It broke, and he spit it out on the sidewalk. His prick roused, he smoothed his hand downward over the swollen cod, as he envisioned her naked, that glorious hair spread across a mattress.

Hector rotated his neck, easing the kinks from his shoulders. Oozing energy, he needed to fight, to feel his fist against flesh. His younger sibling Earl, half-brother if truth was told, and the father's favored, was the target of Hector's pent-up bitterness. He pictured Earl's face screwed with malice as they fought in the hayloft.

Lamps glowed from the windows of the Infirmary across the foggy muddied street spotted with horse dung. He leaned against the doorway out of the rain. His thoughts settled on two days after he discovered Alan a girlie. He'd gone into Gettysburg to watch the troops gathering, his blood stirred at the action. He wanted a piece of it. Then he spotted the copper head of hair in the crowd that gathered, and he tried to grab her. The teacher took her away. The shopkeeper warned him to leave, and he returned to the farm.

The marching Unionists, rifles slung over their shoulders, Alan's new won freedom woke something in him, and he asked permission of the man he knew was his father, if he could enlist. He had never quite understood the boxing lessons encouraged by that bastard, though the fierce plunging of fists to face all part of his youth. Until that afternoon when he begged to enlist and do his duty.

That man snarled, stained teeth barred. "You're a tramp like your maw. Bastard boy you are. No one wants you 'cept me. They want men. You can't even best your younger brother with your fists."

Hector's jaw clenched as he recalled that last conversation, when he learned Smythe wasn't his father. His gaze slid to his ma who stood in the doorway, arms about Giselle's shoulders. She never said a word, simply watched his humiliation. He realized his worth was no better than a punching bag. He remembered the day Smythe tethered Alan to the breaking pole with a yoke on his shoulders. Hector was no better than that foster child was a beast of burden.

That was the night he made his way to town and enlisted as a Unionist. With his knowledge of the terrain around Gettysburg, he proved valuable in the battle that ensued over the next several days.

When the draft riots began in New York City, the President sent the Gettysburg Unionists by boxcar to restore order. It was the first time in his life he learned how others lived and what life was like beyond Gettysburg and Smythe's rule.

Weeks before the war ended, Hector along with hundreds of others, scrambled to find the next best thing. Some were welcome home. Physically fit, Hector had no desire to live under Smythe's roof, even if he were wanted. He liked life in New York City, the bustle, places one could hide and go about their business. Several of his companions were from New York, and through them he discovered camaraderie and a way of life with unlimited possibilities—survival of the fittest, and a hierarchy governed by strength and cunning. The Slaughter House Point Dive Bar and Gin Mill became his headquarters and its owner, Mad Mickey, his mentor. A man with such skillful slyness, Hector was always surprised at the fairness of his decisions, unlike Smythe who favored Earl.

For a month now, Hector had been Mad Mickey's eyes and ears on the streets of the Sixth Ward. In the north end, up on Bowery near Broome, the captains and sergeants of the Sixth Ward were busy shaking hands and accepting congratulations for terminating a riot that had broken out after Molly's Gin House shuttered.

It hadn't taken long for Hector to understand the process. Mad Mickey paid the Mayor to cut a wide berth around the Slaughter House. Mad Mickey wanted assurances the Mayor wasn't campaigning to win the next election using his termination of Molly's as a do-gooder platform. From what Hector understood, the closing of the gin house made perfect sense. A woman's body stiff with death, worms already taken up housing, had been found in the outhouse. Her husband had come around with a knife, slashing drunks lined up inside Molly's, accusing them of using his wife and discarding her. Hector concluded the husband would miss the income she brought him.

Hector shook his mind of the musings bringing him back to the reason he huddled against the door wall, palms under his armpits. The copper gold strands of hair curling out of the hood drew his immediate attention. It was like a beacon screaming of a young lad whose name was Alan. A lad he knew to be a girlie. Purely on impulse, he followed her.

Though it was June, the rain bore down colder with the wind off the East River. He'd wait all night if it took that, though he chastised himself with the unlikelihood the woman was Alan. He played out the scene in the stall the day he put his hand to Alan's chest. Built small, he hadn't expected to feel soft mounds, but they were there, and his prick had responded.

That next morning Alan was gone. Hector recalled the look on the girlie's face when he tried to force her. Shock, fear, he didn't much care. So maybe he found her. Maybe not. Soon enough he'd know if it was the same person, a woman now. He'd have her before the night's end. He faced the wall and pulled himself out of his pants urinating against the brick. A small cloud of steam rose.

"Mad Mickey's lookin' for ya. He's angry as hell."

Hector spun around, buttoning his cod. He recognized Billie's voice. "What does he want?"

"I think he expected you back at the Slaughter House. He's got the Mayor in his office."

Billie glanced around the empty street. The Infirmary glowed with light from within. "What're ya doing here for Christ's sake, ain't ya cold, and wet?"

Hector gave him a scathing glance. "Pretty obvious why I stopped, right?"

Billie shrugged. They headed toward the Slaughter House sidestepping muck along the way.

He figured the copper-headed woman lived near. She walked with direction, as if she visited the Infirmary plenty of times. He knew he could find her later. If nothing else, growing up and living with Smythe, he had learned patience.

Originally built as a four-story tenement, the ground floor of the Slaughter House, joined with the tenement next door, created a large seating and meeting area for customers to drink, dance, gamble, and carouse.

Privies were largely unkempt. Even though they were out back in the rear of the tenement, the stench reached out to dwellers and customers alike. The cellar below the first-floor bar and gin mill was Mad Mickey's office and doubled as storage for his gin barrels. The second, third, and fourth floors rented to his men and their families. Mad Mickey charged fifteen cents a week for a ghastly, squalid one room where the whole family cooked, ate and slept. Diphtheria, yellow fever, and cholera visited the slum with regularity. Mad Mickey's accommodations were the norm for Five Points.

Hector and Billie stepped up their pace, not wanting to further stoke Mad Mickey's ire. Hector didn't have much to report about the Mayor's closing of Molly's joint. It was a simple reaction to a dead body, at least until a possible motive surfaced during the investigation.

They rounded the corner from Bowery down Chatham and over to Pearl. Lamps cast eerie shadows on the cobbled filth of the streets. Horse dung smashed between the crevices, washbowl discards lingering atop already wet stones. Hector leapt to the boardwalk with Billie following suit. Raucous laughter mingled with the tinny pulsing of the piano. Pipe and cigar smoke filled Hector's nostrils. Smoking was the only habit he hadn't acquired since leaving Gettysburg.

"Is he in his office?"

"Was when I left." Billie waved him off and took a chair with one of the other men who swigged a beer. Hector understood Billie's reluctance to join his wife and kids upstairs in their crowded one-room home.

Hector's feet were so big he had to side step on the stairs. A light bloomed from the office, falling across the cellar floor. Hector deliberately made noise descending the stairs. He had no desire to surprise one of Mad Mickey's guards.

The men nodded in recognition. "He's been waitin'."

Hector pulled off his tam and stood inside the door. Mad Mickey sat under the glow of a lantern in the back of the cellar. He and the Mayor talked in low tones. After a few minutes, Mad Mickey waved him in.

"Hector, this is Mayor Reed."

Hector nodded. "Pleased to meet you, sir." The Mayor slid his gaze up and down Hector's length, a tiny smirk at the corner of his mouth, his features dark in the lantern glow. Grunting, his attention honed on the cigar in hand.

The Mayor appeared disinterested, very different from his

commanding presence this afternoon in the streets near Molly's, possibly tired after a long day of civic duties.

Mad Mickey said, "I'm putting you on detail to guard the Mayor."

Hector shifted his gaze to his boss' shadowed face.

"There have been threats to his person. He believes the threats come from the police department, as they seem to come from a source that knows his every move. I'm offering your services for a month. You'll shadow him every moment of every day, unless he's in the privy or sleeping."

Hector knew better than to refuse and listened hard as Mad Mickey continued. "When he's otherwise occupied, you are to stand guard. You'll take up a chair outside his bed chamber door."

Mayor Reed blew a mouthful of smoke into the thick, musky air of the cellar and joined in. "The best time for his relief would be mornings. I do believe I'm safest then. Still at home most days."

Mad Mickey smirked at that. Hector had other plans for his immediate future, and the last thing he wanted was rubbing elbows with this man for a month. Refusing his boss wasn't an option. Against his will, he said, "Whatever is best, sir." In the lamp glow, the cigar cloud circled over the Mayor's head like a specter. A chill ran up Hector's back. He sensed this man was capable of murder.

Business concluded Hector followed the Mayor out of the office, up the stairs, and onto the cobbled street. The Mayor put his foot on the step of the waiting carriage and dipped inside. Hector climbed in the seat with the driver. A half-hour later, they pulled up in front of the finest home in a district Hector had never been.

He jumped down to the street, a footman already at the carriage folding the step down. The Mayor signaled to Hector. "Follow me. I'm tired and will retire shortly. You need to look about the place and decide upon security. I'll sleep better knowing you're outside my door."

Hector took in the surroundings, marble floor; stairs wide enough ten people across could walk up, leading to the second floor. A black man, dressed in black bowtie, white shirt, and fitted black jacket and tails, welcomed the Mayor with a nod, his white-gloved hands reaching for his hat, cape, and gloves. "Sam, show this man around our home, the exits, that sort of thing. Have a chair put up at my bedroom door for him. And don't let it be too comfortable." He took two strides away then glanced back. "Hector, is it?"

At his nod, the Mayor continued. "I am assured if you fail me; your boss will kill you. But you probably already know that, right?"

Again, Hector nodded. He hadn't known, but acknowledgement would reassure the Mayor. He followed Sam into the back of the mansion. The kitchen had a single gas lamp lit on a sideboard, enough to see an exit door. He tried the knob. "This isn't locked at night?"

Sam's white teeth appeared in his dark face. "A kitchen maid stepped out earlier, apparently, she still is."

Hector pursed his lips. "Privy?"

"I would guess. It is not my habit to keep tabs on that sort of thing."

"Are there other doors?"

"In the library. They lead to the garden."

Hector followed Sam through a swinging door that led to the dining room, along a hallway, across the entrance foyer. Two huge panels disappeared into the walls as Sam slid them open. His white-gloved hand motioned toward the end wall, which was mostly a bank of windows affording a view of the garden, the evening cast it in darkness, but clouds moved on to reveal a carefully tended lawn in the full ray of moonlight. Shadows cast long dark lengths across the expanse.

The Mayor was obviously a wealthy man to live in this splendor.

He reached for the knobs and they held, locked. He asked Sam. "Have you a chair I can use?"

The man's white teeth flashed again. "Yes, and I'll show you to the Mayor's chamber."

---

*A*isling worked long hours for five more days until the sick nurse was able to return to the Infirmary. Exhausted, she had managed to study by candlelight when the patients on the second floor slept. Last night before she left, Miss Emily Blackwell gave her the day off, a luxury that encouraged her to sleep later than usual this morning.

Aisling acted as the professor's assistant in the biology lab, and today that class was testing, so she needn't attend. Plumping her pillow, she burrowed into the covers, savoring the time abed.

No longer sleepy, her mind whirled over meeting Kegan, more than a week ago now. She had been too busy with school and work to think of that day. That did not mean she hadn't considered the possibility of running into him again. More like, it is all she thought about with the singular desire of hope.

His distinctive way of inciting her to quarrel puzzled her. She enjoyed the battle of words with him, his features alive with merriment as if he, too, enjoyed tempting her. Exactly the same way he reacted when talking to Alan. He liked to spar, probably the lawyer in him. He most likely had been on the debate team in college.

She threw the covers back and went to her dresser. Opening the bottom drawer, she drew out Kegan's vest. Her heart fluttered as her fingers caressed the rich, dark burgundy cloth, touched by his own hand when he had unwrapped the Christmas present from his aunt. She sat on the bed, flattened it out on her lap, and brushed her hands over the brocade. Her mind went to fairy tale impossibilities—of Kegan's blue eyes sparkling as they waltzed to beautiful Russian music.

A patient on the ward, who, in her early years must have been a beautiful young woman, was dying of consumption. She raggedly talked of the music in her homeland and waltzing with her husband. Aisling envisioned herself and Kegan the way the woman described it with her colorful language, twisting some of her Russian with English making the telling sound like poetry.

Folding the vest, she placed it in the chest and chastised herself for the folly of such dreams. That she planned to visit Father this afternoon had absolutely nothing to do with the tiny hope Kegan would be there.

An hour later Aisling opened the door of the Rectory kitchen. She wore the mauve and cream checkered day dress, her least favorite of the three purchased on the day she became a young lady. Her dresses let out these past two years as she grew an inch taller and the bodice needed loosening. It was not in her nature to complain. So much given her, gratitude remained uppermost in her heart.

Aisling was of the belief her *máthair*, no doubt residing at the right hand of St. Peter, brought loving people into her life, Father, Signey, even Miss Blackwell. She mumbled to herself about Kegan. Surely, her *máthair* wasn't involved in the feelings that surfaced regarding him. The idea almost made her blush.

Determined to prove to herself she was *not* hoping to see him this morning, she deliberately wore her least flattering gown, the mauve plaid. A tiny spark made her believe this was all part of being a young woman.

Signey looked up from writing her weekly grocery list. "I see you took Miss Blackwell's suggestion to stay abed."

Aisling hung her cape on the hook and discarded her gloves. "Habits die hard. I had to force myself to stay put another hour, until Lucy caused me to stir with her interest in the robin's nest out the window."

"Would you like to accompany me to market?" Signey placed the pencil on the table and glanced at Aisling. A long list of items trailed down the paper.

"You'll need an extra pair of hands for the lot. When do you want to leave?"

"Father and the Mayor are meeting now. If you make tea and take it up, I'll finish cleaning and then we can shop."

Aisling put the kettle on and placed Signey's delicious treats, peppered with dark chocolate chunks, on the tray for Father and the Mayor, both cookie hounds. Signey hummed an old tune from her childhood in Italy, broom in hand. The sun filtered through the elm trees outside the window. Robins nested in the branches chirruping their familiar song, adding highlights to the glorious day. The kettle whistled.

Aisling carried the tray along the corridor to Father's office. She heard the deep voices of Father and the Mayor, not exactly arguing, but certainly in conversation on some issue of political importance.

Father stood when she entered with the tray. "Put it here, my dear." He cleared a place on the table between the two chairs in which the men sat. She nodded to the Mayor; and in that moment, her gaze fell on a muscular, tall man in the shadows, standing against the wall, arms folded across his chest, his eyelids lowered, and a distinct vile glower on his face.

Hector.

Coldness hit at her core. Vertigo possessed her, and she slithered to the floor.

Probably moments later—she wasn't certain—awareness came back to her, and with it an alarming sense of fear. She cast a wild glance at the empty corner of the office. Father was on his knees patting her face. She grabbed at his jacket lapels and buried her face in his chest. Desperation pounding her, she could hardly catch her breath. How did that man find her sanctuary? Why was he in Father's office? He could not possibly be searching for her, could he?

Father put an arm behind her and raised her up. "Thankfully the teapot didn't burn you. It swayed the other way when you fainted." His fingers brushed against her forehead. "How do you feel?"

"I don't know what came over me." She fell back against his arm.

"I do. You're working too hard. Sit for a minute, and then we'll try to stand."

Signey rushed into the office. "Dear Mother of God, what now?" She reached for Aisling's arms as she slouched in front of the chair on the floor. "What happened to you?"

She could not look at either of them, not when she needed to lie, and glanced at her hands balled into fists. "I've made a mess of your meeting with the Mayor. I'm so embarrassed."

Signey didn't allow Father to speak. "Don't you go apologizing for interrupting their chatter."

Father's brow furrowed as he glanced about the office, his voice sprinkled with bewilderment. "You cleaned the place out faster than a fire alarm. The Mayor sent his bodyguard to fetch Signey, and then they left, probably wanting to preserve your privacy."

She had not imagined Hector. A shaky hand swiped the cold beads from her upper lip and forehead. She leaned on Father's arm and stood. She wavered, and Father assisted her into the chair opposite Signey. She cast a sideways glance at the corner where Hector had stood. It was dark and empty. Her heart thumped heavily. It was Hector, she was certain.

"Your color is back." Signey took on the manner of Emily Blackwell fussing and nurse like. "What were you feeling when you fainted? Light headed. Weak?"

Aisling's mouth opened, but nothing came out. Astonished and aware of what happened, she kept Hector's identity from them. They would worry sick over her. She tried to think it through. Under the circumstance, she refrained from asking Father if Hector appeared to know her.

The trigger would be her hair color. Then she reminded herself, he *knew* she was a woman. If he did put it together, he could guess who she was. Although many Irish resided in Manhattan, and copper gold hair was somewhat common among them.

She took a deep breath and glanced from Signey to Father. "I'm feeling better. Restored." She patted Father's arm. "You're right. I've put in long hours of study, and it is catching up with me."

He retrieved a cookie from the fallen tray and walked behind his desk. "You'll have to learn to pace yourself, Aisling. I know the effects of hard work but fainting from it is not something I am familiar. But then you are a young woman."

In unison, the women gasped. Did he think females deliberately fainted when faced with difficult work?

"I'm poking fun." With a twinkle in his eyes, he bit into the cookie and walked over to the tray as Signey began cleaning up. "Just a moment." He scooped up two more cookies.

Signey said, "You must have a lot of women fainting in the confessional. You grasp the why of it for sure." She winked at Aisling.

Not one to talk with his mouth full, he glowered at her as he chewed the chunky chocolate treat.

A vision came to Aisling, the expression on Hector's face was one of victory, as in *I got you girlie*. She shifted her gaze away from their probing inspection. She had comforted herself that she had seen the last of him in the alley when the grocer protected her, and Miss Haslett came to her rescue. But, now the truth, like a slap in the face. It *was* Hector who passed by the window of the tea parlor.

She sank into the chair regardless it was soaked with the tea that spilled. A haunting fear washed over her. Was Hector investigating her whereabouts?

The real danger would be if he contacted the Children's Aid Society.

# CHAPTER 14

*T*wenty-three and widowed, Beatrice Molloy, with a backbone rigid as an oak tree, and the resolve of a soldier, firmly planted her dainty feet on solid ground after the journey from Drogheda, Ireland to Manhattan, two entirely disparate worlds, for which she was eternally grateful. Their ship, the *Manning*, moored in the Hudson River near Castle Garden for three days before allowing passengers to disembark. Even though, the country was in mourning for their assassinated President Lincoln, America's Independence was still observed on July 4. Fireworks shot into the night sky, a grand spectacle. A concert on deck included recitations and songs.

A rotting ship in the harbor was purposely set afire as part of the display, flames shooting out the many windows. It had been a partially stuck hazard in the waterway until set aflame, quite unexpected.

Captain Woodward offered her champagne during the festivities and proprietarily hovered the rest of the evening. A soft, bulky man, much older and needing a sharp razor not only on his face but the length of his grey-streaked hair. She avoided him as best she could until the time arrived when the immigration office in Castle Garden allowed her to disembark.

An examination for infectious diseases by a doctor was part of the acceptance into America. She knew she was devoid of any such diseases. What with the cloud of suspicion regarding her husband's rather sudden demise, it was prudent to leave Ireland and begin a new life.

With sadness befitting a new widow, she presented Mr. Molloy's death certificate to the immigration officer. Now, free to search for the only family she had left, Mrs. Molloy pulled out the yellowed letter penned from a charity hospital the summer of 1860. It was from Beatrice's sister-in-law, Agnes Feeney O'Quinn, who was dying. Her child, twelve, was in an orphanage.

The customs officer agreed with her sad journey to America, "'Tis a crying shame, 'tis. Too many families torn apart. Good luck to you, ma'am." He handed back the well-worn letter. "You can begin your search with our blessings."

She swiped at tears with the tips of her white-gloved hand, retrieved her proof of family, turned her back on the circular sandstone edifice of Castle Garden, and secretly praised herself for cleverness beyond imagination; her new life opened before her.

Happy with widowhood, she was grateful Mr. Molloy died before she truly despised him. He demanded liberties against her personal being nightly. In the morning, his cold foot against her backside, he shoved her out of bed, expecting her to attend to the kitchen maid and his breakfast whilst he slept. She oft wondered how he might treat her if she was big with child, but she had not given herself the opportunity to know. This was a man's world, and she intended surviving its many penalties for being born female.

He died of a strange malady that weakened his innards in such a way he was eventually unable to eat anything and drifted toward death. After her husband went to his eternal reward, Beatrice Molloy quickly made plans.

She inherited a small sum from her mother years before and had kept it safe during her marriage. Nevertheless, it was her husband's bundle she gloried in and wondered if he'd shifted in his grave when she discovered the little nook in his office. A year before he died she, quite by accident, heard him gloating over his hoard. She watched while he counted aloud and was nearly rapturous at the sum. It was not much longer after that he had taken ill.

Poor man. Stupid man.

Widowed, young, and with enough coin to keep herself for quite a while, if she lived modestly, she made a plan. Her mother's story shook Beatrice to the core. Beatrice was born in 1842 the youngest of ten. Her mother was fifteen when her first, Gradleigh, was born and forty-eight when Beatrice arrived. Later, when Beatrice was ten, her oldest brother married. He and Agnes had five sons, and newly pregnant with another when they sailed off to New York in America.

Beatrice grew up living in a scrub hut, dirt floor, no windows, but a chimney. Children stacked three to a bed with a fourth crosswise at the foot; the bunks built one upon another. After Beatrice married, she oft pictured her parents coupling in the night. Grunts and creaking woke her, but she was young enough, she had not known the source.

Beatrice's father worked hard, when there was work. She couldn't fault him for their poverty. It was everywhere one looked in the shallows and hills of central Ireland. When Mr. Molloy rode by their hut time and again, her mother would swipe a cloth over Beatrice's face, brush her hair, and then shove her outside to stand awkwardly and wave as Mr. Molloy rode past. After months of this, one day he stopped to chat, her mother standing in the door as he did so. Beatrice's mother lied about her age saying she was sixteen when she was fourteen.

Mr. Molloy did not take long to offer for her. Her parents gained two lambs and a sack of coin for the marriage. Beatrice gained a bed with clean linen and of all things, a pillow. She also luxuriated in meals cooked by a maid. Her sacrifice was, of course, her maidenhead and the nightly exercise Mr. Molloy relished. Giving up her virginity allowed her to wear clean clothing and live in a nice home; Mr. Molloy's use of her young body was another thing. Often her face was stuck in his armpit as his flesh slammed into her. There were times she felt she might suffocate before he finished spilling himself.

One bit of information her mother passed on was the necessity of dowsing herself after Mr. Molloy finished his pleasure. Her mother warned her, one night of not dowsing would get her with a child. Beatrice treated the information as gospel truth and never failed to do so. Some nights she had to pinch herself to stay awake until she heard him snore, then out of bed she would wiggle, no concern for the icy cold in the winter or the bugs in summer. The adversity of her mother's existence drove her to stay childless.

Beatrice took a deep breath as she walked up Broadway toward the Mayor's office. Safe from the fear of hanging, she relished her freedom. It was the first time in all her life she was truly grateful to be alive. Now she could relax to a life of her choosing, with papers she could show, if the need arose, Beatrice O'Quinn Molloy, widow.

Mr. Molloy's stone manse was the handsomest in Drogheda. Pride of ownership came to her each time she had stepped to the front door, etched glass in the top no less. However, the sum left by her husband's hoarding would run out eventually. She needed to plan for her future and gladly packed a trunk and closed the home. Leaving a home that would never be hers wasn't hard; from the beginning, she knew it would stay in his family.

She was convinced there were men in New York who could easily replace Mr. Molloy. Her first stop this morning was the Mayor's office. If he did not have first-hand knowledge of the Gradleigh O'Quinn's perhaps, he could direct her to a recordkeeping office somewhere in the great city of Manhattan. She approached a woman behind a desk. "I would like to make an appointment with the Mayor, please." Her gown of black broadcloth with matching hat and veil would set the stage for mourning, an inducement to assist in her search she hoped. The black brought out the cream of her skin, and set her green eyes flashing.

The young woman asked, "Your name, ma'am?" She nodded to a big, handsome man who entered the lobby and walked directly to the door with the word Mayor painted on the glass.

"Mrs. Beatrice O'Quinn Molloy." Her gaze followed him. "Is that the Mayor?"

"No, ma'am. He works for His Honor."

"I take it Mayor Reed must be in."

"Yes, ma'am. I have his schedule right here, but I cannot make an appointment unless he directs me to do so. If you will take a seat, I will ask. Oh, and may I tell him your business?"

"I am newly arrived from Ireland and in search of my family, the Gradleigh O'Quinn's."

With that, the young woman entered the office door and closed it behind her.

Beatrice glanced about the lobby. Well appointed, marble floors, wide windows looking out on the bustling metropolis. She did not have long to wait.

"The Mayor will see you now, ma'am."

She stood, swept a hand over her skirt to smooth wrinkles, and patted her veil.

Mayor Reed, a balding, paunchy man, stood as Beatrice entered. "Welcome to Manhattan, Mrs. Molloy."

His office was ornate, a shelf with framed awards, mahogany desk, large windows overlooking the city behind his chair. The man she took note of in the lobby stood against the wall in a corner, arms crossed over his chest, a dark-haired, rugged, but handsome sort. "I arrived in your wonderful city a week ago. The fourth of July to be exact and enjoyed your independence celebration from the *Manning's* deck. Quite a sight for a woman from the rolling sheep farms of central Ireland, I can assure you."

He directed her to a chair and sat across from her, not behind his desk. "We pride ourselves on the celebration each year. We are a prospering nation to be sure. Now, Mrs. Molloy, I understand you search for family?"

"My brother, Gradleigh O'Quinn. Perhaps called Gradey. His wife, Agnes, and five sons. Most have copper red hair, curly. I do not know anything about them and am not sure where to begin my search. Perhaps you would be able to direct me." The tip of her little pink tongue wetted her lower lip. Her firm eye contact with him acknowledged his interest in her person.

His gaze traveled over her features and began a descent to her bodice, then drifted back to her face. She forced a blush and tremulous smile as he said, "The name O'Quinn is common in the city. Large families are also abundant. You could inquire at the immigration office. Do you know the year they arrived?"

"Early summer 1848. I remember because I was near seven."

"Do you know the port they sailed from?"

"Dublin." Her tongue darted over her lip again. She leaned toward him, her gloved hand rested on his arm. Certain enticements lured men and she wanted this man to do her bidding.

He nodded to the man in the corner. "Mr. Smythe is in my employ. I will direct him to accompany you to the immigration office and stay with you until satisfaction is given."

Mayor Reed stood, indicating the interview was over. She gathered her reticule, stood, and faced the man introduced to her.

"Hector, this is Mrs. Molloy. I will not need you the rest of the afternoon. I'm quite certain it will take all of that at the immigration center." He said to her. "They are a slow office, not efficient, but they do boast an excellent record file on immigration."

She flashed him what she considered her most beguiling smile. "Thank you for helping me, sir. I'd be lost in this great city of yours without such kindness."

His chest puffed, and he stuck his thumbs into the sides of his vest armholes. "You find your way to my office any time you please, Mrs. Molloy. It is my policy to be of service to my constituents."

---

*A* week after the dreadful fainting episode in Father's office, Aisling still looked over her shoulder, up and down streets on her way to the Infirmary. She chided that Hector did not know where she lived; only that she delivered tea to Father in the rectory.

Manhattan was certainly big enough for the two of them. Her second year in nursing school would end next May with her graduation. She had not made any definite plans, hoping against all else, Miss Blackwell would hire her. Hector would not dare approach her. Yet, a cold shiver sliced along her spine at the evil that smoldered from him, the way his menacing, powerful body braced as if filled with rage. She never wanted to be alone with him again. Once in her life was more than enough.

At home, Signey had the kettle on and the table set as Aisling walked in the door from the Infirmary. A late July storm passed earlier in the day leaving branches down and swishing horse droppings into the gutters. A clean scent filled the air for a change.

Aisling hung her cape on the hook and untied her bonnet. Earlier, she coiled and pinned her hair with a net at her nape. She could almost feel it tighten with the dampness. "It is good to be home. How was your day?"

Signey wiped her hands against the apron at her waist. "My day was unusual to say the least. Father was off right after Mass. The children's choir practiced all morning in the nave and the music was delightful. I believe they are singing for a wedding this Saturday."

Signey warmed leftover soup made earlier for Father's dinner. Her delicious rye rolls, crusted with salt, and a dish of whipped butter sat on the table. Aisling was hungry. She shared her lunch today with another intern who slept in and did not have time to put together a bag.

"Did you say whose wedding?" Aisling was searching in the pantry for an apron, her voice muffled.

"A niece of the Archbishop's. They have not lived here long. From England as I recall. The father works for the *Tribune*. They were Anglicans and converted after they left England."

Tying the apron around her waist, Aisling said, "How nice. I probably wouldn't know the last name."

Signey shrugged. "I certainly don't. It is remarkable because Father wants every detail perfect. He doesn't allow non-parishioners to use his sanctuary. But he can't say no to the Archbishop now, can he?"

"He has no choice in the matter." She drew water for them to drink. The front bell clanged. "I'll get it."

Kegan Galliger presented himself holding a small bouquet of red and yellow coneflowers surrounded by lacy ferns. "I hope I haven't come at a bad time?"

Her heart skipped a beat. "Come in. This is a pleasant surprise."

Signey called from the kitchen. "Do I hear Mr. Galliger's voice?" She met them in the hall.

"These are for both of you. To brighten your late summer evening perhaps." His delightful grin and twinkling eyes intrigued her. This was the Kegan that had not forgotten the vest his Aunt made as a gift to remember his Uncle. Then there was the Kegan who would not wear the vest and gave it to the poor box.

Signey nodded to Aisling to take the flowers. "We were about to have some soup. Are you hungry? Could you sit with us?"

"I don't want to be a bother. Father gave me your address suggesting I visit." His deep blue gaze shifted to Aisling as a grin brought out a dimple.

Flustered, she felt the dratted heat on her neck. "How nice of you. If you don't mind the kitchen, you are welcome to sup with us."

In short order, a third place was set, and the late afternoon drifted by on the wings of laughter and teasing. Aisling enjoyed his presence at their table. He was equally interested in Signey and asked how she spent the day. Signey reported on Father's Day more than her own and Aisling took comfort in how intertwined their lives probably had been for years and years.

On a serious note, Kegan asked, "Have you walked the Ramble in the park yet?"

Signey said, "I've not walked it, but I hear it is very pretty, and the flowers right now should be approaching their finest. Doesn't the Ramble take you through gardens, and leads up to a beautiful bridge?"

He glanced at Aisling. "Would you care to walk with me? We could get an ice at the vendor provided he stays past dark." To Signey, he said, "If we pitch in, the dishes won't take any time. What do you say?"

"No. You two go on. I am ready to put my feet up. Father had so much going on; he tired me out more than usual."

Kegan stood, rolled up his sleeves, and nodded to Aisling. "Let's get these washed. Then we'll go." He stacked the bowls. "The meal was delicious. I don't cook much and appreciate being included."

Aisling teased, "You didn't fool us one bit. A bachelor with flowers in hand, and at dinner time?"

He looked over his shoulder at her, a look of feigned outrage on his handsome features. She added, "Next time, we'll hope you bring chocolates."

Kegan laughed sending ripples of delight through the air. "Greedy little thing, aren't you?"

She reached for the kettle to boil water and glanced at Signey. "Put those tired feet of yours up. I'll bring you a cup of tea."

Within the hour, Kegan and Aisling walked north on Broadway and hailed a hack that dropped them on the southwest corner of Central Park. Kegan assisted Aisling down the step and drew her hand through his arm as they moved toward the southern entrance. Several families walked the paths with babies in prams. Giant elms and oaks dotted the rolling landscape. A glow lit the sky with the sun beginning to slide into the west. A lamp lighter was doing his best to keep up with the approaching evening.

Kegan said, "The Ramble is an interesting woodland walk. I'm keen on sharing it with you."

Aisling clung to his arm as they approached a bridle path filled with carriages and horses. "You enjoy this commerce? I pictured you drawn to quieter places?" It was necessary to wait for a space between traffic in which they could cross.

Grinning, he said, "Picture me do you?"

She tried to withdraw her hand, but he placed his other hand atop hers as it rested on his arm. "I couldn't resist," a soft chuckle mingled with his declaration, "the rub is in getting to the serenity. Hopefully you'll be impressed." A gust of wind blew, and he grabbed his top hat before it tumbled off.

They were able to cross and hurried on their way along a well-worn path, where a lake shimmered beyond the trees and shrubbery. Well-tended gardens filled with white flowers, petals that looked like fluffy muffs swaying gracefully in the breeze. She drew her hand from his arm and walked alongside. Kegan glanced at her and smiled. "I hope this doesn't prove to be too bracing for you."

"Heavens no. The carriage ride was a luxury. Walking is what I'm used to." They passed a small open glade with a stream that emptied into a pond and cascaded into a lake.

"We are almost there. If you glance through that brace of trees to your right, you'll be able to appreciate the bridge."

Aisling picked up her pace, following the path that led directly to a gracefully flowing bridge. "How beautiful."

"It is called Bow Bridge. The final touches made in the last few months. You can't tell now, but the floor is of South American hardwood and in the rain, it turns a deep red."

"It is shaped like the bow of a violin. That must be the reason for the name, Bow Bridge. Thank you for bringing me here. I'll always remember this place." She tugged on his sleeve, "Let's walk across."

He took her hand and squeezed it, not letting go. Half way, they stopped and leaned against the rail to look over the peaceful scene; their reflections shimmered on the mirror-like lake below. The setting sun cast long, low lights across the water, shadowing the trees. She took a deep breath and allowed an inner calm to wash over her. Glancing up at him, she caught him staring. "What?"

"This is the peace after a working day. You, me, this very spot."

His blue eyes locked with hers and he reached over and put his arm about her drawing her an inch closer. She wondered if he might kiss her, instead he hugged her then let his arm drop away. She remembered the last time she saw him as Alan. He was always so kind and interested in Alan.

She glanced about the gently rolling hillside trying to imagine it without the bridge and the gardens. "You've not changed. Seems you were always..." Her hand flew to her mouth, agape with shock.

"How would you know about me *always*?" He glanced down at her. "Father talks of me then?"

"You know he does." Thankful for the straw to grasp, she smiled. "From what I gather, the sun rises and sets with you." What man wouldn't like such a compliment? She fiddled with the clasp on her reticule rather than look him in the eye.

Kegan's voice softened. "I rather think the same of him. Right now, I am far more interested in you. How long have you lived in Manhattan?"

"Almost all my life. I was born on a ship from County Cork. We were immigrants. I take it your family has been here a lot longer."

"Third generation, also of Irish descent, but you can guess at that because of my name. Our ancestors are from Kildare."

A first star of the evening began to twinkle as the purple of twilight blossomed across the sky. She drew in a breath. They were different people with vastly different upbringings. Certainly, not a surprise. She knew that from before, when she was Alan.

He indicated a bench. "Would you care to sit for a while?"

"A little." She settled her skirt, folded her hands over her clutch, and waited. She sensed he had something on his mind.

He sat close, his attention clearly focused on her. His voice was playful yet oddly serious. "It is the strangest sensation, but for some reason I feel as though I've known you a lifetime. There is no sense to it. The only time we met was in Father's office."

Aisling couldn't look him in the eye. A lie would be apparent, and she was not sure how to respond to him. "And you want me to help you figure it out, is that it?"

"You don't know me any more than I know you, other than Father's mention in conversation." He shrugged. "Regardless, it is a compelling feeling, like I'll be the worse for not getting to know you better."

"Ah, so this is a hunt for information about me?" Her fingers tapped the clutch. Was he fishing? On the other hand, was this the mind of a lawyer, seeking facts?

His lips widened over perfect teeth, presenting a smile filled with teasing. Irish humor she knew, with wit and a touch of irony.

"I'm so obvious, please accept my apology." His inspection, darkening like the sky, locked on hers. "I like you. I want to get to know you better. And I'm a fumbling idiot when it comes to this...to my interest in you." He spread his arm along the bench, not quite enough to go around her shoulders. "My mother died when I was sixteen and my father remarried two years later to Martha Homsby, an Englishwoman. My father never said, but I think it was an arranged marriage."

Aisling's brows rose as he revealed his past.

"Just so you know I am not hiding anything from you, I'll also say she has a niece, Eleanor Homsby, who arrived a year ago and lives with them. She came for a visit and ended up with a permanent arrangement."

She grinned. "How old is Miss Eleanor Homsby?"

He pursed his lips that widened into a silly grin. "Twenty or thereabouts."

"The present Mrs. Galliger has presumptions?" It was a question of great interest to Aisling though she tried to act as if it were not.

Kegan drew his arm off the bench. "She may have, but I doused them rather quickly. It appears to have worked because Eleanor no longer hounds me, turning up at every corner of the house when I'm there, that kind of thing."

Aisling lifted her chin and glanced sideways at him. "Perhaps she was lonely and sought friendships her own age. You could have introduced her, taken her about."

He dangled his hat between his legs with his elbows placed against his thighs. "I've unfortunately misdirected our conversation to a less than interesting topic." He rubbed the back of his neck. "Could we get back to us, to you in particular? Because that is where my interest lies. With you, Aisling."

She reciprocated the *interest*. However, she didn't know what to say, but her fingers quit tapping the clutch. She met his intent blue gaze. Honesty blocked the space between them. Hovering in the background, the truth of who she was slammed the fragile space to pieces.

She was a poor orphan, at the mercy of others. There was a dreadful man in her past. A man lurking here in Manhattan, who had learned what church she attends. An, evil man who threatened her once and feared he would do so again. A man who knew she was once Alan.

She liked Kegan too much and was determined to set boundaries right this minute and locked her gaze with his. "We can't be."

Those beautiful eyes clouded with doubt, he bent toward her, and placed his hand over hers. "What are you saying?"

"It is not you. It is...I have... It is not because of you." She drew her hand from beneath his.

His handsome features dissolved into something. Disbelief? Challenge?

"Whatever it is, Aisling, you can share anything with me. If not as a suitor, then as a lawyer. A friend." His jaw tightened.

She glanced away from him and took a long minute to firm her decision. Once made, she faced him. "I'm not who you think I am. There are things I can't share."

His features grew stern. "Do you think I would be here with you, if I wasn't prepared to accept a past, whatever it could possibly be?" He drew a deep breath. "Aisling O'Quinn, I'm not a weak-hearted fool."

She touched his jaw with her gloved fingertips. "I'm aware of the proper man you are."

"Then accept that I want to spend more time with you, get to know you properly, and have you get to know me."

"I already know you're stubborn." She dared not reveal how resolute she knew him to be, one of the many enduring things about him she learned from their conversations as they worked together transcribing documents from the Vatican. And her horrid secrets as an orphan-train child and a runaway that he must never know. She could also reveal the train ride from Pittsburgh to the New Jersey shore with hobos and Union deserters. If she really wanted to shock him, she could reveal that she clothed herself from the poor box—and has in her possession a lovely embroidered vest.

She snuck a sideways glance at him. His handsome face diverted as he glanced at a formation of geese flying somewhere, probably south and barely visible in the darkening sky, but certainly heard.

If the truth revealed itself, it could jeopardize her entire nursing degree, to say nothing of compromising Father's position because he harbored her while a minor.

His voice was rough with declaration. "I am relentless where you are concerned." The warmth of his hand came through her glove.

Aisling stuffed her sorrow deep inside. "I need to return home. Signey will wonder, and I've school tomorrow." She stood, breaking away his wonderful touch. "And I suspect you've a full day too."

They walked in silence to the entrance of the Park where Kegan hailed a hackney. The pools of light from the lamps took her attention, anything to keep from allowing their eyes to meet. He might see into her heart and ignore the words she spoke.

Riding onto Amity, the hackney halted. Kegan stepped down and took her hand—perhaps the last time she would feel his warm touch. At the door, he announced, "I'll be patient. In the meantime, I intend manufacturing time together. You better prepare yourself." He reached behind her and opened the door.

She glanced up at him, and was about to refute him, when he pressed two fingers against his lips and placed them on hers.

"Shh." He winked and was gone.

# CHAPTER 15

*H*ector stepped back into the shadow across from Amity where the copper-haired woman lived. Father O'Mara referred to her as Miss O'Quinn the day she fainted. There was no way Hector could inquire of her first name without raising suspicion about his motive. Certainly, she wasn't calling herself Alan.

Earlier this evening, on an errand for the Mayor, he'd changed his route and strode up Wooster on his way to Second then stopped dead in his tracks and slid behind the trunk of an old elm. Not five yards ahead Miss O'Quinn, or her twin, walked. He followed her for several blocks. She appeared to be in a great hurry and entered a neat bungalow on Amity. He considered it must be her home. Once again, his sense of tracking provided him with results. He knew if he covered the streets within a mile's range of the Infirmary, he'd get lucky.

He now had a name, a home, and a place where she most likely worked. Smug with luck, he knew it was only a matter of time before he had her all to himself, finally. If the young woman was Alan, she wasn't smart enough to change her last name. Puzzling over that, he knew Alan had been smart enough to cover his identity for several years.

The look on her face in Father O'Mara's office when she spied him was worth a thousand bucks. He knew who she was by the scared, shocked-out-of-her-wits look; the same as several years earlier when he shoved her in the chest thinking he pushed a boy.

She dropped like a ton of bricks, sending the Mayor and the priest into frenzy. It was the ultimate proof of her identity. Otherwise, she wouldn't have had reason to react. He had to place his tam in front of his trousers lest the others notice his prick's excitement.

His organ had a mind of its own, for sure, and there was no doubt it wanted her. Right from the start, when he discovered Alan a girlie, it had sprung to life. Most no other woman roused him in that way, especially the tramps in the Slaughter House, unkempt, and smelling of the men they'd just left.

Trollops were plenty interested in him. They had a living to make, but it wouldn't be with his coin. His organ lay flaccid in their presence. No, he liked clean, the smell of soap.

When the Smythes took Alan, Hector was put in charge of making sure the kid did his chores the way Smythe expected. Hector enjoyed his authority over the boy, who mostly kept to himself; didn't speak unless asked a question. The boy was small for his age, and Hector wondered if the orphanage had lied about his age. More like seven or eight to Hector's way of thinking than the twelve written on his papers. What truly mattered was the amount of work he finished in a day, and Alan proved to be quite a worker.

When Hector reached his middle teens, he knew without a doubt Smythe held a grudge against him. He puzzled over it most of his next years. He attempted to talk to Earl about it, but Earl's response was a shrug; except one time after a boxing session, Earl offered to apply oil to bring down the swelling caused by the fighting. Earl never tried to excuse his father's behavior, but he did admit if it weren't for their pa, he wouldn't lay a hand to Hector even in anger.

In the Smythe home, affection was as absent as common courtesy. Some nights, Hector walked the forest at night, oft times sleeping in the barn rather than disturb Earl in their shared loft in the house. Those nights he puzzled over right and wrong, trying to make sense of a father who forced his sons to fight each other. Money was always tight, but they ate well, and had a roof over their heads.

He didn't understand the need to make brothers fisticuff each other, even if it would be a means to earn money in a boxing ring. In his early teens, his refusal brought a belt across his back, causing a jagged tear from his shoulder almost to his waist. The tightness of the scar, when he flexed his back muscles, reminded him. Sometimes it brought gratification to remember he was not of that man's seed.

That knowledge eventually set him free of Smythe's hatred.

When Smythe told him he was a bastard, that his ma had not married the man who begot him, he bolted the farm with no sense of obligation and signed up with the Unionists. He never looked back, to hell with them, with her lying to him. In the days and months to come, Hector recognized why Smythe held a grudge against him. He wondered if it was also the reason Smythe treated his ma more like a farm worker than a wife. He'd never know the answer to that because he was never going back.

Hector's musing includede the foster child Smythe brought into their home, an extra pair of hands for the dirty work on the farm, cleaning the pigsty, mucking the stalls. He knew there was something soft about the boy. He couldn't put a finger to it, more a sense of it.

Within a couple of years, Alan changed, withdrew. Shying from Hector, he wouldn't look him in the eye. When Hector walked the forest in the moonlight, he mulled over this predicament. If there was any humanity on the Smythe farm, it was in Alan. He had an almost pitiable weakness in his nature the others didn't own, almost like a woman.

He watched the boy, fixated on him, especially at the dinner table. Even at fourteen, his face hadn't begun the dark growth; his upper lip remained clean, pale, and soft.

Then came the day Hector received a particularly hard beating from Earl egged on by Smythe, who grinned at his true son with great satisfaction. Smythe slapped Earl on the shoulder, congratulating him on the upper hand. Hector's humiliation caused him to rough up Alan. Lord it over the shorter, lighter lad.

As he remembered it now, two years after the fact, the feeling that shivered through him when he grabbed Alan's chest, discovering a girlie instead, sent his organ into a spasm. Though he'd spilled his seed many times in the forest, never in a girlie. The lids of his eyes lowered as he envisioned her beneath him. His pulse raced at the thought. The memory of that moment never left him.

Alan ran away that night, and two days later Hector left the farm and enlisted in the Unionist Army against Smythe's direct order. Encountering Alan with his teacher in the crowd watching the soldiers march past had been one last attempt to capture her. That damn teacher rescued her, and he lost track of them in the crowd. Until—he could hardly keep the swell of excitement from his organ—he found her again.

Hector shivered at the remembered incident and shuffled on his heel, heading down Broadway. The Mayor expected him to sit guard outside his bedroom. Hector would spin a lie to satisfy the Mayor why he hadn't accomplished his errand.

Miss O'Quinn was as good as his. The net was closing over her. His good fortune at finding her in the most unlikely of places meant they were destined to be together. Her clean scent filled his memory. When he was finished with her, she'd smell like him.

---

*S*igney looked up from her book. "Did you enjoy the park?"

Aisling untied her bonnet and hung it on the hook next to her cape. "There were surprises."

Signey tucked the bookmark into place and set the book on the table. "Anything you care to share?" A smug Lucy-cat smile lit up her face.

"He's interested in courting me." She situated herself on the settee and folded her hands in her lap.

"You've got me on pins and needles. I'm dangling."

"There isn't more to tell. I told him no."

Signey slapped her palms against the chair arms almost coming out of her chair. "What? I'm shocked you would do such a thing."

Aisling's chin lowered to her chest. "I can't tell him the truth of who I was, who I am. And it would be unfair of me otherwise."

"Who you were? Who you are? What the *divil* does that mean, who you are?" Her brow scrunched, and her lip curled on the side.

133

"I'm an orphan, a runaway." It hurt to say, but the truth always stands firm.

"And what does that make you? Unfit? What? I fail to understand your reasoning, Aisling." Greatly agitated, her hands slid up and down the arms of the chair. Lucy was long gone off her lap.

Aisling's gaze unwittingly lowered to Signey. The room grew so quiet, she heard Lucy pad across the floorboards.

"Dear girl. What are you saying?" She hit her forehead with the heel of her hand. "Tell me you didn't scare him off? You've so much sense in you. How could you do such a thing?"

Aisling did not know how to answer.

"Oh, dear me." The older woman's palm now rested over her heart. "He was heartbroken, wasn't he?"

Aisling had to admit how surprised she was at his positive response. Equally, she had been adamant they were unsuited. She spoke, "He said he'd manufacture times for us to be together. He wasn't giving up."

"Well, now. That relieves me." She smiled. "You put a scare into me about your common sense taking flight."

Aisling bit the inside of her cheek, finally admitting, "He said he wasn't a weak-hearted fool to give up so easy."

"I've always taken a liking to the young man. I knew there was something that made him special." A guffaw accompanied Signey's words. "And that something is he likes my girl. He is a man who would know quality."

"I've lied to him and if he ever finds out, he'll change his mind." She breathed deeply.

"You mean about being Alan?"

"I sat across the table from him for months. I deceived him during our conversations all those weeks together, hopes and dreams of our futures, schooling, and families." Her fingers threaded a lock of hair that fell across her forehead. She could not even share with him the vest she kept in her bottom drawer. She did not dare use the Latin terms she learned when arguing a point with him.

Signey leaned toward her. Her fingers gripped the arm of the chair. "Tell him, then. If it is such a burden, tell him. Why do you put yourself through all this?"

Lucy's purr hummed in the silence of the parlor.

"I'm tired. I need to go to bed." She moved to the door and glanced at Signey whose gaze was riveted on her, her mouth agape.

Aisling stated, "If I ever tell him about Alan, I'll never see him again. Right now, I'm too selfish to give up the pleasure of being with him, and all that has come to mean to me."

Closing the door to her bedroom, she leaned against it with her hands still on the knob. Why must life be so complicated? There were only two things she wanted, an education and to be self-supporting. Now it appeared Signey, whom she had grown to love and to whom she owed so much, disapproved of her rebuff of Kegan.

Pushing off from the closed door, she went to the window. The lamp across the street cast its golden glow in a bright circle. A man stepped from the shadow, adjusted his tam, and walked on. No one else was about. She pulled the curtain closed against the darkness and sank onto her bed.

Almost with a mind of their own, her fingertips brushed against her lips where Kegan had left a sweet kiss with his fingertips. If she allowed herself, if she let herself dream, Kegan could be a man to love. As Alan, she had grown excessively fond of him and far too dependent on his opinion. He was her first adult friend, with grown-up ideas. He treated her with respect, even sought her opinion as she translated the documents from the Vatican. Useful and fulfilled came to mind; her hand recorded the documents that decreed St. Patrick's Catholic Church an Archdiocese of New York recorded in English—forever.

Life had been simple as Alan, for sure. There were fewer expectations. She paced the small chamber, back and forth, then again. She liked being a woman though the challenges were greater. She had no one to blame but herself. Greatly surprised Miss Blackwell accepted her into one of the few nursing schools in all the thirty-six United States. She pulled the pins from her hair and let it cascade about her shoulders with a shake of her head and began unbuttoning the front of her bodice.

Next April she would be eighteen, and her *máthair* gone five years then. *Oh, máthair what would you have me do? It seems like I will be giving up if I bend to Kegan's wishes. Yet, a part of me yearns to do so.* She sank upon the bed and envisioned his tall, broad shouldered self, a glimmer of delight in his words, the excitement on his face when he talked to her, the flutters inside when he touched her.

For some odd reason, Conner came to her. A nice young man who had been most attentive to her needs closeted with other men for several days aboard the train from Gettysburg to New Jersey. Though she had not responded, Conner said he knew she was a girl. Unlike Hector, Conner was a gentleman. However, the fact remained, he was a deserter, and she judged him not. She could not fathom Kegan rejecting a commitment. His moral fiber was too strong.

*H*ector Smythe must have dozed off from his nightly guard at the Mayor's bedroom door. The clink of a tea tray roused him in time to open the door for the maid who brought breakfast and biscuits for His Honor.

The Mayor walked out of the water closet, donning a brocade robe and sat next to the fire as the maid stoked it to a blaze taking the chill from the morning air. Hector asked, "Is there anything, sir?"

The Mayor stared at the small flames licking the air. "No, I think I'll have an easy morning and not go to the office until after the noon meal." He tore his gaze from the fire. "Take some time for yourself, Hector. I won't need you until twelve thirty."

Hector nodded and closed the door. His dreams last night made sleeping a restless endeavor. They included Miss O'Quinn. He trumped up the possibility Mrs. Molloy and Miss O'Quinn could somehow be related, a far stretched idea but worth investigating.

Within the hour, he knocked on the front door of Mrs. Molloy's rented home on Unity and requested the maid to deliver a note to her while he waited.

*B*eatrice took her time dressing. The Mayor's henchman could cool his heels. Every bit the gentleman when he escorted her to the immigration office, he'd taken her to tea afterwards then to her home. That was three weeks ago.

She came into the parlor as Hector read a brass plate beneath an oil painting of boats sailing on the East River. "Mr. Smythe, how nice of you to stop by."

He smiled. "Good day to you, Mrs. Molloy. I was near and wanted to pay my respects. Are you able to find enjoyment in our city?"

She settled on the divan and gestured for him to sit. "The immigration office is running circles around me. Mayor Reed was right when he said O'Quinn is a common name. With almost a hundred registered in the city, and others who perhaps moved to other parts of the United States since 1848."

He placed his hat over his knee. "I happen to know a young lady named O'Quinn. She has the color hair you spoke of, but her parents are gone. And I don't know if she had brothers or not."

"The color is common enough in Ireland and America for all I know. Perhaps I could meet her, inquire. A meeting you could arrange. I know you are a busy man in the employ of the Mayor. I hesitate to ask but find that I can't contain my curiosity." Beneath her long dark lashes, she cast him a side-glance and smiled.

"She's a shy thing, but I would be glad to inquire when next we meet. I wanted to know if you were still interested or had made headway on your own."

"Oh, I'm interested all right. Indeed, I am."

She sat in the parlor after Mr. Smythe left and wondered what she would do if it was Gradleigh's child. She also wondered about all those sons. Were they scattered across this great continent? As a little girl, she had taken a special liking to his wife, Agnes. She was a kind woman who had time for her, unlike her own mother who was far too busy scratching out another meal for all the hungry mouths to devour.

Beatrice did not know what she intended, but if the girl was the twelve-year-old Agnes wrote about; she would be easy to control like

Agnes. It would be a feather in her cap to have someone in her thrall, a young person at her mercy. Men were always at ease when they escorted feminine companions, usually bringing along another male. Moreover, in that scenario, there was money to be made. Plenty of it, in fact.

# CHAPTER 16

*K*egan brushed past his secretary's desk, entered his office, and stashed his umbrella in the corner near a hat tree. Miss Hartwig approached as he placed his briefcase on the desk.

"Mrs. Galliger has sent a note to meet her at the Prescott for lunch at 12:30. She requires a response."

"Am I free at that time? I'll need about an hour and a half?"

"You are."

"Then tell her yes."

Obligations from so many different directions beleaguered him, but there was only one direction that sharpened his urge to get involved, Miss Aisling O'Quinn.

He had no reason to want to spend time with her. Other than her sparkling innocent eyes, the color of sapphires, and her quick wit, and bright, beautiful smile from those kissable lips. As long as he was skimming over her attributes, he considered the ease he felt when in her presence. He wanted to hold her hand, laugh aloud with her. Run a fingertip across the bridge of her nose sprinkled with freckles.

Her lashes were light with a reddish tint matching her glorious head of copper hair; curls spilling and tumbling out of control no matter how she may have arranged them initially. He wanted to thread his fingers through the mass, to feel the springy electricity that he knew was in her. His every nerve was alive when he was near her.

Was he a fool? He really knew nothing about her. She was obviously a friend of Father O'Mara's, and, perhaps a distant relative of Signey's. A nursing student. A young one at that, which meant she was a good student. He shook his head with smug instincts. Most of the young women he knew were interested in parties, clothing, and what galas to attend. Miss O'Quinn's interests tended toward cerebral.

He included his father's wife in his speculation. He was certain this luncheon was to discuss his intentions of a possible future with Eleanor. Miss Homsby was the exact opposite of Miss O'Quinn. Father's wife be damned, Mrs. Galliger was no doubt up to a ruse to draw her niece into his circle. He would listen to her out of respect for his father. Then he would put her off with a clever excuse why he could not escort Eleanor to this museum display, or that play.

English bred, schooled in Sweden, aristocratic lineage with an earl for an uncle on her mother's side. Soft gray eyes, blonde hair, statuesque. He sounded like a docent at the art museum looking at *Raphaels*. The idea brought a chuckle. He mused that Aisling would laugh right alongside him. He was not sure Miss Homsby had a sense of humor at all.

He glanced at the clock in the corner. It was almost noon. Half an hour he had wasted on daydreams. The rain stopped leaving fresh, clean air. He needed a good strut along Broadway before meeting his father's wife for lunch.

The maitre d' led him to Mrs. Galliger's table. With a nod or two directed at acquaintances, he wound his way to the back of the restaurant. Mirrors edged the top of the cushioned seating reflecting crystal chandeliers off the upper walls. Tables swathed in white with silver and crystal symmetrically placed, and small glass bowls of red roses centered on the pristine linen. His luncheon companion leaned against the cushioned seat and the *maitre d'* pulled a chair across from her.

He took the hand she offered, "Good afternoon, madam. You are looking rather well today," and bowed slightly then lowered himself.

"How nice of you, Kegan. Your father's son ever more. Etiquette in place, you didn't keep me waiting."

The *maitre d'*, rigid and silent at the end of the table, waited for instruction. Kegan asked, "What would you like for refreshment, Martha?"

"Tea, Oolong. And make sure it is hot this time." She pulled her gloves off and laid them over her small clutch purse.

"The same for me, Ray."

She arched her beautifully shaped brow at his use of the man's given name. "You eat here often, then?"

"Now and again." He opened his napkin and placed it on his lap. "Tell me why you are giving up time with friends to spend your lunch with me. You've made me curious."

She cast him a disparaging glance. "Your father's been after me to make sure you attend the Charity Ball this year. He wants you there and for some reason thinks I have the capacity to wheedle a response from you."

"Is that all? I feared you were going to suggest something unbearably boring, a wet blanket affair of some kind."

He smelled the thyme and basil of the oolong even before the waiter placed it on the table. Mrs. Galliger spoke up. "I'll have the salmon and a small salad."

Kegan requested, "A small cut of broiled beef loin and a salad. That special Russian dressing would be nice."

The waiter nodded.

She did not waste a moment and pouted at Kegan. "You needn't have an attitude about the ball. It is one of your father's proudest functions. So much good is done for the poor."

He held up his hand. "Go no further, please, madam. I'll be more than happy to sit through an evening of glad-handing and congratulations for the endeavors of the wealthy toward the poor and hungry of our city."

Her vision narrowed as she lifted her chin glancing down at him. "Kegan, really." Unfolding the napkin, she placed it over her lap. "The board is honoring no less than twelve charitable organizations."

He toyed with a spoon. "I'm teasing a little. Charitable organizations do need recognition for the good they accomplish. But the money spent could go to the real cause for the people in need."

"Publicity works. The *Tribune* and the *Times* always give us front page coverage, and advertising opens pocketbooks."

He placed the spoon to the right of his plate. "You win, I'm chastised. And to prove that my stubborn resistance is in the past, I'll agree to attend."

She sipped her oolong, looking at him over the rim of the china cup, her gaze partially hooded, as if she played a game with a child. Setting the cup on the saucer, she said, "Then will you hand deliver this, please?" She reached inside her reticule and withdrew a white envelope.

A gold seal stamped on the back and Father O'Mara's name scripted on the front. "It is his invitation, and I know you have business with him," she added.

A notion came to Kegan. "Would there be room for an extra at our table?"

Her eyes filled with surprise, her fork of salmon half way to her rouged lips. "Your father and I, Eleanor, Father O'Mara and you. A sixth would round us out perfectly. A nice idea, Kegan, very considerate of you. Father O'Mara might enjoy bringing a friend."

He grinned. "I do try, Martha. Really I do." He patted the napkin against his smile lest she detect his cleverness.

A week passed before Kegan dropped in on Father O'Mara. When he walked in his office after lunch with Martha, a letter from Lysander Spooner was on his desk. He took a deep breath and turned toward the window overlooking Broadway. It did not bother him that he did not have a corner office. He knew it would come with tenure, and he fully expected to earn the privilege. The offices of Olander, Higgins & Bartholomew, Attorneys at Law, occupied the entire second floor of the building on the corner of Broadway and Houston. The noisy streets bustled with activity now that this morning's downpour subsided.

He slapped the envelope against his thigh. He knew it contained a request for files putting a close to the expenses of the draft riots that lasted one full week in July 1863, ending only after President Lincoln sent in troops to establish order. One of the attacks was on the Colored Orphans' Asylum, which resulted in it burning to the ground.

The rioters were mostly comprised of angry women and children of Irish descent. They found fault with a country that allowed the wealthy to pay for a replacement in a draft army. Irish husbands and fathers, unable to find work, grabbed at the unheard-of sum of three hundred dollars to take the place of wealthy men in the battle.

Ironically, the poverty the Irish lived in that caused husbands to grab at the money, left most of the families without a father—and without an income once the money was gone; which drove the poverty level even higher.

A letter to the editor of the *Times* praised the Irish who began rebuilding for the honor of dear old Ireland, and the Christian teachings professed by all humanity. It was the writer's desire that the same people who caused the destruction are willing to convert the prejudice and crime into a noble monument of liberal reparation and justice; a virtuous notion. To be fair, it was not just the Irish who caused the rioting. Italians, Germans, and Poles were equally as angry over the injustice of the draft.

Olander, Higgins and Bartholomew had taken it upon the law firm to stand behind this declaration and put Kegan in charge of organizing the efforts, the funds, and the initial rebuilding. Kegan did so with a great deal of enthusiasm. Righting wrongs brought on by fear and poverty, it made sense out of ashes to him.

Tearing open the envelope, it was just as he suspected. Spooner's letter asked for a complete itemized accounting of the damage, and the cost of repair. Kegan gladly had Miss Hartwig mail the file to Spooner glad to be finished with a sad chapter about Manhattan's people.

Furthermore, he secretly admired his father's efforts with the annual charity ball. He knew the benefit of the news exposure, too. He enjoyed cracking the marble-like demeanor of his father's wife. Mrs. Galliger's flowery speech was a mite too much. Her florid excess to make a point had the opposite effect on him, and he tended to back off rather than become part of her do-good circle. No doubt, she completed his father's life, and for that, he was grateful.

Well, usually. In the case of her niece, he had no desire to promote interest and kept a wide berth.

Kegan entered the rectory through the kitchen hoping to encounter

Signey. With no sign of her, he continued through the passage into the rectory and the long hallway leading to Father's office. He recognized the Mayor's stentorian conversation streaming into the corridor and rapped his knuckles on the door that stood ajar.

"Come in," Father said. "Ah, Kegan, you are around rather early."

He nodded to Father and then the Mayor, both gripping coffee mugs. In the corner, a large man stood with his back to the wall and a sour look on his face. Kegan nodded to him as well.

"Mrs. Galliger asked me to drop this by." He laid the large white envelope on Father's desktop.

The priest's bushy brows rose. "I'm thinking it is the invite to the charity ball."

"You would be right."

The Mayor chimed in. "A worthy endeavor to be sure."

Kegan offered. "Mrs. Galliger requests you invite someone to accompany you. She is expecting you to sit at their table."

"Ah, well, I'll have to ponder that."

"Your housekeeper might enjoy an evening out." The Mayor held up a plate half full of a cinnamon bun slathered with icing and butter, eager to take another bite.

Well known for his appetite of all things sweet, the Mayor did not disappoint. He often threatened to lure Mrs. Pennino away from St. Patricks. Lively banter on this account between the two men had gone on since Kegan could remember.

Father chuckled. "Mrs. Pennino has an aversion for the *swells* as she puts it. I will ask her, but I won't be surprised if she refuses."

Kegan wanted to suggest he ask Miss O'Quinn if that was the case, but he deemed it prudent not to interject the possibility. He hoped he knew Father well enough that he might come to it all by himself. He said, "I'll leave you to your business. I'm expected in court at eleven and need to read a brief first."

Father tapped the envelope on his desk. "Thank you for dropping this off."

His hand on the doorknob, Kegan said, "I'm simply the messenger. My father's wife is the hostess." With that, he nodded to the Mayor and took note again of the burly, tall man in the corner, who appeared not to have moved a muscle. However, the man's inspection locked on Kegan for an instant, leaving him with the notion he would not want to stumble upon the man in the dark of night.

***

*T*hat afternoon, Father ventured into the kitchen where Signey was whistling. "I've never heard you whistle before."

Mouth pursed with no sound emitting, she blushed.

"Continue. It is a delightful sound. Makes me think of birds."

"You're mocking me."

"I am not." He sat at the table and reached for a pecan sandy, as Signey had labeled them a long time ago. "I'm here to deliver an invitation to the charity ball. Kegan dropped it by this morning."

"For me?" She poured him a cup of coffee and set it in front of him with a spoon and the sugar bowl.

"Mrs. Galliger has asked that I bring someone."

"Well, then, it is settled."

His gaze met hers directly. "This was almost too easy. Wonderful."

"You will take Aisling."

"Ah." He bit into the sandy and nodded in agreement.

"She'll need a gown and proper shoes for dancing."

"So now I'm dancing, harrumph." He sipped his coffee, and then added, "She needs to say yes, first."

Signey's face brightened. "Oh, she'll say yes. What girl wouldn't want to attend a ball? Is it at the Park Hotel like last year?"

Father nodded.

"I won't let her refuse."

***

*A*isling, an open book on her lap, glanced at Signey. Both enjoyed the evening's tranquility. Signey gently rocked in her favorite chair, Lucy, snuggled beneath the wool shawl Signey knitted, purred contentedly on her lap. Needles clicked in a soft cadence with the sway of the rocker.

Aisling offered, "Miss Blackwell asked if I would be interested in attending a seminar this coming Saturday about the treatment for consumption. Well, tuberculosis is the correct term now."

"Of course, you said yes." Signey's nimble fingers fairly flew with the thread of yellow yarn twining with the thread of red yarn joining at the tips of the needles.

"Of course." Aisling leaned her head against the cushion of the sofa and closed her eyes. "The theory of treatment is being challenged by a doctor from Sweden. He will be speaking on Saturday."

"Are all the nurses in training invited to attend?"

Aisling chuckled. "You would ask, wouldn't you?"

"Well..."

"As it happens, I've been the only one selected. There is a tea afterward and Miss Blackwell has invited me to attend that as well."

"Must be the time of year for invitations. Father always enjoys the charity ball. He's received the invitation to this year's event."

"He's in his element with all the gossip and frivolity." Aisling kept her eyes closed.

"It is different this year, and he's muddled." The needles clicked away.

"Why so?"

"He's to bring someone with him."

"Will that be you?"

"You know I don't like all that shilly shally."

Aisling's head rose off the cushion. Her gaze settled on Signey, the needles, and the purring cat. "Is he asking me through you, then?"

"Smart young lady you are."

"I've nothing so fancy to wear. It won't be me accompanying him to such a gallant affair."

The needles stopping clicking. "*Hmm*, what will I do with the purse he's given for purchasing apparel for you, my dear? And, matching dancing shoes."

She pulled herself up straight. "No?"

The needles clicked a staccato. A smile puffed her cheeks. "Isn't tomorrow your easy day? I will go into the rectory in the morning and we can meet at Stewart's emporium at one. How does that sound?"

"You're a fairy godmother of sorts, aren't you now?" Visions of dancing and beautiful music, crystal chandeliers sparkling above swept into her imagination. Would Kegan be there? A hopeful sigh escaped.

"Tch, tch. You're an easy one to love, sweet."

The next day Aisling walked up Broadway but her reflection was on the pre-surgical class she attended that morning. The professor had laid out equipment used in performing an amputation: a long thin knife curved down at the end, bone forceps, shiny saw blades, and a tourniquet.

Wondrously displayed in a mahogany case, Dr. Norton's name engraved on a brass plate across the front. The actual surgical tools for amputation were also on display in the decking area for close observation. She wished she could hold the forceps, feel its heft in the palm of her hand. Someday, after her pinning ceremony, wearing a starched white apron and cap, she would attend a real surgical procedure. At the same table, instruments like these were ready for use, sterile and placed in the order of need. The idea she could attend a surgeon in a hospital arena someday, sent her dreams in a twirl.

Striding along Broadway, she lugged a sack with two books, *The Practice of Medicine*, and *On Anatomy*. Tomorrow, after Mass, she would bury her nose in a chapter of each book before class Monday. However, this afternoon she looked forward to shopping with Signey.

Leaning against the cornerstone of the large department store, Aisling waited. A few minutes later, she spied Signey's full-speed-ahead strut and the fern on her pert little hat waved in the slight breeze.

At that same moment, a carriage stopped at the front doors of the emporium. Two men jumped off the driver's seat. One opened the door for the Mayor who stepped onto the boardwalk and stood in front of where she waited. The other glared at her with a sly smile.

Aisling's blood ran cold. As Mayor Reed gave her a quick nod and asked, "Miss O'Quinn, isn't it?"

Hector's deep voice, came muffled with a twang. "Right you are, sir. In Father O'Mara's office."

The book bag slipped out of her hand to the boardwalk. Hector reached for it. She barely heard his whisper. "A startled girlie, ain't cha?"

His calloused hand brushed hers as he handed it over. She pulled back, and the bag dropped again, his touch burned her skin.

The Mayor handed her the sack this time. Aisling's knees trembled. Signey approached. "I'm late."

Aisling's gaze twitched from the bodyguard's boots, to the Mayor's face, and back to Signey. She tried to catch her breath, stop the pounding of her heart. Her skin crawled with loathing of Hector's deliberate touch, thankful she wore gloves. Glancing at the handles of the book bag where his hand touched, the scene in the stable flashed before her eyes where that same hand had touched her.

The Mayor nodded. "And, I believe you bake the most delicious molasses cookies. In my younger years, I called them *joe froggers*. Father O'Mara is lucky to have such a fine housekeeper."

"Thank you, sir. Nice of you to mention. Miss O'Quinn and I are on a shopping excursion."

"As am I." He looked deep into Miss O'Quinn's face. "You are looking a mite better today than the last we were together." He obviously referred to her fainting spell.

An insufferable fear crawled up her neck. Her desperate side-glance found Signey. "Much better, sir. Thank you."

Hector reached for the glassed door. The Mayor followed the women into the building.

Aisling whispered. "I need to find the necessary room. Quickly."

Signey stopped a clerk and asked the way, and the two women trod the aisle to the stairs and the second floor into a far corner on the right.

Once the door closed behind them, Aisling perched on a chaise, Signey beside her. "What is this all about?"

"Nothing, I...I rushed this morning, and need to catch my breath before we begin."

"Aisling, there's more to this than you're saying." A look of concern crossed Signey's face.

He'd called her *girlie*, the same as that morning in the stall at the farm. She took a deep breath. At least she saw him without fainting this time. He must have heard her name from Father. What did he want with his sly glances, and slick, evil smile? Her flesh crawled, and her stomach roiled.

She could not run away again. Her whole life was beginning to meld into a wonderful future.

"You look quite pale. That big man said something to you, what was it? Did he offend in any way?" She drew off a glove and touched Aisling's cheek.

Aisling looked her square in the eye forcing a smile. "I don't know what you mean. He merely handed my book bag to me. I was winded and needed to catch my breath. I walked fast from the Infirmary."

Signey gave her a side-glance chin down. "Hmm—if you say so."

"I do."

"Well, then we are wasting precious moments."

# CHAPTER 17

*G*rateful for the diversion Signey's take-charge manner provided, Aisling listened as she spoke to the sales manager in women's fine wear. "We're shopping for a ball gown. My niece is going to the Charity Ball at the Park Hotel."

The shop clerk looked Aisling up and down, sizing her for color and the right material. "With your copper gold curls, miss, we could complement with a sage or light blue or even cream. But, with your striking looks, I'd almost say a soft amber or teal."

Aisling touched the swatches thrown over the arm of the chair. Her fingers lingered on the teal. It was a rich watercolor. Perhaps too much though and she picked up the amber, a softer hue. She held it up under her chin and stood before the three-sided mirror, then glanced at Signey with a raised brow.

"Your skin responds to this color." She handed Aisling a swatch of pale green, then quickly removed it. "The amber suits you better."

"Will you be wanting some lace and ruffle? Because if you do, we have received a delivery from Brussels. Tatting in a shade darker than this amber. It would be a striking combination."

Aisling brightened. Her wits aflame with the excitement of the preparation for the ball. "May we see it?"

The little clerk turned on her heel. "Give me two minutes."

Signey said, "Amber woven in brocade. You will not be outdone."

Aisling walked about the perimeter of the show room, picking up other swatches and touched a beautiful, nearly finished gown on a mannequin, all ivory with crystals sewn in a flower pattern on the skirt.

"A ball gown. I still can't believe it." She drew in the clean musky scent of the room, the vibrant colors, the wide carpet on the floorboards, and a large three-sided mirror against the far wall. This space was alive with interest and drama. It captured her imagination, made her feel, well, like a young woman.

"As do most girls, sweet. I confess, when younger, I did, too."

"Did Father say how much to spend? I think, especially with lace, this could be rather costly."

"You do know him. Bless that priest, he handed me the purse and said not to worry," she patted her reticule, "so we won't." Her lips pressed into a mischievous grin, her chin dipped in confirmation.

With a bolt wrapped in tissue, the clerk spread it out on the glass counter then unwrapped the tissue. Delicate, like a spider web, glistening with shiny little beads, the clerk spread a length of the lace over the top of the brocade.

A breath of air escaped Aisling. "It is too beautiful. I think something simple. Maybe without lace."

"I disagree, and I've got the purse. The lace is the finishing touch. We'll have the amber brocade made into a gown," Signey announced. "And, slippers dyed to match."

Two weeks passed in a flurry of fittings, studying for a test on diseases of the heart and lungs, and attending a second tea with Miss Blackwell for a discussion by Dr. H. H. Rogers from the University of Pennsylvania on Microscopic Anatomy.

Kegan Galliger was also on her mind, enough to make Aisling question her own sanity. Father mentioned they would be sitting with the Galligers tonight.

Feeling like a princess, she twirled in the open space in her bedroom sending her beautiful lace skirts about in a swish of amber. Though she was not a princess, she could be the cinder-maid in the fairy tale. Signey finished adding a white silk flower to the tiny waist of her gown.

"The posy draws interest to your graceful form." She stood back and tisked her satisfaction. "My dear, if you don't turn every head tonight, I'll be flummoxed."

Aisling swirled once again, allowing the amber skirt to float outward. "There's one head I wouldn't mind turning."

"That wouldn't be Kegan Galliger would it?" Lucy ran into the room, and jumped on the bed purring up a storm, as though she understood.

Aisling slanted her lids enough to catch a glimpse of Signey's reflection in the mirror. She batted them in an over-done flirtatious way. "Maybe."

Signey laughed in her throaty Italian timber. "He isn't the young man you sent on his way now, is he?"

Aisling shrugged her shoulder. "I wish I could take that back. It is all jumbled up in being the lad I was to him. Awkward, the pants, short unruly hair. This picture I can't get rid of."

"Ah," Signey sighed, "You've doubts, and that is understandable. However, do not cut off your nose to spite your face. He puts me in mind of a young man who knows what he wants, not some lad with tomfoolery in mind."

Aisling ran fingertips across her brow, and then glanced at Signey. "Perhaps tonight I will have an opportunity to make amends."

"Lord above. Letting some sunshine into your life, are you?"

Happiness skidded round about like music in her ears. She had never been so excited about anything to match the evening ahead; Kegan, meeting his parents, Father escorting her, the most beautiful gown in the world. Her heart sang with glorious wonder. "I can't really believe tonight is happening. I'm thrilled and grateful to be a part of it."

Signey reached over and patted the purring cat. "Lucy wanted to know about that young man, too. Wasn't just me perplexed." She coaxed, "Lift the hem let me see those shoes?"

Aisling wiggled her foot in the air.

"They don't pinch, do they?"

"Like walking on air."

A knock at the front door and Signey said, "I'll bet that's the good Father coming to get you. There is not a young woman in all of

Manhattan who can claim the parish priest as escort. You'll be on your best behavior I warrant." She bustled from the room.

Father's jolly, deep voice drifted down the corridor to her bedroom. "She'll not keep me waiting now, will she?"

"No, no, Father. She's all right and ready."

His brows rose as Aisling came into the parlor.

"My, oh my, Mrs. Pennino, what happened to Miss O'Quinn? Won't she be disappointed if I take this lovely young woman to the charity ball and she stays home?"

Aisling laughed. "Flattery from an Irish priest. More like blarney." She gave him a small curtsy. "Thank you for the compliment and for this beautiful gown. I needn't tell you it is the first one I've ever worn."

"Don't remind me of the past. It brings sorrow to my heart." He winked at her. "You've mastered the dancing shoes as well, not twisting your ankle, or tripping."

Signey said, "Now, Father, don't _you_ be bringing the past to mind. She's done excellently, took a shorter walking pace is all."

He held the door open. His carriage waited on the street. Dusk was growing, and the lamps already lit, Aisling hugged Signey goodbye. "You've both made me feel like I'm in the fairy tale of cinder maid. You're my fairy godmother and Father O'Mara is the benevolent king of the castle."

A prophesy in Father's little grin, he said, "You won't have to be running away tonight, child, and leaving a slipper on the stairs. All is well with a bright future ahead. Let us also not lose sight of your attendance to medical school. Surely, that gives you the confidence to attend this affair."

The large ballroom of the Park Hotel, owned by the Astor family, spread out in extravagant splendor at the bottom of the marble staircase. Father O'Mara took her wrap to check and Aisling waited. A deep breath quelled anxiety, soothed her. Signey's use of the term _swells_ caused a giggle. Glancing about the room, beneath crystal chandeliers twinkling with light, she counted twelve in all dangling from the lofty ceiling. The marble stairs, covered in deep red, led downward to a large crowd milling about. Conversation and music from a string band floated upward. Ball gowns of every color of the rainbow were on display in little groups, part of the chatter that swept in the air. Men garbed almost exclusively in black trousers and jackets, crisp white shirts, and little black bow ties.

She spotted Kegan almost immediately. A bit taller than most, he was fully engaged in conversation with two women. The older woman, gowned in a deep blue shiny satin, and the younger in white shimmering ruffles. She looked away rather than have him suddenly catch her gawking. It was not just his handsome demeanor; he also bore a confidence and always a smile. His dark, wavy hair, brushed back off his forehead, curled below his ears. Delighted in the knowledge she was to sit at his table, a feeling of divine pleasure spread through her. So, what if she hadn't been to a ball before? Signey told her that if the gentleman had enough gumption to ask her to dance, he surely would know how to lead. All she had to do was follow in his arms. In his arms! Would it feel like heaven to be in his arms? Truly, this evening was magical.

Father was in his element. She listened to him a half-dozen times or more talk of the families who did so much for the poor in the city. Her biggest thrill, and the opportunity that made her most nervous, was sitting at a table with Kegan's parents. Though she did tell him they were not suited, she could not deny her feelings. He was, after all, the only man on earth she dreamed of in her future. A swell of happiness lit inside her—that little secret buried deep. It was not for sharing.

Kegan's parents were one of New York City's most distinguished Irish families, spearheading fundraisers for the Children's Aid Society and orphan homes. Aisling was an infrequent reader of the *Tribune*, mostly because of her studies, when she did take time she noted the Galliger name mentioned regularly.

Lost in thought, Father's low voice interrupted her musing. "Are you ready to enter the fray below, my dear?" He looked stately with his white hair, black suit, and white collar. His grin put her in mind of the Irish imps depicted in children's books.

"Now or never," she said and took a deep breath. Father crooked his arm and placed her gloved hand there. They stepped onto the carpeted stairs.

On the ground floor, waiters floated about the room carrying silver trays with flutes of champagne. Aisling was content to wrap her fingers about a small clutch purse. Father O'Mara held his glass and occasionally sipped between conversation with Mr. and Mrs. Dudley, parishioners of St. Patrick's, and another couple, Mr. and Mrs. Ellis, parishioners of St. Paul's.

Kegan made his way toward them through the crush of people. Leaving one group, he took a few steps before ending up in light conversation with another. Violins and a harp kept the tempo light and festive.

"Good evening, Miss O'Quinn, Father." He looked at her in a way that brought the dratted heat to her neck and ears, his smile reaching to his dark rimmed eyes.

To her great discomfort, Father added, "This is her first grand affair."

"I am pleased you weren't otherwise engaged, Miss O'Quinn. You certainly are the brightest and prettiest woman in the room."

Pink cheeks and all, she managed to say, "It was kind of you to include me." Butterflies flitted in her stomach.

She glanced at the tables covered in linen, glassware that sparkled in the candlelight, and the majestic display of red roses in the center of each. Her gaze eventually centered on his and the only thing she could think to say was entirely stupid. "There must be two hundred people here."

His eyes sparkled with humor. "Is that really what you wanted to say?"

She was babbling and shrugged an amber laced shoulder. His grin crinkled the skin around his blue eyes. Her chin rose, and she met those eyes filled with humor. "I meant there are obviously many to honor in this great city."

He leaned close, his warm breath whispering in her ear. "I am teasing you."

She felt the blush rise on her cheeks and bit her lip in consternation.

He must realize he flustered her because the timber of his voice softened. "All of New York's dedicated organizations and their leaders for the welfare of children are here. Can I assume you have a personal interest?"

A personal interest? Suddenly, she felt exposed, and cast a wary glance at Father. "I...I..."

Father saved her. "Aisling has assisted me over time and become quite knowledgeable about the plight of orphans and their needs."

"Of course." Kegan said. "My father is a second generation New Yorker. His ties to Ireland however, are very strong."

"Your mother..." She glued her eyes to the clasp on her reticule.

"Her family were second generation from County Kildare.". Kegan glanced at the two women drawing near; the same he conversed with when she arrived.

The blue gown and the white gown. "Miss O'Quinn allow me to present my father's wife, Mrs. Galliger, and her niece, Miss Homsby."

Aisling gave a slight nod. "How do you do?" When she and Kegan sat on a bench at Central Park, he had talked of them. Miss Homsby's gaze honed on Kegan, her interest palpable.

Mrs. Galliger's curiosity swept the length of Aisling's gown. "What a lovely creature you are." Her brow wrinkled at Kegan. "How ever did you meet her, you naughty boy. She is the reason you wanted a sixth, is she not?"

Kegan laughed outright. "Martha, I can't pull the wool over you, can I?"

Mrs. Galliger said, "Eleanor, you will need to strike up an acquaintance with Miss O'Quinn. It appears she knows the right salons."

Miss Homsby's gaze blinked off Kegan and honed on Aisling without skipping a beat. "Your gown is striking. Takes a certain kind of young woman to wear that color with your hair. Most wouldn't dare."

Aisling took the glimmer in her eye to be teasing, certainly not malice. "Thank you. I have never worn anything so lovely before. I have Father O'Mara to thank."

Father harrumphed. "I've no need of gratitude; the sight of you is enough."

Kegan's eyes must have caught her pink cheeks because he chuckled. There was nothing for her to do but raise her chin and bare the flush.

Miss Homsby said, "I would be more than excited to visit the shop where your gown was made. Perhaps we can schedule a day next week?"

Kegan interjected. "Aisling is in nursing school during the week."

"Really?" Miss Homsby leaned in, her eyes narrowed, and all her focus was on Aisling. "You must entertain me with your reasons for attending a nursing school of all places. I would think it dreadfully boring, to say nothing of disease ridden."

A tall, barrel-like woman, gowned in black with a matching feather waving from her graying hair joined their little circle. An air of crisp authority in her tone as she nodded to Kegan. "A fine affair, Mr. Galliger."

"Miss Helberg, good evening. I presume you know Father O'Mara, and this is Miss O'Quinn." He added to Aisling, "Miss Helberg administers the Children's Aid Society and is involved in the orphan trains."

Aisling froze, and all recognition washed back time. Every tiny bit of her twelve-year-old self suddenly remembered this woman. She struggled to act natural. Even Father would not know what this woman represented to her.

Kegan said to Miss Helberg, "I'm certain you already know Mrs. Galliger and her niece Miss Homsby."

The women nodded and smiled at each other as Kegan explained to Aisling, "Miss Helberg is one of our honorees this evening. Her hard work and dedication are unparalleled in her efforts to save orphans."

The woman was much heavier than Aisling remembered. She met Miss Helberg under unspeakable conditions nearly six years ago. The woman represented a past that clung to Aisling like a funeral pall. Forcing a conciliatory nod, her grip tightened on Father's arm.

The woman stared at her. "You have the most remarkable eyes, dark like sapphires. I knew a lad with your coloring. Can't recall the name, but I never forget a face." She reminded Aisling of a time she prayed to forget.

Miss Helberg sipped her flute of champagne and explained to the small group. "I began my career with the Aid Society as a matron, got to know the orphans quite enough. The lad was one of our little alone people, as we used to call them. Poor children all, my heart ached for the poverty in which they lived."

Aisling was aware of Kegan's attention directed at the woman, when he mentioned, "Miss Helberg has dedicated her life to the Society. She's deserved this honor for a long time, wouldn't you say, Martha?"

Mrs. Galliger agreed. "She was my first choice in voting."

Aisling inhaled and tried to bring a measure of calm to herself. She didn't trust herself to respond, and squeezed Father's arm that held his wine glass, whispering, "A sip please?"

His brows rose, but without a word, he handed over the goblet, scrutinizing her.

The master of ceremonies requested guests take their seats. "The chef has declared dinner is to be served." Miss Helberg excused herself and retreated to the guest of honor table on a raised platform in the front of the ballroom.

Kegan led them to their table. Introduced his father to Aisling, and then pulled out a chair for her between Father and himself.

On the verge of a powerful surge of anxiety, Aisling's mind raced, her heart thumped, she drew a deep breath. She knew Miss Helberg too well, uncommonly well; she had practically been chained to her until the Smythes took her. Spreading her napkin across her lap, she squeezed Father's forearm again; attempting to quell the anxiety that threatened. His kindly visage and smile of encouragement, comforted. He understood her predicament. She silently praised God that Miss Helberg was not at their table.

Mrs. Galliger interrupted her jumbled musing. "Miss O'Quinn, do I understand correctly you were born in Ireland?"

"I was born aboard a ship from Dublin. My parents were from Fingal."

"I was hoping we might have some commonality. My ancestors hail from Dublin, although I was born in England. Their estate burned, and they relocated near London. Mr. Galliger's family is from Kildare. Quite south of Fingal."

Conversation stuck in her throat. Kegan's family was nice, but she was out of her element. What would they think if they knew the part Miss Helberg had played in her life?

Dinner passed in a maze of roast pigeon, fried potatoes, beef olives, two different red wines, and thin slices of fruit bread slathered with soft butter.

Barely touching the offerings, she nervously moved morsels about the gold-rimmed plate with her fork. Her unease caused a fear that tormented. She wished she could talk it out with Father, but right now that was impossible. She glanced about the table. Miss Homsby appeared to have Kegan's rapt attention.

She could not fault him. Miss Homsby obviously held a place in society. Educated, beautiful, the ease with which they conversed most apparent, their string of conversation floated to her. She caught words of legalities, masterpieces, distant cousins. Aisling was powerless to compete with that history.

The main course finished, the Master of Ceremonies called Miss Helberg to the podium. The black feather in her coiffure bobbed above her staunch demeanor as she navigated the few steps to accept the award.

Aisling calmed from her earlier nervous bout. Yet, deep inside a great dread, a foreboding grew. Meeting Miss Helberg stirred the ashes of her past. Like a specter flying overhead, waiting to spread the truth, to enlighten, to unmask the imposter.

The woman began by drawing attention to the beginning in 1853 of the orphan trains that carried homeless children to the west, the poverty of little ones on the streets scavenging for food, parentless for one reason or another. She painted a picture of devastation and rescue. Childless people in the west gladly accepted the bedraggled urchins scooped up off the streets of Five Points. Thousands saved, fed, housed, and schooled by God-fearing pioneers who opened their homes and hearts.

Aisling's skin prickled with a growing dire sense it was wrong to have come here. Clarity rushing in at her pretense that she was something she was not. With Miss Helberg on the stage, waving her award in the air, and Kegan at her side, all his attention on Miss Homsby, doubt slipped about her like a shawl. What made her want this evening with the gown, and the thrill, and, yes *him*, when the truth of the matter was she was little more than a scamp on the filthy streets of Five Points, her *máthair* barely months from dying. In her mind, she was twelve, running the cobbles of Five Points, searching for food. Her hands fidgeted in her lap. She should never have come here.

Miss Helberg raised her voice. "Amongst us tonight we have a perfect example of the good accomplished with your donations to the Children's Aid Society. Mr. and Mrs. Galliger, will you please have Miss O'Quinn stand."

Aisling's blood drained. The sound in her ears rang like a death knell. All faces swiveled to the Galligers' table. Kegan looked at her as if she had two heads. Father stood and pulled her chair back. Placing his hand on her arm, she shakily stood, pleading with her eyes. He whispered, "I'm here, child. Hold on to me."

She leaned heavily on him for support when Miss Helberg's voice resounded across the banquet room. "I give you Miss O'Quinn, a perfect example of the poverty and neglect in the slums of Five Points experienced in one so young. I caught her stealing fruit from a vendor. She was near twelve and dressed as a boy. I forced her to take me to her home.

"Her tenement lay up several flights of rat-infested stairs, where her mother shivered under a thin blanket. With her mother's consent, I, myself, put her on a train to a better life."

Miss Helberg smiled and glanced about the audience, half of whom were riveted to Miss Helberg, the other half glaring at Aisling with obsessive curiosity, mouths agape as if she was an animal in a cage; an oddity to pick over and sneer.

Trembling, she clung to Father, and set her gaze on a spot on the wall above Miss Helberg. A sea of gawkers, horrified to have her in their midst, swam beneath her sight. Mr. and Mrs. Galliger, and most especially, Kegan, part of the maze of derision she could not face. In her heart, she feared what she would find if she did.

In this moment, anxiety spread with the absolute conviction they would never suit as a couple. Had it come to him yet, she was Alan? She gripped Father's arm fearful she might swoon. Miss Helberg's lively gaze burned into Aisling. Her voice rang out across the tables. "Miss O'Quinn, do you recall attempting to run away from me? And my struggle to detain you?"

Wrapped in her delivery, she did not wait for Aisling to respond, and continued to regale the spellbound audience. "She would not be here today if not for my determination to stay with her until a family finally took her. The train made half a dozen stops before she fostered out.

Gettysburg, the last stop for that train. She was fortunate at the end of the line; there was a family and a home that welcomed her.

"Until tonight I did not realize that male child was Miss O'Quinn. Five years ago, I feared she would not find a family willing. Sullen and belligerent, no doubt learned in the tenements. As luck and good people happen, she was taken in. And, of course, they had the option to put her on another train had she, well *he*, not worked out."

The heat from Father's arm that slipped about her shoulders, sustained her; she trembled with mortification. Miss Helberg's lips moved, but Aisling could no longer hear her. The woman's face contorted with her oration as she placed shame. Snippets came to her; *belligerent, thief, sullen.*

Father's hand gripped her shoulder; she continued to rivet her sight to the wall, anchored by his strength. The tension in his fingers as they gripped her shoulder, told her of his own apprehension. Attempting to face her truth, she peeled her gaze from the spot on the wall and hesitantly glanced about the circle of their table. Mr. and Mrs. Galliger, grim faced, stared at her. She could not bear to look at Kegan and instead focused on the vase of red roses in the middle of the table.

Miss Helberg began winding down, her voice less strident. Her arm extended pointing to Aisling. "This is what your donations bring us. Young women and men who are now fit for society. Not the filthy scavengers we were forced to step around before 1853, but capable young people who hopefully live their lives as Christians." She held the award high. "I gratefully accept this on behalf of all the dedicated workers at the Children's Aid Society."

The applause proved deafening. She had given them quite a show worthy of their time and donations.

Shakily, Aisling reached for the arm of her chair and sank into it, attention glued to clutched hands in her lap. A side-glance at Miss Homsby, her rouged lips smirking with the knowledge she, Aisling, was not worth cultivating after all.

She still could not look at Kegan. She had lied to him. Omission is the same as a lie. She represented herself as someone she was not; someone who overstepped her place. Who did she think she was? When all was said and done, the dirty scoundrel Miss Helberg tried to help stood in finery beyond her station. Her heart pounded the ringing in her ears louder. She squeezed Father O'Mara's arm, whispering, "If you will excuse me. I need to find the power room."

He immediately stood, and a sense that Kegan stood as well. Shamefaced, she still could not glance at him.

Father intervened, "I'll walk you to the corridor."

"I can find my way." From beneath lowered lids, she noted Mr. Galliger also stood. Exposed as an imposter, her shame fell over her like a heavy, dark cloud. Kegan's hand lightly touched her arm, but she ignored him, and walked away. The flame of humiliation burned her cheeks. How could she let this happen? How could she think herself good enough? An Irish tenement dweller, a thief, a liar; she summoned strength to carry herself to the hallway.

A damning censure became the penance she rightly deserved. Her sense of smell overly acute in the moment, chocolate parfait distributed to the tables, made her feel nauseous. The gorgeous amber gown swished between tables as she made her way to the back of the hall.

Do not faint; get to the foyer—fresh air. Her mind raced with the impulse to hide, to be free of discrimination. The outright rebuke renewed the fear of standing time after time on train platforms. The humiliation and rejection, which had confused her, because all she really wanted was her *máthair*. At the time, she prayed rejection would return her to Five Points. Her twelve-year-old self had been so wrong.

Aisling reached the foyer, a marbleized room with columns reaching above winding staircases to the second floor, and wide double doors ahead of her; an escape from this hall of disapproval and reprimand. She glanced back to the banquet room. Thankfully, Father had not followed her, nor had Kegan. Why would he, when the realization hit him that the lad who scripted his legal documents two years ago, was she.

Stepping outside inhaling the fresh, crisp air, she placed a palm against a post, and pressed her forehead against her arm. The burden of such disgrace was too much for her.

"Some come down for you, girlie, the truth of who you really are exposed to all those you wanted to count as friends. Duped 'em good, you did, by the looks on their faces. Same as how you duped me on the farm."

Hector.

Lamps hung to either side of the doors cast him in semidarkness. She took two steps toward the entrance. He stopped her with a hand on her arm.

"I won't hurt you, Miss O'Quinn. I admire you, fooling my family as you did for food and shelter."

Her gaze shifted from his dark visage to the doors and back again.

"You'd go back in there knowing they all laugh and ridicule you for what you were, a runt tomboy, and mucking cow dung on a farm?" His face was shadowed, his voice smooth. He continued, "If you like, I'll walk back with you, and they can see what hard working folk aspire to. We'll show them we're the best of what is."

A sob caught in her throat, her wrist hid her gaping mouth. His hand slackened on her other arm and she hugged it to her waist.

"I'll stand up with you, Miss O'Quinn. I ain't ashamed of my background. Look at me now. The Mayor's bodyguard, couple of years a Unionist. Got my own place; don't wear second hand clothes."

She gulped a deep breath, trying to gain control. Unfortunately, Hector appeared sensible in the aftermath of humiliation. "You would have me believe we could be friends after...after what you threatened to do to me?"

"You mean in the stable?" His brows furrowed. "Young and angry I was. And stupid. I lashed out at someone smaller than myself was what I did." He took a step away from her and let his hands drop to his side. "I mean you no harm, and I could sure use a friend. It is lonely in this big city." His gaze slid away from her and roamed over the road and the buildings across the way shuttered against the night.

Almost in a whisper, he added, "Remember when Smythe ordered you to clean the pigsty. It was knee deep in filth and you balked at entering the enclosure?"

He locked eyes with her. "He grabbed you by the collar, dragged you to that damn yoke on a pole, and tied you by the neck. Forced you to walk the paddock in a circle for two days, with no water and no food."

She nearly gasped. "I remember you snuck a dipper of water to me, claiming I would live through it because you had when you were younger."

"That's my point, Miss O'Quinn. You did live through it. We both did. Even the whipping he gave you when you fell down."

She remembered it all. "He told me he'd break me like the animal I was."

Hector's voice filled with venom. "He most likely added, 'You'll thank me for your chores when I'm done.'"

Aisling shook her head in remembrance. "Giselle climbed the fence and stuck her tongue out at me. Her pink ribbons ruffled in the breeze. I'll never forget that moment."

"Try remembering that you lived through it, and you will live through this, too."

Mired in disgrace, and memory, Aisling's feelings toward Hector shifted a fraction. He had reached out to that fragile lad. If Smythe had known...

A shaft of light spread over them as the door to the hotel opened, silhouetting Kegan's frame. "Miss O'Quinn. Aisling, is that you?"

"I'm here."

He let go the door and walked over to her. "We were worried when you didn't return." He registered surprise she was not alone.

She said, "This is... Hector is..."

Hector held out his hand. "I'm a friend of Miss O'Quinn's and wanted to make sure she is all right. Hector Smythe."

They shook hands and Kegan said, "Kegan Galliger. I did not mean to intrude. We were concerned." His questioning gaze held to her. Even in the dimly lit space, she could tell he was confused. He said, "Dessert has been served."

"Will you give my regrets to your parents? Please tell Father I'm being escorted home by Mr. Smythe."

Kegan's surprise evident in the rise of his brows as his gaze wandered back to Smythe, then back to her. "I had hoped to dance with you and enjoy a pleasant evening in your company."

Her fingers twisted together. "You want to dance with me after all that." She glanced over her shoulder at the closed doors. Her huge dose of self-pity would not allow that.

"I'm taken by surprise. I admit. It is apparent we need to have a meaningful discussion, but this isn't the place or the time for that."

"You boil my public humiliation down to a meaningful discussion? Do you not realize what happened in there, in front of your family and friends?" Remorse washed over her.

"Aisling, don't. Whatever happened in there was obviously your life that is in the past. I'd rather dwell on the future." He reached for her hand, but she stepped back, withdrawing from him.

His hand in midair, he glanced at the tall, thick-shouldered Mr. Smythe once again. "Have we met?" The only light came from the moon and the flickering of light from sconces on either side of the doors.

Hector shook his head and scrunched his jaw. "Not that I recall, Mr. Galliger."

---

The hopelessness Kegan witnessed on Aisling's face before she left the table took him a minute to decipher before traipsing after her. When Father whispered, "Go after her," it was the moment he spurred to action.

A negative, puzzling aspect nagged, but he could not reason it out. Aisling was exceedingly upset, that much was obvious. He knew her well enough to know if he took her in his arms and tried to comfort her, she would balk, stiffen, and declare herself capable.

Besides knowing her that well, he would not dare be so demonstrative in front of this man, Mr. Smythe, a figure he had taken an instant dislike to, although Aisling appeared quite comfortable in his presence. That alone irked him. He thought he knew everything about her, but he had not known an iota if Miss Helberg spoke the truth. Furthermore, this smug, rather arrogant man, whose arms threatened to burst the seams if he so much as flexed his muscles, appeared to have some sort of relationship with her. He would be out of place to ask where or how they had met. It would mean interfering with her privacy. Any other time, his question might draw a saucy smile. The more he looked at her, the more inconsolable she appeared.

Warring with his emotions and a sense of her troubled heart, he did not know what to do but follow her desire.

He offered, "Let me call our carriage. I'll take you home."

"No, Kegan. The walk will do me good."

"Then I'll walk you."

Mr. Smythe quickly interjected, "I'll see to her. She'll come to no harm with me."

Kegan's irritation bristled. He managed to keep his hands from fisting. She had not come to harm with *him* as far as he knew. Who the devil was this rogue?

She said, "You could do me a favor."

"Anything." He was greatly relieved to do something to ease the horror of the evening for her.

"You could retrieve my cloak from the check-in."

He spun on his heel. "Give me a minute."

# CHAPTER 18

$\mathcal{K}$egan rushed out the double doors, Aisling's cape over his arm. Glancing to the right and the left, he dashed across the portico and took the steps two at a time reaching the walkway. Aisling and Smythe were nowhere in sight. He ran to the corner and found it deserted except for an open-air carriage only the driver onboard.

With a sinking feeling in his chest, he spun back to the other street, sprinting to the corner. Several people were about, but no two matched Hector and Aisling. She sent him on a fool's errand to rid herself of him. As the truth dawned, he handed the cloak over to the clerk, and mumbled the owner would retrieve it herself.

His jaw clenched over the strange evening, beginning so perfectly. Aisling was adorable in the soft amber gown with her copper gold curls. He ached to hold her in his arms and waltz, whisper in her ear, her sapphire orbs twinkling with delight. Arriving at his table with a heavy heart, he quietly whispered in the priest's ear. "She's on her way home. A Mr. Smythe, a friend accompanied her."

Father's vision narrowed. "I would know if she had a male friend. Signey would have told me." He placed his palms flat down on the table as if to stand. "Did you meet him, then?"

Kegan leaned closer, his voice softer. "Most assuredly. She adamantly rebuffed my offer of a carriage saying she preferred to walk and that she needed the air."

Father drew his hands from the linen. His brow eased of furrows. "She's had quite a shock tonight." He toyed with the stem of his wine glass. "I would have left with her, but the look she gave me; I knew she needed a moment alone to compose herself. I did not realize she planned on leaving. Did this Mr. Smythe appear to be a gentleman?"

"He's familiar but can't place why. Articulate, soft, but firm, speaking as if he knew her quite well. She was the one who said he'd walk with her."

Father nodded, and then looked slant eyed at Kegan. "I would think you have many questions."

"I do. But this is not the place." Father chuckled when Kegan rolled his eyes to the right where his father's wife and her niece sat. "May I come by in the morning?"

"That would be best." Father drew the wine glass to his lips.

Kegan's minutes with Aisling and retrieving her cloak caused him to miss the rest of the awards ceremony. So much for not wanting to churn the whole of Aisling's heartbreak, he could scarce keep it from buzzing in his head and his heart.

Mrs. Galliger tapped him on the arm with her fan, he turned a blank face to her. "Are you going to sit sour faced all through the dancing?"

"I beg your pardon?"

"You've a long pout over Father's guest? She is ungrateful to have run off without a by your leave. But then, what manners would she learn from a rag-a-muffin life?"

He glared at her, a caustic retort on the tip of his tongue. "You are assuming, Martha. It doesn't become you."

Her eyes widened as the fan fluttered beneath her chin. "Hardly. Miss Helberg wouldn't fabricate in front of this gathering, would she?"

"Holding one's counsel until the facts are in, might be wise given the circumstance where Miss Helberg made her revelation." His jaw clenched to the point of discomfort.

"You have your mind set, and that's good enough for me." Mr. Galliger slipped his hand on his wife's arm. It had the required effect of quieting her.

"Unlike others in this room, I'm not at liberty to have an opinion yet." Kegan forced civility. He hoped that after leaving the rectory tomorrow morning, it would be with consoling facts.

Martha's vindictiveness had not ceased, in spite of his father's attempt to intervene. "I think you've been duped. It is time you ask Eleanor to dance. Put your mind to someone who will leave you with a smile on your face." She tapped the fan on his sleeve. "Quickly before she knows I've suggested it."

He could hardly refuse, knowing Eleanor's ear strained in their direction.

Eleanor gracefully came within the circle of his arms as they swirled into line and waltzed about the room with the beautiful *um, pa, pa, um, pa, pa* beat of the music. He could not fault this lovely victim of his stepmother's match making. During the dance, visions of a copper haired, saucy young woman blurred his thinking.

---

*A*t ten sharp Kegan rapped on Father's office door.
"Come in."

Kegan entered, slid his briefcase next to a chair opposite Father's desk, and plunked down. "I hardly slept with concern for Aisling."

"Then you'll be needing tea, or coffee." He looked at his watch. "I can't imagine where Signey is at this hour."

"Probably got her hands full mothering Aisling," said Kegan.

A brisk tap, tap of shoes hit the hallway floor echoing in rapid staccato toward his door. Signey entered without knocking, stirring the air with her haste. "Where is my girl? I better be told she spent the night here." Her quick glance took in both men. "I've been worried sick, so tell me, where is she?"

Kegan jumped up. "She's not at home?"

"That's what I'm saying, young man. Now, where is she?" Signey

169

paced to the side of Father's desk, shaking a finger at him. "I've a bad feeling. What happened last night?"

Father peered over the rim of his glasses at her. He stood, causing his chair to almost fall back. "I wish I had your presence of mind then I could have calculated the whole of last evening's nightmare before it happened."

"Dear Mother of God." Signey reached for a chair next to Kegan and practically fell into it. Her face puckered into a frown. "Tell me all of it?"

"Calm yourself. We'll talk this through, the three of us." Father pulled his chair back and sat.

He rehashed the whole of Miss Helberg's acceptance speech and the emotional cost to Aisling.

Kegan added, thick remorse in his words, "Miss Helberg asked my parents to have Aisling stand." His hand swept over his brow. "I'm sick with the memory of her, innocent, lovely, standing there, about to be—" His fingers rubbed his brow.

"Publicly humiliated." Signey's quivering chin lowered.

Kegan sighed. He paced to the window and back again. "This is one of those questions that in hindsight will appear rather stupid; but Alan and Aisling are one and the same, right?"

Father and Signey nodded with resignation.

Signey said, "She is ashamed to have misled you. Believe me; I've heard the worst of it from her over and over. She wanted to tell you and feared your reaction if she did."

Father added, "And most of what Miss. Helberg said is true."

Kegan spouted, "Most? What part wasn't for the love of Christ?"

Father peered over the rim of his glasses and gave him a warning look. "Aisling, Alan at the time, found herself in a bad situation with the foster family who took her in. The family lived on a farm in Gettysburg. She was desperate and made her way back to Manhattan to find her mother. I kept her occupied while I searched for her mother and assigned her to you to transcribe the Vatican documents."

"Did you know she was a young woman?" Belligerence laced Kegan's words.

'No. Months passed before I suspected." Father cleared his voice. "One day I popped in to your workroom and saw such a look on Alan's face I couldn't shake it. I talked it over with Signey, and the next morning we asked her directly if she was a young lady. She didn't deny it."

Signey spoke up. "That's when she came to live with me, after we discovered the truth of her."

Kegan gaped at the two of them, hands on his hips artless as a bumpkin. "What was the look?"

Father cleared his throat. "Close to adoration as you explained something or other."

Silence fell upon them as they allowed him to absorb the information. He fought to understand what Aisling had endured. Realizing how unaware he had been; as if they had just met. And, then he reminded himself, he had just recently met Aisling; it was Alan he knew so very well.

He is over the moon for a young woman who lied about her identity, her background, who she was, and where she came from.

He also knew she brimmed with trust, kindness, and sympathy for others. Her values were strong. He glanced at the two other occupants of the office. With silent intensity, they waited for him to say something.

One thing he knew; the respect he harbored for her was greater than anything he had known for another person. However, her lying was hard to accept under any condition. Didn't trust him. Couldn't put faith in him. It is why she rebuffed him in Central Park. Clarity like the sting of a bee brought home the fact she was an injured soul who hid her feelings rather than discard them. This meant he did have a chance with her.

"We'll find her." Like a knife, Kegan's voice sliced the silence.

Signey's words filled with sadness. "If she doesn't want to be found, how is that possible?"

Kegan said. "I'm of a mind not to involve the police yet. We know she was last with Hector Smythe. What do we know about him? Anything a'tall?"

Father said, "Isn't that the name of the Mayor's bodyguard? Large and stout, dark kind of man. Sullen."

Signey gasped, "That man standing in that corner caused her to faint." Her finger shook as it pointed to the damning spot in this office.

"You're saying she knew him?" Kegan's voice slithered like venom.

Father interjected, "She didn't acknowledge him. I passed her exhaustion off that she was working too hard."

Signey gasped. "The day we shopped for her ball gown. Aisling dropped her book bag—he was there with the Mayor, picked it up, and handed it over. He said something that frightened her because she had to find the necessary room and calm herself before we could shop."

"What did he say?" Kegan barked.

"She wouldn't repeat it, said it was nothing, scoffed at me. We went on with our shopping."

Kegan asked. "You didn't think her reaction odd?"

She stood, put her hands to her hips, and leaned into him. "How was it he was at the Park Hotel, of all places for such as he?"

Father said, "His job is to guard the Mayor."

"Why does he need guarding?"

Father shook his head. "Some threats or another. I've not the whole of it."

Kegan added, "I'm speaking out of order here, but let's assume the Mayor is in cahoots with Mad Mickey, the owner of the Slaughter House Point Dive Bar and Gin Mill."

"Five Points is a rough neighborhood. It is also where Aisling lived with her mother." Father glanced at Kegan. "Hector works for Mad Mickey you say?"

"I'm not sure I have all the facts, but there is an investigation, and the Mayor has been seen at Mad Mickey's establishment a time or two. He could have met Hector through Mad Mickey, which would not be a good reference for Hector to oversee Aisling's security."

"Just what I was thinking."

"How does this bring Aisling into *that* man's circle?" Signey's voice squeaked with shock.

The two men exchanged a withering glance.

"Well?" she demanded.

Father said, "Kegan and I need to pay a visit to City Hall. Perhaps the Mayor can shed some light on Smythe and point us in the right direction."

Kegan suggested, "Is it possible Aisling knew Hector from somewhere else?"

Signey's hand flew to her breast. "Can I take comfort that she's with a friend then? Or, must I now despair that she's landed in trouble?"

"To that, we'll have to wait." Both Kegan and Father headed for the hallway.

---

*F*ather stood in front of the secretary's desk in the mayor's mahogany paneled office, surrounded by oil paintings of the Hudson and East rivers. He was not taking *no* for an answer. "Young lady, this is an important matter. I will wait for Mayor Reed in his office then."

She came around her desk and headed for the door. "If you must, Father, but you could have a long wait."

"That'll be my problem, then won't it?" He shrugged his shoulder at Kegan to follow.

Both men took chairs along a wall of books. Behind the desk was a bank of windows overlooking Broadway. With nothing to say at this point, Kegan glanced at the titles of books on a shelf, and Father stood at the window perusing the street below. An hour passed with two impatient men continuing to linger.

Their ears perked up when they heard the drone of a man's voice and the secretary announcing visitors.

Mayor Reed, jovial as always, entered his office with a big smile, his bodyguard close behind. Father and the Mayor greeted each other. Hector nodded to Kegan and backed into a corner, hat in hand.

"To what do I owe this honor?"

Father began by reminding the Mayor of Miss Helberg's award and the attention she brought to Miss O'Quinn.

"Yes, yes. I think the woman intended to demonstrate the merits of her orphanage's work. Making Miss O'Quinn a public example was too much under the circumstances. It was obvious the poor girl felt publicly exposed. Had her laundry waving in the faces of all assembled?" He jammed his thumbs into the sides of his vest. "I hope she's been able to calm down. Come to think of it, I don't recall her dancing about with the younger set."

"Because she removed herself." Father said. "I thought she was going to the powder room. Kegan found her outside with..." Father swiveled in his chair and glared at the man in the corner. "With Smythe there. We've come to ask him a few questions about last night."

Hector stepped forward alongside the Mayor's desk. "Anything you wish to know, sir, I'm glad to help."

"For starters, how do you know Miss O'Quinn? We weren't aware she'd taken an interest in anyone."

Hector shifted one foot to the other. "I met her through the Mayor is all. It would be quite something to be an interest of Miss O'Quinn's, but that is not the case, sir. Acquaintances at best."

Kegan did not see it that way. "How did you happen to be with her outside on the steps of the Park last night?"

He shrugged. "I witnessed her distress, clear as anything on her face. I was concerned and followed her."

Chagrined, Kegan bit his tongue. *He* had not gone after her right then. He sat uncomfortably in his chair and waited—for what, for God's sake?

Father interjected. "Tell us, if you will, what happened on the steps."

Smythe pondered a moment. "She was upset, nervous, her hands trembling like, shaky. Trying not to cry, I think. We were not out there but a few minutes when Mr. Galliger arrived. She said more to him than any conversation she had with me up to that point. She was angry, and sad, told Mr. Galliger I was walking her home. She wanted fresh air. She sent him for her cape. The minute he walked into the building she grabbed my arm and said quickly, get me home."

He folded his hands together and glanced at them a moment. "I knew she was terribly troubled. I didn't know where she lived but, of course, she showed the way."

Kegan interrupted. "I wasn't gone but a few minutes. Tell me how you managed to be out of sight so quickly. I ran to both side streets searching for you."

Smythe's gaze traveled to the silent Mayor then back to Kegan. "Well, sir, bothers me to say this, but I'll be honest. She wanted to avoid you at all costs. It is what she said. And when your footsteps were heard coming down to the street level, she ducked us into the shadows of the building on the side street."

Noting the strain on Kegan's face, Father urged, "What happened next?"

"We walked to her home on Amity. A light shone through the front parlor. Didn't see anyone, but the curtains were drawn, and I did not want to appear nosy. I left her with her hand on the door handle. She didn't smile, didn't invite me in, said thank you. And I left."

Kegan, hands jammed in his pants pockets, paced as Smythe answered. He leaned toward the man. "You didn't wait for her to open the door?"

"I saw no reason. She lived there, and someone was clearly inside."

"You weren't curious about that someone?"

"Wasn't none of my business."

"Yet you considered it your business to follow her outside at the Park Hotel and question her about what occurred?"

"Her face showed hurt." Smythe glanced at the Mayor then back to Kegan.

"And you know her well enough to discern hurt, do you?" Kegan spun back to the window and added, "I think you aren't telling us the whole truth."

Smythe sputtered. "What's a man to do here? I assisted a woman in distress, now you accuse me of lying?"

Kegan glared at Hector. "After you left her standing on the porch, where did you go?" He hoped the look on his face reflected the rage he felt toward Smythes nonchalant care.

Hector sheepishly glanced at the Mayor. "I am bodyguard to the Mayor, sir. I hot footed it back to my job."

Father glanced at the Mayor, who then spoke. "He was gone for a while. Didn't mark the time. To my recollection, I don't think it could have been more than an hour at most."

Kegan dropped in a chair, elbows to his knees, and pushed out a deep sigh.

Father stood, and Kegan immediately unwound from his dejected posture. "Thank you for your time, Mayor Reed." He gave a nod to Smythe. "We are stymied as to her disappearance."

The Mayor offered, "If I...if we hear anything, we'll get in touch with you immediately, of that you may be certain." He shook his head in dismay. "Sometimes their emotions rule. I'm sure she is trying to come to grips with the situation, is probably feeling shamed, and doesn't know how to rectify her behavior at this point."

Father and Kegan nodded and left. On the walk back to the Parish, Kegan said, "I don't trust him."

"The Mayor?"

"Smythe."

"For what reason?"

"He mentioned he didn't know where Aisling lived. I distinctly recall a man who fits his size and demeanor follow Aisling and me one night when I visited Mrs. Pennino's home, and we went for a walk. Why would he lie about that? Why even mention it? Unless he's hiding something."

"You're sure it was him following you?"

"Not a hundred percent. It was dusk; lamps were not all lit, enough to think it could have been. Same walk, long leg jut, hands crammed into pockets, a tam. To some degree, I am a sleuth; it is what led me into law. It was not because of Miss O'Quinn that I kept an eye on him. It occurred to me I was being tracked. A specific case I am working on made me wary. I waited for a while after Aisling was inside, and whoever it was turned down the backstreet. At the time, I shrugged it off; but now I wonder if he was following her."

"So why would Smythe lie? What would he be hiding?"

Kegan mused, "I don't know, though I aim to find out. And this afternoon, I'm going to begin with Mad Mickey."

"Leave Mad Mickey to me, I won't say he owes me anything, but we do have a rather particular acquaintanceship, and I will lean on it. Hard."

"If he's your preference, then I'm going to visit the nursing school. Wouldn't it be a good day for us if she was there?" He nodded at Father as they reached the corner. Kegan traveled north, and Father ventured south.

---

*M*ayor Reed leaned over his desk, both hands palm down atop a stack of papers. "I covered for you, Smythe. You have one minute to tell me the truth of last night."

Hector jutted his chin and lowered his gaze. Jamming hands in his pockets, he cleared his throat. "None of your business, sir."

"When you're on my dime, it is my business. Don't get cocky with me. You won't last long in your line of work I promise you that."

"Sorry, sir. It is that..." He removed his hands and let his arms fall to the sides in supplication. "Well, I miss my lady friend, and seeing as I wasn't too far from her home, I stopped by on the way back to the Park Hotel." Hector lifted his gaze to the Mayor. "Miss her bad if you get my meaning."

"A young buck like you, I bet you do. Don't ever lie to me again. Mad Mickey won't take the information that you were off the job for what...was it three or more hours you were away from your duty to me?"

"Probably about all that, sir."

"Mad Mickey will have your hide if he is made aware of your dereliction to duty. He recommended you for this job. He's a man of his word."

"It won't happen again, sir. And, goes without saying I'll expect you to dock my pay."

Mayor Reed glared at the upstart, his vision narrowed with assessment of this young hack. "Yes, it goes without saying."

---

*F*ather walked south on Broadway. At the corner of Anthony, he veered east toward Mad Mickey's establishment. Over the course of the last two and a half years, since Aisling came into his life, there were times she allowed emotions to rule rather than reason. Was it possible she had a relationship with Smythe with none the wiser?

It was hard to believe Aisling knew nothing of the man, and only knew him as the Mayor's bodyguard.

Why would she put herself in his care? What was he missing? She barely had time to herself with schooling, studies, and her internship. Did she befriend another student? Someone she could run to in time of trouble. He would talk this over with Signey and find out what she thinks.

Moving out of the bright sun and into the musky gin joint, his vision took a moment to adjust. Mad Mickey leaned against the bar with one elbow, twirling a cane in his hand. Gleaming white spatter dashes on his shiny black shoes, and tailored coat, he looked as out of place as Father must with his white collar and long black religious frock.

"Saving souls, are you Father?" Mickey strutted toward him.

Father cast him an easy smile. "I'm not above saving a few here and there. However, it is you I seek."

Mad Mickey stepped back, a hand to his vest. "I've been above reproach, no need of the confessional."

"You're sure, are you?" He laughed outright. "Then you're a better man than I. 'Tis another matter that's on my mind."

Mad Mickey spread his open palm to the door of his office. Father knew of another office the man used, more than likely for nefarious dealings, hidden down two flights of stairs, below the acrid scent of stale beer and thick, cigar, and pipe smoke. Obviously, Mad Mickey did not deem his arrival to be anything of great import. He appeared rather jovial.

Settled in their chairs, Father got right to the heart of his visit. "I have taken a young lady under my protection, an Irish lass, whose parents have been long gone. She disappeared last night and was last in the company of one of your employees." He did not want to label the man a thug, not yet, anyway.

Mad Mickey's brows lifted. "A name for this employee?"

"Hector Smythe."

The man took a deep breath. Obviously, the name rang a bell. He said, "Yes, he works for me. What's he done besides being in the presence of this lass?"

"Honestly, I don't know that he's done anything. I would like to know something about him and decide for myself if I think he's lying or not."

The man burst out in raucous laughter. "They all lie. Every damn one of them." His arm swung out moving the air above his lap. "Look about ye, Father. I employ at least fifty, more so now that the war has ended. Better to have them employed than on the streets causing mayhem."

"You are to be commended. I believe you are right. You do not need the confessional. You need a blessing. Though, I've no holy water on my person."

"You go too far with your flattery, Father."

Bending his elbows on the arms of the chair, Father leaned forward. "Are you saying Hector was a Unionist?"

"In the infantry that was brought in to assist in the draft riots. If you recall, once that settled, Manhattan was full of men who could not find jobs, did not have the resources to move out of the city. Hector came to me begging for work. I kept him busy enough with this and that until Mayor Reed had a problem." His lips pursed. "I could probably tell you what, seeing as you've taken your vows..." He eyed the priest. "...I think I'll not share his private concerns."

"All to the good, all to the good. Keep on with what you were saying about Smythe."

"Not much to say. I assume he's not been derelict in his duties or I'd have heard."

"Is there nothing else, anything a'tall?"

The gin joint owner tented his fingers under his chin, growing pensive. Father let him think and kept quiet.

"An odd sort of a man in one respect."

"What might that be?"

"Well, a man of the cloth might not like to hear this. The type of women who frequent my place, I'm sure you're..."

Father waved his hand. "I wasn't born yesterday. And I do hear confessions daily."

"Hector steers clear of them. Cuts a wide path. He's a good-looking sort in a rugged way and hasn't chosen a one of them. I do know, for the past two months, he's been spending his nights on a chair outside the Mayor's bedroom. If I see him, it is usually in the morning."

"Hmm. That is strange."

"One more thing. A woman came looking for him several days ago. A pretty, well dressed, and determined a woman as I've encountered. In this business, I know the ways and wiles. Not bragging, Father, stating facts. This one had an agenda of her own; and I think she met Hector somewhere, because she sure knew who she wanted to talk to."

# CHAPTER 19

$\mathcal{B}$eatrice swept the flowing skirt of her morning wrap away from her legs as she paced up and down her bedroom. Stupid, stupid, stupid what folly of Smythes to bring that hysterical girl here.

Distraught, the foolish thing couldn't control her emotions; nearly incoherent with her explanation. Beatrice held little sympathy for a weakness that would render someone incapable of calming herself. For all the drama, she finally made sense of the occurrence that rendered Aisling inconsolable. It boiled down to public embarrassment.

A tap on her door and Beatrice, in a fit of peevishness, said in a low growl, "Yes?"

The maid's head popped around the corner of the bedroom door. "A visitor, Mrs. Molloy. The same what was here last night?"

"Put him in the parlor. Then come back and help me dress." Under her breath she swore, "Cursed man. He'd better have an explanation for all this. Damn him."

Not inclined to greet him in her morning wrap, Beatrice threw open the mahogany doors of the wardrobe and pushed aside each gown until her gaze fell on blue muslin, embroidered with ferns and butterflies on the sleeves and vest. Bent on making an impression on Mr. Smythe, she tossed hanger and all on the bed, then sat in front of her three-way mirror and quickly applied a teensy bit of rouge. Brushing her luxurious hair back away from her perfectly formed shell-like ears, she caught up a length and dug a pearl comb into its thickness to keep it upswept, and repeated combing on the other side. Untying her robe, she allowed it to slither to the floor as she waited for the maid to ready her corset and crinolines.

Breathless from the rush, Beatrice entered the parlor. Smythe, tam in hand, stood at the window; her caustic voice filled the silence. "You don't appear to have lost any sleep last night?"

Somber as a ghoul, he glared at her. "Morning to you, Mrs. Molloy. I wanted to check in on Miss O'Quinn."

"She isn't up yet." She snarled, "I'm barely up. After all the histrionics and tears, I could hardly settle into sleep." She edged closer, like a cat on the prowl. "What were you thinking bringing her here in such distress?"

"You could be family. It is what she needs right now." He stepped back, clutching his cap as if she intended biting him.

"With questioning, that should become apparent soon enough." Exasperated, her gaze drifted upward.

The girl's room was up the staircase on the left, and Beatrice's chamber directly below. The walls and ceiling were not so solid she could not hear the incessant, wearying sounds of self-pity.

"She's got the color hair and the last name. I would think you've got enough to suspect it anyway." As if on edge, he shuffled his boot on the black and red pattern of the carpet. "She jumped at the prospect of coming here rather than going to her place. I tell you, the girl's bewildered, bad."

A knock sounded on the parlor door, and the maid's head popped around the opening. "Miss O'Quinn's up, ma'am." She opened the door all the way.

Aisling, clothed in a woolen day wrap Beatrice had given her late last night, shuffled into the room in her bare feet, appearing more dead than alive.

"Thank you for this, Mrs. Molloy." She patted the wrap, as her gaze shifted to Smythe. He looked serious, his dark brows knitted, and his lips clenched. She nodded to him.

"How do you feel, my dear?" Mrs. Molloy's voice dripped with honey.

"Exhausted. My eyes burn." She wished Hector wasn't here. Though he had been most kind last eve, she really did not want to be in the same room with him, especially because she was vulnerable and sad.

Mrs. Molloy led her to the sofa. "You cried your heart out way into the night. I am not surprised. We'll have tea." Aisling sat, and Mrs. Molloy nodded to the maid who had not moved from the open door. Then she bade Smythe sit in a chair opposite.

Once all were settled, Mrs. Molloy asked, "Aisling, does anyone know where you are? Your family?"

Her teary gaze shifted to Hector. "No." She asked him, "Did you go back to the...the...hotel?" She could not say *ball*. *It* implied a gay, happy affair. The evening was anything except that.

"I had to. I was on the job. Mayor Reed expected me. I got docked my pay for being gone so long."

"Oh, I'm sorry. Somehow, I will make it up to you. I promise." She tucked the edges of the woolen wrap about her feet, and then leaned her head against the back. Her throat tightened.

An acute sense of bawling came over her. She was a dead weight. If she walked into a lake, she would sink to the bottom. Perhaps that would be the solution to her heavy heart.

The maid entered, set the tray on the table between the three occupants, and left. Mrs. Molloy poured and inquired of Aisling if she wanted cream, lemon, or sugar. At Aisling's refusal, she handed her the saucer and cup.

The steam touched her face. The tip of her tongue burned, she swallowed anyway. The scorch meant she could feel. The weight crushed down on her again, and with trembling hand, she bent to put the saucer on the tray. Hector quickly took it from her.

She drew her fingers up the open sleeves of the wrap. Her head drooped, and tears welled—overwhelmed, weary and bereft.

Mrs. Molloy asked, "Aisling, are there people who need to know where you are?"

Her voice cracked. "No. No one. They're all dead."

"No family?" Mrs. Molloy glanced at Hector with raised brows. "None?"

Hector asked Aisling. "Do you mind if I tell her how we met?"

She shook her head.

"Aisling came on an orphan train when she was about twelve."

"What's this orphan train?" Mrs. Molloy asked.

"A train loads up with orphans and takes them west. It ain't all perfect, they get fed, and the farmers get much needed labor."

She could feel Mrs. Molloy's assessment on her. Her perfume assaulted Aisling's dour, gloomy heart, a sugary scent that pushed through her stuffed nose. She almost spoke, her voice raspy, her throat sore. Mrs. Molloy touched her upper arm. "Were you going to say something? I'm listening, my dear."

"I stole fruit from a vendor. A matron caught me and forced me to my home. She saw *máthair* on her cot." A sob caught her, and she quit.

"Your mother, then. I haven't heard that word in a long, long time. Do you remember her given name?"

She whispered, "Agnes."

Aisling still did not raise her head when the woman said, "I'm almost afraid to ask."

At that, Aisling met Mrs. Molloy's gaze, when the woman asked, "What was your *athair's* name?"

"*Máthair* called him Gradey." Her lids closed to better envision the memory—*máthair* at the cook stove stirring, *athair* at the table a cup in his big calloused hand. "I can't go on. I can't do this. I'll be back in the room." She staggered to her feet, tightened the woolen wrap about her, and lunged off to the stairs.

---

*B*eatrice and Smythe watched her go, bare feet shuffling across the floor. She said, "Poor, forlorn young woman, battered by the social structure of Manhattan socialites. Except it wasn't a socialite who told her story, was it? Last night you said it was a matron from the Aid Society?"

He nodded, and Beatrice continued. "Most likely a woman with much the same background as Aisling, bringing her down to the level where she belongs. That's where I'd bet my money."

"Cynical you are. Puts me in mind of a true Irishwoman."

"You were at the event; you heard that woman. You're the one who told me what she had to say. This young woman, wallowing in her piteous state, doesn't deserve to have her laundry hung out for all to see. A part of me feels badly for Aisling."

"And the other part?" he challenged, "You want your pocketbook lined, is my guess."

"She confirmed our relationship. My eldest brother was Gradleigh. Gradey we all called him. He married Agnes. They had five sons when they left on the ship for America. There are many years between Gradey and me, he being the first and me the last of ten. I was nothing except a beggar child traipsing after him. I remember Agnes. Sweet, soft spoken, she always talked to me when we were together. She would take me on her lap. Though my mother was fifteen when she married, she was old and worn out by the time she gave birth to me. Agnes kind of filled that role until they married, then she had her own to care for." She trailed a finger along the back of the settee as she spoke. "Then they sailed for America."

Smythe asked, "So, nothing all these years? No word?"

She went to the mantel, opened a wood box, and pulled out a letter. "I've got this. Agnes wrote when Gradey died in some sort of warehouse union fight. He was a butcher and worked down on the docks along the Hudson River." She flipped it over and drew her finger across the name and address along the front. "Doesn't say much other than he died." She glanced over at Smythe. "In some ways this letter defined me. It is why I didn't fight it when my mother insisted I marry. As if my life ended, and I didn't care who took me."

"That's a reason to marry?" He looked at the scone in his hand. "How old were you?"

"Fourteen." She couldn't help the smirk on her face. Like most men, he would feel victorious at getting a young thing, virginal.

185

"Kind a young, weren't ye?" He bit into the scone.

"If you knew anything about Ireland in the fifties, you would have gotten into bed with anyone if your next meal depended on it." Her coy look slanted to him. "My reward was linen on the bed, a maid to cook, and fancy clothes."

Smythe bit his bottom lip. When he spoke, his voice held a hint of sarcasm. "And you'd be the woman to leave Aisling with?"

"You're the one who brought her to me in the night." She toyed with the lace on her sleeve.

He stood then, hands jammed in his pockets. "Here's the deal, Mrs. Molloy. I have plans for Aisling, and they don't include where she's come from but where I think she should go. And that's with me." He jabbed a thumb in his chest, the cords in his neck tightened. "I need time to get a place of our own. I'll pay you to keep her here, watch over her, and make sure she doesn't leave."

"Now, how will I manage that? She's practically a grown woman. How old is she?"

"Near eighteen."

"It is clear she's a mind of her own, even if she's beleaguered right now. We O'Quinn's don't give up easy."

"Seems she has, can hardly talk without crying."

"And you're the man to bring her out of this are you?" She slanted him a coy look again and ran a hand across a pillow with buttons and tufts decorating the back of the settee.

"We have a long history. Long before all this. You help me, and I'll pay you decent."

She tapped a finger on her chin, continuing to slant him a look. "There is something I'd like from you, something you could do for me."

He stood in silence waiting for the shoe to drop.

"I'd like to get to know the Mayor better. On an intimate basis." She slipped the finger down her chin and along her throat to the top of her bodice, where she tapped herself with its tip.

Smythe knew her type. "I'd be happy to pave a relationship with the Mayor."

"Wonderful".

A laugh bubbled out of him. "I don't admit to much influence with him."

She swayed to the door, her hand on the knob. "You can rest assured I'll keep your little friend under control. And, don't forget, this agreement includes a decent amount of cash, too, should it benefit me."

A head taller, Smythe's glance swept over her features as she warned, "Don't think for one moment I'm not capable of retribution should you cross me or break our contract."

"It never entered my mind, Mrs. Molloy." He nodded and walked out the door.

———

*A*isling woke again before noon. For an instant, her surroundings confused her until memory clouded heavy with grief. She could not face Signey, couldn't allow her to smooth the hurt away. Father, well, that dear man wanted the best for her, clearly. The truth, she was not meant to step into a role that took her above her station.

Drawing her legs from beneath the comforter, she dangled them off the mattress. The curtains, heavily lined velvet, shut out the day. She leaned over and drew one aside; the blinding light hurt her eyes and she dropped it back in place.

Pulling a woolen wrap across her shoulders, she padded downstairs toward sounds in the kitchen. The maid prepared a tray. "Morning, miss."

Aisling nodded. "Is Mrs. Molloy in?"

"This is for her. She's in her bedroom."

"Let me take it to her." The maid gave her a little curtsy and dug her hands into the sink where dishes waited.

"Come in." Mrs. Molloy said.

"I wanted to bring your tray because I need to talk to you."

Mrs. Molloy gazed the length of her. "That would be appreciated; you've been closeted since you arrived."

Aisling sat on the end of the bed, gathering the wrap about her shoulders. Not as robust on top as Mrs. Molloy, it hung loose. She was an exact opposite shape. Mrs. Molloy was almost the same height,

187

except Aisling was thin, especially compared to the voluptuous figure. Mrs. Molloy had curves everywhere. She drew a withered breath. "I've given my circumstance some consideration and have made a decision."

Mrs. Molloy looked over the rim of her cup. "Go on."

"It is obvious I can't go back to my life. A foolish notion I could be somebody I'm not." She gulped a sob, clearly still emotional.

"And who are you, Aisling?"

With a deep sigh, she relayed her circumstance beginning with the years at the tenement. Then mentioned Gettysburg, though leaving out the reason she ran from the farm. Her return to Five Points to find her *máthair*, and these last years spent with Father and Signey and attending school.

"What did you learn of her? I presume she died."

Aisling nodded. "Shortly after I was put on the train. All the while I missed her, and she was already in heaven."

"Yes, well, you might consider she's in a better place, as we Irish are fond of thinking."

Aisling's fingers spread across the design on the bed cover. The idea of her parent in heaven did little to ease her heavy heart.

Mrs. Molloy asked, "I wonder, why you think you are so different? Why you struggle with what that horrid matron had to say?" At the look of shock on Aisling's face, she quickly added, "Mr. Smythe told me of your years on his family farm, working as a lad, fooling them all."

Aisling couldn't keep the disgust from her voice. "Those curious faces assessed me, like an animal in a cage, an oddity. They gawked as she raged on about me, filling their ears about my filthy dress, my thieving, my *máthair* who spent her time abed. I saw it plain as day etched on their curious faces. Poor, ragged child, stealing to eat, feeding her lazy *máthair*, an object of censure and ridicule. Probably the worst of it was the bold pity."

Mrs. Molloy grimaced. "You've fancied most of it. How could you possibly know what was on their minds?"

"The dress I wore last night, that beautiful creation?" Beatrice nodded. "Father paid for it. I was almost a fairy princess in it. I'd never ever worn anything like that." The hurt in her heart rushed to get out.

"I stood on display in that gown, feeling ever so pretty, lovelier than ever in my life and listened as Miss Helberg told them who I really was."

"Which is what?" Cooled, Beatrice sipped her tea.

"A pretender, a farce. She made me feel like the child who wore rags, a child taken from her dying *máthair*. Never mentioning it was against my will. I distinctly recall my *máthair* telling her to keep me for two months 'till she got better, but that woman put me on the train anyway."

Mrs. Molloy said, "Yes, your past is a blight." She neatly folded the napkin after pressing it to her lips then shoved the tray to the other side of the bed. Clasping her hands, she said, "You don't know me, and you've told me in essence what she said about you. Do I look like I'm ridiculing you?"

"No..." Aisling shook her head. "No, I don't think you are."

"There is a reason for that."

Aisling swiped her wrist at the corner of her cheek. "I don't understand."

"I believe you are my niece. I believe we are related. I think last night was meant to happen. However, would we have met other than fate that brought us together?" She paused a moment then added, "You suffered great humiliation, your friend tried to help you, and another door opened for you."

Aisling stared. "What makes you say such a cruel thing?" She shifted off the bed ready to leave the bedroom. She rushed across the room and reached for the doorknob.

"I attended your parents' wedding, at our parish in Fingal, St. Mary's. When they left Ireland, they had five sons. You and two of your brothers have the hair of Gradey. I have a letter from your mo....*máthair* informing me of your *athair's* death in the warehouse. I can show it to you." She slipped from beneath the covers and pulled a worn letter from the bedside drawer.

"I received this in the Fall of 1860 from the Little Sisters of the Poor." She held it between her forefinger and thumb dangling it in Aisling's face. "They write about a twelve-year-old, put in an orphanage. I came to search for the child. I found you because Hector said he knew a young woman, O'Quinn, with copper gold hair."

Aisling's hand had long since dropped from the knob on the door. She slowly faced Mrs. Molloy. "What color were my *máthair's* eyes?"

"Soft gray. Kind."

"What were my brothers' names?" She crossed her arms; teetering on the suspicion this woman might be a relative after all.

Mrs. Molloy smiled. "Truly?" Jutting out one of her hips, she slapped her hands on them. "Well, I burped Alsandair many times, diapered Conlaodh many times, too. Donn, Flann, and Liam were born about the time I married, and my husband took me away."

As she talked, Aisling slowly moved back to the bed and sat on the edge. Tears began again, and she let them go. A different kind of sadness, not the one of last night's degradation.

"You've the same hair as your father, and Alsandair and Conlaodh. Your *máthair* probably told you this many times through the years."

She toyed with a loose thread on the blanket. "No. Very little. They named me for a dream or vision. They said they needed to think of the future, not the past."

Mrs. Molloy nodded in agreement. "Gradey would think that way. A means to cheer his little wife. She must have been devastated."

Aisling's tears came in a flood. Her mouth drooped, breathing long and low with the sadness of it all.

---

*B*eatrice watched the young woman and her sorrow, her lost family, and her lost dreams. Aisling would be putty in her hands if she played this right. Young, rare looks and a quick mind, a seemingly well-bred lady fit for society despite the fact she has lost her confidence.

Aisling was far too good for the likes of Hector, absolutely. Beatrice calculated that the girl's devastation would pivot in her favor.

Perhaps even jerk the girl out of her doldrums, lift her spirits. What wealthy man wouldn't like to be in company with two young, pretty women squiring him around this bustling city of theaters, restaurants, balls, and famous people? A man with plenty of means to pay.

She reached for a handkerchief. Handing it to Aisling, then hugged her. "Now, now. You have sniffled enough. I have not any doubt you are my lovely, forlorn niece. And I plan to take care of you."

"I can take care of myself."

Beatrice could tell from Aisling's manner that she was not completely comfortable yet. Beatrice attempted to show a motherly demeanor. "I have no doubt of it. You are an intelligent young lady. The die is cast, my dear. I have no one in my life except you. The fairies have brought us together. Think on it. I was in Ireland, you here in America, and here we are in my bedroom together. Does that not tell you something? Perhaps 'twas your sainted *máthair* who arranged our meeting?" Beatrice could tell she'd reached the girl with *that* little bit of cleverness.

Aisling's blue eyes, glistening with tears, peeked over the tip of the handkerchief, and searched Beatrice's face. "I need my clothes."

"How do you propose to get them?"

Aisling lowered the handkerchief. "Monday morning Signey is at the rectory from eight in the morning to sometime about six when she leaves. I can let myself in and gather my things before she arrives."

"You don't want to thank her for all she's done? Sounds as if she's been kind to you." Beatrice held her breath as she watched Aisling consider the idea. It would ruin her plans for this young woman to encounter either the housekeeper or the priest, certain they held deep sway.

Aisling's gaze dropped to her lap. She twisted the handkerchief between her fingers. "I can't explain it. She is a truly loving person. This thing inside me is not about her. It is about me, my failure to be what I want, not society's pre-set conditions of what I should be."

"And the priest?" Beatrice's hand swept a length of curl off Aisling's shoulder.

"He's wonderful, reminds me of my *athair* in some ways." Her eyes brightened. "He'd have had words with that matron. Well, I think he would have, I'm not certain."

"Should you write to him? He's probably worried about you."

"No."

Taken aback with the force of that one word, Beatrice's mind twirled with what it meant. Her brow must have quizzed because the girl said,

"I've not sorted the whole of it yet, last night and the meaning of such ridicule."

Sad countenance and all, her shoulders slouched with an inability to reverse her despair. "If you are willing to help me for a time, and let me stay with you, perhaps I can come to an understanding about the whole of it all. I love both Signey and Father, but I have to work though this disgust shadowing me."

A stroke of luck came to Beatrice when the girl intended to put distance between her and those two people. It had to be the shame she feels toward herself. Beatrice knew about self-abasement. She knew most folks try to hide it from others. She looked at that copper gold head of curls as the sniveling girl's head drooped. Shame was a dirty little device to use for her own benefit. She had not come this far to give up on her goals. The belief that one deserves to be humiliated and rejected would be quite useful in handling her from this moment forward. She obviously wasn't hardened by life yet.

Beatrice said, "Let's look in my closet for something to wear while you get your own clothing. I agree with you about the priest and his housekeeper. You need to discover who you are on your own. Not someone else's idea of what you should be."

Beatrice felt victorious when Aisling gave a timid little curve to her sad mouth.

# CHAPTER 20

*D*ressed in a makeshift outfit from Beatrice's closet, Aisling wrote a letter to Signey including Father in the address. She explained herself to the degree she could and make herself understood, without being slobbery and sounding lamentable. Except that is exactly what she did feel, inadequate.

Because she did not want Signey or Father to search her out, she told them a good friend had put her up, and she would contact them when she could. She added I love you both; I need time to sort it all out—who I really am.

Adding a postscript to Kegan, she sealed it and walked to the little house where she had been so at home, retrieved the key from beneath the mat, and let herself in. Lucy always greeted her, and she wondered where the orange tabby had got. Not wanting to linger in the parlor where too many safe, comfortable evenings spent with Signey, she hurried to her room.

There was Lucy curled in the middle of the bed. The only recognition the tabby gave her was to raise her head and blink. No purring, as if Lucy knew this was not going to last. The ivy papered walls, the white iron bed, braided rugs, and Aisling's heart clutched. A wonderful, comfortable space Signey had provided was not enough to arm her against contempt.

Pulling her valise from beneath the bed, she filled it with necessities. Her movements were jerky, unsettled. A moment of hesitation seized her. Signey did not deserve this. Of course, neither did Kegan or Father. She needed to step back and figure out what she wanted—well, precisely how she could make a livelihood. Which, of course, meant her schooling.

She made her decision and knew it to be for the best. Miss Helberg flashed in her mind's eye. Her finger pointing into the crowd, everyone gawking at the dreadful sight, a ragged child gowned as a pretender. The memory, so vividly clear, drove her to fold inward, pull back from others. Beatrice would help her. She was a lifeline amongst her misery.

Entering the kitchen, where months and months of laughter spread across the table like linen, flew in her face, and clutched her heart. Kegan sat with them not long ago, brought her flowers, wanted to stroll Central Park. Admitted he wanted to court her. She swept a wrist over her eyes and shook her head.

She slumped against the wall when thinking of that. He wanted her in his life, and even then, she knew enough to pull back.

Propping her note against the salt and peppershakers on the kitchen table, Aisling glanced around one last time. Lucy sat in the doorway to the hall, staring at her, no purr, and no tail swishing the floor. Signey probably waited up quite a while for her to come home.

A niggling in her mind caused her to wonder if this was a bad decision. Yet, the humiliation of who she was weighed her down. The filthy tenements, rats scurrying in the hall, garbage everywhere; the stench, scummy puddles dotting the cobbles; and the odors, putrid excrement mixed with lentils and porridge that assailed one's nostrils.

That was home her first twelve years, the tenement on Mulberry, situated at the bend, and four flights up. That is what she came from, and that is the last she saw of her *máthair*, lying midst all of it on the little cot in the corner, shivering. Why it came to her now, she could not explain. Except Miss Helberg had stirred the ashes of her life.

Closing the door, locking it, placing the key under the mat, Aisling took a deep breath. There was one last thing she needed to do this morning. She walked up ten blocks to Fourteenth, then east to the Infirmary for Indigent Women and Children.

Miss Emily Blackwell greeted her and told her secretary not to disturb them. "You surprised me this morning when you didn't come to school. I don't believe you've missed one day since you enrolled."

Aisling stood with valise in hand. "I've come to explain myself, if I may?"

Miss Blackwell indicated she take a seat, and behind her desk, did the same.

"I've changed my living arrangements and need to ask your approval about my schooling, to ask if I may take some time off."

At this Miss Blackwell's dark, heavy brows rose. "Your graduation is only months away, early May. Why would you jeopardize this opportunity?"

It had been a good mile of walking, allowing Aisling to come to some sort of hope about Miss Blackwell and the finish of her education. She said, "More than anything in the world I want to be certified as a nurse. This dream has not changed. I—circumstances have changed for me, and I need a little time to get settled."

Miss Blackwell placed both her palms down on her desktop and leaned forward. Her black bushy brows almost met in a V-shape over her long nose. "I considered you one of the most serious of students. I am disappointed in your request to take time off, regardless the situation." She paused a moment. "Has someone died?"

"No."

"Have you been put out by Mrs. Pennino?"

"No."

"Then I take it, the nature of your request is frivolous." Her forehead scrunched.

Aisling pulled her gaze off the frown. "It is too personal a situation for me to be completely forthcoming with what has happened."

"Hmm." She drew her hands from the desktop to her midsection and entwined her fingers then leaned back in the chair.

Aisling added, "I am more serious than ever to continue my education. I love nursing and working with you in the wards. I do not want to lose this opportunity."

"Hmm."

Aisling waited for her to say something. When she didn't, Aisling continued. "You know I haven't any family. This morning I learned my father's youngest sister arrived from Ireland. She has asked me to live with her. She's a widow with no children."

"Mrs. Pennino will miss you, of that I'm certain."

Aisling nodded.

"What does she think of your aunt?"

"They haven't met."

"Hmm." Her thumbs circled as her fingers continued to twine at her midsection.

"How much time do you think you will need?"

Aisling's heart jumped. "A few days, a week at the most."

"How did you meet your aunt?"

"She came from Ireland to look for me. She knew my parents had died." Another long pause. Aisling added, "She received a letter from the Little Sisters of the Poor, telling of my *máthair's* passing, and me in an orphanage."

Miss Blackwell swiveled her chair to face a bookshelf. She stayed that way for several minutes, the great clock on the mantel ticking away the silence. Voices in the hallway, as footsteps scurried about in the performance of their duties, which were constant with the Infirmary's fifty beds usually filled. This was part of Aisling's schooling done 'on the job,' so to speak. Students assisted with bedpans, food trays, washing of limbs and hair, writing letters to loved ones.

The swivel chair creaked, and Aisling looked up. Miss Blackwell said, "I'll not question why she waited several years before coming to get you." A long pause cautioned Aisling to hold her breath.

Miss Blackwell continued. "I'll grant you seven days, Miss O'Quinn. Only because you are a star pupil and there has not been cause for one black mark on your record. I know this because the board reviewed this soon-to-graduate class, and you appear to be the front runner, both in grades, ability, and demeanor." Her thumbs got busy again. Apparently, she had not finished. "Of course, there are seven more months ahead of you, and anything can happen in that length of time."

"I am so grateful, Miss Blackwell."

The woman stood, Aisling followed suit, grabbing her valise. "I'll work twice as hard when I return."

"No need for dramatics, Miss O'Quinn. We all need to put our attention to other matters from time to time." She nodded, giving Aisling leave.

Aisling stood to leave, and Miss Blackwell stopped her. "You had a visitor this morning. Mr. Galliger. He said Father O'Mara had him looking for you."

"Kegan Galliger?" Aisling faced Miss Blackwell, stunned by the news.

"Yes, that's the name. When I mentioned that you were late coming in, he left without leaving a message."

"Thank you, Miss Blackwell. I'll return Monday next." She needed to get outside, take a deep breath, and gather her wits. Kegan came looking for her. Kegan. He must know who she is, or rather was, by now, probably had sorted it all out with Father and Signey at this point—the boy who dressed from the rag box, Alan; the liar who sat across from him for many, many months as they transcribed the Vatican documents. A part of her was thrilled, a part horrified that he looked for her. Of course, they worried where she had got.

A moment of doubt crossed her mind about the way she cut it off, severed ties. Nary a word to Father and Signey was not fair, she clearly knew this, and hoped her note would calm them. If her *máthair* were alive, she would have guidance. Perhaps the next best thing is Beatrice. At least now, Aisling had a little time to think.

*U*sually, when the maid brought the Mayor's morning tray, Hector could leave for two hours. This morning the Mayor slept in, an unusual occurrence, and one of great distraction for Hector. He planned to look for an apartment. No way could he take Aisling to Mad Mickey's establishment. Not after Saturday's disgraceful reminder of her early life. He needed a nicer place, one where they would live together. He wasn't at all sure how long Mrs. Molloy would keep her.

A maid approached with the Mayor's morning tray, and Hector

opened the door for her. His Honor sitting up in bed propped with several pillows, fluffed out the napkin on his tray, tucked it under his chin, and said, "You must have plans? Does it involve that lovely Mrs. Molloy? Because if it does, you've overstepped yourself." He reached for a wedge of buttered toast.

Hector's stomach growled. He shifted on his feet. "Don't know why you'd say that, sir. Sorry if I seem distracted."

The Mayor sipped tea. "Have you heard any scuttlebutt about the missing girl?"

"None, sir. I've been on duty, not about the streets." He tried not to scowl. The Mayor scrutinized him, from his shoes to his hair. It made him feel uneasy, as if the man read his mind.

"Well, then you probably haven't any information about Mrs. Molloy. I'd be interested if you did. Took a fancy to her myself."

Hector couldn't help but tip on the balls of his shoes, his hands clasped behind his back. "She's definitely a looker I don't mind saying. Far more in your league than a fellow like me, that's for sure."

The Mayor bit into another wedge of toast.

Hector added, "When I took her to the immigration office, she asked a lot of questions about you. If you were married was one of her questions."

The Mayor stopped chewing at that. Crumbs tumbled onto the napkin under his chin. "You don't say?"

"I told her if you were there wasn't a Mrs. about the place. She asked if there was someone special in your life."

The Mayor swiveled his hand as if prompting him to say more.

"I told her I wasn't privy to your private life, though seeing how hard you work, I didn't think so."

His Honor brushed the crumbs off his napkin letting them fly over the tray and bed covers. "You wouldn't happen to have an address for her, would you?"

"I do, sir. She had me take her to the home she is renting. It is off Sixth Avenue, up on Nineteenth. I can get the number."

"Do that." He set the tray over, pulled the napkin from under his chin, and threw the covers back. "You take another hour for yourself this morning. Meet me in my office about 1:00 let's say." He shooed Hector off with a wave of his hand.

---

*C*oncern over Aisling churned Kegan's thoughts, made him restless. With the lack of any hint as to her whereabouts during the brief and terse encounter with Miss Blackwell, he arrived at his office, and attempted to busy himself shuffling papers when Father walked in and closed the door.

"I've a little news, how about you?" Father placed his black bowler on the desk and brushed a hand through his white hair.

"Nothing. Absolutely nothing. It is as if she has disappeared into thin air. I can't figure out where she would go. I don't believe Smythe's got her someplace, bound and gagged."

"You've certainly allowed yourself to wallow in the worst of it. My news will possibly take thinking in another direction about the man. He might have a female friend."

Kegan dropped the bundle of papers on his desk and gave Father his full attention.

"Mad Mickey was amiable enough and fairly forthcoming about his employee. He avoids a certain kind of female who frequents Mad Mickey's place. Steers a wide path to avoid them. Oddly, a few days ago, a well-dressed, handsome woman came looking for him. She asked for Mr. Hector Smythe, knew exactly who she was looking for."

Kegan shook his head. "What does that mean to finding Aisling?"

"Well, it means our Smythe has a life we wouldn't be inclined to ascribe to him. He's a rough rogue, comes from a mean life I would gather. Mad Mickey seemed to think it odd, a woman of her class walked into his establishment, and asked after the likes of Smythe."

"I wonder how we might try to find her," Kegan said, as he shifted through an index of cards on his desk. "Here's the name of a good detective. If this woman is in the city, he'd find her."

Father held his hand up. "Let me ponder the situation a moment. I do not want anyone to know exactly yet that Aisling is missing. No need to attach notoriety to her just yet. We've a good lead with Smythe. Her disappearance points to him."

Kegan, hands on hips, paced back and forth between the walls of his office. "You are right of course." He stopped marching back and forth and glanced at Father. "I can't get the look of her out of my mind. The picture of torture. What must have gone through her mind in those minutes of standing there?" A hand swept through his dark tousled hair.

"You've a growing attachment, I gather."

Taken unawares for a moment, Kegan gaped at the priest. "Unfortunately, I do, though she rebuffed me. I vowed I wouldn't give up, and then this happened."

Father sat in a chair across from the desk and crossed his legs, drumming his fingertips on his knee. He waited for Kegan to settle. "Had I known, I could have prepared you better. The more Aisling grew into her new life, the more she became aware how sad her circumstances were. I saw it every time I talked to her. On one hand, she is proud to be in school, and at the head of her class. On the other, she comes from— well, you heard it all two nights ago. She would see you as someone unattainable."

"Though I spoke of my feelings?"

"Well, she's unaffected, not naive, rather more an elegance of thought. I do not know this for a fact, however I believe your family would be the factor. She craves family, maybe more than she cares to eat or sleep. She's not been able to put it behind her. It was drummed into her that she came after five sons who died in the crossing from Ireland. Your family and what they represent would overwhelm her."

"She accepted you and Signey without a problem." Kegan cradled his head in his hands as he leaned into his knees.

"Neither of us was a threat to the vision in her head of what could be possible. Truth be told, Kegan—"

At this, Kegan's head rose, and his dark features scrutinized Father.

"—I think she formed a strong attachment to you when she was Alan."

A long moment of silence followed the declaration. Suddenly, Kegan shot up off the chair. "You've given me hope. I've not called a man of the cloth a fairy dreamer before."

"Then don't start now, young man. Let's put our heads together and figure out where she's hiding."

Father walked Kegan to the door. As they approached, it banged open practically nicking Kegan in the arm. Signey, clearly out of breath, gasped, "I've got a note. You'll want to read it."

The duo followed Signey back into the office and shut the door. Signey, indignant with pursed lips, handed the note to Father, who deferred it to Kegan, who opened it with a tremble of his hand.

*Dearest Signey and Father,*

*I know you must be worried about me. I am staying with a good friend. I am safe and would feel terrible if you worried about me, please do not.*

*I need time to sort myself out. I think I have been in a dream these past two years, and Miss Helberg brought back the reality of who I really am.*

*I love you both, I will keep in touch. I plan to ask Miss Blackwell for a short leave from school.*

Kegan clutched, she had not added him to her note, until his gaze fell to the postscript. *Please tell Kegan I am sorry for duping him. He deserves far better than what I have to offer. Tell him he always made me feel special. Ask him to forgive me, if he can.*

Kegan looked over at the two people who loved Aisling. Hope and a sense of relief brightening their faces. He took his cue from this and handed the note to Father. "Well, she clearly explains herself."

Signey, arms folded over her chest, gray tendrils fallen from her chignon, argued. "Does and doesn't. Remind yourselves, I was in the parlor Saturday night, and she didn't come in while I was awake. None of her clothing was gone in the morning. Her ball gown not in the closet." She stepped closer to the men and unfolded her arms, pointing a finger into Father's chest. "This wasn't planned by her. She didn't get the urge to leave until that horrid woman spoke out against her. So, I ask, how did she manage to make arrangements in such short time?"

Folding her arms back to their staunch placement against her ample bosom, she glowered. "Tell me that, if you please," she said with a nod of disgust. "Furthermore, she packed her valise when she left the note. Her clothing is gone. She's made some sort of permanent arrangement." She stopped for a short breath. "I'd like to know with whom."

Father and Kegan exchanged dark looks. No one spoke for a minute or two. They paced, and after a few minutes, almost as if on cue, each spoke at the same time.

Father acquiesced to Kegan, who said, "I still say Smythe is at the bottom of this. He was the last one with her, and she asked him to take her home—which, of course, we know he didn't."

"I absolutely agree. That fierce looking man—Hector Smythe. I saw the fear on her face on two different occasions." Signey pointed to the far corner in the rectory office. "The first time he was lurking in that corner." Her shoulders hunched. "Can't recall if I mentioned the second time when we shopped for her gown. Bold as brass he walked up to her on the street. Her fright was such she dropped her book bag. We had to go to a room and sit a minute until she got over it. She told me she had a busy day and was tired. I saw her sweet face wrinkled with fear."

---

*B*eatrice was not home when Aisling arrived. The maid expected her by early evening. Aisling unpacked her things then lay across the bed. The maid did not sleepover; she came daily from her home in Five Points. That touched Aisling. Beatrice's rented home was a few blocks into upper Manhattan. The air was fresh, not of soot and other foul things.

A man's deep voice lively with exclamation, filtering up from the parlor, roused Aisling who had drifted into a nap.

She glanced in the mirror, tucked several strands back in place, smoothed out her skirts, and descended to the parlor. A well-dressed man, starched collar under his jowly chin, and far too much after-shave, stood in the center of the room with a drink of dark liquid in his glass.

His hair was shorter than fashionable, with muttonchops, and a large mustache that curled to his cheeks. He regaled a tale to Beatrice, who appeared enthralled as she looked at him, and sipped her drink; her cheeks burnished a bright red.

At her entrance, Beatrice said, "Edward, I'd like you to meet my sister, Aisling."

His evenly matched teeth glistened in the light as his broad smile settled on her. He made a slight bow. "Lovely to make your acquaintance, Aisling. An unusual name. Irish, I believe. You are the image of your sister's description. Perhaps even more lovely."

He moved too close as he spoke, invading her personal space, and she stepped back. And, *sister*, what was that? She gave him a small nod. "Nice to make your acquaintance, Mr.—"

"Edwards. Edward Edwards. I don't apologize. My parents stuck it on me."

"It is nice to meet a friend of my sister." She glared at Beatrice whose features were giddy, with too much rouge on her lips, and long dangling earrings. Two small feathers had been added to her swept up hair.

"I've promised to take Beatrice to dinner and am delighted to have you join us."

She tried not to sigh. Exhausted from everything that had happened in the last two days, her gaze shifted back to Beatrice. "I need to catch up on some things that need my attention. But, I thank you though."

Beatrice rose off the settee, set her glass on the side table, and touched the arm a moment as if regaining her equilibrium. "You simply must come with us. Edward is being so kind. And, we can all get to know one another over a delicious dinner." She took three steps toward Aisling and put her hand to the back of the settee, further stabilizing herself. Aisling wondered if she'd tripped over the rug, perhaps tangling in the long fringe on the edge.

"I am clumsy."

Edward came forward and placed his arm about Beatrice's shoulder. Surprised when she did not flinch, Aisling wondered if he was a familiar and good friend. "I won't take no for an answer, little missy. Get your wrap; we will be on our way. My carriage is on the street."

Grateful for the swaying carriage maneuvering the bricks, Aisling gave it credit for keeping her awake. Maybe after she fortified herself, she would perk up.

Beatrice had little to say during the short ten-minute ride to the restaurant on the main floor of the Park Hotel. Liveried men opened the doors and handed them from the carriage.

Anxiety hammered through every limb in Aisling's body. This place was where her nightmare began. She visibly balked and stepped backward almost tripping into the gutter. Mr. Edwards must have realized her hesitation because he grabbed her arm forcing her along the walkway. Entering the brightly lit foyer, he handed their wraps to a footman. As if he sensed her hesitation, Mr. Edwards glared at her. His beady glance burned into her. She tried to catch Beatrice's eye, but she behaved as if in a world of her own.

Double doors opened when they arrived at the dining room. Conversation burst from the large room, violins, and a harp barely heard above the din. Tables teaming with people further reminding Aisling of two nights ago. Was she going to relive that humiliation, her copper curls marking her?

Their table tucked in a corner gave her pause for a silent prayer. Mr. Edwards seated them and ordered a bottle of wine. Obviously, a special vintage, because when the waiter delivered it wrapped in linen and poured a small amount in a glass, Mr. Edwards treated it like the holy grail and sipping, rolled it on his tongue. He nodded approval and ordered their dinner without discussing preferences for either Beatrice or herself.

She glanced at her *sister*, who for the most part was rather quiet considering all the chattering Aisling had heard earlier from the parlor. "Beatrice, you'll have to tell me how you met Mr. Edwards."

The waiter leaned over to pour wine into Beatrice's goblet. She whispered, "No."

Mr. Edwards cajoled. "Now, now, Beatrice my dear, I want a gay companion this evening, drink up. It will give you vitality, make your wit sparkle."

Beatrice glanced at her beneath lowered lids as she placed her hand in her lap. When the waiter came around to Aisling's chair, she said, "I have allergies to the drink and get quite ill."

The waiter withdrew the bottle, and circled around the table to Mr. Edwards, filling the bowl of his stemware.

"Allergies? Have you been to a specialist?" he barked.

He had a peculiarity; when he took exception to something, his speech held a hint of brogue, like an angry Irishman. Rather snobbish, her chin rose. "There was no need. My reaction was a rash." No one was going to force her to drink. And, if her *sister* could fabricate, so could she.

He interrogated Beatrice as if she was to blame. "Did you know about this? Seems you might have mentioned it." The glare he sent her matched the challenge in his voice. There was that definite hint of dialect, English spoken by an Irishman.

"I forgot, Edward." She delicately shrugged her shoulders and gave him a radiant smile. "She's not as used to grand outings as you and I."

His toothy smile rotated to her. "We'll have to familiarize her, then won't we?" He paused a moment, drank from his glass, and then said, "Which recalls, a house party this weekend. I insist you both be my guests. My carriage will pick you up at seven Friday evening. Bring whatever you need for two nights. Also, if you ride, you will need an outfit. There will be other guests. We customarily dine at nine on Friday and Saturday evening."

Beatrice beamed and said, "Why, Edward, how wonderful." She patted Aisling's hand. "Isn't this grand?" Her pretty face lit with excitement. "Of course, we would love to attend. Where is your home?"

"It is north of Manhattan along the Hudson River. An hour's journey. Shouldn't be too inconvenient for you." His dark gaze shifted from her to Beatrice and back again, lingering on Aisling, until she looked away, a cold chill edging up her spine.

The evening with Beatrice and Mr. Edwards ended on a sour note when Aisling requested to return home. Mr. Edwards had plans for the three of them and acted like a spoiled child when she refused. Beatrice, other than scrunching her brow at Aisling, and pressing against Aisling's leg with the toe of her shoe, remained silent.

Aisling ignored her. She was more than tired and emotionally drained from the last three days. She wanted quiet and a bed. Mr. Edwards stayed in the carriage, when the maid let her in, he slammed the carriage door, and off they went. She had no idea when Beatrice arrived home. Once her head nestled into the pillow, she did not remember a thing.

---

*I*n the brisk, sunny autumn day, Aisling walked from Beatrice's up Broadway. Kegan dominated her thoughts. Her heart flip-flopped when Miss Blackwell mentioned he had asked for her. The night of the ball, when he first saw her, a sparkle gleamed. The intensity of his cerulean glint caused a tingling sensation. He made her feel as if she could conquer the world.

Of course, then the crushing moment when humiliation struck. Kegan had come after her. Her frenzy had blocked clear thinking. Since that night, she pondered his actions often enough. Why she should care so much was puzzling; her feelings ran rather deep; they frightened her. Everyone who crept close could die or leave.

Beatrice, on the other hand, did not inspire esteem. Aisling was not convinced of their supposed relationship. Beatrice's lies on several occasions confirmed her caution. When Beatrice offered her shelter even before the possibility they could be family, Aisling questioned the woman's motives. Otherwise, what possible reason would she have to befriend Aisling?

Tomorrow evening a carriage would take them to Mr. Edwards' estate. Beatrice made it quite clear Aisling owed her this; with all Beatrice provided her, her presence was the very least she could give in return.

The entrance to Central Park came into view and Kegan came to mind. She wandered the same path, trees now practically shorn of their leaves, a few tenaciously clinging. A light breeze tumbled the rest across the expanse of green. He had taken her hand at one point and squeezed. She remembered her heart flipped, a blush warming her face. Black lamps along the path, ready to throw their golden circles with nightfall. *The* most romantic evening of her life, until she ruined it by rejecting his suit.

Wandering far into the park, she came to bow bridge, and leaning against the railing glanced at her watery image. Kegan had been in the reflection the last time. A cloud rolled in front of the fading sun causing her image to become ruffled. An omen, surely.

Squirrels bustled, cheeks full collecting oaks' fare. A hawk sailed overhead, mayhap in pursuit of one of the little critters. She was a mess.

Her regrets confused with rambling misdirection. Yesterday, Beatrice demanded Aisling accompany her shopping. Apparently, the wardrobe Father and Signey so generously allowed her would not do for such a grand affair as Mr. Edwards offered.

The only permissible garment was her charity ball gown, and Beatrice had the maid clean the hem, and freshen the lace. She also proclaimed the shoes were near ruined. Well, of course, she had walked two miles or more that night. The maid said she could clean them. Wearing the gown would be irreverent. She should have returned it to Signey's when she left the note.

That gown represented mixed emotions. Excitement, the possibility of dancing with Kegan, her first time ever at a ball—she refused to despair over that part of the evening; could not allow herself to dwell on him. Except, she did.

Aisling had begged off shopping. Listless, tears done with, sadness lingered like a pall. Someday, maybe, she would be beyond all this. Just not yet. At least school beckoned on Monday, after the long, long, long weekend at Mr. Edwards's estate.

# CHAPTER 21

The Mayor's butler banged a fist on the bedroom door, causing Hector to jump off his chair. He'd fallen asleep while on duty. In his scramble to stand, the chair tipped over and he landed on all fours before gaining his footing.

At the Mayor's muffled summons, the butler entered the darkened chamber, opened several of the heavy velvet drapes, allowing light in and apologized for waking him in such a crude fashion. "The messenger said it was urgent, sir." He handed over an envelope with The Mayor written in bold letters. The sleep fell from his face as his eyes widened.

Mayor Reed adjusted his glasses on his nose and tore open the letter. A minute of heavy breathing was all that Hector heard. He watched as the man reread the note.

The Mayor threw it at Hector. "I assume you read well enough."

Hector picked up the parchment off the floor where it landed. Thick bold characters, lettered across the page. DO NOT ALLOW THE VOTE TO BAN WOOD FOR BUILDING MATERIAL OR THE DRAFT RIOTS WILL BE CHILDS PLAY.

Hector blinked and reread the threat. The Mayor barked, "The hell! Those wealthy downtown traders push this reform. There's no stopping them."

He slid out of bed and scratched the back of his head as he paced. "It is the beginning of construction below Canal Street. The fools who want to stop using wood will never get their say. It is downright dangerous the way immigrants pour through our open doors." Mumbling almost to himself, he added, "Fires daily. The only way to stop them is quit using wood to build. There's the rub, hundreds of men will be out of work. I suspect that threat came from one of those."

Hector remained silent. His job wasn't to act as the devil's advocate. As much as he wanted the job, he didn't much care if the Mayor received a death threat or not. His job was to make sure he survived.

The Mayor glanced over the rim of his glasses. "I suppose we should double up on guard duty. No reason to become a sacrificial lamb over immigrant living quarters, eh?"

Hector said, "Should I contact Mad Mickey?"

"I'm not a fool, Smythe. No use going all out. You've kept to my agreement with your employer. I'll add fifty cents to your weekly pay and cut your time off to an hour in the morning and an hour after I go to bed at night. Should allow enough time to tip that honey of yours if you're quick about it." He grinned at Hector, his meaning clear.

Cutting his hours meant he wouldn't have much time to find an apartment, the raise in income would allow him to look in better neighborhoods. He wanted better than what he and Aisling came from.

---

*K*egan came out of his office to hand a letter to his secretary. Thomas Hightower, unmarried and never known to pass up an opportunity to chat with a pretty woman, leaned against her desk engaged in friendly conversation. The two men were friends at Harvard graduating from law school in '61.

Flashing a grin at Kegan, Thomas stepped back from the desk allowing him access to his secretary. When he finished, Hightower said, "I was on my way in to ask if you are free this weekend?"

"Come in. Tell me what's on your mind."

Kegan closed the door and motioned for his friend to sit across from him.

"You remember my Uncle Harry?" At Kegan's nod, Hightower continued, "A friend of his is new in town, has an estate up river, and is giving a weekend party, horseback riding, boating. He would like to meet up-and-comers, his choice of words by the way, and asked me to bring a friend."

"Nice of you to think of me." Probably do him good to get out of town. His father had invited him to the house, and he wished he had a reason not to go. Eleanor was beginning to show a more than casual interest in him, and he did not want to have 'the talk' with her, about his lack of feelings toward her.

Hightower perked up. "Really? I was prepared for a turn down."

Kegan came around his desk and slapped his friend's shoulder. "Have more faith than that. I'm always ready to best you at riding and boating."

"Dirty pool. We should be a couple of years from that kind of one-ups behavior."

"I think you're turning into an old man." Kegan chuckled at the look on his friend's face.

Hightower sputtered. "Old man? You are the one who would rather work than play. When is the last time you took a pretty little thing to dinner?"

Kegan's breath caught before he attempted to defend himself. And, Thomas guffawed. "Did I just touch a nerve?" His brows rose up in question.

Kegan opened his mouth, and then shrugged his shoulders. "What?"

Hightower's mouth gaped. "You've got yourself rebuffed. Unbelievable. That's a first if ever there was one."

Kegan said, "Your imagination has gotten the best of you. Worry about racing that little sailboat you've bragged about."

"Should we ride up together? I won't be able to leave until later Friday evening."

"Then come by. I'll be ready. Does your Uncle Harry's friend have a name?"

"Mr. Edwards. Edward Edwards to be precise. He is rather wealthy —made off the war. Restructured a cotton-gin factory into a munitions plant, or some such. An enigma, even Uncle Harry knows little about him. I've met him twice, always with a striking woman on his arm. Never the same woman either."

Kegan grinned. "Well, I'll have to keep an eye on Mr. Edwards and watch how he navigates the waters he sails."

When Thomas closed the door behind him, Kegan glanced out the window overlooking the main street below. Rebuffed was a mild word, compared to how he felt about Aisling's rejection of his stated intentions. He could not get her out of his mind. Then Saturday evening happened. Miss Helberg called on her to stand, and she did so; unsuspecting he thought, until she appeared to freeze. The look on her face made him cringe. Like a cloud passing over, her pretty face changed. Forlorn came to mind, vulnerable surely. Her fingers whitened with the clutch on father's arm. The revelations of her earlier years devastated her.

Well, she certainly had the upper hand now. Hiding, God knows where.

*F*ather O'Mara was reluctant to show an attitude toward Signey. The disruption in his household was in its third day; he missed hot tea first thing after Mass, he missed cookies, or at this time of year, her pumpkin bread filled with walnuts. He missed the cheerful voices that echoed from the kitchen when Aisling came by. His cassock flapped about his long legs as he strode the hallway toward the small chapel. He knew where Signey was spending most of her day.

Peeking inside the chapel door, sure enough there she was on her knees at the Blessed Mother's altar. At the sound of the door opening, she crossed herself, stood, and faced him. "Father, I was just now coming with your breakfast. Time gets away from me."

"I know, Signey. Not to worry. If I could boil water, I wouldn't bother you a'tall." He was grinning.

"As soon as I have enough time on my hands, that'll be the first thing I do, teach you how to boil water. Now, give me a few minutes and I'll be along."

They went their separate ways. Within ten minutes, Signey carried a tray to Father's office. The door was ajar, and she walked right in and set it on the edge of his desk.

"Tell me, is there anything new?" Wiping her hands on the apron, she glanced up.

"The Bishop has given me the burden of overseeing Cardinal Westmore's visit to our fair city. That blessed man has more things on his 'needs' list than any of God's other living creatures." He reached for two sugars and plopped them in his cup.

"No, no. About Aisling."

"I know who you meant. I am trying to lighten your fears. The note she wrote should have alleviated them." He leaned against his elbows, toying with a pencil. "I know her as if she was my own niece. That is precisely why she wrote that note. To rid us of anxiety."

Signey twisted her fingers together. "It is that man, Hector Smythe, behind all of this. I know it. He's evil."

"I planned to visit the Infirmary this afternoon and ruffle a few of Miss Blackwell's feathers. How about if I report to you the minute I'm back?"

Pursing her lips, and with lowered lids, she said, "I suppose you'll be needing a slice of pumpkin bread when you show up?"

His head already bent to the task on his note pad, he cajoled, "What a delightful surprise then."

---

*B*eatrice waltzed into the parlor and plopped packages on the floor and settee. She hummed an Irish tune from her childhood. The maid hurried in from the kitchen, wiping her hands on the apron, and then reaching to help with the packages.

"Is Miss O'Quinn in?" Beatrice drew off her gloves and handed them to the maid.

"Yes, ma'am. In her room, she is."

Beatrice gathered up four of the packages and glided toward the staircase. "You can bring tea to Miss O'Quinn's room."

After a knock and no response, Beatrice entered; Aisling laid on her side starring out the window. "You didn't respond."

Aisling sat up, her face wet as if she'd been crying. "Perhaps I wanted some time alone."

"To mewl away the afternoon?" She set her armload on the chair. "Come look what I've brought you."

Aisling swung her legs off the bed. A low sigh escaped. She did as told.

"I decided to spare you a shopping trip. I already had an idea what would look good on you." Beatrice removed the lid off the largest box. She withdrew a sage green gown with a lace skirt, square cut neckline, and perky short sleeves that puffed. "What do you think of this little treasure?"

Aisling's eyes rounded, wet as her cheeks were. It was lovely. She reached over and traced her fingers across the puffed sleeves. "Beautiful. The color is lovely." Her hand drifted to her side. "You shouldn't have. I can't repay this kindness."

"Yes, you can." She laid the gown across the bed and then put a finger under Aisling's chin, lifting her somber face. "You can be a charming companion this weekend."

Aisling stepped back. "I'm not of a disposition to attend this function. I know it means a lot to you. I'll not know anyone. Besides, I've an odd notion where Mr. Edwards is concerned."

"What might that be? You hardly know him."

"From what I understand, you hardly know him either."

"What are you suggesting?" Beatrice smirked as she drew a pair of long white gloves from a box.

Aisling's quick tongue cut to the matter at hand. "I am inferring that we've been invited to a home where we will not know any of the guests. I'm not exactly comfortable being in a circumstance like that."

"Afraid to meet new people? You surprise me to no end. Your father was so cheerful with others, always willing to meet and greet."

Aisling twisted her fingers together then glanced at Beatrice. "What if some of the same people are invited who were at the charity ball?"

"Ah. So that's it. Well, my girl, you face them square on and dare them to say something. That's what you do. I've not been *born to the manor* either, you know. And I won't let anyone curse me because of it." She patted Aisling on the arm. "Where is your self-worth?"

Aisling thought for a moment. She probably left it on the platform at the train station in Gettysburg because that humiliation still haunted her.

"You do owe me, Aisling. I've taken you in and bought you clothing fit for this gala weekend. I am doing this all for the memory I carry of your dear departed *máthair*. She was kindness itself when I was a child." Beatrice carefully spread a cream-colored shawl on the bed. "The least I can do is show kindness to her beloved *inion*."

The sting in her eyes melted to tears spilling. She'd not been called daughter in their native language since her *athair* died. Not even her *máthair* had used the lovely word. The sound was sorrowful, even with the flicker of happy memory it evoked. With a sense of manipulation, she glanced at Beatrice. "Tell me why I am to be your sister to Mr. Edwards?"

As smooth as silk, Beatrice answered, "I'm sorry if that offended you, dear. I didn't mean harm. You are a beauty, and I wanted Mr. Edwards to perhaps see that in me, a sameness of sorts."

Flabbergasted by the admission, Aisling did not feel pretty, yet Beatrice lied. She had not a clue how to respond.

"Is it all right with you if I don't rectify my little slip to Mr. Edwards?" Beatrice's voice sounded tiny, like a child who took a treat without asking.

Aisling nodded, even as she also knew it was not a little slip, it was an outright, deliberate fabrication.

"Good then. Let's look at the other things I purchased for you." Beatrice lifted the lid off another big box.

Troubled by her vexation at Beatrice, she glanced at the bountiful array of clothing. Her emotions stuck like a lump in her throat and brought on a headache. She was amidst a dual role that was the opposite of honor and integrity, and the weekend had not even begun.

---

*H*ector walked almost at a run to Mrs. Molloy's home. He hoped to spend a few minutes with Aisling before his damned watch. The additional fifty cents a week was almost a king's ransom. Even if he had been able, he would not have turned it down.

Mrs. Molloy did not invite him in. She stood at the door, opened a few inches and told him Aisling had already retired for the evening. He didn't believe her and wanted to muscle inside but reconsidered. "I'm not getting as much time off work as I did. It's important that I talk to her."

"What's so important, Mr. Smythe? You've no claim on her yet. We have a bargain, and I've not heard from the Mayor, which tells me you did not put a bug in his ear."

His jaw clenched, his glance moved from the top of her gown upward to meet her cold stare. "I did. He's received a threat and keeps close right now until resolved."

"So, don't expect me to hold up my end, until you've seen to yours." He slid his boot in the door before she could slam it shut.

He leaned in. "I've told you my plan to set Aisling and me up. I want her assured I'm doing all I can with the time I've got." He grimaced, spittle mixed with his warning. "Don't think of crossing me. You'll get the short end. I intend having the girl, and no smart-ass floozy is going to keep me from her." He stuck his finger in her neck. "Got it?"

She didn't back down and stomped on his foot. Her slipper against a hard-toed boot made a silly attempt. "You don't know who you are threatening, sir. I'd watch my back if I were you."

He wanted to rip the door from her hands and strangle her. Getting a grip on his anger, he pasted a thin line of a smile on his face. "You take care with that young woman who belongs to me or you won't be worth two cents when I'm done with you."

He pulled his boot out of the door, jammed his hands in his pockets, and walked back to the Mayor's home. The night air was coming on, cold and blustery.

# CHAPTER 22

*T*he smartly outfitted carriage Mr. Edwards sent for Aisling and Beatrice sported a shiny black lacquered finish with a matched pair of blacks, a driver, and a groom. Beatrice sauntered to the conveyance. Aisling grudgingly succumbed to the elegance of his gesture, running her gloved hand along the black leather interior, and the glass windowpanes.

With child-like delight, Beatrice stuck her elbow into Aisling's side as they heard the groom strapping their two trunks to the back. Aisling was surprised they had not shared a trunk. Beatrice insisted on her own separate traveling case.

A crack of the reins and they were off heading north on Sixth Avenue where it intersected with Bloomingdale then drove northwest for the remainder of the drive. Homes and buildings became sparse in the countryside the further they rode. Beatrice glanced at her watch neatly pinned to her day gown. In the few short days Aisling had known her, she realized Beatrice's impatience with most things. Mr. Edwards had said an hour or little more.

"I do hope we'll have time to change clothing before dinner." Beatrice tapped her gloved hands together.

"I believe Mr. Edwards mentioned nine for dining. We should have plenty of time. He's rather organized about the whole of our visit, don't you think?"

Beatrice pulled her attention from the passing countryside. The Hudson River was in view at intervals between great stands of trees. "Yes. I'm simply excited, and nervous, too."

"You must like him rather much and want to make a good impression. I think his regard for you is high or he wouldn't have asked you to be a guest at his home."

Beatrice searched Aisling's face. The glow of the lantern made the inside of the carriage brighter in the failing light outside. "He's a wealthy man. What woman wouldn't want to make the best of it? Perhaps I'll meet a really special gent this weekend."

"But you liked Mr. Edwards?" She was surprised at Beatrice's revelation.

"He's a means to an end, my dear. These next three days should set you up, too. Pretty as you are, young, you'll get plenty of attention. Take my advice and choose to your liking. It might prove to be a means to an end for you of long lasting duration." She patted Aisling's gloved hands then added, "Your Mr. Smythe is not the man for you, though he believes he is. No, your future is with a man who has wealthy friends, and travels in the best of circles."

"How would you come to such an astonishing idea about Hector?"

"He told me so. Said he planned for the two of you to live together."

Aisling stiffened. Her hand flattened against her chest. "That's shocking. Preposterous. I can't believe he would suggest such an outrageous idea."

"Now, now. Men get fanciful ideas when they want a woman. Perhaps he was blustering for my benefit?"

Aisling assumed, after his kindness last week that he had changed. "Well, he's quite mistaken. I've absolutely no reason to ever see him again."

"He came by last night after you'd gone upstairs. I didn't let him in. He stuck his boot in the door, reached through, and jabbed at me with threats."

Aisling squeezed her arm. "I'm so sorry, Beatrice. Truly. He can be menacing. His father taught him to box. I know he can carry out a threat easily enough. I will certainly avoid him as best I can. At least we've the weekend free of him."

"I don't want to have to call a policeman. Neighbors think such bad things when one has to resort to that."

"Nosy neighbors, maybe. Police make us feel safe."

Beatrice's gaze fell on the countryside, rolling hills, lambs frolicking off in the distance. "Yes, well we might get lucky, you and me. Our circumstance might land us in a safety net filled with the means to secure a wonderful future."

"And how do you think this will happen?" Aisling teased.

She looked askance Aisling, the corner of her red lip wiggled upward. "I've ways and wiles, my dear. A recent widower, lonely and in need of comfort might think me the cat's meow."

"You know of such a man? I take it he will be attending the evening meal."

"I'll find out soon enough. I've my ways. They have a certain look about them. He will have one too many drinks, trying to be social now he is widowed and feeling awkward. Keep alert tonight. We'll talk in the morning about what you observed. Think of this adventure as a lesson in furthering your future."

Aisling wished she had been firm about not attending this farce of a weekend. How did she get in the middle of something of which she had no desire? How did that happen to her?

Kegan Galliger popped into her head. She knew he wouldn't get himself into situations he had no control over. He knew the details of her past and has her all figured out by now. She tried to comfort herself that he would take great purpose to avoid her. Achingly, there was no solace in the probability.

She took her glove off and smoothed her hand over the walls of the carriage: diamond-pleated burgundy velvet, elegant and comfortable with rich russet leather appointments. Mr. Edwards lived in a grand style. If Beatrice got her wish, she would be living far above anything Aisling envisioned.

The carriage slowed as a huge stone gate crested with the name Elmhurst came into view. The gates opened with the help of two liveried servants, smart in their burgundy and white.

Along the gravel road, bordered by a hedge, stately elms marched beyond the privets, their color changing with autumn. The largest home Aisling ever imagined peeked at them from time to time behind the hedging and trees. Apprehension crept along her skin. This was of the kings and queens she read about in novels. Fanciful turrets with an asymmetrical outline loomed against the darkening sky. Candlelight glimmered in a hundred windows, winking at her in recognition of her utter ignorance. She had only herself to blame.

As the carriage crunched across the white gravel and came to a stop, a great clatter arose behind them. Glancing out the rear window, she counted six more carriages rattling their approach. Elbowing Beatrice, she gasped, "Look."

Beatrice clapped a gloved hand to her gaping mouth. Even she, with her years of experience in the great world, appeared surprised. That was little comfort to Aisling, who hoped to lean on her *sister* for advice over these three days. This weekend could be disastrous; Aisling with no social experience at all; and Beatrice, far too eager to meet strange men.

Ten servants stood at attention along the gravel that extended to several sweeping stairs leading to the front door. As soon as their carriage stopped, the door opened, and the step put in place. A gloved hand reached inside the carriage and Beatrice put her hand atop and stepped out, swishing her skirt free of wrinkles. Aisling did the same. The butler immediately introduced them to a maid, Gwen, who curtsied and asked that they follow her. Two male servants carried their trunks.

With each step, Aisling's awe increased. This was an estate worthy of royalty, with its park-like landscape and now this remarkable Gothic facade. Mr. Edwards was looming into her imagination as more of a surprise than ever. She had sensed a pompous bully. Perhaps she jumped to a misapprehension. Beatrice grabbed her hand and squeezed as they walked under the entryway and through the open doors to a marbled foyer. "We are surely in for a spectacular weekend," she whispered.

As if hearing the exchange, Gwen announced, "I am to serve both of you." She bowed her head slightly. "I'll take you to your rooms where you will be able to freshen and prepare for the evening. If you have any questions, please ask. Naturally, the dress for this evening is formal." Her left brow rose as if expecting questions about the attire. When neither Aisling nor Beatrice commented, Gwen moved toward the stairs.

Beatrice and Aisling exchanged glances. A cat-like smile spread across Beatrice's face. She squeezed Aisling's hand once more then let go.

After two flights of marble stairs, a sturdy balustrade on which to cling, and mirrored walls shimmering with the flickering light of gas lamps, Aisling heard Beatrice's ohs and ahs, as Gwen led them along a corridor laid with a black runner woven with red, green, and gold flowers. Alcove after alcove, Aisling wondered why they were in a wing so far from the living quarters.

The little parade rounded a corner and the third door down on the right Gwen stopped. Opening the door, she stood aside and gestured for Aisling to enter. "Which trunk is yours, Miss O'Quinn?"

Halfway into the beautiful chamber, Aisling questioned, "Aren't we to share a room?"

"Oh no, miss. There are enough rooms for all at Elmhurst. Mrs. Molloy will be down the corridor from you. Mr. Edwards chose a special room for her."

Beatrice pointed to Aisling's trunk. "You may set this one inside." She smiled at Aisling. "I'll come by for you on the way to dinner."

Gwen added, "I'll assist with your hair and dress at seven thirty, miss. Plenty of time to meet up with Mrs. Molloy."

Chagrined, Aisling closed the door after them. Opening her trunk, she took out the only gown deemed fitting for this evening, her amber charity ball gown; thankful Beatrice insisted she include it in her packing. Smoothing the wrinkles as she laid it out, feeling the soft elegance of it, she couldn't stop the image of Kegan sitting next to her; his strong hand brushing hers, the deep timber of his voice.

She had to quit dreaming and glanced out the window at the park. Two stories below a fountain spouted water that spilled gracefully down two tiers. Benches scattered about. A large patio with low baluster circled out away from the outer walls of the mansion. Pots and pots of flowering asters and zinnias blossomed in reds, oranges, and yellows. The forest beyond reflected the same colors as the flowers. The scene was pure autumn.

What would the arrogant Mr. Edwards think if he knew a girl who mucked out horse stalls was a guest in his palatial estate? She grimaced and glanced about the elegant room. The bed was a four-poster encased in heavy draped damask of muted pastels that also matched the bed covering. A two-step stool would assist getting into bed.

The fire grate glowed with coals taking the chill off. Someone had been considerate enough to put a vase of roses on the table between two chairs gathered close to the fire. Rubbing her arms, her gaze slid over every detail of the huge chamber. What a waste of space not to share with Beatrice. Certainly, she was not one of Mr. Edwards' favorites; however, she tried not to believe he deliberately stuck her so far away.

She poured a glass of water from a pitcher that was delightfully scented with lemon slices; another lovely gesture on her host's part. She certainly was at cross-purposes with her feelings about him. Had she unjustly vilified Mr. Edwards? Just because he put roses in a vase, didn't mean he was nice.

Aisling sat in one of the matched chairs, put her feet on the ottoman, and laid her head back. The warmth of the fire reached her and within seconds, she drifted to sleep.

*Hector* had one hour and did not waste it apartment hunting. He headed straight to Mrs. Molloy's. Fed up with her lording it over him about who Aisling could see and who she couldn't, he aimed to set the record straight.

The maid spoke through the door without opening it. "Mrs. Molloy isn't home."

"I've come to talk to Miss O'Quinn. Tell her Hector is here."

"They've both gone off."

Was this another stall? "Yea, well when can I come back?"

"Sunday afternoon, late. Maybe then Monday."

"They've gone off where?" Was she lying? He dug in his pocket and pulled out a crisp dollar fresh from the Mayor's bankroll. "I'm slipping this under the door for you if you tell me where?" He flashed it in the glass of the door, and then tucked it under the door. "You gonna tell me or not?"

"They got invited to a friend's place up the Hudson for the weekend. Big doings for Mrs. Molloy."

"If you got more to tell me, I'll give you another."

"I know his name." She was smiling at him through the glass.

He dug in his pocket once more and pulled out another bill, waving it in her face.

"Mr. Edward Edwards."

He tucked it beneath the door, and she grabbed it. He said, "Anything else of use?"

"It is called Elmhurst, about an hour or so up on the Hudson."

He grinned, pulled out another bill, and tucked it under the door. "You've been helpful." He winked at her. "Enjoy your weekend with the old crow gone."

She laughed outright as he stepped rather lively down the walkway. He felt his hard-earned pay well spent.

---

*A* soft knock at the door, and Gwen entered with a tray. Aisling slowly opened her eyes and looked about. "Tea?"

"Yes, miss. Time to do your hair."

Her watch pin lay on the table, and it noted half past seven. "I slept for more than an hour." She reached for a steaming cup and added a lump of sugar.

Gwen laid out Aisling's brush and some pins on the dressing table and, with teacup in hand; she sat on the padded seat in front of the mirror.

The maid commented, "You've beautiful hair, miss. I don't know if I've ever noticed the color before."

"Thank you. A family trait I've been told." She sipped. "Have you been at Elmhurst long?"

"No, miss. Less than two months."

"Does Mr. Edwards entertain often?"

"On weekends. He likes to have his friends about." She pulled the few pins Aisling had used this morning, and then began brushing out tangles. "I think an up do would go nicely with the neckline of your gown." She glanced over at the bed. "That is the one you intend wearing this evening?"

"Yes. I'm frightfully short on gowns. I will be wearing it again tomorrow evening. Do you think that will be a problem?"

"No, miss. Mr. Edwards does keep a closet of gowns for young ladies who visit and feel as you do."

Aisling sipped her tea and considered what the maid meant. "He invites ladies of modest means then?"

Holding a length of hair in her left hand, Gwen brushed out the tangles. "Yes." She smiled to herself, and Aisling caught sight of it in the mirror. It set her to pondering the remark. "You are smiling?"

"I shouldn't say. Every so often, there are those who don't even know which fork to use. The gowns they wear from the closet don't give them knowledge of table manners, don'tcha know."

Aisling caught Gwen watching her in the mirror as she talked. Was the maid warning her? A creepy sensation gave her cause to wince, because not long ago Gwen would have been describing her.

Gwen added, "I didn't mean anything by my remark, miss. I know you're different from most who come. Why, your gown says so if nothing else. Finer than most."

Aisling did not respond and drew the cup to her lips.

Gwen swung the fistful of hair up and twirled it atop Aisling's head, then secured it with pins. She gently pulled a few strands along the hairline down around her ears and nape. "Your skin is unblemished and soft. This arrangement will show your neck to full advantage. Will you wear ear bobs?"

Thankful for Beatrice's shopping spree, Aisling retrieved a cloth pouch from her trunk and spread two pairs on the dressing table. Gwen immediately picked out the gold dangles with a tiny butterfly on the end.

"These will complement perfectly, miss. The amber gown, and your copper hair, you'll look lovely."

The maid then assisted with the corset and underskirts, tightening and tying. "You don't need this corset, miss." Aisling pictured Alan and all the years spent as a youth. "It has been drilled into me that no proper lady goes without one."

"You'll need assistance later readying for bed." She spread the gossamer gown on the floor, so Aisling could step into it, then Gwen drew it up over her skirts, so she could slip her arms into the short sleeves.

Aisling glanced into the mirror again. The memory of a week ago flooded back. Father waiting for her in the parlor and Kegan at the Park Hotel. There was a fairy tale aura about the whole of it until...she sighed. Time to grow up and put childish dreams away.

The maid curled the springy locks around her finger, and then allowed each to dangle along her nape. Aisling asked, "You won't be available?"

"Definitely, miss. The bell pull is in that corner." She nodded toward the wall where the fire grate glowed. "Yank and I'll come."

"Has Elmhurst been Mr. Edwards' home his whole life?"

"Oh, no, miss. He moved in at the time he hired the staff. Two months ago."

"Will his family attend this evening?"

"He's alone, miss. A shame, too. This large home and all. I think it is why he entertains. Could be why he invites women without husbands." Gwen patted the back of her hair. "You look lovely."

"Have you finished with Mrs. Molloy?"

"Long ago, miss. She went down before I came to you."

---

*A*isling walked over to the grate after Gwen left. Beatrice obviously disregarded the fact that she had been averse to coming here. She was not of a mind to enter the affair downstairs alone. If she had brought a textbook with her, she would sit by the fire and study.

Tomorrow it would be a week since Miss Helberg recognized her. She spread her hands toward the warmth of the grate. Had she given too much emphasis on what others think of her bedraggled past? The maid transformed her, much as had Signey. Her illusions of grandeur attending the charity ball, sitting with Kegan and his family were the real failing. All Miss Helberg did was remind her of who she was, and where she came from.

What would her *máthair* say right now? Aisling surprised herself with a disgusted snort. She would say, *get up lass and be about whom you are. The truth being you are right as rain and smarter than most.* Aisling flapped her hand in dismissal and caught her reflection in the mirror. For one split second, she saw her *máthair,* arms akimbo, blowing out a breath that rattled her lips in a funny way. *Get on with ye, lass.*

Armed with the tender memory, Aisling opened the door, and stepped into the corridor. It was going to be a long walk toward the sounds of music and conversation, and that was fine with her.

Following the thread of violins, she picked up the sound of a deep bass. At the top of the stairs, gloved hand on the baluster, she took a deep breath. The prittle-prattle of discourse drifted from the west wing beyond the marbled foyer. To her left was another corridor. Obviously leading to the servants' end of the estate and she decided to enter a room with those more her kind than people like, well, like their host. She would say she was lost.

The woolen runner ended at a door that was ajar. A staircase, hardly wide enough to bring up a tray, beckoned. She descended four separate flights. The lower she went the more discordant the mixture of sounds from the kitchen. Opening the door at the bottom, she stepped into a corner of a simple dining area teeming with servants. It quickly became apparent who was in charge, as the butler, the same one who welcomed them when they arrived earlier this evening, stood in the middle of the bustle directing the help, as if he conducted an orchestra. All noise came to a halt, and everyone gawked.

"I've lost my way."

The butler regained his composure and came toward her. "You most certainly have, miss. Allow me to show you the way." He glared at his staff. "No need to quit, I'll return shortly." Extending his arm, he showed her the way and followed in her wake.

"I'm sorry to cause inconvenience. I followed my nose rather than my ears." She cast him a smile.

He did not as much as nod, kept on at an even pace out of the working wing of the estate, toward where Mr. Edwards entertained.

They arrived at the foyer with the marble staircase to her right and a brightly lit room straight ahead with finely polished wood floor, gleaming with gaslight flickers from three enormous chandeliers. Vases spilling with roses, no doubt from a greenhouse, stood on pedestals arranged about the perimeter; and a seven-chair ensemble played at the far end.

"Here we are, miss." He stepped aside at the threshold of the ballroom.

"I appreciate your rescue." He bowed slightly and left. Aisling sidled to the nearest wall. A footman offered a tray of assorted punches. Not wanting to make a fuss, she took a cup and held it in her hand. Perhaps thirty or so people milled about, mostly talking in small groups. No one waltzed, though the music was delightful. A harp with its deep, rich sound blended well with the intimacy of violins. She could not find Beatrice. Moreover, as she glanced around the large room, she suspected there were far more men than women in attendance. Setting the cup on a side table, she slowly made her way along the wall hoping to find her *sister*.

———

*A* drink half way to his mouth, Kegan gaped at the vision of unmatched, graceful elegance making her way about the ballroom. In utter disbelief, he considered he drank too much punch, yet knew he held his first cup. He would know her anywhere, of course; the enchanting and fair Aisling. Wearing the same gown as when she sat next to him at the charity ball. A russet, golden beauty. Her slender neck and lovely face with a crown of hair the color of bright rubies glistened in the gaslight and candlelight. His breath slowed as his gaze held to her.

She looked lost, and miserable.

What in the name of God, was she doing here? Whom did she know at Elmhurst who would have vouched for her attendance? Surely not Edward Edwards. A notorious womanizer, how in hell would he know Aisling?

In his astonishment, he watched as she patted her neck with gloved fingertips, amazed him he had not drawn a similarity. It was a gesture Alan made, numerous times when puzzled about transcribing. Spurring his memory, he saw it clearly, as if it were yesterday, Aisling dressed as a lad for safety to navigate the lawless streets of Five Points. She must have quite a story to tell. He hungered for every word. Would she even speak to him? He'd come to realize this past week that he wasn't one of her favored, someone that put her at ease, or she felt safe with, someone in which she could confide.

She did not mingle, rather floated about in the background, slowly making her way where? She stepped to the side of the music platform and listened. Her gloved hands folded together in front of her, as she observed. Her sweet face one of enchantment. The slightest curve on the side of her mouth warmed him. How many times had that same look appeared on Alan's face when he unscrambled a paragraph from the Vatican documents and then correctly rewrote the passage? He looked at the transformation across the ballroom floor, aghast he had been so blind. Incredulous that he thought himself a rather astute detective, was good for a laugh.

This past week, in the frenzy to find her, he now tried to understand the dramatic change. Stunned, his heart quickened. She was the single loveliest woman he had ever laid eyes on. She sat across a table from him for months and months and he had never really seen her. What did Father say to him—something about adoration on her face? A chill ran over him. He had to be the blindest man alive.

Kegan stepped backward into a corner. How had he missed her beneath the boy's clothing? His investigative mind failed him at an obviously critical time in her life. He wanted desperately to go to her now, restraint kept him in check. An elderly gentleman, Kegan could not put a name to him, stepped toward Aisling, engrossing her in conversation. She smiled and answered his question when another gentleman joined the conversation. Her brow furrowed, she took a step back and glanced about. She was clearly uncomfortable with the attention.

Kegan set his empty cup on a passing tray and stepped behind a column hung with velvet drapes. A servant carrying a tray of hors d'oeuvres stopped, and Aisling choose something to nibble as she inched away from the two men and along the perimeter of the crowd.

He wanted to drag her out of this den of iniquity. Did she have a clue with whom she was keeping company? Had she come here to—*NO!* He would never believe that. He raked a hand through his hair as if obliterating the insanity. How in the devil did she get an invite to an Elmhurst's *soirée*? He stepped back from the edge of the room and glanced about. She was nowhere in sight.

"There you are. I've been looking for you." Hightower replaced his empty flute and grabbed another off a passing tray. "Wondered where you got to, old man."

Kegan teased, "I can tell where you've been. Aren't we were racing in the morning? You won't be in any shape."

"That was all your idea. I've got other plans that should earn me a long morning abed." He polished off the champagne in his flute.

"Sorry to hear that. I had plans to recoup my loss from the last time we were here; I used that little boat, *Morris*, or, *Mystery*? Cannot recall the name. Wanted to give her another try."

"You mean the time I ended in the surf and you had to haul me out?"

"As I recall, you had a snoot full the night before and weren't on your best game."

"That was well over a year or more. I might not be on my best game tomorrow. How about Sunday morning? I've got my eyes on a little something I saw wandering about, so I won't be rising early." He winked at Kegan and grabbed another flute from a footman. "The weather should hold through Sunday."

"Suits me fine. Say, Thomas, I'd like to ask if you know..."

At that moment, the dinner gong rang. Kegan stepped back, allowing the guests to move forward into the dining room, the doors opened wide. He did not want Aisling to notice him. He wanted to watch her and figure out why she was here. Besides, the last time he was with her, she as much as told him to get lost. Thinking of which, Smythe was not in the crowd, which meant the Mayor was not here either, because that would be the only way Smythe could gain entrance.

Aisling walked slowly on the arm of a man Kegan did not recognize. A dark blond woman, with too much bubbly in her clung to Mr. Edwards' arm as they made their way forward. Mr. Edwards nodded to him in recognition as he passed.

The massive dining room held one long table, seating close to forty people. Seven candelabra illuminated the center of a red cloth spread on the table that glistened with silver and gold-rimmed china. He watched where Aisling and her escort would sit before he took his place and ended up at the opposite end of the table on the same side, keeping her unaware of his attendance.

Edwards raised a toast to his guests welcoming them and announced a special meal his chef prepared, which progressed as usual, each course larger than the previous and each accompanied with a complementing wine from Mr. Edward's stock. Kegan could only wonder how Aisling handled the amount of drink consumed.

She was not his responsibility. Why should he care? The violinists now played from a corner of the dining room. Edwards certainly knew how to entertain. Kegan was not blind to the goings on after hours, though he had never taken part. The woman Edwards escorted to a place on his right was pretty. She appeared drowsy, or perhaps too much champagne. He wondered how Edwards chose his women.

After they supped, china and silver removed, Mr. Edwards once again stood and offered brandy and cigars for the gentle men who were interested. He directed them toward his library. His housekeeper led the women to a parlor where they could assemble.

Edwards motioned for his butler. Apparently, the blond-haired woman seated to his right needed assistance, and the butler led her out of the dining room. He noted her wobbly walk. Understandably, the butler would safely escort her to her room, and no doubt, would call the maid assigned to her.

Kegan slowly made his way toward the library, knowing from previous occasions the layout. He stood in the shadows until Aisling passed through the hallway toward the parlor. He watched as the women chatted amicably. Aisling appeared preoccupied, her attention on the marbled floor rather than conversation with others.

He could tell something bothered her from the slight droop of her shoulders and the way her fingers tapped against the skirt of her gown as she walked. She lagged behind the others when they entered the parlor. Thinking she was unnoticed, she stepped toward the grand staircase and without a backward glance, ascended. Something in him reacted to her evasiveness.

He waited until she entered the hall going toward the east wing, then he took the stairs two at a time. The corridor was empty, and he moved quickly along the carpeted hall until he spotted her then stepped into an alcove watching as she continued. When she was almost out of sight, he scurried along, ducking into another alcove. He was amazed at how far lodged she was from general company. Almost to the end of the corridor, she stopped and reached for the doorknob, then entered the chamber. He noted which door she used then made his way back downstairs to the library.

Was she going to ready herself for the rest of the evening's goings on? One part of him would not believe it, another part recognized why all these women were here. Surely, they were aware of the situation. Aisling was by no stretch stupid; although he quickly admitted, she was naive. He understood she had been sheltered from society's manipulations.

By the time Kegan arrived at the library, Hightower, who could have been an entertainer in another life, was in full charge of regaling the men with a story of a case he handled regarding a dead body stuffed in a trunk and hauled about like a sack of grain.

The owner of the trunk, and not related to the dead man, wanted the return of his trunk. However, the police considered it evidence in the obvious homicide. In the end, though the owner's wife, cuckolded him, stuffed the drunk into the trunk, where he died of asphyxiation. She allowed the trunk to sit in their apartment until she could arrange for supposed thieves to remove it to another location.

The brunt of the tale that Hightower found so funny was; the husband did not give a whit that his wife committed adultery; it was the trunk that held sentiment.

He ended the story by saying, "Remember gentlemen, women are scheming, wily creatures. Keep your possessions close, and your women at arm's length."

Applause and laughter concluded his tale. Finishing off his brandy, he sauntered over to Kegan. "Do you have plans for the night?"

Kegan knew what he inferred and shook his head.

"Shame. Some intriguing pieces. I'm particularly drawn to copper-headed one."

"Well, let's hope a trunk isn't involved in your exploits."

Hightower put a hand to Kegan's shoulder. "Funny you are old man." He held an empty goblet. "Think I'll get another, how about you?"

"I've my fill, imbibed too much during that delightful meal. Mr. Edwards doesn't stint on his parties." He leaned in close and lowered his voice. "Tell me, which woman fascinates you?"

Hightower's vision narrowed, and he pursed his lips. "The prettiest one in the room. I've already told you the color of her hair. Why do you ask?"

"Curiosity. How do you know Edwards?"

Hightower got a silly grin on his face; he was clearly on his way to oblivion. At least Kegan hoped so. "My uncle, you know that. Otherwise this is the second time I've met him."

Kegan laid a hand to his friend's shoulder. "As you know, I've only made his acquaintance this afternoon. He's a curiosity."

Hightower bent his head and glanced into Kegan's eyes. "You, old man, are the curiosity. Always trying to figure people out, puzzles are your game. Me..." he hiccupped. "...me, I'm just out to enjoy life." Another hiccup, and this time his grin dove for the rim of his flute and he downed the entire contents. "Ah, this should cure..." he hiccupped. "...get another."

He toddled off in the direction of a footman with a tray.

Mr. Edwards asked his butler to pass around the coffin of cigars. "Brought back from Cuba. A fine mellow smoke."

As the butler made the rounds, almost every man took one. A footman walked behind with a lighted taper. The library would fill with smoke and his clothing reek of it on the morrow. It was a beautiful evening and he stepped out the glassed doors to the patio of a mind to stroll about. The moon was nearly full and lit the walkways.

He inhaled deeply and slipped his hands in his pockets, slowly touring the grounds, and deep into contemplation about Aisling and her appearance at Elmhurst. Hightower had Aisling in his sights. Did she know of the activity within the walls of this Gothic revival estate? What the men expected of lovely, young women, single and unescorted? He suspected even those with spouses might indulge. As smart as Aisling was, he was certain she would not have a clue. His biggest puzzle, figure out how she was invited. He could not ask Edwards.

What to do? He strode along the gravel path toward a large gazebo with a bridge that crossed over a small body of water. His mind wandered over the work waiting for him back in his office, his father's wife, and her rather obvious matchmaking pursuits. The last though not the least by far, Aisling's living arrangements, her discomfort with a past that obviously weighed like rocks on her mind, and his regard for her that frankly weighed like rocks on him.

Too restless to sit, he strode the interior circle of the gazebo. He glanced back at the estate, shadowed by the cirrus clouds passing across the moon. Several rooms on the second floor, emitted light. On the third floor, Aisling's wing, a light illuminated what he guessed was her chamber. It was the only room lit. Was she ensconced in an empty corridor for a purpose?

*A*isling rang for the maid and began pulling out hairpins. A light knock on her door and she bade enter. The door opened in a rush and, glancing into the mirror, she spun about. "What do you think you are doing here?"

Thomas Hightower held up a magnum of champagne. "Thought you might be thirsty." He skipped a step forward and regained his bearing.

"Are you out of your mind? Leave this room." She stalked to the door tearing it open.

He hiccupped and smiled. "Not on your life, my little beauty. I've come for some reward having found you in the most unlikely of places."

"I beg your pardon." Where was Gwen? "Get out of this room. Now!" she tried not to scream.

"Needn't get all huffy." He glowered at her. His breath stunk of drink. "You shouldn't be so picky."

Gwen peeked around the doorjamb. "Miss?"

"Help me please. Do come in. How do we convince this, this...drunk to leave?"

Gwen walked over to him and took hold of his arm. "Come this way, sir. I am sure you have lost your sense of direction. Mr. Edwards entertains gentlemen in the library."

He threw a scowl at Aisling. "You'll not be back. Mark my words." His voice slurred. His arm held high with the magnum swinging from his fist. "Would have wasted the night on you. Better spent on an appreciative Cyprian."

Gwen tugged on his arm. "This way, sir. Mr. Edwards calls for you." She winked at Aisling and in a low voice said, "I'll be back shortly."

Aisling closed the door. Her knees shook, and she plopped into one of the chairs in front of the grate. What was that man thinking? He paid her attention earlier, nothing exchanged between them to encourage this. Thank heaven Gwen appeared when she did and handled him with expert care.

It made her wonder if this was the objective for the weekend. Did Beatrice know? The last she saw of her, Beatrice was leaning on the butler, as they walked out of the dining room. She would speak to Gwen about her aunt's whereabouts.

The first time she met Mr. Edwards, Beatrice had been woozy, too. The man encouraged her to drink. A pattern was presenting, and she needed to be cautious. Tomorrow, she would demand he allow them to return to Manhattan. Yet, she was wary of causing a scene. Once was enough to witness his temper. However, she was not at all sure Beatrice would agree to leave.

A knock, and this time Aisling did not open it. "Who is it?"

"Gwen, miss."

She opened the door. "I'm glad you're back. Did that man give you any trouble?"

"None I'm not used to. I led him to the library. There were some gentlemen who teased him when he stumbled in."

Aisling asked, "Do you know the room Mrs. Molloy is in?"

"Yes."

"Could you take me to her, please?"

"I checked on her before I came to you, she's sound asleep, miss." Gwen went to the bed and pulled down the sheet and blanket, plumping the pillows. "I think...."

"Yes, she likes the bubbly drink."

With pursed lips, Gwen nodded in agreement.

"Well, then you can unhook me, and I'll do the same. It has been a long day."

Gwen pulled the remaining pins from Aisling's hair, took a brush to the locks, then unhooked her gown and hung it in the wardrobe. Aisling was not used to someone helping her undress. Gwen stood ready to put the night rail over her head, it fluttered down around her ankles. "Will that be all, then?"

"Yes and thank you." She caught her reflection in the darkened window and giggled. "I'll be perfectly cozy in this." She referred to the night rail, a checkered, red and white flannel, perfect for an autumn night, and the chill that permeated the bedchamber.

With her hand on the door, Gwen added, "I'll bring a tray about eight, and then help you dress. I'll also bring you news of Mrs. Molloy."

"Goodnight and thank you again."

Aisling grabbed the cream shawl Beatrice purchased and wrapped her shoulders in warmth. She wasn't tired considering the commotion Hightower wrought on her already frayed nerves and the oddity of the dinner party. She simply needed quiet. What a day. It did not suit her at all. Nestling into the chair, she rested against the comfort. The fire provided soothing warmth, and she snuggled into the shawl and her flannel gown in the room grown smaller with the lengthening shadows. It wasn't too much later she nodded off.

*A*isling awoke suddenly. The coals where mere embers with little glow. A rustling sound alerted her she was not alone. Wary, she pretended to be asleep and with narrowed eyes tried to glance about.

A man's voice, soft and low, said, "It is near eleven o'clock."

A rush of fear swept through her. Her breath suspended, as she slowly grew accustomed to the dark. An outline of a figure in the chair opposite became clear. "Who are you?"

# CHAPTER 23

"*K*egan Galliger."

Her heart fluttered. "What!" Her voice squeaked at least one pitch higher than normal.

"Shall I add more coals to the grate, or light a lamp?"

"Both. Neither." Her outburst squeaked again as she became horridly aware she was not properly attired for company, most especially that of a man. Of him!

A soft laugh and the figure stood. With a taper from the coals, he lit a gas lamp. As the light took hold, she gasped again, fingertips to her mouth. "It *is* you."

"I said so." He bent to the fire, added a few more coals from the bucket, then sat in the chair opposite.

"How did you get here? What are you doing here? I can't believe it is you." Her outburst sounded mild considering the erratic beating of her heart.

He chuckled softly again. "I have surprised you then?"

"To put it mildly." She slouched against the cushioned chair, her guard softened. He was not a threat. Except for the fact that he knew about her former life, she welcomed him with open heart, especially considering the last time they saw each other.

Kegan noted the sleep fading from her delicate features. "I apologize for shocking you. I am a guest this weekend and saw you tonight. Considering the way we parted, I kept in the shadows rather than face you. You can call me a coward."

Her chin rose at that. She brushed hair off her forehead. Not quite sure what to say. Afraid that maybe he would want answers and she was unprepared to talk about the whole of it ...to him, tonight, ever.

"Tell me who invited you here?" His fingers drummed the arm of his chair.

"It's not your business."

"You were charitable to send a note to three people who care deeply about you. Who is the friend you mentioned in the note you left at Signeys? The friend you are living with—is it Mr. Edwards?"

She shivered in what he considered repulsion, and made another guess, "Thomas Hightower?"

This time her chin dropped against her chest, her eyes closed in disdain.

"Well, damn it, Aisling. Tell me who then, who are you living with? Who brought you here?" His attitude soured. He quit drumming the arm of the chair and fisted his hand.

"I don't have to tell you anything."

He placed his palms on his knees and leaned forward. "No, you don't. However, I believe you have not a clue what this weekend means to the men who come here. Because of that, I think you need protection. Which is why I'm spending the night in your room, and why I want to know who you are living with, and who invited you?" His voice was menacing, low, and argumentative.

"I'm living with my sister, and she asked me to accompany her this weekend."

"Who?" He hadn't expected a lie.

"Beatrice Molloy. My aunt. My father's sister. She introduced me to Mr. Edwards as her sister. She intended painting a pretty picture for him of two sisters, making her younger, closer to my age."

He glared at her a moment almost afraid to ask. "Is she a blonde?"

Aisling nodded.

"She drank too much at table, didn't she?"

She hesitated a moment. "I think so. He encourages her, and she wants to please him."

Her checkered night shift made her look childish and adorable. Frustrated, he got up and put his hand on the mantel, his other in his pocket. The flickers of fire became a focus. "Aisling, I'm not the one to have this talk with you. You sent me packing last week when you had me run for your cape." He cleared his throat and took a deep breath. "Nevertheless, it is in your best interest for me to be frank with you." He glanced over at her. He had her full attention, sleepy though she looked. "Have you a clue what this weekend invitation means?"

Her voice grew soft in the shadowed space. "You mean did I take note of more men than women in attendance?"

He nodded. "That's part, not all."

"Last night a man came to my room as I prepared to retire. Luckily I had already called for the maid and she led him away."

"A tall, sandy haired man, in his cups?"

She nodded. "He called me a Cyprian."

"That's because he intended taking advantage of you. He believed you willing to oblige him."

Those brilliant blue eyes grew wide. "You mean—that is to say—he wanted..."

Kegan grimaced and nodded, certain she put it all together. A student of nursing should come to the expected conclusion, right? "Hightower will be mortified when he learns you are not one of the party of women who come here for reasons other than polite society."

"Oh my." Her hand cupped her mouth. Her eyes, filled with sudden knowledge, locked with his in the semi-dark chamber.

Kegan plopped into the chair, weary of the whole of this night. "This is why I am spending the night in your room."

Gripping the sides of her head, as if to cover her ears, she gasped. "Because you expect me to do *that* with you?"

His palms shot up in supplication. "Absolutely not. I had a strong suspicion you needed protection." His mind nearly froze with her disgust. She had used the word *that* as if it meant filth or death, something other than love, for sure.

A deathly scream rent the air. Chilling in its eerie shriek. Kegan shot out of the chair and demanded, "You stay put." He pointed a menacing finger at her, and the door banged shut with his dash into the dark hall.

---

*a*isling sprang to her feet and drew the shawl close. Putting her ear to the chamber door, the corridor was strangely quiet. Then she detected scuffling and muffled footsteps of some sort or other; and, another unearthly scream, shrill then silence, sounding as if it was near, just on the other side of the door. The skin on her back crawled.

The distinct outcry sounded like an animal in great pain. If anything happened to Kegan. She shrugged off the fear not allowing herself to think of the worst. Beatrice? She could not be sure where her room was located.

Reaching for her watch pin on the bedside table, it was almost midnight. She wished she could lock her door. Glancing about the room for a weapon, she picked up a long rod with a rake at the end meant to move coals about in the grate. With some heft to it, she knew it might come in handy.

The coals diminished to mere embers, the night chill seeped along the floor. Of all the disagreeable circumstances, she did not know whether to cheer Kegan's presence or rue Beatrice's insistence she accompany her to this estate. Again, she put her ear to the door. Deep voices mumbled in the corridor. She considered why she had been invited and gripped the rod with both hands.

The knob turned, and she backed against the wall, the poker at the ready. The outer part of the chamber was dark except for the golden glow from the grate. She shut the valve off the gaslight earlier, right after Kegan dashed out. Better to catch an unaware perpetrator in the dark and bash him.

The door swung open, a pool of lantern light spread into the room, "Aisling?"

"Thank God it is you." The look on Kegan's face was ominous, dark with worry. She lowered the poker. "I was fearful of who might intrude."

He smiled, "You prepared for any eventuality."

She stepped away from the wall to place the poker in the stand.

"After what you told me about this weekend, I am on my guard for certain."

"Yes, as you should be." He set the lantern on a side table and shoved his hands in the pockets of his trousers. "There's been a horrid accident. A woman is dead."

Shock registered on her face, and her hands, as if in prayer, covered her gaping mouth.

"I believe it was she who screamed. Her room is down the corridor, from where we heard the sound. Edwards has sent for the police. We are all to stay put exactly as we were when the screams were heard." He glanced about the room, a serious look on his face. "It means I am to stay with you until we are questioned and allowed to depart."

Grateful for the order, she wanted him to hug her, hold her close, and comfort her. She did not deserve any kindness from him, not after the way she had treated him at the Park Hotel. She could still wish for soothing. Her heart hammered. A woman dead. She wrapped her arms about herself and stared at the dying embers.

"Ah, this may appear questionable to you, but do you need assistance with your clothing? I requested a maid for you, though none of them will come near the corridor."

Her throat knotted. She faced him. "The...the woman's out there?"

He nodded. "Can't move the body until the police arrive and look over the scene."

She fell backward into the chair and buried her head in her hands. A horrid mischief if ever there was one. Murder, a man to assist in her dressing, nearly abused by a drunk, and Beatrice—with a gasp, she asked, "What of Beatrice? I don't even know where her room is, I should go to her."

He knelt in front of her and clasped both her hands. "Aisling, I've more to tell. I don't know how to say it." His gaze searched her face, like begging. He wetted his lips, his grasp tightened. "The woman, the dead woman is a

blonde—"

"What are you saying? It cannot be Beatrice; she practically passed out from drink. She is sleeping. The maid, Gwen, ask her. She checked on her before she came to me."

He swept her cheek of a lock of hair and kept his warm palm on the side of her head, a tender gesture considering the fear in her heart. "Dearest, the woman is the same one who sat with Edwards during dinner. The same one the butler escorted to her room for imbibing."

"Did he say this?"

"No, he wouldn't look at her. This came from the butler." He cupped both palms on her cheeks. "I'm so sorry to have to be the one..." Brushing his lips against her brow, he said, "Knowing this woman was your aunt, I can hardly fathom what must be in your heart."

Tears slid down her cheeks, and he wiped at them with his thumbs. She barely whispered, "We met the night of the charity ball. Hector took me to her. He suspected we were related, and as it appears we are...were."

He drew her to him, cradling her in his arms. "I can't imagine what you've endured in your short life, Aisling. What must be an impossible hurdle for you."

She stayed within the safety of his embrace for a long time, swiping at her tears with his handkerchief. Finally, sodden with grief, and a tingling of sinful relief, she said, "I've not been honest with you."

His soft laugh tickled her ear. "Is this a confession?" He drew his arms from her and sat back on his haunches, then took his seat in the other chair.

She cast him a weak smile and dabbed at her cheeks. "I'm sure Father and Signey have told all of it to you. Miss Helberg certainly opened all my early years for everyone to chew and gossip about. I was overwhelmed and disgraced beyond belief that she revealed my life to all those people."

His elbows rested on the arms of the chair, fingertips tented under his chin. His voice was tender in the midnight of the room. "When it came to me what was unfolding that evening, I must tell you I admired you more than any single person I've ever known. You are the most remarkable woman in the world, Aisling." He lowered his hands. "My regret is that you hadn't trusted me enough."

"I'm learning about trust. It takes a while. I'm slow."

Again, he chuckled. "Trust has to grow, coming in little patches. But, you slow? Not one whit, dearest."

A blush grew up her neck to her face. He called her dearest twice. He complimented her rather extravagantly. She had been so wrong about him; it saddened her to think she spoiled their time together. Her gaze fluttered to the coals, barely a glow of light now.

Following her gaze, Kegan got up, raked the embers, and added more coals. Voices rose in the corridor. He said, "Can you dress yourself? I believe we are about to be investigated."

She sprang from the chair, grabbing the shawl as it slipped. "I can manage quite well." She quickly chose garments, then stepped into the privy closet, and closed the door.

------

*F*ather paced Miss Blackwell's office. Apparently, there was an emergency somewhere within this healing facility, which was full of women who had medical needs. She had dashed off asking him to wait, if he had time.

Something had drawn Aisling to this care facility and its miraculous work. The swell of pride circled in his thoughts as he considered the young woman who brought so much to his life, and, Signey's too. Aisling wanted to care for people, and yet found it difficult to care for herself. He knew that now. He had spent a goodly number of hours this past week justifying her actions. Aisling was due back Monday, and he wanted to be here in this office to talk to her before classes began. He was going to ask permission of Miss Blackwell, if that would be possible.

He simply wanted to tell her he loved her.

Miss Blackwell arrived in a huff. "Sometimes common sense eludes us when it is needed more than ever." She shook her head. "Please sit Father. I have ordered tea. I want to take quick advantage of a few minutes of uninterrupted time with you before another disaster strikes." Her features softened as she sat on her side of the desk.

Miss Blackwell was a medical doctor first, and a fine businesswoman. But, it was the numerous charitable acts for which she was admired. Her Godly reputation was well known. He said, "I've a request."

"I'm assuming you want to discuss Miss O'Quinn?"

"Not so much discuss as to ask a favor. She has had quite a shock to overcome and needed some time to come to grips with it. She left a note with Signey saying she was with a friend and safe." He set his bowler on the table and reached for a cup of tea Miss Blackwell poured.

"In her note, she wrote she would be back in the classroom Monday. May I come to your office early Monday morning and talk with her before she starts her week?"

"Of a certainty, Father. You didn't even need to ask."

"There is a definite possibility Signey will be with me. I understand you are neighbors and know each other. We've both been quite worried about her."

*W*hen Father arrived at the rectory, he entered through the kitchen door. Immediately confronted with Signey beating a mound of yeast dough within moments of its death, he glanced at her beet red face, and wisps of hair usually in a bun, hung in disarray. She had worked herself into lather.

"My, my, what was that going to be, if I might ask?" He pointed his bowler at the flattened mound on the flour-ridden table.

She mumbled something.

"What?"

"Hector's face, that's what!" She punched the mound with her fist, twice.

He backed away from the table and placed his bowler safely out of harms reach. "What has that man got to do with something that should bake into a cinnamon raisin bun slathered in white sugar icing?"

"He's from Gettysburg, that's what." He winced at the punch she gave the yeast dough, hoping she did not break a knuckle.

He reached over and grabbed her arm. "Tell me what's happened. You've learned something?"

She swiped an arm over her brow, pushing strands of hair off. "More than I want to know, for sure."

He spun about, spotting the teakettle. "Let's have a little sit down with tea. Both of us have things to share."

She wiped her hands on her apron and took another deep breath. "Right," as if comforting herself.

He moved bowls off the little table where they usually sat, dusted the chair of flour so his cassock would not make him look like the pastry chef in his own kitchen, and sat. "Do we have any pumpkin bread in the pantry?"

She gave in and grinned at him. Some of her anger dissipated. "You sit and wait your turn."

He glanced around the room. There were no others about. At least that meant he was first in line. His large hands folded in his lap. There was an end in sight to all this and it would be a happy one, he prayed.

Tea poured, bread cut and slathered with soft butter, he asked. "What of Hector, then?"

"He's got to be the man who accosted Aisling when she was a lad. You know, the reason she had to leave the farm, one of the older boys discovered she was a girl and attempted to—"

He held up a fist of half-eaten bread, "Right." He leaned closer. "You think he's the one?"

"I went to Mad Mickey—"

"You did NOT!" He dropped the half-eaten slice to the plate. "YOU were at that gin establishment ALONE?" He almost screeched, his cheeks puffed with the effort.

"I most certainly was," defiance glistening in her eyes. "He knew Hector was from Gettysburg. He lived on a farm there and joined a regiment the day of the battle. Then his regiment came here to quell the draft riots. That's how he got here." She drummed the tabletop with her fingertips, almost as if she expected him to pooh-pooh her discovery.

He admired Signey's spirit too much to admonish her and said, "That certainly explains her faint that day in my office. She saw Hector in the corner."

"Fainted with fright. Passed right out from eyeing a man who would have..." Well, she could not continue along this line, and took a deep breath, "That explains her other reaction." She sipped her tea.

"Go on, don't leave me hanging..." Father twirled his hand as if to wind her up.

"I've told you before. We were at Stewart's for her ball gown. The

Mayor got out of his carriage, and who was holding the door for him? Hector, that's who! Aisling saw him and dropped her book bag. He handed it to her, and her hands were shaking. She told me later she did not know what came over her. I finally put it together and know what came over her. Hector, that's what." She pursed her lips with assurance.

The idea swam in Father's head. Could Aisling be staying with Hector? Highly unlikely given what they knew. He would have to remain calm through today and Sunday, until he could stand before her and ascertain her welfare early Monday morning in Miss Blackwell's office. It was so important to him, he asked Father Brown from St. Jude's to say his eight o'clock Mass on Monday.

Patience was one of the seven pillars of virtue that determine if an act is good or bad, right or wrong. Barometers of Catholic tradition and the Gospels. Unfortunately, it was the one he lacked, and had worked toward his entire life. Sighing, he finished the pumpkin bread, sipped his tea, and glanced across the table at Signey. She was waiting for him to say something, surprisingly patient.

He obliged, "Can you arrange to go to the Infirmary early Monday morning before coming in to the rectory? I am meeting Aisling in Miss Blackwell's office at that time."

A big grin spread her cheeks into a warm smile. "I'll try to find the time." She patted her chest over the place where her heart fluttered with longing.

They had not a clue about the friend with whom Aisling had taken up residence. Their combined horror was it might be Hector. Would Aisling have gone willingly with such a man?

Kegan was the last to see them. He reported they appeared at ease together; then she left a note. Patience! A lost virtue if ever there was.

---

*S*aturday morning dawned with the murder of last night like a dark pall hanging over Aisling's bedchamber. Kegan had refused to leave her alone and spent the night in the chair. The butler informed them they would be next in the interrogation of Mrs. Molloy's death.

Their morning chocolate barely cooled when a knock on the door announced the arrival of the Police Lieutenant, Mr. Séamas O'Flannery.

The butler introduced the lieutenant. "Mr. O'Flannery, Mr. Galliger." He gave a slight nod, looking rather haggard.

Lieutenant O'Flannery entered and took out a pad and pencil. "Now then let's get down to the facts." He looked at Aisling. "Miss O'Quinn?" At her nod, he glanced at Kegan, "And Mr. Galliger?"

"Yes."

"You were the pair who responded to a scream?"

Kegan answered. "We both heard it. I was the one to enter the hallway. The time being a minute or two after eleven."

"How much time would you say between the scream and your leaving the room?"

"Mere seconds."

"Did you see anyone?"

"I had an eerie sense someone was to my immediate left. However, the faint light at the end of the corridor to my right was what drew me, that and the sense the scream came from that direction."

"What did you do then?"

"A door was ajar at the end of the corridor, casting enough light for me to notice a figure dash out of the room toward the stairs at that end. I came to find out that Mrs. Molloy had summoned her maid, who, upon entering the room and finding it empty, went to the privy closet. A man came at her with his fist at the ready. She screamed, and he ran out. He did not touch her. However, she was badly frightened."

"Then what?"

"About that moment, there was another scream. I looked down the hallway and saw something lying on the carpet, just beyond this room. I discovered it to be a female figure and quickly determined a faint pulse that ebbed as I held my fingers to the carotid artery. I was about to turn the victim over when someone ran away from me. I could not tell who it was, but I believe it was male because of the heavy pounding of the feet. He escaped in the dark. I concerned myself with the victim, so stayed with her."

"What else might you have noticed?"

"A strong odor of spirits and a sticky substance. In the dark hall, I wondered if it might be blood. However, once I returned to Miss O'Quinn's room and glanced at my kerchief, there was no blood. It was then I realized my hands were covered in liquor, perhaps brandy."

The lieutenant busied himself with penciling details of Kegan's description. Finished, he said, "Who did you encounter when you went into the bedroom at the end of the corridor?"

"I didn't even get a chance to ask her name because of the second scream."

"Were you able to determine if the second scream was a woman's or a man's?"

Aisling spoke up. "It was definitely a woman's scream. High pitched and filled with outrage or fear."

Mr. O'Flannery asked, "And where exactly were you when all this occurred?"

"I was sitting opposite Mr. Galliger in that chair." She pointed to the overstuffed chair on the left.

"And where was Mr. Galliger?"

She pointed to the other chair. "In that one."

"Had the two of you been drinking alcohol?"

Her eyes narrowed the tiniest little bit. "Since dinner hours earlier, neither of us had eaten or drunk anything."

His intense gaze shifted back to Kegan. "Do you agree, sir?"

Kegan nodded with a wry twist to his lips, and noted her little hands fisted in her lap. Did the lieutenant have to ask such pointed questions? Well, he did. This was a murder investigation after all.

The lieutenant inquired, "By your addresses, I presume you are not married."

Aisling and Kegan exchanged glances, with Kegan answering. "We are not but allow me to explain my presence in Miss O'Quinn's room at the hour mentioned."

The lieutenant lit up. "I'm all ears."

Kegan said, "My invitation for the weekend came from a college friend, whose uncle once lived here. The uncle rented it to a Mr. Edwards who met my college friend, Thomas Hightower, and asked him to assemble some friends for a weekend of sailing and fun. I agreed to come with Mr. Hightower. We arrived about six yesterday evening."

The lieutenant, eyebrows raised; his nose in the air as if he smelt a disagreeable odor. "And, you, Miss O'Quinn. How did you come by your invitation?"

"My aunt, Mrs. Molloy. The...the victim...was a friend of Mr. Edward's, and he invited both of us."

"Had Mrs. Molloy known him long?"

"I'm thinking not. I hadn't known my aunt but a few days when the invitation was delivered."

The lieutenant's brows, now drawn together, and nose lowered, honed squarely on her. "How is that, you didn't know your aunt?"

"My family came from Ireland in the forties. Both of my parents passed away one after the other, and I was twelve. I've never been to Ireland."

Kegan leaned over and held her hand. "It is a painful story, sir."

He glared at Kegan. "It is also a murder investigation, *sir*." His emphasis made clear he was not going to back down on the question.

Aisling, knuckles white with her tightened grasp, whispered, "I'll be quick." Her gaze met the officer. "I've been away since my *máthair* became too ill to care for me. When I returned to New York, I began living with Mrs. Pennino, Father O'Mara's housekeeper. One day I met Hector Smythe, who works for the Mayor, who would visit Father in his office and always bring Mr. Smythe with him. Mr. Smythe took me to meet Mrs. Molloy. Somehow he knew her and decided she and I were related."

"Far-fetched tale if ever, miss. And you fell for it?" The lieutenant chortled. "I would have given you more sense than that."

For some unexplained reason Aisling did not take offense, and added, "She certainly had sufficient proof. Knew all my brother's names. Showed me two letters, one from my *máthair* saying my *aithar* died. She claimed to be his youngest sister. I recognized my *máthair's* hand as further proof. I had no reason to doubt her. She also received a letter from the Little Sisters of the Poor telling of my *máthair's* passing and of a twelve-year-old in an orphanage."

He was penciling her story as fast as he could. Detailing it for further attention later, she supposed. A quick glance at Kegan, who studied her intently, caused her an unsettling moment. Had she said too much to the detective, who sought a perpetrator? Suddenly, she grew even more grateful Kegan had spent the night.

Done penciling her facts, the lieutenant's interest was once again on Kegan. "The figure you saw dashing from the room at the end of the corridor, man, or woman?"

Kegan, focused on the commotion in the corridor, did not hear the question. It was obvious several people were in the area, and apparent Mrs. Molloy's body had not been removed yet.

"Mr. Galliger?"

"Sorry, you asked if I saw a man or woman." At his nod, Kegan reiterated the entire circumstance. Once done, he glanced at Aisling who looked dazed. He was sure she also heard the commotion in the hallway. He reached over and took hold of her hand.

Lieutenant O'Flannery laid the pencil down. "You've had a difficult time. You do appear a stalwart sort. Would you know where the maid might be now?"

As Kegan let go of her hand, Aisling said, "My guess would be in the kitchen seeking solace."

"Does the maid have a name?"

"Assuming the maid was in my aunt's chamber, it would be Gwen. She is also my maid."

"You didn't know where your aunt was staying?"

"No. I was the first given a room, and then Gwen took my aunt to her room. Frankly, I was put out to discover we weren't sharing a room." She fidgeted with her hands then added, "I'm guessing, but I think my aunt knew of the arrangements because she insisted we each have our own trunk rather than share. I was not happy with the separation from her."

The lieutenant, who had dropped to his haunches to write, stood, perhaps to stretch his legs, and walked to the windows that overlooked the gardens below. "A good-looking woman such as you shouldn't have been surprised at the sleeping arrangements. It is a well-known practice for men of a certain culture to make visits during the night."

# CHAPTER 24

*A*isling glared at the lieutenant about to retort.

Kegan interjected. "I beseech you, lieutenant. Miss O'Quinn is of impeccable reproach. Innocent in all of this. Her instincts were already alerted when brought here against her better judgment."

The lieutenant smirked. "And that's why you happened to have spent the night in this room with her. To protect her innocence or to avail yourself of her services?"

"How dare you!" Aisling, fists clenched, heat swiftly rose to her cheeks. She felt like belting him in his smirk.

Kegan's hand held to her arm. "Don't. Allow him his indecent speculations. We know better. I certainly know you and the strength of your moral fiber."

The lieutenant opened the door to the corridor, and sounds of muted conversation drifted in. Aisling could not look out the open portal and went to the windows. Kegan stood between the two, waiting. The lieutenant said, "Stay put. I'll be a minute or two."

As the officer closed the door behind him, Kegan briskly stepped to Aisling and put his hands on her shoulders, turning her about. "He's agitated you. I am sorry to say, it is part of his job. Until he gets to know you better, he's simply trying to figure you out."

Spiteful and cranky, she said, "He didn't attack *you*. Is this a gender issue?"

"Ah, a feminist reaction. Perhaps you should delve into politics rather than medicine." He chuckled.

He eased her anxiety, and frustration. She hardly knew her father's sister. Barely had time to understand what brought her to New York. Beatrice was gone before Aisling had a chance to learn about their family, things that parents would not have told a young child though would be worth a great deal to an adult.

"Thank you for your care, Kegan. I am grateful. Last night was horrid. I am relieved I did not have to be alone. The idea of her out there on the carpet, dead." A shiver coursed through her. "Unbelievable, even now. Poor woman. I cannot help my feelings. I've had time to think and my mind keeps going over and over some of the things she said to me."

"I'm listening, if you care to talk." He stood next to her at the window, hands jammed in his pockets.

"She harbored an angry outlook on life, on men, which was at cross purposes to her admiration for Mr. Edwards. Everything he suggested, she agreed to without a word of protest."

"Give me an example."

"Well, her drinking. He encouraged her to imbibe far more than she should. Almost as if, he wanted her to be nonsensical. Last night was not the first time she was in that condition when with him."

"What do you know of Mr. Edwards?"

She considered the question. "Probably less than you."

"I wonder about his background, where he comes from. Hightower mentioned the south. He thinks the man made his money refitting a cotton factory into a munitions factory. Of course, that doesn't explain why he would rent an estate in New York."

"Maybe he needed to get away. Maybe he's not who he says he is."

Kegan's features were lively with amusement. "Aren't you the one to question?"

Heat rose up her neck. "He gives me the creeps. He tried to force me to drink. I told him I have an allergy. It is not even that. I think he's someone who goes to great lengths to disguise who he really is."

"You believe he's hiding something?"

"I do, yes. What and why I've not a notion."

"How do you decipher such a feeling?" He leaned in with a teasing twist to his smile.

"I hid behind lad's clothing for almost five years with good reason. It protected me."

"I loved that lad. Did you know that?" His gaze riveted to her perhaps searching for Alan beneath who she was now. His declaration was unexpected. His voice softened. "Maybe I do know how to decipher such feelings, because there was something about Alan that compelled me to care deeply for him. A sensibility that I have transferred to you over time. Perhaps I've been drawn to you because of that earlier awareness."

A knock on the door, interrupted a tender caring that touched her heart. As much as that lad her been who she was, Kegan cared for him, too. It mattered a great deal, more than she could put into words.

Gwen said, "Sir, miss, Lieutenant O'Flannery asks that you meet him in the large parlor."

---

*A* special delivery handed to Father made him check the time. Saturday about three o'clock, he had not expected any more posts for the rest of the weekend. He was familiar enough with Kegan's hand, he knew before unfolding the letter, and tore it open.

*Father Declan:*

*My news will no doubt shock you. I am with Aisling. She sends her love and appears to be in excellent health. We are in upper New York at an estate on the Hudson, Elmhurst. I will not go into details, but a murder has occurred, and we are unable to leave until the investigation concludes.*

*The murdered woman has proven to be Aisling's father's sister, Mrs. Beatrice Molloy, most recently from Ireland with proof of her identity, so far as can be believed. Mrs. Molloy is the same person Aisling took up residence with since the night of the charity ball.*

*I will not leave her side until this is solved. I will keep you informed as further developments occur. Funeral arrangements need to be handled. Though she was Catholic, Aisling does not know if she registered at a church in Manhattan. The body is to be transported to the morgue in Manhattan later this afternoon.*

*Regards, Kegan Galliger*

*P.S. please share with Mrs. Pennino, who I am certain is as worried as you about Aisling's welfare. Aisling asks if you could inform Miss Blackwell, as she is expected at school Monday morning and may not be able to be there.*

Father whistled a long thin sound of relief and ran out the door, down the hallway, cassock flapping about his long legs, and into the kitchen. "You must read this."

Signey wiped the suds from her arm and with skepticism scrunching her salted brows, began reading. She scanned the note to the signature, then back to the beginning. "I'm speechless. Dumb founded."

"That girl has not led a normal life in all the time I've known her." Father sat at the table, hands folded on top.

Signey sighed, "Well, she's safe as can be under such circumstance. I'm grateful Kegan is with her."

"Now, how do you think that happened?" His bushy brows were halfway up his forehead with the question.

"You can be sure it is a good thing, Father. No sense in blowing it all out of proportion."

"An aunt? Murdered? How do you think that happened?" His brows did not move.

"Well, she'd be an immigrant come as hundreds of thousands of others have come. As to her death, that would be left to the police. We need to light a candle at St. Joseph's little altar."

"An estate in upper New York, and on the Hudson no less, how do you think that happened?" His brows lowered causing his vision to narrow as if daring her answer to be as easily explained as the others.

"That I've not got a notion about, Kegan is with her, and that reassures me."

"Well." He stood and tucked the letter in his pocket. "I'll go to the Infirmary and hope that I find Miss Blackwell in as good a mood over this information as you appear to be. All due respect for the deceased aunt."

He whistled as he banged his way out the kitchen door, a relieved cleric on a mission.

---

*H*ector tried as best he could to ignore his growling stomach and the chill of the night air. He found shelter in a woodsman's cabin meant for cleaning kill. He was certain it belonged to Elmhurst and was grateful for the cold that kept the stench at bay for the most part. Several ham hocks dangled from the rafters, and some birds, still feathered, hung by their feet, waiting for the honor of being the main course in the fine Elmhurst mansion of Mr. Edwards no doubt.

If he didn't sneak out before daybreak, he might be stuck inside this shack until dark. During the night, he heard mumbling and the snap of footfall, and figured they hunted him. He hoped the maid was too frightened to give a description. Her scream still rang in his ears. He spent the night under a pile of burlap bags and was able to drop a rake over the lot in a corner. Sometime during the night, the door opened, and a ring of lantern light swooped about. He'd been lucky they didn't have time to get sniffers. Those damn bloodhounds would have found him in an instant.

Damn Mrs. Molloy for her conniving. He hadn't trusted her, little good it did. The last time they talked, she must have already made plans for herself and Aisling. She is a man hunter; he knew that the first moment.

His fingers ran over the knife handle shoved in his boot. Slicing off a fat piece of the ham made his mouth water. There were no windows in the cabin. From inside, all he had to go by was his hearing. About the time, the hunt moved on a storm had come up. He couldn't tell if men prowled the grounds or not. Limbs thudded to earth in the cracking wind.

A slit under the door and a few knots in the walls lightened with the rising dawn. Throwing off the burlap bags, he stood and crept toward the slim shaft of gray light beneath the door. Opening it, he peeked out, glancing about the wooded area. Hungry as he was, he glanced at the ham, and standing on a stool, sliced off a good-sized chunk.

Leaving the cabin, he closed the door, and ruffled the ground where his footprints dug into the softened loam. Dragging a large branch behind, he made his way into the dense brush. He didn't even want to think of the wrath that waited for him at the Mayor's office.

He hadn't hurt the woman, not even touched her. Why in tarnation did they hunt him? He couldn't fathom the manpower used for no good reason. Had to be trespassing, what else? He didn't waste any time moving off the grounds.

---

*A*isling settled herself in a chair and watched as last evening's guests slowly made their way into the parlor. Kegan had whispered that he heard the lieutenant require everyone to stay for two or three more days until he finished his interrogation.

Kegan winked at her from across the room. He appeared to be in heavy conversation with Hightower and another man she did not know. Even in the middle of the day, Hightower looked rather peaked, probably from the evening spent in far too much drink—and, no telling what else of interest he may have found.

Mr. Edwards hadn't shown yet. Two young women, near enough that she could overhear, spoke of breakfast in their rooms as if it was a luxury. When in fact, she knew it to be inconvenient for the maids who were averse to walking the corridor where her murdered aunt laid for the rest of the night. Aisling lost all appetite, except for a few sips of tea. Her aunt's demise, Lieutenant O'Flannery's subsequent questioning, and the mess in which she found herself erased any desire to eat. She missed Father and Signey. If it were not for Kegan, she really did not know what she would do.

The lieutenant walked in as though he had been running. Several uniformed men in his wake. From where Aisling sat, in front of a huge bay window, the gurney on which lay Beatrice's body waited for a carriage. Four men slid the corpse onto the back, and then closed the panel. Her stomach churned. Before they arrived in the parlor, Kegan had taken her to the cellar where her aunt's body laid waiting for the carriage from the morgue.

It was difficult viewing her remains, Beatrice still wore the gown from last night. The sight of her clutched at Aisling's heart. She swept her hand along Beatrice's upper arm noting the marks a strong grip would leave.

Someone had handled her roughly before she died. Otherwise, she would not have bruises. Aisling had smoothed the blond hair off Beatrice's highbrow.

In the span of a few days, Aisling learned how fussy she was with her appearance. Beatrice had been living and breathing less than twenty-four hours ago and filled with excitement over meeting a new beau. A man she could plan a life with, someone who would love her, and she could love.

Aisling was not sure what to make of her feelings. She had not known her father's sister only a few days. It was not like her to drown in pity. Yet, Beatrice was family.

After they viewed the body, Kegan showed her the letter he wrote to Father O'Mara. With her approval, he would send it off. She was grateful he asked about a funeral. Where was her brain that she could not think? A numbing sense encased her, as if she was somewhere else viewing all this from afar, most certainly not a part of the scene.

A prickly sensation ran up her spine as she also considered the man who killed Beatrice most likely was still at Elmhurst. She wanted to stand and stare at each face and try to figure out, if she could, who it might be. The man, who might have been the one for Beatrice, became her killer instead.

Three women stood near. She glanced up at them as the drone of whispers and giggling from behind their hands reached her. Did they not know her last-living relative was murdered last night? Did they not care a woman was dead?

The lieutenant shouted for attention. Someone clapped hands and a pall fell over the assembled. "Now, then. Sirs, ladies, we have an ongoing investigation with the murder of Mrs. Beatrice Molloy. We will require your continued occupancy at Elmhurst for another day or two while we finish the interrogations." A rather loud buzzing spilled about the room with his announcement.

Mr. Edward Edwards entered followed by his butler. His brisk stride as he approached, was a spectacle of sadness. "Mrs. Molloy was a beautiful creature, lively and witty. I am sorry for your loss, Miss O'Quinn. Do allow me to assist you in any way as we get through this sad business of finding out who doused such a bright light and gay companion." He inclined his head, and the large mustache twitched on his cheeks.

"Thank you," was all she could manage. Her dislike of him caused her to consider his words false; she shook her distaste off as a personal irritation with him.

He moved on, the butler in tow. The room quieted when he spoke to her. Now the lieutenant recaptured the moment.

"You must keep to the grounds. Mr. Edwards has arranged a schedule by which I will talk privately with each one of you. He will alert you to your time of day and where I will be carrying out the business at hand." With that, O'Flannery picked up a pad and a book from the table and left the room, his contingency quickly marching after him.

Kegan made his way across the room through the guests who formed little conversational circles. "A walk about the grounds would be good for both of us. I believe we have a rather nice autumn day, and the trees are coloring. What do you think?"

"I suppose you are right. Fresh air might be the tonic."

"Can we meet in the front foyer say ten minutes?" He drew his fob chain from his waistcoat, and she glanced at her lapel watch.

---

*W*hy is it, after a storm the sky is serene, bright blue maybe a few wisps of cloud, as if yesterday was as normal as blueberry pie. Grateful she brought a quilted hood, and snug in her cloak, she and Kegan, who had donned a black frock coat and matching leather gloves, strode a well-worn path along the cliff overlooking the Hudson. A few sailboats on the water; geese in *vee* formation flapped and honked.

So far, they walked in silence. What was he thinking, this handsome man, with his bright blue eyes that matched the sky? She appreciated a good walk, especially in air with a brisk feel. Perhaps more that she walked with him, just the two of them; there was comfort in his presence.

"I think Father Declan will arrange for the care of your aunt's remains. He's good about that sort of thing." He glanced at her as he spoke. "That should be some comfort for you."

"To be honest, I hadn't given it a thought until you wrote it in the letter. I am ashamed that I didn't think of the need." How could she be so uncaring?

"I am wondering about Smythe—Hector. Was he a longtime friend, do you know?"

"Beatrice arrived early in July. Less than a week later, she processed through Castle Garden, and they directed her to a home for rent. Most immigrants were not so lucky. To answer your question, I believe they met through the Mayor. She started her search for family at his office. It was by that chance she met Hector."

"Were they romantically involved?"

"At first I might have considered the possibility. It appears Hector was...was interested in someone else." She hated difficult situations that made a flush creep to her face and was thankful for the quilted hood.

Kegan stopped and gave her a sharp, penetrating look.

She could sense the question forming in his head, as if a mist of curiosity emanated from him. "Am I right in thinking that someone is you?"

Her gaze drifted away from him to the river shimmering through the forest of trees. She shrugged.

"Aisling, help me. I am trying to figure out some puzzling things. You might not even realize you hold answers that will help solve your aunt's murder."

"His, well, yes, his attentions focused on me."

Kegan grimaced and the words came out awkwardly. "I can hardly blame him. You are a very special young woman."

Rather than meet his inspection, she pulled dead leaves off a small twig.

He placed his hands on her shoulders and drew her close. "I am so sorry, Aisling."

She struggled against him. "Don't pity me."

He tightened rather than loosen his hold. "Allow me to comfort that young lad, Alan, who had no one." His large hand pulled her head against his chest his other arm around her waist. "I can't fathom all you've endured."

The feel of him, his resolute convictions and strengths, clutched at her heart. She silently wept. Drawing back a few inches, he looked down at her, red eyes, tears welling, and gently dabbed her cheeks. "You'll have to get used to me because I'm not going anywhere without you."

His gaze swept her features; he leaned close and kissed the corner of her mouth. The potent scent of him, zesty rather like lemons, almost caused her to swoon.

She blinked, sending another wash of tears that now straggled down. "Hmm, more tasty kisses," he said, as the fingers of his palms slipped inside her hood and cupped her face.

This time he kissed her lips, softly moving over the edges nibbling the delicate plumpness. She did not resist when his lips parted hers, opening to his deeper plunder. Her knees weakened, and she drew her arms up to his shoulders giving into the ecstasy. A low sound rolled from his throat, and he pulled back enough to lock onto her startled gaze as if searching for something. Reluctantly, for she did not want to relinquish this kiss, he ended the sweet interlude.

As he drew away, his palms still cupping her cheeks, his rumbling voice whispered, "Where did you learn to kiss like that?"

Her eyes twinkled with brightness from the earlier tears. "It simply came to me." She laughed softly, and the cold crept in without the nearness of him. A skittish feeling swept through her. She would never have imagined a kiss would make her feel like this and pried her gaze off the curve of his mouth, where a tiny shadow of dark grew on his square jaw.

He vowed, "I'll want to do that again."

Even with the chill of the day, a heated blush coursed upward. She turned away, so he would not realize the yearning she felt. "I think we need to get back to Elmhurst." Glancing at the sky and the dark clouds rolling in, she added, "Our beautiful day is changing."

He took her hand and placed it on his arm. "How did Hector feel about Mrs. Molloy bringing you here?"

So, back to the business at hand. She was beginning to understand how driven he could be. "I don't believe he knew anything about it. I tried to avoid him when he came to the house. I suppose she could have told him." She saw concern in the scrunch of his brow. "Why, what are you thinking?"

"A long shot, perhaps. Could he have been angry with her and followed you here?" Kegan swept a low hanging branch aside for her to walk ahead of him.

"Absurd. Truly."

"Men can be moved by less than jealousy when a beautiful woman is involved."

The past spun about in her mind. The horrid scene in the stable with Hector. Discovering him in town the day Buford paraded his troops before the battle. Kegan stopped, and put his hands on her shoulders, tipping her face upward.

"You've not told me everything, have you? I can see it in your expressive eyes, consternation."

She moved her chin away from his hand. "I'd rather not say."

"If it helps figure this out, perhaps you should. A woman is dead, and if the killer is simply killing women, then you can keep your secrets. If he intended to kill Mrs. Molloy, then it could lead me in the right direction."

With more of her past coming to light, it mattered what he considered, the picture he would carry in his mind.

"Nothing you can say will shock me, Aisling. As a lawyer, I have heard it all. As your friend, I want to know all there is to know about you."

"I'm not some silly little coy girl. It is not pleasant to remember." She took a deep breath. "You already know I ended up in Gettysburg on a farm. The farm had two older boys, Hector was one of them."

# CHAPTER 25

*H*is breath caught, as she sidestepped away from him to finish. He put his hand on her arm stopping her. Much too sharp, she protested, "No, I don't want you to look at me. Simply listen."

He moved slightly, inches only, and she began, "One of my duties was to clean the stalls and feed the horses. Mr. Smythe taught his two sons the art of boxing each morning using their fists to beat on each other. Up in the loft, I could hear him coaxing them to pummel the other. Time and again, this happened, and Hector, the elder, always lost. He had a surly manner, and it was customary for him to take his frustration out on me, he would be angry, sour with his words. He shoved me..." She hesitated.

"We were both shocked, his hand pushed against me...my...top...he knew instantly I wasn't a boy. He told me to take off my pants."

Kegan groaned, his hand cupped her shoulder. She took a deep breath. "I was saved by his father yelling for him. He told me he'd get me later and if I refused, he'd tell his father I'd been allowing him all along."

Placing his hands on her arms, he faced her, and lifted her chin so their eyes met. "And you ran away that night. The night before the Battle of Gettysburg."

She nodded as he enfolded her in his arms.

"You are a precious gift, Aisling. Intellect, compassion, sympathy, and mighty strength, all rolled into one delicate looking woman. I am a fortunate man to be included in the circle of your life." He pressed his lips against the top of her head and held her tenderly. She needed this, had for months, years.

Reluctantly, she inched apart. "You've given me comfort from a burden I've carried a long time." She took her glove off and placed her palm against the chafe of his jaw. "You are a very compassionate man."

They walked on in silence for a time. Then Kegan asked, "Your encounters with him here in town must have been shocking, thinking you had left him in Gettysburg."

"To say the least."

"Can you explain to me that awful evening at the Park Hotel when I went looking for you and there you were companionable with Smythe?"

She cast him a glance, biting her lower lip. "Knowing what I've told you, it must appear hard to understand. I decided between the lesser of two evils in that moment. I had to make a choice, and I took Hector at his word when he apologized for his behavior in the barn. I sensed a much nicer man standing on the portico the night of the charity ball."

"And he had already met Mrs. Molloy through the Mayor and understood who she looked for, and he gambled on it being you. It is all beginning to make sense now. Could he have been setting another trap for you?"

His question should not shock her; after all, his mind had been trained to consider all possibilities. Her gaze swept off toward the forest of trees swaying in the late afternoon breeze. When would there be peace in her life, order to her days, school, and her studies?

Her gaze came full circle and she locked onto his eyes; he was eager for her answer. "I hope you are wrong about him. Even though I want nothing to do with him, I do not wish him ill. I would like to think he is becoming a better person for his tribulations. He was raised by a cruel man."

They strolled back to Elmhurst. Tea served at four o'clock, and it was half past three. Neither of them spoke. The quiet between them comforting, companionable. As if, they had known each other for a long time.

The second they entered the marbled foyer, it was obvious trouble was afoot. Cursing and shouting split the air from Mr. Edward's library; several different voices rose up in anger. Kegan said, "You wait here, I'll be a moment."

He strode directly to the library and opened one of the double doors. Angry voices tumbled out, loud and accusatory. "...not me...who...a liar and a murderer...don't dare..."

Aisling rushed to the door and stood behind the open portion. The lieutenant, Mr. Edwards, Kegan...she almost screamed...Hector!

In the past two hours, she and Kegan talked of Hector. She stormed into the library.

There were four police officers, two with darkly bruised faces, another two holding Hector's arms. He struggled against attempts to bind him with handcuffs.

Mr. Edwards had his back to her. "Ye a liar I say. A damn good one, too. Dy ye not deny ye're the killer of my dear, beloved friend?" He swerved his body away from Hector and she gasped at the sight. Mr. Edwards had shaved off his facial hair. His large curling mustache and muttonchops were gone, his face beet red with anger.

Lieutenant O'Flannery punched his arm in the air then downward. "Let it be, Mr. Edwards. You are not the police. He is innocent until proven guilty. Let it lie I say." He stood between the two men, glaring at Mr. Edwards.

"Dy ye've not got all the proof ye need, ye bloody sod?"

Aisling had heard a slight brogue from him a couple of times though nothing this pronounced. Then, she had not known him this angry either. She glanced at Kegan who shook his head, and rolled his eyes at her, probably pleading with her to leave the room.

The lieutenant glanced at her in surprise. "This isn't a place for a lady, miss. You'd best wait in the parlor."

"May I know the circumstances under which this man was found?" She pointed to Hector.

"Running through the woods, attempting to get off the estate."

"Is there more proof than Mr. Edwards' accusatory statement?" she asked in what she hoped was a firm voice.

Mr. Edwards venom honed on her. "Ye meddling where ye ain't welcome, miss. Ye should be off saying a prayer for yer sister." He put an emphasis on the last word, apparently knowing Beatrice was not her sister.

"Mrs. Molloy was my aunt, my father's youngest sister. Moreover, I do not think of my questioning as meddling. I am more entitled to hear the goings on of this investigation, far more than you, because she was my relative." Her chin rose, daring him to contradict her. The lieutenant cleared his throat. Kegan shook his head; a gleam in his eyes relieved her. Hector appeared to calm, though his breathing snorted heavily.

"She was a s——" Mr. Edwards almost slandered her dead aunt.

Kegan interrupted him. "Here, here, Mr. Edwards. Watch what you say of the dead."

The angry Mr. Edwards swung his shaven face toward Kegan. "I'll not be shut up in me own place." His ire was rising by the minute.

Aisling wondered why this was so personal to him. He was far too dramatic and should be grateful for the possibility a killer might already be in custody. She looked at the lieutenant. "Did Hector admit to killing my aunt?"

Hector spit out, "I did not kill anyone. I came looking for her, I admit. She wasn't in the room. Ask the maid. She knew I didn't find her and when the maid screamed, I ran out as fast as I could."

Even though Kegan stood across the library from her, she noted the questioning furrows on his brow. He always got this little faraway look in his eyes when he pondered. An idea was coming to him, perhaps something Hector said, perhaps not. Poor Hector. She did not believe him capable of killing Beatrice. Oh, she knew his anger well enough, nearly four years of it; as time passed, the ire grew into a man's ferocity. Murder? She was not convinced he would do such a thing.

Mr. Edwards crossed over to the lieutenant and shoved a finger into his chest. "Ye get that scum behind bars, or I'll have ye put in jail meself, mister. I've got connections in the city, and ye'll never have it so good again, mark my words. Now get that filth out of me home." He jabbed a thumb at Hector and banged his way out of the library, slamming the heavy oak door. The thunder of his inner fury echoed in his wake.

Lieutenant O'Flannery ordered his men to take the handcuffed prisoner back to the shed, tie him to a chair, and two officers were to stay inside with him through the night. The other two were to stand guard, on both sides of the door.

Hector called out, "Miss O'Quinn, I swear I didn't kill her. I didn't even see her. Help me please. Aisling, help prove I didn't do this." His voice faded as they shoved him out the double-glassed doors that led to the patio.

Kegan took her by the arm. "I want to have a few words with the lieutenant. Will you wait for me outside?"

Her brow rose up. "Something I'm too delicate to hear?"

He chuckled. "Okay, then. Come with me."

"I'm teasing. I actually prefer to wait in the parlor across the foyer."

Ten minutes later, Kegan found her thumbing through a book of travel on England. She glanced up at his approach. "I've ordered tea for the two of us apart from the others right now."

His lips pursed, and he nodded. "They found Hector lurking in the woods. He'd almost made it to the road when they captured him. In light of our conversation this afternoon, it's almost providential."

A servant brought their tray, and Aisling set about pouring. "Except that I don't think he's guilty."

"I may be off guard. I'm going to put a lot of faith in what you think." He sipped the hot brew and sighed lightly. "Besides, I believe he wasn't after Beatrice. I believe he was after you."

"I might agree with you." Her lips curved. "You do enjoy your afternoon drink, I see," then she tasted her own.

"Your revelations earlier today, regarding Hector makes me curious why you think him innocent."

"Mostly because I saw how he was with his little sister and his mother. No matter what his father or brother did to him, he was gentle and caring with them."

"He would have hurt you perhaps beyond repair."

"I think it was bluster. Oh, at the time I did not. Since he re-entered my life I have had occasion to think about that. He was as injured by his father's rejection as I had been when forced from my *máthair*. He lashed out. I have noticed a significant change in him the few times we encountered each other, mostly in Father Declan's office. He was quite solicitous that night of the charity ball when he took me to Beatrice's home. It was kind of him. If he meant me harm, it could have been accomplished that night." Had she made sense, won him over?

"If not Hector, then the killer is at large, perhaps one of the guests who are sequestered as we are." With finger and thumb, he rubbed the space between his eyes. "I'll be in your room again tonight."

"I'll have a blanket and pillow ready for you on the chair. No use suffering for your good deed."

A teasing glimmer brightened his eyes. "One good deed deserves another." His attention lowered to his cup, she caught a mischievous smile playing on his lips.

"Well then, I'll make sure it is a soft down pillow rather than feathers."

He chuckled.

---

*D*inner was a somber affair, conversation hushed except the snickering between three young women at the end of the table. Within twenty-four hours the outlook of everyone at the table had grown pensive, and the desire to head homeward probably uppermost.

Aisling noted the excessive consumption of wine. Burgundy and white liveried footmen, at attention against the wall of the dining room, refilled crystal goblets almost immediately when drained. Mr. Edwards must have directed them to do so. Not just the gentlemen, women, too. Perhaps they intended forgetting last night and the murder. On the other hand, perhaps they attempted not to dwell on what might happen tonight as they slept. She was grateful she could count on Kegan's presence in the dark hours.

Mr. Gault set his goblet down, interest keenly on her. He chose a seat directly across from her last evening, too, and introduced himself then. "Mrs. Molloy was your sister. A shame. She was a lively conversationalist. How are you coping through all this?"

"As well as can be expected, sir. She was my aunt, not my sister."

His puzzled gaze went directly to Mr. Edwards who sat at the end of the table. "I was led to believe otherwise."

"Some confusion to be sure. Mr. Edwards has been informed of the truth." Mr. Gault swung his gaze back to her.

"At first glance, you've not the look of her. More an attitude than a physical resemblance, I believe."

"That happens in large families to be sure." Aisling was uncomfortable with his scrutiny. She noted he drank several glasses of red wine, and dinner was only on the third course.

Another man sat next to Mr. Gault. Though she had not met him, she knew his name to be Martin. He asked, "Your aunt was recently come over from Belfast was it?"

Aisling was about to reply when Mr. Edwards, who obviously followed their conversation, answered in his deep baritone. "Drogheda. She was from Drogheda."

He knew a great deal about Beatrice. Why did that surprise her? Though her aunt had declared to look for someone younger, she was quite taken with him. As obnoxious as he appeared, she had doted on him, did everything he asked.

Aisling glanced back down the table and asked, "Mr. Edwards how is it you would know that my aunt came from Drogheda, when I'm certain she told me she lived outside Dublin?"

Without the muttonchops and the big bushy mustache, his smirk was evident. "Well then, it appears she was more trusting of me with specifics rather than generalities, wouldn't you say?"

The hint of brogue was gone from his speech. "It appears so." She sipped from the water goblet.

Mr. Edwards lowered his drink, "Mrs. Molloy did tell me you haven't been to Ireland. You might not know Drogheda is north of Dublin. So to say you are from one place could imply the other as well."

Aisling had nothing to say. She glanced his way before patting her lips with a napkin.

The assembled guests took their time eating, drawing out the ritual longer than the previous evening. Aisling guessed it was a better use of time, now that Mr. Edwards had cancelled tonight's entertainment, a show of respect for her aunt.

As the women excused themselves, Aisling walked past the always-mirthful trio. A flaxen haired woman, striking in emerald green, asked, "Miss O'Quinn, would you care to join us in a game of cards in the library? We need a fourth."

Pleasantly surprised, she said, "I would like that. Thank you."

She asked the butler for a piece of paper and wrote Kegan a note. *I received an invite to play cards in the library.* She folded the note and scripted his name across the front. "Please deliver this to Mr. Galliger."

She entered the library and went directly to the card table, her chair waiting. "Sorry, I've forgotten your names."

"Alice Dickinson." A robust, cheerful woman, Aisling smiled at her.

"Call me Jayne Miller." A young woman about her same age with chestnut hair and wearing a flattering green gown.

"I am Suzette O'Malley." The only description that came to Aisling was sultry.

She settled in the fourth chair. "What will we play?"

Suzette, the one who invited her, and obviously, the leader of the trio, said, "You must know how to play euchre? Right?"

Jayne and Alice nodded. Aisling said, "I'm a quick learner."

Suzette explained about the black and red jokers that can become bowers, how to call trump, and how many to deal.

Aisling asked, "Can we play a fun round?"

Suzette shuffled, and then asked for a cut. Aisling obliged, and the cards dealt.

The women placed five cards in their hands and did some shuffling about. Aisling followed suit as best as she could with the little understanding she had. Jayne was to be her partner, as she sat directly across the table.

To score, each team used two fives. Red for Aisling and Jayne, black for Suzette and Alice. Jayne began with a pass and explained why, pointing out the face-up ten of clubs. "If I said pick it up to Suzette, then it would be up to you and me to take three tricks, with clubs being trump. If we didn't make three tricks, they would get two points for trumping us."

In short, after two hands played out, Aisling found the nerve to call trump and make it, to everyone's delight. The score was two to four in her and Jayne's favor when Suzette asked, "How did you come to meet Mr. Edwards?"

"Through my aunt. I'm not exactly sure how they met, though."

Suzette dealt a new hand. Hearts were called, and she laid her nine of hearts on a club lead, giving her the trick. "Isn't he a little out of your league."

Jayne piped up. "She means that in the kindest way, Aisling. You don't appear the sort for one of his wild weekends."

Aisling glanced at each woman, who appeared very interested in how she might answer. "I really didn't want to come. My aunt was determined. I think she had a crush on Mr. Edwards to be truthful."

Little murmurs drifted around the table. Suzette said, "He certainly appeared interested in her. He's quite a catch from what I've been told."

"How do you come to know him?" Aisling glanced up from the new cards that Jayne dealt.

"I don't really. Mr. Gault introduced us."

Alice added, "And when Suzette was invited she asked if she could bring two friends." She giggled, "We do everything together. Ever since childhood, we've been a team."

Aisling asked, "You really know nothing about him, then?"

Like birds on a fence, they shook their heads in unison.

"Where is he from? Is he English or perhaps Irish? What business is he in?"

The birds glanced at each other. Then Jayne piped up. "I think he's English. At least I did until I saw his face shaved."

Alice added, "He doesn't own this home. He's rented it for a month or so. I overheard two men discussing the rental price and what a great deal Mr. Edwards received."

Suzette, who mostly appeared uninterested in the conversation, dropped a surprising bit of information. "He wasn't interested in your aunt. I happen to know he spent last night in someone else's room."

Aisling looked at her, tried not to show her surprise at how betrayed Beatrice would feel if she had known. She could not have though, she was murdered. Aisling decided Suzette, or one of her friends, must be the woman with whom Mr. Edwards spent the night. How else would Suzette know?

Perplexed, she asked, "A man wanders into a room and stays the entire night?"

"You really are out of his league, aren't you?" Suzette's voice held a superior tone.

Aisling could feel the heat climbing up her neck—of all times to look like a ninny. "You make it sound as if he wanders the corridors and knocks on random doors." She could hardly put voice to it. "A woman sits in her room waiting to be chosen?"

Suzette's brow rose, and she glanced at Aisling over the four cards left in her hand. "My dear, you are unpracticed at the art if that's what you think. We are in the minority here in case you haven't realized." Her glance swept each of her friends who offered pretty, little coy smiles. "If a gentleman is interested, he'd better be quick with his decision."

Aisling knew the truth of that. Hightower had practically followed her up the stairs last night. She willed herself not to reveal disgust.

Jayne, who habitually softened her friend's sharp tongue, offered, "Not all of us fancy the gentlemen who attend. I like men my age. That lawyer from Manhattan for instance. Sure would like to know where he was last night." She giggled at her admission. "The knock on my door was from a textile manufacturer from Queens. He's promised me a tour if I ever make it to his ward." She giggled again. "His hands are so smooth because of the lanolin," she added with a note of superiority.

Aisling looked hard at the cards still in her hand. She found it disconcerting to play and talk at the same time, especially when the talk was so absorbing. A blush creeping up her cheeks was immensely inappropriate when one wishes to appear worldly.

Alice tittered, "Aisling it is your turn."

"Oh." She laid down a queen of spades, not being able to follow suit, then glanced at Alice, because she found difficulty in looking at Jayne after her admission. Her heart was heavy for the pleasant young woman; saddened to think of the life she led.

The game ended with Aisling and Jayne behind by four points. No one suggested a second game, for which she was grateful. "Thank you for including me. Perhaps if we are here tomorrow night, we can do this again?"

The trio nodded. Jayne's lip grimaced. "After two nights, I'm ready to go home. Money isn't everything."

Aisling glanced at her lapel watch rather than stare at Jayne. A quarter past nine, and knew it was time for these women to be in their rooms waiting for a knock. "Good night, then."

She started up the main staircase, and then considered some reading material and retreated to the library to look for a book. Her hand on the latch, she was about to open the door when it swung in, practically dragging her with in.

"Wasn't I thinking about you? Miss O'Quinn, is it? Right?" Mr. Martin, the man who sat across from her at dinner, next to Mr. Gault.

Flustered, she scrambled to keep from tripping. "I've interrupted. Sorry. I was after something to read." Her gaze darted about the room. It was empty of anyone else. "It isn't necessary." She fled to the stairs.

He came after her. "Wait. I've something to ask of you."

Her hand on the rail, and four steps up, she said, "Sorry, I've no answers. Good night." She took off in ascent. Once she reached the top, she glanced down and caught the last of him heading into the parlor where she left the three giggling women.

In the corridor, candlesticks and a bowl of matches were on a side table. Grateful because the corridor was long and rather dark, she lit the candle and made her way toward her room. As she passed the second alcove along the way, Kegan startled her by moving away from the little nook to stand directly in front of her in the carpeted hall.

He said, "Give me the candle."

She handed it to him. "Thank you for meeting me, I was a trifle unnerved."

He set the candle on the floor, took her by the shoulders, and pushed her up against the wall. With both her hands in his, he spread them above her head and planted a kiss on her lips that took the breath from her. She closed her eyes and gave into the sensuous delight. A far different kiss than the one this afternoon. This one was confident, insistent. A weakness overcame her.

His thumbs caressed her palms, his breath on her cheeks as his lips left hers and traveled a path along her face, over her eyes, and back to her mouth. His body pressed against her or she would have slithered to the floor in a swoon. She wanted this to last forever; pure ecstasy, as she never had known, and his spicy scent filled her with the manliness of him.

His lips near her ear whispered as he kissed the tender area, "Stay calm."

*Calm?* The length of her trembled with excitement.

# CHAPTER 26

"*Y*ou've got her. How fortunate you are." A baritone with a hint of brogue.

Kegan squeezed her hands then let go. He faced Mr. Edwards. Aisling noted pure disgust on his face, even with the insufficient flicker of candle light. She struggled to remain passive, though her heart hammered. She could have collapsed when he let loose of her. Mr. Edwards' voice jerked her from the ravishment of Kegan's kiss.

"I'm not usually in this part of the house. Didn't know the corridor was this dark." He gave a slight nod of his head. "Good night then." He left them standing there.

Aisling had been holding her breath, and now realized it as a low sigh escaped.

Kegan picked up the candle, reached over, and took her hand. "Shall we?" He led her along the corridor and entered her chamber. The gas light cast a golden glow. Kegan must have lit the grate its warmth was welcome. She surmised he had waited for her from the preparations. A pillow and comforter nested on the bench alongside the chair he occupied last night.

Aisling stood in the middle of the chamber trying to understand the last few minutes, knowing what she really wanted was for Kegan to kiss her like that again. Instead, she asked, "Mr. Edwards thinks you've knocked on my door?"

He chuckled. "You've gained a wealth of knowledge about the goings on in little more than a day."

"It has come to me, with this knowledge that Hightower actually knocked on my door last evening."

A distinct edge to his voice, he grumbled, "He offered to apologize to you."

"What would have prompted such an offer?" Her thumbs twiddled.

Kegan looked up at her from beneath a lowered brow. "About the time I had my fist at the ready."

She reached for his right hand, drawing it to her lips and placed a kiss on his knuckles. "You take my breath away. Thank you."

Glancing at him, she noted a look of awe on his face as he stared at the hand she kissed. "You needn't be so dramatic. I appreciate your chivalry, last evening and again this evening."

"If that's the case, then you still owe me one more kiss." He grinned.

Ignoring him, she said, "Playing cards with three women who apparently are regular guests is enlightening. Although, I must say, I'm saddened to think they believe it enhances their lives."

"I took the liberty of ordering up sherry. You mentioned an allergy, perhaps it doesn't sound appealing?"

She cast him a slanting grin. "I had to invent that, so he wouldn't badger me like he did Beatrice."

He shook his head. "Why am I not surprised. Then I'll assume you would like a dram before we tuck in?"

"That would be nice, thank you."

Seated across from each other, in front of the grate, Kegan could not take his eyes off her. Was something on his mind? Did she even want to know? After the way he kissed her in the corridor, she could hardly think of anything else. Even if his intention had been to deter Mr. Edwards, he must know a great deal about what goes on at Elmhurst on weekends.

"I need to apologize for being so forward and possibly rough with you out there." He nodded toward the door and the corridor beyond. "Mr. Edwards showed quite an interest in you at dinner."

She took a tiny sip of the sherry, disappointed he was sorry. "He was probably disconcerted that I brought him to task over where my aunt lived in Ireland."

"Oh no, Aisling. You are not getting off quite that easy. Mr. Edwards enjoys these weekends for one reason only. I fully suspected he had his attention honed on you."

"I know that's why you kissed me." Like a coward, she slid her gaze to the bright glow of embers.

He set his half-finished sherry on the side table. "I had to do something to save you from him."

"An act of valor, then." She finished the sherry in one gulp, and her gaze met his.

He winced. "Call it what you want. Delightful as it was, I wanted him to think you had already been spoken for."

"You mean like knocking on my door."

He finished his sherry in one gulp, stood, and restored the libation in both glasses. "What should I have done? I told you last night it was why I came to your room. I know this isn't who you are. I like who you are, I would not allow anyone to spoil you, or bring you harm. Damn it all, Aisling. You matter a great deal to me. I tried to tell you the evening we walked through Central Park how I felt about you. Do you recall giving me the heave ho?"

She set the refilled glass down. Her heart skipped, her breath quickened. It was a good thing she was sitting. For once in her life, she could not think of what to say.

He hammered on. "On the portico of the Park Hotel, seeing you with Hector, I couldn't believe my eyes. Then when you sent me on that fool's errand, I considered you preferred him to me, and..." He strode to the grate, brushed a hand through his dark wavy hair sending it off his forehead.

"...and I tried to forget you. A useless endeavor if ever there was. Forgetting you is not in the cards. Everywhere I looked, all I could see was your lovely face, your beautiful hair, the way you talk with your hands, and that sassy grin that quirks up the side of your mouth." He ran out of steam, picked up the sherry, and drank it in one gulp.

Silence reigned except for the crackle of the coals. Rendered speechless, she felt he voiced his heart, and all she could think was how she did not deserve him. And, if she said so, he would be angry that she spoke of insecurity, because she already knew he did not think like his stepmother, or Eleanor Homsby.

"I...I...you..." She took a deep breath, her struggle intense. "I never dreamed...well, I did, do...dream about you. I think about you all the time. I have never forgotten each hour spent with you in the rectory. Generous, kind to a fault...I could go on about how I created a deep friendship with you in my heart. It kept growing and growing. I would go to bed at night, and after prayers, think of you, your sparkling smile, your wit, how you challenged my learning of Latin. And, then..." She swiped at a tear. "And then I would think of the boy I was to you. A homeless little rag and you were so sympathetic."

She glanced at him. He had taken the chair opposite and crossed his legs. Her voice was almost a whisper. "You were so far out of reach."

The silence encased them. In some ways, making her feel like they were very close. He listened to each word with care. She knew he did because she knew his goodness. She also knew she couldn't end her tirade this way. "When Father and Signey figured out I wasn't a boy, the rock on my heart lifted. Out of their great generosity, they opened a world that is beyond anything I ever dreamed. A home, schooling, the ability to become a gir...a young woman. And, I considered the possibility of seeing you again. It scared me, also made me eager, anticipating what you would think or do." Cautiously, she slid her gaze to his. "A thrilling and terrifying prospect."

He chuckled at that. "I disappointed you when I didn't recognize you."

She nodded and swiped her cheeks with her wrist. The worst of it was over, because he knew the rest.

Kegan crossed over the space between them and knelt before her. Both hands on the arms of the chair, he leaned in. "I cannot imagine what must have gone through your head as that woman—Miss Helberg —destroyed every wall you built to survive in a world that sometimes isn't as nice as it should be. If I could magically erase that night I would."

He reached over and gently traced her jaw with his fingertips. "You are precious to me. Both of you, Aisling—Alan." He leaned in and pressed his lips ever so lightly against hers, then said, "It occurred to me our first son should be named Alan."

She sat bolt upright, almost knocking him over. "What did you say?"

He chuckled as he retook the chair across the way. "You heard me."

Aisling counted the chimes drifting up the corridor from the clock on the main floor. Eleven o'clock. The announcement that their first son would be named Alan made her heart skip a beat, because the meaning went deeper than the name. It meant he considered a lifetime with her. She softened inside, in her heart and soul, a peacefulness that covered her like a cashmere shawl. He must love her even if the words were not spoken. Mustn't he?

Her foot set to jittering beneath her skirts and she wanted to laugh. "You appear to have a strong partiality to the name Alan."

His eyes reflected the small flickers of the fire. "One would think so, wouldn't one?" His fingers steepled.

Her soft laugh tinkled in the air. If she was not careful, she might float upward with the sound.

After a minute or two of silence, she asked, "Who do you think murdered Beatrice?"

"I am mulling that as we speak. There were two screams."

She nodded. "The first one was further away than the second."

His lips pursed. "If Hector is telling the truth, he was with the maid, and within a minute or two, the second scream appears to have been Beatrice. Therefore, Hector could not have killed her. He was running down the back stairs away from the maid when the second scream rent the air."

"One of the women I played cards with, Suzette told me she knew Mr. Edwards didn't spend the night with Beatrice. She seemed certain who he was with but did not give a name. I suspect he was probably with her."

"Which one is she?"

"The striking flaxen haired. One might call her sultry." Pensive a moment, she let him be as he pondered.

Suddenly he interjected, "If Beatrice occupied the room at the end of the hall, and Mr. Edwards was with another, we need to find out where that room is and its proximity to this corridor."

Aisling said, "Allow me to add what I'm thinking as long as you might consider him a suspect."

Kegan, hands on knees, sat forward in his chair as she continued. "I lived my first twelve years in a tenement filled with families from Ireland. One certainty I have is an ear for the Irish tongue. I believe Mr. Edwards has gone to great lengths to be someone he is not. He speaks perfect English, except when he's riled. He drops back to speech that appears to come easily as though he's as Irish as I am." Kegan started to say something, and she held up her hand. "Such as, he pronounced Drogheda exactly as it should be, not like someone who isn't familiar with the name. In addition, in his anger this morning, when the police brought Hector into the parlor, Mr. Edwards slipped into familiar Irish idiom, saying *dy ye*, rather than what we might say, *do you*. One more thing, this morning, he shaved off his face hair. I am certain an investigator would discover he has changed the color of the hair on his head, too. So, I asked myself, why would he do that and hide his Irish background other than he has a deliberate reason."

Kegan was immensely attentive to her discourse, and she continued, "Beatrice arrived in Manhattan several weeks ago. What if Mr. Edwards followed her from Ireland? I truly believe he is hiding his Irishness. He always encouraged her to drink too much, disguised himself, until today, because he no longer has need. Like he didn't want her inspecting him too closely?"

Kegan shook his head. "My goodness, Aisling. Not only do I think you should be in politics, I think you should also get a law degree."

A little smile curved her lips. He thought her clever did he, she quickly added, "He also knows Drogheda is north of Dublin. Which anyone who cared would know, but so would someone who lived there."

He interjected, "It shouldn't be difficult to find out when Mr. Edwards came to this country. We have the finest immigration registers. I guarantee when he arrived and where he came from is documented." Kegan lowered his brow at her. "Dying his hair could be a simple matter of vanity; I don't think it is a clear intention of murder."

"It is not the coloration; it is the timing. If he did murder her about eleven or so, when we heard the second scream, then he shaved upon rising this morning. Because the one person who could identify him is now dead."

"It does appear more than mere coincidence. What motive would he have?" Kegan leaned against the back of the chair, his hands sliding from his knees to the chair arms.

Aisling remembered the feel of them on her cheeks as he kissed her, warm, caring, protective. What a moment to think of kissing. She blinked, forcing her to the present. "Edward's anger at Hector seemed out of proportion if you consider his own disrespectful behavior toward Beatrice. He ordered her about, treated her as if she hadn't a brain, and urged her to drink more."

"Because of his ill-treatment of her, you think it would make more sense if he showed understanding of Hector's actions?"

"I think that angry display was intended to direct everyone's attention away from him and on to another. He took advantage of Hector in handcuffs, already a suspect."

"If you are really on to something here, we have a serious problem. The first one is keeping you safe. He did pay you an inordinate amount of attention at dinner tonight."

She said, "The trio informed me that we women are in the minority. We can expect men to knock."

"I'm not even talking about the others. I'm specifically referring to Mr. Edwards. Aisling, this is not something we can treat casually. If he is Beatrice's murderer, you might be his next victim." Kegan reached over and put that warm, caring hand over hers as it lay in her lap. "I think he followed you up the stairs and along the corridor tonight."

"Why would you suspect that?" She felt safe, more so with Kegan next to her.

"I'm speculating. We don't have any proof positive of his motives."

"I thank you for that. You had me worried for a moment."

He squeezed her hand then settled back in his chair. "We'll have to prove who Mr. Edwards spent time with last night, and how long he stayed."

Aisling grinned. "You might have to work your charms on the giggling trio at breakfast. Perhaps you can find out all the details."

He stood and reached for her hand, drawing her up then slipped his arm about her waist. "Will you always encourage me to use my charms on other women? Because I find that frightfully modern coming from the young woman I would rather charm."

She shied her cheek away from his warm breath. "You can start with the one named Joyce Miller, short dark hair. She proclaimed a fancy for you tonight during cards, wished you would knock at her door."

His arm quickened on her, his hand tipped her chin. "Is that so?"

Tantalizingly near, and so tempting, she stood on tiptoe, placed her lips to his. For the last hour, she had wanted to do this and leaned heavily into the circle of his arms.

Morning came through a small crinkle of the drawn drapes. Aisling lay against the pillow watching dust motes drift past the brilliant shaft. Of a sudden, realization came to her and she rose up.

At that moment, Kegan threw off his blanket and reached for the bucket of coals immediately refueling the grate, then said, "About time you woke. What a sleepy head you are."

"You waited in the cold so as not to make noise."

He rang for the maid. "I'll freshen up when Gwen arrives. We'll catch up in the dining room." In a big hurry, hands jammed into pockets, he paced in front of the grate.

She yawned and asked, "Has something happened as I slept?"

"No. I woke with an agenda bouncing in my head. I simply want to get on with the puzzlement of Mrs. Molloy's murder and get both of us back where we belong."

She held the blanket up to her chin as she sat on the mattress against the pillows. A chill crept over the entire room. "You haven't slept well in two nights. I'm sorry to be such a bother."

He ignored her comment. "Lieutenant O'Flannery mentioned yesterday that he would arrive this morning even if he hadn't a confession from Hector. In light of our conversation last night, I'm inclined to think he hasn't got one."

"How do you plan to check on Mr. Edwards if the lieutenant won't allow you to leave?"

"I'm not leaving here without you in any case. That's not an option."

A knock at the door startled them. Gwen entered. Her little white cap atop her head bobbed from Kegan by the grate, to Aisling in the bed. She stammered. "Sorry, miss, shall I come back?"

Kegan spoke hurriedly. "Come in. As a matter of fact, Gwen. It is Gwen?" At her nod, he continued, "Two nights ago, did you ready Mrs. Molloy for bed?"

"I told the officer everything I know, sir."

"Well, then tell me too."

Gwen's gaze shifted to Aisling, then back to Kegan. "She came in from dinner under the weather, if you get my meaning. The butler brought her."

"And, did he stay?"

"No, sir. He was agitated. Almost shoving her in a chair, nodded to me as if to say she was in my care, and left."

"What happened next?"

"Mrs. Molloy wasn't of a mind to retire for the night. She waved me away. Told me to come back after midnight, and if she wasn't in her room, to go to bed."

Kegan moved a step closer to her. "You told me, when I ran into the chamber, that she had rung for you?"

"It came from Mrs. Molloy's room. She had said she might ring me; I thought she came back to her room earlier than planned."

Kegan glanced over at Aisling whose attention was on the maid. He said, "How much time transpired between the ring, and when you entered the chamber?"

"I was helping cook cut up chicken for today's supper. I had to wash, wipe, and dry off. Then put on a clean apron, as mine was bloody. It took a few minutes to be sure. Five, maybe ten."

Kegan considered perhaps longer because she also had to climb the stairs. "Thank you." Solicitous of Aisling, he asked, "Will you be all right if we meet in the dining room in twenty minutes?"

"I will be fine. You go on. Won't take me long."

As he pulled the door shut, she swung her legs over the side of the bed and threw the covers back. "Well, what to wear today, considering my few options."

Gwen chortled. "Yes, miss."

$\mathcal{F}$ather Declan pulled the chasuble over his head and carefully hung it in the closet. The Ladies Altar Society bestowed it on him in honor of his feast day and he always wore it on special occasions. Today was special because Kegan wrote of Aisling's safety, and they would be in Manhattan probably tomorrow. He untied the cincture and hung it on a peg inside the closet. Next, his white Alb that he also put on a hanger, so it would be ready and unwrinkled tomorrow morning. He untied the amice, folded it, and placed it neatly in the drawer in which it belonged. He liked to appear tidy and careful with his priestly garments. Some ladies of the Altar Society might take it in their heads to reprimand him for carelessness if he did not. God forbid *that* should happen. It would bring back memories of his mother and him when he was a messy lad.

He washed his hands in the basin and looked forward to breakfast. His intention was to begin the week with renewed vigor now that he was calmer knowing his two, young people were in company together.

A couple waited for him in the hallway and he directed Mr. and Mrs. Contadina into his office. "Your visit is timely as the Baptismal documents arrived yesterday. Your registration at St. Patrick's is ready to sign."

They had arrived from Italy more than two months ago and wanted to register at St. Patrick's. Father requested their Baptismal certificates from their parish back home before he could do so. More and more families, good people like this couple, arrived in America in pursuit of a better life. He wished them fulfilled dreams. His policy clearly meant to assist in finding living space, clothing if needed, food always, and a place to bring concerns and worries.

With his many years as pastor, he could assess their chances of surviving; and, this young couple appeared to be fine. Mr. Contadino's profession was woodworking, making handcrafted furniture in his northern Italian providence; Mrs. Contadino worked as an apprentice in a doctor's practice.

Once the couple mastered more English, they would really be on their way. The first time they came to him, he put them in touch with a diction teacher. Their improvements were clearly recognizable.

Hand-in-hand they left the rectory, and Father couldn't help feeling a sense of satisfaction. Even though he knew, there were many who never thrived.

Nearing nine o'clock, the growl in his stomach caused him to make his way to the kitchen.

"I don't suppose you've heard a thing over the weekend?" Signey asked as she set a plate of walnut pancakes in front of him." His nose tweaked with anticipation.

He had no need to ask of whom she spoke. Kegan and Aisling were all she spoke of since the letter arrived. After a quick blessing of the food, he attacked the steaming cakes topped with warm syrup and melting butter. "I'm off to the coroner's office after breakfast. I have some questions about this aunt of Aisling's; perhaps I will get some answers. Kegan supplied me with an address where Aisling lived with her. Apparently, there is a maid, who no doubt needs informing of the sad matter at hand."

"I've preserves to put up today. Can't keep the tomatoes any longer, or the pickles. Otherwise, I'd have liked to see the place where Aisling settled the days away from me."

"Now, now, Mrs. Pennino, I don't want you to fret over that again. You know the why and wherefore of the matter." He made a sound much like a contented cat as the forkful of pancake found its mark.

She bristled. "Mrs. Pennino is it? Tells me you've decided all's well, and I'd better do the same." She went to the sink and began pumping water into a pot. "It is not as easy as you make it."

"If Kegan hadn't been with her, we'd both be up the Hudson this minute." The last forkful of pancake entered his mouth, followed by another murmur.

"More coffee?"

He nodded as he wiped crumbs from his chin. "It is always sad to inform someone of a death, even if it is the maid." He gulped the cooling brew, then slid the chair out, and looked around for his bowler, grumbled, decided he had not brought it with him, and marched back to his office.

Father twisted the knob of the bell on the front door on Nineteenth Street and waited for Mrs. Molloy's maid to answer his ring. A little bird of a young woman opened the door inches and peered through the crack. She surveyed his bowler down his face to his white clergy collar, and then looked back to his face. "What can I do for you, Father?"

"It is my sad duty to deliver some information to you, miss. Do you mind if I come inside?"

Her brow wrinkled in question, but she opened the door gesturing for him to enter. She did not invite him into the parlor and stood on the apron of a foyer with hands folded in front of her. He removed his bowler and said, "Your employer has met with a sad accident."

"Mrs. Molloy?"

He looked at the hat in his hands. "Do you have family near?"

"I've me mother and da on the east side."

"That's good then. What I've come to tell you is that Mrs. Molloy died Friday night, sometime during the night." He had no desire to say murdered. He did not want to frighten the young woman, even though the coroner was specific on the matter. He waited for her to understand what he said. He wasn't sure his words registered, she simply looked at him as though he had not finished.

He added, "Her body is at the morgue and identified. As you must know, Aisling, Miss O'Quinn, went with her to Elmhurst up on the Hudson."

She nodded. "Will the miss be living here, then?"

"No, I don't believe so. She lived with Mrs. Pennino before she came here. That's her home where she belongs."

"Who will be coming here, then?"

"Mrs. Molloy rented this home. It will be turned back over to the owner." He glanced about the parlor, then down the hallway, kitchen at the end, and a doorway leading to the left. A staircase led to another hallway. He assumed bedrooms were up there.

"I would like you to write down your parents' address, in case I have need to talk to you at some point. Your name is?"

"Ruth Sims, Father."

"I wonder if you can tell me if Mrs. Molloy had any visitors that I should inform of her demise."

"Just two that I know of. A Hector Smythe and a Mr. Edward Edwards."

That took the air out of him, he dissembled. "Do you know the nature of their acquaintance?"

"Mr. Smythe brought Miss O'Quinn here late the first night of her stay. He cared for her a great deal, from what I gather. Mr. Edwards' interest clearly was Mrs. Molloy. Sent her flowers he did, took her to fancy dinners."

Father smiled at Ruth. She was clearly gaining trust in him. "I wonder if you would know how Mrs. Molloy met both men. Did she talk about them?" He walked into the parlor as he asked the question, drawing the maid with him.

"It is not nice to speak ill of the dead. Me mum taught me that, Father." She gave him a rather stern glance, as though he of all people should know *that*.

He tried not to feel chastised. "That is why I'm not asking you to besmirch. Mrs. Molloy died under strange circumstances and I'm trying to figure out what may have happened."

"Oh. Like an investigator?" she said with a cheery lilt.

"Exactly."

"Well, both of the gentlemen argued with Mrs. Molloy. I could hear back in the kitchen. They shouted at each other. Mrs. Molloy became angry at the times Mr. Smythe showed up. She spoke unkindly to him when all he was trying to do was help a poor girl regain some sense of herself. He was all about Miss O'Quinn getting out of the doldrums. I'm a lowly maid, and I could hear it in his voice."

"And, Mr. Edwards, what was his demeanor?"

"He acted like he doted on her. Then I got to thinkin' why did he force the drink on her if he liked her? She didn't like the drink much; he got her to do a lot of it. Several nights I had to walk her to her bedroom and get her ready for bed after she flopped into it, the covers beneath her and all."

Father picked up an object from the mantel and inspected it —a porcelain figurine of a woman. "Would you say she was in his thrall?"

# CHAPTER 27

*R*uth Sims stood, hands crossed in front of her starched apron, a little white cap on her head. She looked like a proper lady's maid. "Me mum would most definitely tag her that way." A hand flew to her mouth to hide a sudden giggle. "Well, would'ja know. I'm becomin' me mum, because I agree."

He tried not to laugh and placed the figurine on the mantel. "I'm sure your mother is a very nice woman. So, to her credit you are like her."

Ruth must have agreed, because she quickly added, "Mr. Edwards was the one invited her to his place up north. He wanted her to come badly and allowed her to bring her sister with her, so she wouldn't refuse."

"Sister?"

"Miss O'Quinn."

Perplexed, he asked again, "She's Miss O'Quinn's sister? Who said that?"

"Mrs. Molloy." She paused a moment. "You're puzzled. It is how Mrs. Molloy introduced Miss O'Quinn to Mr. Edwards. I was in the room serving cakes when she said it."

"Hmm."

"Should I pack up? I'm not exactly sure what to do."

"Not just yet. Tell me, did Mrs. Molloy keep papers, or a journal? Something that might explain her background. Where she came from, perhaps her family?"

"Came from Ireland first of July. Her ship anchored beyond Battery Park for almost a week until allowed in to shore. She was foully put-out."

"Would you know how she met Mr. Smythe?"

"It was the day after she employed me. Might have been at the Mayor's office, because she got up that morning and was in a great rush to be on her way."

"She had an acquaintance with the Mayor, then?"

"Seeking relatives, she was, and figured he could help her."

Father pondered that bit of news. Was this how she met Hector? He would keep the Mayor out of it for now and said, "You've been more helpful than you can imagine. Now, about correspondence..."

"I can bring you her writings. There is a drawer full, if you like?"

"If you show me, that would be easier, Ruth."

"Her room is in here." She led the way down the hall and opened the door to a bedroom. A clean, well ordered bedchamber, flowered wallpaper, rugs on the floor, a large four-poster, and two gaslights, one by the bed, and the other at a desk. He walked directly to that piece of furniture and stood a moment trying to get a sense of the woman who most recently sat at the chair putting her dreams on paper. At least that is what he hoped to find.

A quill and a bottle of ink placed off to the left. If she did journal, it would be at this desk.

Ruth asked, "I don't want to sound like I'm not sorry she died, but do you know if I'll get paid for the week's wages?"

"Perfectly understandable. Yes, you will be paid what you are owed and coach fare to your parents' home, too."

That took away the somber look on her face. "I'm sorry she died. I hope it was peaceful."

"If you don't mind, I'll begin this unfortunate task and call when I'm done."

She curtsied and left him to poke about in a deceased woman's past.

An hour later, finished with reading Mrs. Molloy's letters and journals, he folded and tucked them back in the drawer. Aisling will be intrigued to read the bits and pieces of her family and life in Ireland. He bid Miss Sims good day and headed to the rectory.

It was as if Signey sat in the hallway waiting for him. He could hear her solid heeled shoes on the flooring as she approached his office.

"Did you find anything?" She settled into a chair opposite his desk, and he could do none else than begin answering her questions.

"Hector took Aisling to Mrs. Molloy's home the night of the charity ball. He was interested in her welfare, I believe, and I think Hector and Mrs. Molloy may have met at the Mayor's office. She referred to Aisling as her *sister* in front of the maid, Ruth. So, what do you make of that?" Without waiting for an answer, he continued, "A Mr. Edward Edwards was apparently caught up with Mrs. Molloy and invited her to his home. I believe Mrs. Molloy was the one to secure an invite for Aisling."

Signey's rapt attention reminded him of a hound on the scent. She mused, "Hector found a connection between the two women. I would be surprised if there was a real blood connection. Cannot for the life of me believe that? Aisling's whole family was gone, years ago. Her parents came over alone, with only their infant daughter, and no other family members from Ireland. Aisling told me about her past. There was never a mention of a sister. And she certainly would have known."

A knock at his office door, and a post-boy glanced around the door, which slanted ajar. "A delivery, Father."

"On a Sunday afternoon?" Father took his glasses off and glared at the boy. "What is to become of our world?"

"It is a Special Delivery, Father. Good day to you." He placed the white envelope on the corner of the desk, nodded, and left the room.

Signey leaned forward her nose twitching with curiosity.

"Hmm, let's hope it is from them."

She grimaced. "It better be good news."

*Father - Mrs. Pennino:*

*Aisling and I are in good spirits as much as can be expected under the circumstance. Hector Smythe is suspected in the murder of Mrs. Molloy. Aisling does not believe him guilty, though we do not have any proof to the contrary.*

*In any event, we may be detained another day or two. I will keep you informed.*

*Regards, Kegan Galliger*

Stunned, both Father and Signey rent the air with their voices. "Hector?"

Father stood, his chair almost tipping. "I'm going up there. I think I've got information that should be brought to the investigator's attention."

"You can't leave me dangling." She practically jumped off her chair and put her hands on her hips, scowling at him.

"Mrs. Molloy has quite a past and some things she wouldn't want known. It appears she left Ireland in a rush so not to possibly face the criminal justice system for murder."

"No!"

"And she is an aunt of our Aisling. She's sister to Aisling's father."

"No!"

"How this involves Hector, I can't figure." He scratched his head and then smoothed out the hair.

"And you think you'll do some good going up there, getting into the middle of it all?"

As only Mrs. Pennino could do, she ruffled his feathers, and even caused him doubt. "I suppose I could send them a note, and I wouldn't have to ask Father Brown to cover tomorrow's Mass for me then."

"You never fail to be the voice of common sense, Father."

———

*A* note from Mr. Edwards interrupted Aisling's morning sipping the cup of chocolate Gwen brought. She instantly lost interest in her tray. He requested she join him near the carriage barn for a morning ride. She dared not tell Kegan, he would want to accompany her, and this might be a great opportunity to ask a few questions of her own.

Minutes later, she strode across the gravel toward the barn. A large man, she could not mistake Mr. Edwards from a distance. He stood next to a handsome curricle with stylish yellow wheels and framework, black leather hood, and jet-black horse. She held his note in her hand.

"Thank you for answering my note, Miss O'Quinn. We have not had a chance to talk since your...well, since Mrs. Molloy's accident. Perhaps you will take a maiden tour with me." With a great deal of pride, his glance shifted to the elegant curricle. "This beauty arrived yesterday. We'll have a chance to better acquaint. Without others about."

She could not muster a smile and toyed with the note in hand. "I suppose it wouldn't hurt to discuss matters." She gathered her cloak close and put her foot on the step before he could assist her.

Mr. Edwards energetically jumped in and took his place. She grasped the handle to her right, and the note fluttered out of her hand floating to the ground. He snapped the leads sending the horse forward.

Her bonnet slid off her head, and she re-tied it. "What did you want to discuss?"

"I am sorry for your loss, and the loss of my dear companion. Talking about her with you might relieve my sadness. There's something about you that brings her to mind."

He really did want to talk. "Tell me, Mr. Edwards, how long had you known my aunt?"

"Time is relative, don't you think?" He cast a somber smile. "It is the essence of that time that matters. How long had you known her?"

"I didn't even know she existed until a week ago."

"Orphaned you were at a young age, is that right?" He snapped the black into a cantor, perhaps testing the vehicle's sturdiness.

She pondered his question, wondering about his reason for asking. "Young, yes."

"My new ride is comfortable, wouldn't you say?"

"Very much so. And such a lovely day, too." She inched her way to the end of the shared cushion. He was a large man and took up more than what might be his half.

"Your father, Gradleigh O'Quinn, he had the copper hair like you?"

This was eerie. Her blood ran quick. "How on earth would you know that, Mr. Edwards?"

A chuckle came from his throat, deep and wily, not mirthful. "Mrs. Molloy of course. How else?"

She needed to get a grip. Of course, it would have been from

Beatrice. Attempting to put a nicer tone to her voice, she took a deep breath and reconsidered what the mystery was about this man.

Mr. Edwards slackened the rein in his right hand and slightly pulled the left. They drove into an outlook over the Hudson River, breathtakingly beautiful on this excellent day. Wind-blown sails scattered the boats about the river. He laid his hand over hers, which fisted in her lap. "Let's walk out. After, we'll head back to Elmhurst."

She did not wait for him and alighted in a jaunty manner. Her bonnet slid off and hung by a ribbon.

He came around the back of the curricle. "May I?" His hand reached out.

He surprised her. "May you what?" Her voice snapped.

"Touch that lovely hair of yours, unadorned, shining in the sunlight. I've wanted to do this from the moment I met you." His beefy hand reached out.

She stepped away and tucked her hair beneath the bonnet. "Mr. Edwards, really."

He had the decency to blush. "I don't know what came over me. Sorry." His palm fisted and dropped against his side.

"I think we should go back. Mr. Galliger is expecting me."

"What does the young lawyer mean to you?"

"He's a friend. We've known each other a long time." Mr. Edwards slanted a skeptical look. Her blood was racing, soon coloring her neck and face.

"I'm surprised you met me alone." He stepped closer. "You entertain in your room without a maid. Leads me to believe you are more like your aunt than I first suspected."

The heat rose up quickly, inflaming her. "I'll not be riding in your fine carriage." She spun on her heel and practically ran away from him in the general direction of the estate.

She walked at least twenty or more minutes before she realized he didn't call out to her and had not driven past. She certainly was not frightened, though he did give her the willies. He was a strange man. It would take her at least an hour or more of walking. She quickened her pace grateful for the sunny, brisk day.

Kegan paced the entrance to the carriage house. She could spot him from the distance as she strode up the drive, bonnet in hand. The wind kept taking it off; she untied the bonnet rather than fight the wind. A footman was unhitching the curricle with the yellow wheels. She wondered how Mr. Edwards drove back, as he had not passed her on the rutted road.

She knew the moment Kegan saw her, because he jogged over. "You left without a word."

"Didn't Mr. Edwards tell you? That's his curricle the groom is unhitching." Kegan glanced over his shoulder then back to her.

"So, this note must be yours then? It was fluttering about the yard."

She nodded.

"Why didn't you return with him?"

Censure punctuated his words, and she narrowed her gaze. Ordering her about, especially on the heels of Mr. Edward's odd behavior, did not sit well with her now.

He cleared his throat. "What I meant to say is I've been worried."

"No need. It was a lovely morning for a walk."

"You could have met me as planned in the dining room, and we could have gone together."

"Yes, but I didn't, so we couldn't." She brushed past him and into the front door of Elmhurst.

---

*A*isling went directly to her chamber. She needed the ability to lock her door. Doomed if she allowed Kegan to sleep on the chair, possibly doomed if she did not, unless she had a key.

A sharp rap at her door, followed by, "It is me."

Recognizing Kegan's voice, she opened the door.

His face was dark with consternation. "What was that outside on the gravel? What happened with Edwards?"

Closing the door, she leaned against it and sighed. "He's odd. Nothing happened, just a feeling I get." She was weary from her long walk. "He knows you've spent the past two nights."

"You've led me to believe you care little what he thinks."

"Well, the way he said it bothers me, makes it like it is something other than the innocent truth." Here came the heat up her neck. Drat. The chairs in front of the grate beckoned, and she sat, Kegan followed suit.

His hand rubbed across his brow and pinched the bridge of his nose. "Aisling, we know the truth. We know my presence is a necessity. He is attempting to manipulate you."

"In any event, whatever damage might occur already has." She flung her hand, like a butterfly in the wind.

"What damage? He is a man who rides roughshod over others. It is his way. He isn't really concerned whether I stay here or not, other than he might like to catch you alone."

Tears threatened to fall. How long ago since she was in charge of her life; strong like her *máthair* before she became ill; strong like Signey, whom she missed. Kind like Father Declan, whose presence was always calming.

She confessed, "I'm not feeling nice right now. You'll likely catch the brunt of anger that man stirred up if you stay."

He shot up out of the chair and paced to the grate, then to the wardrobe and back again. A hand swept over his brow again. "When was the last time you were in control of your life?"

Dumbfounded, her tears no longer threatened. "Are you trying to make me laugh? Because right now, as much as I do want to have some say in my life, the last thing I have energy for is a challenge from you."

"I'm serious, Aisling. When was the last time you felt capable of directing what you want out of life?"

She tried to think. A minute passed. "The last day I was in school, over a week ago. Miss Blackwell announced I'd passed an important exam, one that would allow me to intern in the hospital and still continue with my studies."

He leaned against the mantel, arms folded, smiling at her. "Well, then, we'll get you back to that place. That's a promise."

His firm response, coupled with sympathy and fortitude made the tears brim. She wanted to believe him.

# CHAPTER 28

egan smiled his voice teasing, "I do have good news. Lieutenant O'Flannery announced he is allowing us to leave in the morning.

He will have finished interviewing the last of the guests by tonight. Perhaps he'll have all the answers he needs to actually think he has the killer in jail already."

"That's something at least." She slid her gloves off and placed them on the arm of the chair.

"I sent Father and Signey another letter and apprised them that Hector has been jailed as a suspect in Mrs. Molloy's murder."

For a moment, all the weariness of the past three days clouded the air. "Don't be surprised if Father shows up."

"Funny, I had the same idea. His presence would actually be a grand diversion." He had not moved from the mantel; a quiet and solid comfort. There was a definite sense of strength about him. Amidst death, murder, and wicked indulgent lives, he surrounded her with security.

She owed him so much and rued her snappish tongue. "I went with Mr. Edwards because I needed to settle some questions I've had. I came away with more questions. He mentioned my *athair* by name, and remarked on my hair, how it matched his."

Kegan's interest validated with the rise of his brows.

"He told me Mrs. Molloy had spoken of the comparison. I didn't for one minute believe him."

"What are you saying?"

"Let's suppose he followed Mrs. Molloy here from Ireland. Maybe they were lovers, and she escaped him, or something."

"As I mentioned before, it will be an easy matter to find out if and when he came to America. It is a matter of record."

"What if he used fake papers?"

"Well, that would be a problem, let's give it a try just in case. When we arrive in Manhattan, my first order of business will be to visit the immigration office."

"I'd go with you, but I have to get back to my studies. Miss Blackwell is probably already fuming." She ran her fingers over the folded gloves on the arm of the chair. She missed her lessons.

He pushed away from the mantel. "Shall I enlighten you about where Mr. Edwards spent the fateful night?"

She perked up. "Do."

"According to Miss Joyce Miller, who spilled everything on her gossipy little mind, the sultry flaxen haired bragged about Mr. Edwards visiting her Friday night. It was well past midnight when he arrived, and he stayed through until dawn, leaving before the maid arrived with morning cocoa. She didn't make a showing until almost noon, having slept in from her amorous night."

Aisling picked up the gloves on the arm of the chair and inspected them. She could not look at him. "What else did your informative Miss Miller have to say?"

"She suggested we play cards this evening. I told her I was already engaged." He smiled when she glanced at him. "I received a pretty little pout."

A light rap on the door, and Gwen entered. "Lieutenant O'Flannery has asked everyone to meet in the main parlor."

"We'll be right there, thank you." He asked Aisling "Was there anything else?"

"Does the time work out with Edwards? You fixed my aunt's death

295

at a bit past eleven, right. So, he could have done it."

"What motive? The police will need a motive."

"For heaven's sake, what motive does Hector have?"

"Between you and me, we could find one. What I do not know is if the police are investigating Edwards. We need to either confirm or let go our suspicions where he's concerned." He held out his hand. "Shall we go down?"

---

*A*s soon as they entered the parlor, Aisling walked over to the three women with whom she had played cards.

All seated on the divan, Aisling took a chair that was positioned at a ninety-degree angle. Jayne leaned over, whispering, "This might be good news. We might be allowed out of here."

Suzette hushed her with a scowl.

Jayne leaned closer. "She doesn't want Mr. Edwards to hear me. He's taken a liking to her and she wants to keep it that way."

Aisling nodded in understanding. "Would he have another of these weekends, then?"

Jayne shrugged. "Who knows? He indicated to Suzette he might take up with her on a permanent basis. He suggested they could be a couple. I gather he's planning on moving."

The murmur of conversation came to an abrupt halt when the butler rang a little bell. Lieutenant O'Flannery stepped into the circle of the guests gathered. "I've good news. It appears we found our suspect to be guilty and have no further need of questioning. Mr. Edwards has informed me dinner will be served almost immediately; and with that said, I'll give you all leave to go to your homes." The conversation buzzed about the room. "I have your addresses on file, should there be need to corroborate in the future."

At that moment, the buzz of conversation increased, as men and women paired and moved toward the dining room. Kegan offered Aisling his arm. "Shall we eat before leaving?"

"I don't actually know how I'm to get back to Manhattan. I arrived in one of Mr. Edward's carriages with my aunt, and am hesitant to ask him, especially after the uncomfortable ride with him earlier today."

"I expected you would ride in my carriage. There is one problem—Hightower came with me. Rather than cause you inconvenience, I'll tell him to find another conveyance."

"You would do that for me?"

"Aisling, don't you know yet how I feel about you?"

His brilliant blue gaze cast on her with such declaration, she could have kissed him. Instead, she placed her hand on his arm and squeezed. "One good turn deserves another. Hightower can ride with us. He did not harm me. I understand, given what the weekend was supposed to accomplish, why he would have thought otherwise about me. Though won't it be too dark to travel?"

His eyes twinkled. "You want one more night of me, do you?"

The blush came so quick, her cheeks burned. "I was thinking of our safety in the dark, *sir*."

"Isn't your safety in the dark something I've been guarding?"

She might swoon blast him. She tried to slip her hand off his arm. He held it firmly. Mirth danced in the corner of his eyes, making him even more handsome, as if that could be possible.

---

*a* group of eight hastened to their rooms after eating. At least half of the guests lingered in the dining room, in no apparent rush.

Kegan hurried to his room to pack, with plans to meet Aisling in the foyer. Aisling went directly to her room and asked Gwen to pack her things. Laying out her wrap and bonnet on the bed, she told Gwen she had an errand and would be gone but a few minutes.

She took the servants' staircase down to the main floor slipping past footmen and maids into the hall that would bring her to the main part of the estate. Her intention was to rifle through Mr. Edwards' desk. She wanted to discover who he really was and searched for writings and agendas.

Laughter and gaiety spread across the foyer coming from the dining room. Her aunt was a wisp of memory to the weekend guests. Someone had died, certainly not anyone of consequence considering the frivolity.

Silently cracking open the library door, she stepped inside closing it behind her. A gas lamp on a table afforded enough light for her to rummage about. Without a moment to lose, she pulled out the middle drawer in his desk and found pens and a small ruler. Opening a side drawer crammed with invoices, she closed it and opened the drawer opposite discovering a stack of letters. A moment where she considered the invasion of Mr. Edwards' privacy passed quickly when the memory of Beatrice's body on the gurney overcame a sense of wrong; Aisling decided that defended her actions. Mr. Edwards did not strike her as someone who was honest, and she needed to discover why her intuition was so strong.

She opened the letter on top. It was from Mr. Gaunt who had sat across from her at the dining table, full of anticipation for the weekend, and promising to make sure on the delivery of a special wine from France. She replaced it and drew one from the bottom of the stack, glancing at the signature at the end of the missive. It was signed James.

James asked if Mr. Edwards knew when they could expect him to return home. The sheep fattened nicely for the coming winter. D'Alton was quite ill, not expected to live. The rail link to Dublin had an accident, and repairs were already underway, might take another week or two before it is back up and running. Certainly, it would be in repair when next Mr. Edwards arrives home. He signed it, Godly speed, James.

Aisling re-read the letter. It sounded like a letter from home. She glanced at the postmark. Drogheda, County Louth. She practically fell over the swivel chair behind her. He was from Drogheda, as was her aunt. No wonder he knew where her aunt was from. She tucked the letter into her pocket, closed the drawer, and left the room, scampering to her chamber through the kitchen.

Gwen met her in the corridor. "Mr. Galliger has already taken your bag to his carriage. He awaits you, miss." She handed over Aisling's cape and bonnet.

"Thank you for all you've done, Gwen. You take care. Sometimes things are not as they seem, and we need to be on guard. Heed what I say for I believe you to be a nice person."

"Yes, miss. I want to say I knew you were of a different sort than the women who come here on weekends. I knew right off and am glad your friend kept watch for you." She gave a small curtsy and they parted.

Aisling, surprised at Gwen's declaration, hurried along the corridor and down the main staircase. Kegan, hat in hand, waited in the foyer, along with several other gentlemen. All she wanted to do was make haste and leave this jaded, woeful place.

"Are you ready?"

She nodded and glanced about the marbled entrance. Mr. Edwards was coming straight at them. "You are taking advantage of Lieutenant O'Flannery's dismissal."

Kegan reached out his hand. "Thank you for an interesting weekend."

"You didn't sail yesterday. A beautiful day for it."

"Well, it didn't seem..."

"Yes, yes. I agree. Next time, perhaps. Hightower kept himself occupied—hardly saw him a'tall." He turned his pink jowly face on Aisling. "And, you my dear thank you for accompanying me this morning. Will you inform me when arrangements are made for Mrs. Molloy's internment?"

She fiddled putting on her gloves rather than look at him. "Should I send the information here to Elmhurst?"

"That will be fine."

He raised her hand to his lips. She tried not to jerk away from his touch.

They were off.

Kegan pulled himself into the carriage. Aisling noted Hightower's absence. As if reading her mind, he offered, "He made other arrangements. Needed to be in Manhattan by late afternoon. I did not know when I spoke earlier he had already left. Was he at dinner?"

"I honestly didn't look for him." She clasped her gloved hands together. The cadence of the carriage, the canopy of overlapping oaks and elms with the paintbrush of color on their tips, and light fading with the approach of evening. The tension in her shoulders slipped away. She was ever so glad to leave this stronghold of iniquity.

Warmed by Kegan's declarations over the past three days, her mind and heart tangled with promise, excitement, and the real possibility of love. Tonight, she would sleep in her room with a light heart.

Kegan stretched his long legs out, crossed at the ankles, his arms folded against his chest. He appeared at ease, comfortable against the button-tufted leather cushions. Two lanterns swayed with the movement of their transport, the lights increasing with the onset of evening.

For the next two hours or so, they would still be together, the two of them; cozily ensconced within the safety of his carriage. She had gotten used to his nearness, his attention and embraces, his kisses. Oh my! And, the whiff of citrus that surrounded him, like the oranges Signey cut up for breakfast.

Gratitude for his presence this weekend blossomed in her heart, a glorious imagining of her life—their future—spread warmth through her. The urge to touch him was so strong; she reached over and patted his arm.

His warm gaze rested on her. "You are deeply pensive."

"Thinking of you, and how you've been my protector this weekend. How grateful I am. I don't deserve your friendship, or your consideration."

A long moment passed, and then he said, "Let me be the judge of that."

"I found out something about Mr. Edwards. He's from Drogheda."

"In Ireland? He might have known Mrs. Molloy."

"Precisely what I'm thinking."

"How did you come across this information? Dare I ask?" It was dark enough she couldn't watch his lips curve. She distinctly heard delight in his words.

"When I left you to pack, I went to his library. He was occupied in the dining room and I took the liberty to look around." At the shock on his face, she added, "Okay, snoop. I found this in his desk drawer." She drew the letter from her pocket.

"It is too dark to read, tell me." His voice sounded weary, she hoped it wasn't because of her trespass. He uncrossed his long legs.

"It was written by a James. Informative items, train accident, some man in ill health, sheep are all fat and ready for winter. And, when are you coming home, hope it is soon. The postmark was Drogheda, County Loath."

"And your aunt was from Drogheda."

"Exactly."

He said, "First thing tomorrow, I'll check the manifest for the ships that arrived from Dublin. I recall you saying she arrived July 1."

"Yes, the tag on her trunk said *Manning*, which I think would have been the ship, and the date June 1865. That should help when we go to Castle Garden."

Kegan patted her hand. "I'll go. You need to set things right with Miss Blackwell."

"She's heavy on my mind. You're right, I will do that instead."

He situated his right arm along the backside of their leather bench. His fingers played with curls dangling over her nape. "Now, what else can you think of regarding Mr. Edwards and Beatrice?"

His touch sent remarkable sensations through her. She knew his penchant for solving mysteries and tried to keep on track with her answer. "She acted smitten, and much as if they had met recently. She was quite giddy with their friendship, head over heels about the invitation to Elmhurst." She tucked the letter back in her pocket.

"Take special care of that. It could be used in court, especially with the postmark dated and designated." His fingers caressed her nape, lightly tracing toward her left ear.

"Do you think I should visit Hector and perhaps lift his spirits?" Why didn't he lean over and kiss her?

Restless, he removed his arm from the back of the bench, drew his legs upright. "Aisling, the letter isn't proof of anything. We need to find a motive. Not try to lift Hector's morale only to have it dashed again."

How could Kegan's mind be on the case against Edwards, when all she could think about was kissing? She nodded the truth of Hector's confinement, yet she couldn't help remembering how Mr. Smythe treated Hector, and the sadness of such hateful behavior.

"I know you think him innocent, and he may well be. As they say, let sleeping dogs lie. He isn't any better or worse off at the moment."

"You're right. I'm impulsive, too much so."

301

He laughed outright. "I'll add that to my list of things to ponder when I can't sleep at night."

It was good to hear him tease. So, she kept him awake, did she? Pleased with herself, she peered out the window and grinned until her cheeks hurt, even though she would have preferred one of his kisses. "Do you think the maid, Ruth Sims, would like Beatrice's clothing?"

"You'd have to ask her. Putting the items to use is right."

She pictured Beatrice in her low-cut bodices, feathers in her hair, strings of pearls dangling about her neck, silky hose embroidered with birds and scrolls. Aisling could not envision herself wearing any of the satins and brocades. "Well, then perhaps I'd be interested in another weekend at Elmhurst and parading around like the others."

"You are a little minx, aren't you?"

She slanted him a wily glance, though she was sure he couldn't detect it in the gloom.

He said, "Do you have any idea what went through my mind when I saw you Friday evening, wearing the same gown from the ball? I wanted to claim you for myself. I wanted to grab your cape and whisk you out of there. I was dumbfounded to watch you in polite conversation with one of the men. I wasn't the only one who took note of the lovely, young russet-haired woman. I admit a furor rose up in me."

A warm feeling enveloped her—almost, but not exactly as good as his kiss. It was so nice, just the two of them in the carriage as if they had a long history. This is what families do, how husbands and wives get on. Her heart flip-flopped. This was normal. "I had nothing else to wear. Ruth cleaned the hem and stitched a seam to make it presentable. Beatrice insisted I wear it."

"I could tell you were unaware of the attention you drew. It has occurred to me this past week that dressing as a boy since you were young, might have made it difficult to transform to a young lady. You made it appear natural. You are a very feminine and striking beauty. When I saw you, I had no doubt your door would get a good many knocks."

Again, she sensed the humor in his voice. "I'm happy to have obliged your sense of deduction, sir." She opened her gloved hands and placed them on her thighs. "I, ah...I don't think it is a good idea we share this little bit with Father or Signey."

"Our secret, then?" He chuckled.

"Yes and thank you." Her gloved hands rested against her bodice. "Speaking of which, I hope we won't be rousing Signey by the time we arrive."

"I sent a messenger before we went in to dinner."

"You think of everything. I don't know how I'm going to manage without you underfoot every hour of the day."

"One thing for certain, you are a survivor, my darling. The ease with which you navigate through life, and all you've endured getting to this point, you'll manage fine."

And, with that, his arm went around her, and his other hand lifted her chin. "I can't help myself any longer; my urge to kiss you needs immediate attention."

Her hand found its way to his upper arm. She almost purred with delight.

---

*T*he carriage rambled toward Manhattan. The sky reflected a glow from the street lamps. The closer they rode, the brighter the sky became. It was near ten-thirty as they passed Central Park, then within a few miles, left on Amity. Kegan rolled up the canvas on the side window as they neared the city, and Aisling could see the parlor lamp lit in Signey's home. It glowed with welcome. She was arriving home to her safe harbor.

A sacred moment of remembering came to her of the time she climbed the stairs on Mulberry Bend thinking her *máthair* was waiting, after the long and somewhat frightening journey from Gettysburg. This arriving home, was happy.

Kegan patted her hand. "Glad to be home, are you?" He knew what was going on in her heart. He understood. She placed her hand atop his and squeezed, and the carriage pulled to a stop.

The front door opened even before the driver secured the reins and alighted to drop the step. Father and Signey were silhouetted against the brightness of the parlor lamps. A lump caught in her throat. Kegan scrambled out and gave her assist. She fairly flew off the step, up the short walk, and into their open arms.

Kegan spoke to his driver and stepped inside with the trio.

A rich floral scent of black tea, and lemon cake led them down the hall to the kitchen. Signey held Aisling's hand and did not let go. Curious Lucy sat at the door to her bedroom. Her yellow cat eyes followed Aisling into the kitchen still she kept her distance.

Father declared, "I'll wait not a minute longer to get the whole of the weekend. However, before we begin, I need to say something." He met Aisling's gaze. "You, my dear, are precious to us. If you haven't learned that in the past two years, I'm perplexed as to what will convince you."

If he had asked this a week ago, her answer would have been far different. In one week's time, some of life's lessons had come hard and vicious.

Father's brows practically met in the middle of his forehead such was his concentration. He stood over her, hadn't even waited for her to sit down. He leaned in, intent on her words.

Her voice filled with emotion. "I owe both of you my deep regret and apology for running away, hiding actually." Kegan handed her a handkerchief. She dabbed at her eyes.

"I think I was trying to escape myself. I was ashamed and had no right to self-pity. I know that now. My parents were hard-working, loving people. They suffered horridly in ways I hope I never have to endure. I shamed their memory by reacting the way I did to Miss Helberg's acceptance speech." She took a cautious breath. "I'll not fail your trust and love again."

Kegan patted her arm. Father's scrunched brow did not ease; it appeared he wanted more from her, expected more. Lucy's tail swept the floor at Father's feet, as if she was as agitated as he seemed.

"I do have need of the confessional, Father." Did she ever, stealing, and conniving her way through the weekend.

His brows lowered to their original place above his eyes. "That can wait until tomorrow. Signey's cake won't stay warm much longer, icing is still soft the way I like it."

Chairs scraped the floor as they each took their place. Kegan excused himself a minute and took a piece of cake, and a cup of tea to his driver, returning quickly to the warm kitchen, where the questions had already begun about the sister-aunt in question.

Father and Signey's interest in Beatrice Molloy, and what they heard, both fact and fiction, reminded Aisling of how Kegan and she tried to ferret out information and innuendo over the weekend.

Signey asked, "You never heard her name mentioned once as a child?"

She shook her head, her mouth full of delicious lemon cake frosted with creamy butter icing.

Father said, "There are letters in her rented home. In time, you will have to go through everything and decide what should be done." After another bite of cake, he added, "I've talked with Ruth Sims. She's agreed to stay on until you decide what to do with her things."

Aisling said, "Thank you for taking matters in hand."

"It is almost as if she never intended to see Ireland again." Father sipped his tea. "I would wager everything of value to her is in that home. Ruth Sims is quite capable." He glanced over the rim of his glasses as he stirred sugar in his cup."

"First things first. Tomorrow I must go to school. Miss Blackwell will dismiss me if I lose any more time."

"And what are your plans for tomorrow?" Signey asked Kegan.

"My law office and the immigration office. The letter Aisling has in her possession demands we verify Mr. Edwards date and time of entry into our country."

Father moved his chair back. He leaned over and kissed Aisling atop her curly, copper-gold head. "I've made tentative arrangements for a memorial service for Mrs. Molloy."

He swiped his fingers on the napkin, adding, "And don't ever think of scaring the dickens out of us again with such foolish notions." He briskly asked of Kegan, "May I take advantage of your carriage and beg a ride."

With a nod, Kegan stood along with Father. "Thank you for the delicious dessert, Mrs. Pennino. It was a nice homecoming." Father placed a hand on Aisling's arm. "Perhaps now we can settle into humdrum and sameness for a while."

She put the napkin to her mouth with a little cough, nodding in agreement. Father eyes gleamed with perception; she knew there was no use hiding the truth of the growing involvement between her and Kegan. Father and Signey exchanged glances.

The women walked Father and Kegan to the door. The driver handed his plate and cup to Signey thanking her and opened the carriage with step in place. Waving them goodbye, Signey and Aisling hugged.

Signey said, "I've missed you so. Nearly broke my heart." She stepped back and smoothed a lock of hair from Aisling's forehead. "But I understood sweeting. I knew what was going on inside you."

Lucy rubbed against her gown, purring as she did so. Lucy and Signey sympathized and she was very grateful.

She really was home. Surely, her sainted *máthair* had a hand.

---

*M*onday morning Kegan was at the counter of the Immigration office at Castle Garden and introduced himself, saying, "I'm assisting the local authorities in a murder investigation and need to look at records for a Mr. Edward Edwards, who may have arrived from Ireland sometime in July of this year."

"Is this the name we should be looking for?" The officer took the piece of paper Kegan offered, with the name and possible dates.

"We aren't certain. More like a needle in a haystack. What we do know is he most likely followed Mrs. Beatrice Molloy who arrived July 1 on the *Manning*."

"That narrows it nicely. I'll send a messenger to your office with the information."

"Perfect." He extended his hand.

---

$\mathcal{A}$isling paced in front of Miss Blackwell's office door. The woman was in a meeting and Aisling waited impatiently. A hundred things to say crossed her mind, yet she was skeptical about revealing too much.

A young woman, gray woolen skirts swishing with her hurried shuffle, burst from the closed door, swiping her face with the back of a gloved hand. On her heels, an assistant, pad of paper and pencil in hand, announced, "You are next, Miss O'Quinn."

Entering Miss Blackwell's inner sanctum, she closed the door.

"Come, come." Miss Blackwell waved her hand. "Sit." Her hands folded together, elbows on her desk. "It is good you are back, you're quite behind your class."

Aisling nodded. "And I'm prepared to get right to it."

"Good then." She scrutinized Aisling. What was she looking for? Horns? She added, "You don't look any the worse. Must have been a nice time getting to know your aunt, was it, newly from Ireland?"

"It was eventful." Her voice came out hesitant, guarded. She bit her lower lip and glanced across the desk to her supervisor.

"I've not known you to be coy, Miss O'Quinn."

The words shot out of her mouth. "She was murdered Friday night."

# CHAPTER 29

$\mathcal{M}$iss Blackwell's mouth gaped.

Aisling spewed, "The police believe they have the killer. I do not think he did it. I think another man did, a man who may have followed her from Ireland. I believe they knew each other—"

"Hold it right there, Miss O'Quinn." Her palm faced Aisling's blast of explanation, and she shut her mouth.

"This is the aunt you met?"

Aisling nodded, still biting her lip.

"And here you sit, ready to honor your dedication to school and duties. Is she even buried yet?"

Aisling shook her head. "An autopsy was performed."

"Are you returned to Mrs. Pennino's home?"

Aisling nodded, easing up on her lip.

"For good this time?"

She nodded.

"Well, then keep me apprised of the situation. I think your place is at home right now and the burial of your aunt. Do not worry about your schooling. It is here for you." She stood, fingertips placed like little tents on the desktop, a determined look on her face.

Aisling sobbed. Her relief was palpable; in a swift motion, she went around the desk and hugged Miss Blackwell.

In the awkward moment, Miss Blackwell peeled Aisling's arms away. "Now, now. Take care. I'll stop by Mrs. Pennino's on my way home tonight and check on how you are doing."

Aisling left the Infirmary feeling a great deal better than when she arrived. She did not want to go to Beatrice's house by herself, out of necessity she would manage. She needed a steady, plodding approach to the next few days. Burial arrangements were in order and Father would know all about that. Surprisingly, with all the thinking and talking to herself, she found herself at the kitchen door of the rectory, rather than Beatrice's home.

A racket spilled from the pantry. "Drat!" At the sound of Signey's disconcerted voice, Aisling peeked around the doorjamb. Several sacks of rice had fallen off a top shelf upturning a stack of pots on their way to the floor.

Signey stepped down from the stool. "Why aren't you in school?" She maneuvered her way out of the closet, red faced, strands of hair loosened from her bun.

"Miss Blackwell was so kind. She has given me leave to attend Mrs. Molloy's burial."

"A sad thing for you to do. Let's take a break from this mess and visit Father. He's not left on his duties yet."

Two men, dressed in police uniforms, hats tucked under arms, faced Father at his desk.

"We will need a signature for verification, Father."

Hearing this, Aisling and Signey entered without knocking. "Here is the young woman who is relative to Mrs. Molloy. Aisling O'Quinn. She'll do the verifying."

The two officers glanced at them. One was Lieutenant O'Flannery, not exactly a man she wanted to greet. "Miss O'Quinn." A grim set to his square jaw, he nodded to her.

Father said, "The autopsy is concluded, and they need a signature that Mrs. Molloy is who she said she was before we can bury her."

Signey wrapped her arm about Aisling's shoulder. The officer asked, "Can you do this, miss?"

"I can't honestly say she's my father's sister. She did know everything about my family that I knew from stories my parents told me. Based on her word, I surmised she was an aunt."

"No likenesses of any sort?"

She shook her head. "My parents didn't talk much about life in Ireland. I do not ever recall hearing about an Aunt Beatrice. I plan to go through her things and hope to find verification she really was my aunt."

"The body can keep another day or two. It is in a cold room below the morgue. When you find your proof, stop by the station, and ask for me."

"Do you know how she died?"

Lieutenant O'Flannery glanced at Father, and then answered Aisling. "A broken neck. Someone strong is most likely the perp."

Aisling pictured the darkened corridor, the scream that ended abruptly. "Hands were used, not a rope or scarf?"

"The bruises are consistent with hands."

Father said, "I have a few hours now. We could go over Mrs. Molloy's things. The three of us might find something of use. When I was there yesterday, I read letters that might have the information you need."

All in agreement, the officers left. The trio donned outerwear and walked to the home on Sixteenth Street. The day was windy a northerner blowing. Winter was approaching. They might even see sprinkles of snow by night.

Ruth Sims answered the door. Recognizing Father and Aisling, she let them in. Father introduced Signey, and Aisling explained what the police required.

Father asked, "Was there anything I may have missed?"

"She had a small trunk. I don't know what's inside."

Father carried the trunk to the parlor, along with the contents of the drawer in Beatrice's bedroom. There was also a carpetbag filled with papers and books that Ruth carried into the parlor. "Will you need anything else? A pot of tea to get you through?"

Signey smiled brightly. "I can certainly use a cup. I'd make it myself."

"I've barely anything to do, ma'am. I welcome the chance to be busy." The maid gave a little curtsy and left the parlor.

Father said, "Let's make piles. Business information on that table." He pointed to a drop leaf. "Personal matters over here." His shoulder shrugged in the direction of a mahogany gate-leg. "And, anything that you deem suspicious on any account, place on the divan next to me."

Three hours later, two pots of tea, and scones, the trio found only one item of significance. A wedding certificate issued in St. Mary's, Mallow, County Cork, between Miss Beatrice O'Quinn and Mr. Ian Molloy.

"Will this satisfy you? What do you think?" Father handed the certificate to Aisling.

Quickly scanning the scripted document, she exclaimed, "She *was* an O'Quinn. I remember my *athair* talking of his childhood in Mallow. He learned to swim in the Blackwater River that ran through the town." She sighed. "Bits and pieces of their lives, that's all I have. My parents were married in my *mathair's* parish, St. Brigid's in Fingal. That's one of the bits I know for sure."

Father recapped, "This certificate tells us Beatrice lived in Mallow, and her maiden name was O'Quinn, two significant clues that she was your aunt."

Signey added her own ideas. "In these times, that's all most of us have. Bits and pieces of who we were, where we came from. The world is in an uproar. I can't imagine what will happen next to change our lives."

Glancing at his housekeeper, Father's brow wrinkled. "You're referring to Lincoln's assassination, aren't you?"

She nodded. "I didn't get to watch the funeral train, couldn't get close to the tracks that day. I might seem oddly attached, but I am quite thankful to be part of Mrs. Molloy's burial."

Aisling carefully listened to Signey and understood about the need for the ritual. She did not remember her *athair's* burial and was not here when her *máthair* died.

Signey added, "It is an important part of saying goodbye. Even though you've only known she existed hardly more than a week ago, this is the right thing to do, especially now that you have proof of her identity."

Aisling dropped her gaze to her hand, the marriage certificate still in her grasp. "I don't even know if my parents kept theirs. Or what happened to it."

Signey said, "This rite of passage for Beatrice Molloy might allow you to put a good many things to rest."

Aisling glanced at Father. "Would it be possible to bury her near my parents?"

"I'll look into it. If anyone can make that decision to have her in St. James' Cemetery, it would be the funeral director, a good old man of the sod himself. There'll be no fuss I would think." He folded the marriage certificate. "I'll show this to Lieutenant O'Flannery."

*W*hipped by a northerly wind, St. James' Cemetery looked like a somber painting with snowflakes floating, trees stark against the gray sky, conifers green and staunch like pillars. Using thick straps, six men from the funeral home lowered the casket. Kegan, Mr. and Mrs. Galliger, and Signey were present. Upon noticing Ruth Sims, who stood off from the little gathering, Aisling went over to her and encouraged her to join the rest directly in front of the casket. Signey whispered to Ruth that they had room in their carriage. It was too cold to walk home. At the last minute, as Father prayed, Thomas Hightower arrived. He doffed his hat to Aisling and stood at the edge of the mourners, next to Mr. Galliger.

In the carriage on the way to the burial plot, Father had mentioned the Galligers expected her at their home for lunch.

"Me? Alone?"

"The Archbishop is making a stop on his way to another parish. I must be there. Signey would not allow Himself to arrive and not partake of some of her treats, as she put it. So, you will be on your own." He chuckled. "Though being in the care of Kegan isn't exactly being on your own now, is it?"

Beyond caring what others fancied about Miss Helberg's revelations,

Aisling did care a great deal what Mr. and Mrs. Galliger thought of her and was surprised when, at the gravesite, their presence was gratifying, as if they wanted to assure her of their support.

The numbness was not from the cold, it was another kind of daze; empty insensibility. This was her first visit to the gravesites of her parents, and now an aunt—her family. Someday when she earned an income, she would put stones on the three graves. She made the Sign of the Cross along with a silent promise to make that happen. The stones would give her more resolve about the trio of family who lay beneath the cold ground, with its patches of white already blanketing them.

It was not until the carriage left the cemetery, that she realized Mr. Edwards had not shown. As Kegan escorted her to his carriage, she made mention that Mr. Edwards asked specifically to be informed of the date and location.

He said, "Something may have interrupted his plans. Or, he may have decided it wasn't such a good idea to attend."

She nodded in agreement and looked through the window at the passing gravesites as the carriage exited the burial ground.

"In spite of the circumstances, my father and Martha are looking forward to visiting with you." He held her gloved hand as they sat on the leather cushion.

"I agree. The impression I made the night of the ball needs repairing. And their invitation is a comfort."

He squeezed her hand. "You take my breath away. Do you know that?"

 

The grand foyer with its staircase winding to the upper floor, and parlors to the right and left, awed Aisling. A butler nodded to Kegan as he held out his hand for Aisling's dark woolen wrap. Snowflakes drifted to the floor as he took it from her. "Mr. and Mrs. Galliger are in the main parlor, sir. You are expected."

Kegan led Aisling toward double mahogany doors, one slightly ajar. He knocked gently and stood back allowing Aisling to enter ahead of him. Greeted warmly by both, Mrs. Galliger offered a chair next to her in a little circle near the blazing fire.

Mr. Galliger moved to the side of the fire, and Kegan joined him.

Mrs. Galliger said, "You've had a great many difficulties, Miss O'Quinn. Now, a tragedy this past week. We sympathize with you. It is complicated, to the point of daunting to make one's way in the world having lost both parents at such a young age, we can't imagine." She paused a moment, focusing on Aisling. "I have a reputation for getting right to the point. May I with you?"

Startled, Aisling almost did not agree, curiosity overruled fear. She glanced at Kegan who was in conversation with his father. "Of course, Mrs. Galliger. I know my actions were bizarre and must have appeared unbelievable. You were kind enough to have me as a guest at your table, and I to this day I haven't thanked you."

Mrs. Galliger waited until the maid placed the tray on the table in front of them. "Miss Helberg meant well. She intended, I believe, to show the good works of the Children's Aid Society. Her method wasn't the most delicate of approaches."

Aisling said, "I first met her when I was twelve. She caught me stealing from a vendor's cart."

"I take it you have improved your manners?"

Aisling glanced at Kegan then back to Mrs. Galliger. Much to her surprise, the woman had the most impish grin on her face. Aisling suddenly realized this woman liked her. She was teasing.

"One can only hope." Her face softened. Mrs. Galliger put her at ease.

"Kegan has mentioned some of your background. And, of course, Miss Helberg. We are not responsible for how we are born. The truth is children have little to say in circumstances such as yours. You can't possibly be held accountable."

She turned to the men. "Tea?"

They stepped forward taking their cups and saucers. As Mrs. Galliger handed Aisling her steaming cup, Aisling said, "Your understanding means a great deal to me."

"You've earned far more from us than mere insight, my dear. Kegan informed us about your university studies in nursing, and your desire to devote time to underprivileged children."

Kegan added, "She is an inspiration." He winked at her in front of the Galligers.

In the carriage on Aisling's arrival home, Kegan put his hand over hers. "Are you relieved?"

"You arranged this afternoon, I know you did."

"No, I didn't." His eyebrows rose, his eyes wide. "Truly."

She knew that little smirk.

He came to his own defense. "The morning after the ball, both my father and Martha inquired of your welfare. I had to admit I did not know. One thing led to another, and with all Miss Helberg revealed, it painted a picture that brought out their protective nature. They care about you."

She said, "It's you they care about."

"And it's you I care about." His voice filled with warmth and strength. Love, too, because he had revealed himself.

He added, "I've made my wishes known to you, Aisling. And I don't give up."

"I'll never understand why."

"You're real. You mean every word you utter. You are determined, honest. And, I think you are the most charming woman I've ever set eyes on."

She leaned over and brushed his cold cheek with her lips.

Even though the weather was rather frigid, and sleet pelted the windows of the carriage, inside was cozy and warm. It helped that the soles of their shoes rested atop warmed bricks, and Kegan had drawn a throw over their laps.

He walked her to the door, slipped inside, and took her in his arms. She melted against him as their lips met. His arm drew her close, a sweet, tender moment bringing closure to an afternoon of gratitude.

He whispered as his cheek rubbed hers, "I love you, my darling."

She almost swooned into the moment. Her heart quivered with the same affection for him. Despite the bird of omen that will undoubtedly swoop down crashing this all about her.

Kegan rode his carriage to the immigration office. Mr. Knapp met with him almost immediately. "I'm wondering how the search for Edward Edwards' records is going?"

"It is right here, somewhere." Mr. Knapp shuffled files about. "Aha." He glanced through a few pages. "I would have delivered this, but it appears we haven't a match."

Kegan took the pages, and began perusing, suddenly glued to the name Edward. The name was not Edward Edwards, it read Edward Molloy. He glanced up at Mr. Knapp, who said, "Surprised myself. Could that be the same person? The dates coincide; but the name is wrong. It wouldn't be the first time someone lied to gain entry."

"If I'm reading this correctly, Mr. Molloy arrived on the next ship from Ireland after Beatrice Molloy."

"That would be right. She arrived July 1, he arrived July 11."

"May I keep these?" He waved the pages in his fist.

"Yes, I had copies made in case the name change worked for you."

They shook hands, and Kegan raced back to his carriage. He needed to hear Lieutenant O'Flannery's ideas on the discovery. This was much more than a mere coincidence. This meant something. What, he was not sure. Was Edward Beatrice's husband, and she ran from him. No! She would have recognized him. They were together for days, a week or more. How could she not recognize him?

If they were married, why did she run from him? Did he abuse her? Did she abscond with the family fortune? Perhaps not. It was obvious Mr. Edwards lived quite well. What was he missing? What piece of this isn't he getting?

Thumping the roof of the carriage, his driver stopped. Kegan jumped out. "I'll walk the rest of the way. You can wait for me at police headquarters." He was simply too unsettled to sit any longer.

---

*L*ucy rubbed against Aisling's skirt, purring up a storm. She rather liked Mrs. Galliger, direct, no subterfuge. The grand society woman had put her at ease almost immediately.

Ten days ago, she was dressing in a gorgeous gown eager to attend a ball and dance with Kegan. Odd how one could change in so short a time.

A sudden restlessness seized her. Signey would still be at the rectory, so Aisling kept her cloak, boots and hat on, closed and relocked the door. Lucy poked her head through the curtain at the front window.

With the burial several hours ago, a tug on her heartstrings led her to Beatrice's home. Meeting her aunt was the closest she had been to her parents in years. Since the day she was put on the orphan train, early summer 1860. As she bustled along the street, wind blowing her cape, she realized that was more than five years ago.

Ruth met her at the door, cape about her shoulders, and hat on her head. "Oh, miss, I was on my way out."

"Would you mind terribly if I stayed for a bit? I can lock up and put the key under the mat."

Ruth drew her inside. "The burial was hard on you."

Aisling welcomed the warmth after her walk. "Unsettling. I certainly don't want to keep you from your mission."

"If you don't mind then, I'll be on my way. I expect I'll be at least two hours. I'm visiting a friend who had a baby and I'm freeing up some time for her to do errands."

"My aunt feels more alive to me here. I lost her so quickly. Truth be told, I feel funny admitting it." She began untying the bow under her chin.

"Stay as long as you please. And if I haven't come back, leave it as you said."

Aisling removed her cape and placed it over a rocking chair to dry out from the sleet. She stood a long moment in the parlor glancing at the bits and pieces of Beatrice's life. Not much to be sure. A small box on the mantel, which she already knew held the letter her *máthair* had written of her *athair's* death. Her fingers slid across the humped top of the box as if she could touch them.

Resting her hand on the mantel, she tried to get a feel for her aunt. A whiff of her aunt's scent remained, lavender and something else almost like cinnamon. Two of her bonnets hung on hooks by the door, peacock feathers on one, a bird, and flowers on the other. She was fond of flamboyance.

Aisling's glance toured the room, recalling the morning she came down the stairs in her aunt's robe, barefoot. Hector stood nearby—she suspected they had been arguing about her. Her head ached something horrid and after a few minutes, she returned to her room rather than listen.

Beatrice's bedroom was along the hallway toward the kitchen. She put her hand on the knob, and for a split second, thought she heard rustling within, turned the knob and threw open the door. The bed was neatly made, everything in order; much better than if Beatrice still lived. She was careless where her things landed. She owned a lot of shoes, clothing, bonnets, reticules, and shawls. Aisling knew the poverty in Beatrice's formative years. She remembered her *athair's* stories. The excess probably derived from her earlier deprivation.

The lamp on the street outside the bedroom window came alive, flickering within its glass globe, evening coming on. She meandered to the parlor and sat on the divan. Her elbow rested on the arm, and her fingers sifted through her curls as she tried to recall Beatrice's voice.

Aisling had an innate sense about people, and after the long ride in the carriage to Elmhurst, she gained some measure of understanding about Beatrice. Her gaiety was forced. Sadness consumed her, and she needed others to draw it out and replace it with fun; perhaps to cover up a deep insecurity.

Mr. Edwards must have been that person for Beatrice. Except when Aisling had been with them, she saw a darkness creep upon Beatrice. Mr. Edwards demanded she drink beyond her capacity, on two occasions that she knew of; and he ordered her meal without her consideration. As if he owned her rather than nurtured her.

That reflection made her think of Kegan. He was the opposite of Mr. Edwards. There was no linking the two of them. Massaging her forehead, she glanced out the window. It had grown darker. She got up and lit a lamp, then went into the kitchen to rummage about. Nothing appealed to her, wasn't much to find; a bowl with two eggs, a large russet potato, a pot of jam. Ruth must be eating elsewhere. Aisling supposed she would soon move to her parents' home.

The front door flew open and Aisling replaced the pot of jam on the shelf. She called out to Ruth, "I'm in the kitchen.

# CHAPTER 30

*M*r. Edwards stood in the kitchen doorway. The chill of the night gusted from him, snow dust on the shoulders of his cape and brim of his hat. "Just the woman I'm looking for."

Shock took hold. Aisling stepped out of the pantry. Her hand shook, and her fingers curled into fists. She said, "You aren't at Elmhurst."

"Your message about the burial didn't allow me sufficient time. I came as quick as I could."

"I'm sorry about that." Unfurling her fingers, she swiped palms along the sides of her skirt. "Shall we go to the parlor?"

He stood to the side and allowed her to pass. As she did so, he grabbed her upper arm and drew her up close. "I'm compensated with your presence." His breath reeked of cigar smoke and drink.

She tried to twist free. "Let me pass."

His large hand tightened. "We'll get on, you and me. I fancied you from the start. Your *sister* paled in comparison."

This time she jerked free and backed down the hallway toward the front room. He did not move, and his presence filled the entire opening; a large fierce specter.

Could she make it to the door? Though she preferred a

confrontation with him rather than avoid the unspoken between them. His proximity, and what his intentions were, bewildered her.

Surprisingly she was not frightened; she felt like insulting him but held her tongue. He repulsed her with the stench of liquor, his beefy self, like a battering ram, barreling over people. She knew he was a liar, and pretty much had him pegged as Beatrice's killer.

She sat on the divan and watched as he shrugged off his cape, grabbed his hat, and tossed the articles on the arm of another chair. He had not wiped his shoes on the mat, they dripped with mud and wet. He almost fell into the chair opposite. There was no graceful way for a man his size to ease. He appeared weary. He must have just driven down from Elmhurst.

With his presence so near in the low-lighted room, she skimmed over the realization he was from Drogheda, and here he sat. Why?—the all of it; his pursuit of Beatrice, his treatment of her. She needed to take command of his proximity and beware. More than anything, she wanted to understand his motivation.

"Can I get you some tea, Mr. Edwards?" She was not going to allow his size to intimidate her.

He shook his head. "I'd be wantin' a whiskey. Beatrice would have known that." His gaze searched the room coming to rest on the cabinet where she kept liquors.

Aisling ignored his blatant request. "I'm sorry you had to come all this way for nothing. Especially when the weather wasn't in your favor."

He shrugged, the corner of his mouth pinched. His eyes were dull, tired, perhaps.

She inquired, "You hadn't known my aunt long, had you?"

"Why would you be askin'," a cunning slant to his voice.

"Beatrice must have told you how she and I met, how we were related?" A conflict of emotion kept her seated when something else urged her to run out the door.

He pulled a flask from his pocket, untwisted the top, and raised it up. Completely ignoring her question, he said, "How about a sip or two?" He got up off the chair and took a step forward.

She put her hands up palms facing him. "No, no. You know I don't."

His great bulk ungracefully fell back into the chair. "Blood related it is so, 'cause I think yer a liar like her, that's what I think." He gulped a portion and put the cap back on.

Her mind buzzed with possibilities. Had he enough of the alcohol to allow her to question him further? All caution to the wind, blazing ahead, she asked, "Why did you shave the morning after Beatrice's murder?"

"What makes you think she was murdered?" He cast a furious glare through narrowed eyes, and his fist clenched around the flask, as it rested against his thigh.

She picked at small specks on her skirt as if they mussed the wool and dropped them on the floor. She did this twice before answering him. "The lieutenant said so."

A low growl rolled out his throat, his jaw rose up. "She could have fell. She was a drunk."

Aisling took offense at that. His own lack of moral fiber left no room for him to condemn her. She shook the last of the imaginary specks from her skirt and glared at him, locking her gaze on his face. "There were bruises on her arms and neck. The doctor who did the autopsy said the bruising was consistent with a twist and jerk to her neck before she died. I think that's conclusive evidence to claim murder."

"Ye might be too smart for yer own good, little missy." He pulled the top off the flask and took another lengthy gulp.

She sat up straight, rethinking the distance between them. His brogue was in full force. He was a brawny, ruddy-faced bully. Beatrice's last few minutes with him before she ran into the hallway must have been brutal.

He was a chameleon, changing right before her. "I wonder why you put on airs; when it is clear to me you're Irish. Your complexion, no longer hidden by face hair, and I've recognized the Gaelic on your tongue almost from the first we met."

His great bulk came out of the chair in one quick maneuver, and put her at a disadvantage, looming in front of her chair. His nearness smothered her. Yet her common sense had taken flight, and she goaded him. "You kept her drinking against her will. Why?"

He guffawed, she clearly saw the row of his teeth, and the pink of the roof of his mouth as he leaned in above her. He said, "Where's my letter?"

Not prepared for this question, her mouth gaped. "What letter?"

"From James. The one you stole." He blocked her from getting out of the chair and took another swig.

"You are mistaken." Her mind buzzed with entrapment.

He barked, "Drink this," shoving the flask in her face.

"I'll do no such thing. I've not the constitution for it, unlike you." Why did she add that last with his dangerous mood?

"Spunk, like her. You're of the same makin'." He dropped into chair, like a jack in the box, unsettled. Up, down. She breathed a sigh of relief wondering what made him nervous.

"You're of a mind ta blame me, aren'tcha."

A knot formed in her throat. Her brain screamed caution. "What I do know is Hector would not have killed my aunt."

"I'm your suspect, is that it?" His left brow rose as he glared at her, daring her.

"You don't have an alibi." His distance, though not great, made her feel more comfortable.

"Snoopy aren't ye. Suzette took my horn off that night."

Suddenly wary, she bit her lip trying not to mention that Kegan had inquired of Joyce Miller and discovered Mr. Edwards did not arrive at Suzette's room until midnight. The clock in the foyer had already chimed eleven within minutes of the deadly scream.

A big grin parted his fleshy pink lips. "Better if I'd been spent the night with you."

Ignoring his crudity, she snapped, attempting to goad him into revelations. "I believe the police need motive. What possible motive would you have, Mr. Edwards?" As she said the words, like lightening, his mask fell. Her mind raced with possibilities. He absolutely must have known Beatrice in Ireland. They had a past, perhaps fraught with loathing, or a fixation of some sort. She hoped her face wasn't mirroring her speculation and pressed fingertips to her forehead.

"What nonsense have you conjured in that copper head of yours?" This time when he stood and came at her, his large beefy hands fell to each side of the chair arms imprisoning her. "What do ye think ye figured out, me pretty little lass? Eh?"

"That I'm missing an appointment with Father O'Mara at this moment. You will have to excuse me. I mustn't keep him waiting." She expected him to take his hands off the chair, so she could stand.

"You'll not be goin' anywhere. Least ways without me." He uncapped the flask and shoved it at her. "Drink this or I'll pour it down your creamy little throat." Venom sluiced his command.

With a shaky hand, she reached for the flask. In one defiant move, she tipped it upside down and emptied the contents on her dress and his arm. His ham-like fist grabbed her upper arm, dragging her from the chair.

In a frenzy, he dragged her into Beatrice's bedroom. She screamed, and he slapped her across the face. She tasted blood and kicked at his legs. Throwing her on the floor between the bed and the wall, he placed his foot on her back as she struggled to get away; his size against her, and his abundant strength. She heard cloth tearing; next, he jerked her arms together, tying them behind her. He wrapped strips about her ankles, hobbling her.

Flipping her over, she screamed in terror as he shoved a length of sheet into her mouth and tied it uncomfortably tight.

He stood up to his full size, now that he secured her. "As I said, you're not goin' anywhere without me, lass."

He drew another flask from his pocket and drank. Swiping a wrist across his mouth, he said, "I think yer made of finer stuff than yer sister. We'll get on." Leering at her tied helpless and gagged, he winked at her. She banged her feet on the floor, and made a sound that didn't go anywhere, except inside her head.

He threw the coverlet from Beatrice's bed over her, and then slammed the door shut. Helpless, she lay there. If he wanted her dead, he would have done it by now. He wanted her drunk, like he wanted Beatrice drunk. What was she missing about him—them?

Surely, someone would come looking for her. Ruth. Dear Mother of God—Ruth was going to walk into this mess and what would he do to *her*? Likely, the same thing, and she tried to calm her breathing, tried to assess her situation. The stench of liquor was gross. She wiggled and fought the constraints to no avail; liquor was not the only thing assaulting her.

Not a sound came from the parlor. What was he doing? Had he left her? She did not hear the front door shut. Would he drink himself into a stupor? She could only hope.

Disgusted with herself, smothered beneath the blanket with the putrid stink of liquor, what made her think she could get a confession out of him?

*K*egan knocked on Lieutenant O'Flannery's office door, tried the knob, and entered. The room was empty. He returned to the front desk, inquiring of the sergeant on duty. "Is O'Flannery in?"

"Ran an errand. He'll be back soon."

"Is it possible to check in on Hector Smythe while I wait? I'm his lawyer."

The sergeant looked him over and satisfying himself grabbed a ring of keys. "Follow me."

They entered a long hallway, unlocking two different gates, rounded a corner, and the sergeant pointed to the second cell on the left. Kegan walked to it. Hector was lying on a cot and at sight of him jumped up. "Come to gloat?"

Kegan glanced back at the retreating sergeant, and then said, "Keep your voice low. I am your legal counsel as of now. How you are doing."

"Who's paying you?"

"You are when you get out."

"Pretty optimistic. They think they've a good case against me." He stuck his thumb in his chest.

"I might have uncovered some information that will shed light on another suspect. And, as I was in the building, I wanted to see how they are treating you."

Hector sagged against the iron ribs of the cell. "No one believes me. I set myself up pretty good. Wrong place, wrong time."

"Yes, I'd say as much." Kegan leaned close. "You do know Miss O'Quinn is off limits for you." More a statement than a question.

Hector took in a deep breath. "I always knew it."

"Then we are in agreement. And, for your information, she believes you innocent."

In amazement, he pushed away from the iron bars. "She does?"

"Right from the start. Said a lot of things about your earlier life, also said you weren't a murderer."

Hector's lips thinned out. "That means a lot after what I tried to do to her."

Kegan noted the handcuffed ruffian. "I should think so. She's a good woman to have in your corner."

Hector's chin sagged. He lifted his hands and swiped at his cheek.

Kegan said, "I sent a note to the Mayor saying I will handle your case if it comes to that. I do not believe it will. He told me to tell you that your job will be waiting for you when this all gets sorted out."

"I don't make enough to pay you." His gaze squarely on the floor.

"We'll figure something out, Hector. What I do know, if Miss O'Quinn thinks you are innocent, that's good enough for me."

From the end of the hall, the sergeant yelled, "Time."

Kegan nodded to Hector and spun on his heel.

By the time Kegan got back to O'Flannery's office, the lieutenant was at his desk. He shut the door and took the chair opposite the officer. "I've uncovered some information you need to know." He handed off the copies of immigration papers pertaining to Edward Molloy's entry to America and gave the lieutenant time to read them.

"What precisely are these saying to you, Mr. Galliger?"

"That he may have had motive to murder Mrs. Molloy. He never said he was from Ireland, in effect lying about that. He arrived in Manhattan ten days after Mrs. Molloy. I believe he followed her from Ireland. Drogheda to be exact."

The lieutenant stood. "You want me to haul in the man for questioning? Is that it? What would you expect me to ask him? Why did you not mention you are from Ireland?" He shrugged his shoulders in irritation, and possibly from overwork. The daily drudgery of human behavior that comprised his line of work never ended.

Kegan stayed seated, trying to keep a handle on his growing impatience. "Surely you see a discrepancy. Another fact, the night of the murder, he spent with a woman, Suzette. He went to her room near midnight, plenty of time to have murdered Mrs. Molloy at eleven."

"Kills one, and then beds another—all within an hour?"

Kegan tried to maintain his calm. "Like as not. I believe that's what the evidence points to."

"A prostitute is going to be your witness? She'd look good on the stand, would she not?"

Kegan scraped the chair as he rose. The lieutenant was as stubborn as they came and could not get beyond the collar he already made. He considered the case a slam-dunk. "I would like to think you more open-minded. An innocent man is going to be on trial and a murderer on the loose. You will be responsible for that." Kegan slammed his hat on his head, picked up his briefcase, grabbed the papers off the lieutenant's desk, and cast him an infuriated glare.

"And for your reference, I've been retained as Mr. Smythe's lawyer. Moreover, as long as you have him under lock and key, I want the handcuffs removed. Is that clear?" He stomped out of the office.

Like a petulant child.

He needed Aisling. She would be in school, or at the Infirmary. He considered stopping in at the rectory. What he finally decided to do was go to Mrs. Molloy's home. He dug out the address from his briefcase and told the driver, then got in his carriage and rewound the last twenty minutes with the lieutenant.

By the time the carriage stopped in front of Mrs. Molloy's rented home, he had a full-blown anger to vent. He was not sure what he would uncover. It sure beat twiddling his thumbs in his office.

When he knocked on the front door, no one answered. He recalled a maid would be in residence for a week or two. He knocked again and saw a shadowed movement through the curtain. Still, no one came to the door. He tried the knob and it opened.

Mr. Edwards stood in the hallway a gun in hand, pointed directly at him. "Didn't expect ye." He gestured with the gun. "Take a seat."

Kegan stepped inside and closed the door behind him. If anything,

Mr. Edwards holding a gun at him confirmed his worst suspicions. "You killed Mrs. Molloy, didn't you?"

At that moment, a thud hit the wall, then another, then another. Edwards growled, "Stop that, you little bitch." He banged the wall with his fist punching a hole in the board.

Wordless, Kegan set his briefcase on the floor and moved toward Edwards. The man's attention came back to Kegan. "Stop right there."

Kegan did as told when another thud hit the wall. It came from a room off to the side of the hallway. Another thud.

Edwards kicked open the door and yelled, "I tell ye ta cease."

Kegan lunged for Edwards' arm that held the gun. The man tossed him off as if he was a bug and sent him sprawling against the wall on his back. Kegan jumped up. "What's going on here, Edwards? What are you hiding?"

Edwards pointed the gun squarely at Kegan's head. "Get in there." He waved the gun into the bedroom.

Another thud. Someone under a blanket was hitting the wall. Petticoats ruffled around black shoes and two slender legs wrapped in woolen stockings and tied at the ankles. The maid?

Edwards grunted, disgusted like. "Pull the blanket off, then." He pointed the gun directly at the woman.

Kegan bent over and gently drew the coverlet off, gasping, "You're supposed to be in school!"

Aisling's golden brows scrunched together. She mumbled and hit the wall with her shoes. Rolling his eyes, he quickly responded by reaching behind her head to find the knot. Edwards did not tell him to stop, and he unbound her mouth, and pulled out the cloth. She gasped and took a deep breath. "You took forever."

With Edwards pointing a gun at his back, Kegan gave her a look that said *be careful.* Unbinding her arms, he rubbed some feeling back into her hands. He helped her to sit and unbound her ankles, then threw the blanket on the bed, helping her to stand. She stunk like a brewery.

At gunpoint, Edwards motioned them to sit in chairs in the parlor. Kegan wanted to grab Aisling's hand, when Edwards leaned against the wall and repositioned the gun directly at her. "One move and she gets it." He ground his teeth and planted his feet wide apart; an unsteady man wielding a weapon.

"You murdered Beatrice," Kegan growled.

"Earned it, the bitch did." Edwards' words slurred.

"How's that?"

"Killed me brother, poisoned him. Slow and sure over weeks until he died in his own vomit."

"Ian Molloy?"

Not taking his inspection from Aisling, his shoulders slumped, and he nodded.

"Can you prove that?"

Edwards' lips drew back, baring his teeth, and he gave Kegan a chilling look, like his eyes turned to ice. "A big, robust man, he was and not getting well, shriveling to a shell of what he was. She showed no concern for him. Proof enough. The bitch didn't like being tied to an old man. She poisoned him. Wasn't till she fled Ireland I found a bottle in her cupboard and took it to the apothecaries, had it analyzed. Arsenic, a slow, certain death. She left for America the day after he was buried." He pulled off the cap on his flask and gulped a mouthful. The gun still aimed on Aisling.

"You aren't going to get away with three murders, Edwards. Justice will be served." Kegan glared at him. He wanted to reach over and grab Aisling. The best he could do was keep the attention on himself. Defiance glistened in her eyes; she did not appear frightened, or cowed. God Bless her, he hoped she would have enough sense to keep quiet.

"What about me brother? What justice did he get? Gave her home, clothes. She was a rag mop when he wedded her, gave her his name, food. What about him?" Edwards was between a sob and a guttural roar. The hand with the gun wavered as he talked.

Kegan figured the navy Colt had six rounds. He had no way of knowing how many chambers were spent, and he was not going to goad the man into firing.

Aisling spoke up. "If her husband gave her so much, yet she did what you say, why do you think she would kill him?"

Lost in consideration, he shrugged with weary resignation. "I think I proved it since she was more than eager to have me take her places, buy her things. All I know, she killed him for money and moved here when he wasn't cold yet." He ground his teeth, his nostrils flared. "Taking me only family away."

Aisling knew what hurt, the words never again spoken by a voice you had heard your whole life, a face you looked at every day, your past gone with their memory of you as a small child. Her voice cracked when she asked, "Wasn't there an investigation in Drogheda? If you suspected her, wouldn't the police—"

His neck corded, teeth grinding. He shoved the Colt inches from her face. "They wouldn't listen to reason. Wheedled 'em with her slutty ways. It is how I knew to lure her. She likes men with money."

Aisling glanced at Kegan. "It is why you grew a beard and mutton chops, so she wouldn't recognize you?"

"Why I kept her drunk, too. She likes her drink, that one."

"Liked, Mr. Edwards? Remember, you killed her. She's gone."

Kegan threw a sour look at Aisling, his brow scrunched.

She did not say another word.

Edwards said, "Me dearly departed brother didn't deserve death. She got good as she gave." He pinched his nose with finger and thumb, possibly to squelch tears, his voice tightened with emotion. "An eye for an eye." Tears brimmed anyway. "Her fairy ways and dreams of fate didn't save her this time. Wasn't it perfect she died on a Friday the Thirteenth?"

Kegan threw himself the few yards between them and tackled Edwards legs throwing him off balance. The colt registered once, twice, three times, before Kegan fisted him in the face. Aisling jumped up, grabbed the poker from the fireplace, and hit him over the head with all her strength.

The gun dropped from his hand to the floor. An anguished cry came from him as he grabbed his head.

Kegan grabbed the gun. Two shots left. He held it steady on Edwards as the man lay on the floor holding his head in pain, blood dripping through his fingers.

### *Seven Months Later May 1866*

*M*r. Molloy's trial and conviction for involuntary manslaughter in the fourth degree was no longer newsworthy. The District Attorney's office had willingly accepted a plea for a minor offense. Much to Aisling's sense of fairness, this action was common in New York's legal system in the mid-1860s in cases of high crime.

With a vast degree of humility, Edward Molloy was deeply grateful for the narrow escape from the hangman's noose. He agreed to plead guilty to the lesser charge with the understanding, after his three-month incarceration, he would sail to Ireland and never set foot in America again.

Today, the Fifth of May, Aisling graduated from Miss Blackwell's nursing school, achieving honors in her studies.

With women beginning to earn medical degrees, an ancient rite of passage was renewed. During the Crusades, monks received a Maltese Cross for their efforts with injured and suffering crusaders.

Aisling earned her Maltese Cross in the form of a pin bearing the Red Cross of St. George, as part of her nursing degree.

The nursing pin was a great honor. Aisling glanced into the audience; lined up in the front row, Kegan, Mr. and Mrs. Galliger, Signey, and the dearest man in the world, Father Declan O'Mara. As the highest ranked student nurse in her class, she walked to the podium to give an acceptance speech.

Her love for Father and Mrs. Signey Pennino was the cornerstone of her three-minute oration. The two people whom she felt were the ones deserving recognition for their selfless love and caring for the past three years.

Miss Blackwell, seated on the platform, was the first person to congratulate Aisling after she stepped down. "What are your plans now that you've read volumes and studied into the wee hours all these years? I think you won't be missing it a'tall."

"You're right about that. I have an interview this afternoon. If it goes well, you will be among the first to know." Aisling smiled at her benefactor. To think a chance meeting of a neighbor, Miss Blackwell, the week she moved in with Signey, led her on this path.

After a peck on her cheek, Kegan reminded her, "Martha expects us at three." He followed the kiss with a brush of his fingertips across her cheek. "I'm bursting with pride." His blue eyes glistened with merriment. "I want so badly to take you in my arms and kiss you properly right now."

The blush he received was answer enough. Father and Signey were making their way toward them. The Galligers planned a late luncheon to celebrate her graduation. They would all be together, including Miss Blackwell. Kegan offered to drive them back to the rectory until the appointed hour when his carriage would return.

Aisling refused his offer. She preferred to walk. Kegan and she talked of this moment months ago and he knew where she headed. To the others she was rather mysterious and told them she would meet up at the Galligers in time for the festivities.

Aisling progressed south toward Fulton with a determined gait. She was more than ready to pursue her future. Since her arrival in lower Manhattan from Gettysburg, she had deliberately avoided the second ward. The memories of leaving her sick *máthair* always left her wanting. Her mission right now, she hoped, would ease the burden of that day in June 1860 when she was twelve and the matron caught her stealing.

She came to realize how that day changed the trajectory of her life.

Today, diploma in hand, she trekked on toward the Children's Aid Society and Miss Helberg's office. She intended to face her past head on.

The shock on Miss Helberg's face was significant. Aisling was quite sure the matron never dreamed of seeing her again after the night of the charity ball. Moving a stack of papers from a chair, the matron said, "Please sit down, Miss O'Quinn." She placed the arm full of documents on a shelf, and then took a chair opposite. "This is a real pleasure. Is there something I can do for you?"

Aisling smoothed her skirt. "I've come to apologize to you."

Clearly baffled, Miss Helberg said, "Me? Whatever would you have to apologize to *me* for?"

"Something I'm sure you aren't aware. The Charity Ball where you received an award for your dedication to the Children's Aid Society, you gave an acceptance speech. And, in that speech you had me stand, as you recalled a young girl who paraded as a boy and stole food because she was hungry."

Miss Helberg's gaze fell to the hands in her lap. It took her a moment to find her voice. "*You've* come to apologize? I should have apologized to you, six or seven months ago now, is it?"

"No. I have it right. I am the one, for the anger and rather vicious feelings that rose in me that night. Reminded of my poor upbringing, my bereaved parents over the many losses they incurred. It was difficult for my *athair* to step forward into his life in this country. His heart was broken. When he died, my *máthair*, with a young daughter to support, was overwhelmed. It was a tragedy, unfortunately not a singular one."

"My insensitivity—"

"Was the truth. That's what you shared, the truth. When I came back from Gettysburg, and Father O'Mara discovered who I really was and gave me the opportunity to become a young woman, it was like a butterfly leaving the chrysalis. I began to think I was somebody different, better.

"The reality is my parents gave me a future. They suffered and died young. They left their country behind, and any dreams they had of a life in Ireland, to give their children a better one. I take it especially personally because on that ship, I was a daughter born after the loss of five sons.

"I had no right to wallow in pity and shame because of my background. They crowned me with a name that means dreams or vision."

She spread her arms out, fingers wide, and shrugged her shoulders. "Who am I to deny my parents' vision for a fulfilling life? So, I've come to apologize to you for the ill feelings I harbored and to ask a favor."

Miss Helberg got up and rang the bell on her desk. Her secretary came to the door. "Tea for two, please, Ella." Then she sat back down. "If it is within my power, the answer is yes."

Aisling laughed. "We are going to get on quite well." She handed over her certificate of graduation from the nursing school. "I am now qualified to nurse and wonder if I might work in your girls' orphanage. I would especially like to be with children who are going to be on the orphan train."

"I am thrilled at the prospect of you working with these children. My answer is absolutely yes." Miss Helberg rifled in her desk drawer and drew out a yellowed envelope. She handed it to Aisling. "I think you'll enjoy this letter and what it has to say about you. Your former teacher, Miss Haslett wrote to me two or so years ago inquiring about a lad with copper-gold hair. His name was Alan O'Quinn. She wanted to know if I knew where he was now."

Aisling remembered the remarkable woman, and her ability to put Aisling at ease during the wagon train trip to York. All Miss Haslett had requested was for Alan to write to her. She reached for the envelope and said, "This is how you put together who I was at the ball, isn't it? It wasn't the color of my hair?"

Miss Helberg nodded with a glint of a smile crinkling her cheeks. "The color of your hair confirmed the information in the letter."

At three o'clock sharp, Aisling presented herself at the home of Mr. and Mrs. Galliger. The butler took her cape, hat, and gloves, saying, "Allow me to add my congratulations on your very honorable graduation." Surprised his face did not crack with the smile he gave her, she thanked him and followed his direction to the large parlor, a lovely, comfortable room she had been in several more times since the day of her aunt's burial.

Kegan's face spread into a lovely smile when the butler announced her. He set his punch down and came to her, kissing her on the cheek in front of everyone. She shied that he would be so intimate publicly, the second time today. Her glance quickly went to Father, who beamed, then Signey, her blue eyes twinkling. Miss Blackwell was engaged in conversation with Mrs. Galliger, they greeted her as she entered.

It was as if her eyes opened and she could feel what they saw; a young woman freed of sorrow, strong and independent—plucky. Something happened in Miss Helberg's office that allowed her to detect a future filled with promise and a life of fulfillment.

Kegan asked, "Can I get you a glass of punch?"

She nodded as the Galligers and Miss Blackwell approached.

Miss Blackwell took her hands and squeezed them. "I am so proud of you, as I daresay everyone in this room is. You set a task for yourself and achieved it. I count you as one of my stars."

Overwhelmed, Aisling blinked back a sting in her eyes. "Such a compliment, Miss Blackwell. I will treasure it always. And, to think none of this would have happened if a cat hadn't brought us together."

Signey chortled at that. "Lucy got out. Remember?"

Miss Blackwell said, "I believe I do. It was a chilly autumn day and your cat didn't have a key, so I had to take her in."

A joyful murmur spread among the others. They knew the champion of women's and children's medicine, a woman who had dedicated her life to nursing and the exemplary teaching of such, had given her seal of approval to Aisling.

Mr. and Mrs. Galliger waited until Miss Blackwell stepped back. Mr. Galliger said, "We wish to add our congratulations. You are an extraordinary young woman, Miss O'Quinn, one who has also captured the interest of my son. Though I'm not sure that is your greatest achievement."

The others chuckled, as did Kegan who passed a cup of punch to her and winked as he did so.

Mr. Galliger continued, "Martha and I wish to donate to some charitable organization in your name, to suitably recognize your earlier life and what we are all guessing might be your bright future. It will be your decision which organization."

She was stunned. Her hand holding the cup trembled. Kegan quickly retrieved it. "I...I don't know what to say." Tears welled up, and she took a deep breath attempting to quell her surprise.

It did not work, and she dabbed at her cheeks with fingertips until Kegan handed her a handkerchief.

Gaining control, she said, "I do know what to say. Such an honor. I guess this is as good a time to tell you..."

Father interjected, "Oh, oh. Here it comes."

Signey reached over and squeezed her arm. "We knew something was going on."

Aisling flashed them a big grin. "Yes, something has been on my mind, and I rectified it before coming here." Her gaze met Kegan's, and he nodded with pride flickering across his features.

"I met with Miss Helberg this afternoon. I asked her forgiveness for my anger toward her when she exposed my past. And, I asked her if she would allow me to work with the girls' orphanage, especially with those intended for the orphan train." Aisling shrugged her shoulders, palms up. "She hired me."

"Am I to understand this is the charitable organization you would like us to give the donation in your honor?" Mr. Galliger asked.

She nodded. Mr. Galliger reached for her hand, and gallantly placed a kiss. "You are a singular most lovely and decidedly determined young woman, Aisling."

Mrs. Galliger hugged her, and Aisling responded, "You are wonderful to think of this. Miss Helberg will be ever so grateful. Your goodness inspires me. It will bring care and comfort to the children."

The butler announced lunch, and they all walked in. Kegan placed Aisling's hand on his arm as they followed. He whispered, "It is all coming true for you. Which means for us."

She blushed. It crept beyond her collar, flashing on her cheeks. Her heart burst with happiness. This man had planted himself right in the middle of her life.

Once at the table, Kegan stood and raised his goblet. "I wish to ask a question of Father in front of this notable gathering."

With open surprise on each face, he knew he had their attention, as he stood in the center of the placement, Aisling directly across from him, he said, "Father O'Mara, I seek your permission to openly court Miss Aisling O'Quinn, with the direct purpose of a proposal once Aisling settles into her endeavors."

A hush ensued. Father stood, raised his own glass. "With my blessings, young man. With my most sincere blessings."

Kegan's twinkling blue regard shifted to Aisling. "I told you he would be agreeable."

Her heart so full, all the people who mattered surrounded her, tears gushed, and she busied herself swiping at them with the dinner napkin.

# HISTORIC MENTION

In 1853, Charles Loring Brace and a group of businessmen formed a new organization to help care for the neglected children of New York City. They called it the Children's Aid Society (CAS) with Mr. Brace as the First Secretary. This care led to the 'free-home-placing-out" of over 250,000 orphaned, abandoned, or homeless children between 1853 and the early 1930s.

Children, in groups of ten to forty, and under the supervision of at least one agent, traveled on trains to selected stops where families willing to foster looked them over. This effort was the precursor of modern day foster care.

Agents would plan a route, send flyers to towns along the way, and arrange for a "screening committee" in towns where the children might get new homes. All towns had to be along the railroad line. When a child was placed, a contract was signed under the condition the child was schooled during the winter months until eighteen years of age.

The first group of children went to Dowagiac, Michigan in 1854, and the last official train ran to Texas in 1929.

By 1860, over 30,500 miles of track had been laid and eleven railroads met in Chicago, enabling the CAS to place children throughout the country as it could be reached by rail.

At one point, ten thousand vagrant children lived in eleven wards in New York City. Over three thousand children, of whom two thousand were girls between the ages of eight and sixteen were regularly trained to thieve.

New York was unable to deal effectively with the tides of immigration that tripled the city's population. Industrialization and the Civil War induced adversity and encouraged epidemics such as cholera, typhus, trachoma, and favus.

Delinquents, prostitutes, beggars, and drunkards dwelled in contaminated tenements and rat-infested slums. Five Points was one of those slums, and the most notorious.

Sixteen thousand criminals were arrested in 1853 in New York, one fourth were less than the age of twenty-one, and eight hundred were under fifteen.

For more reading on this sad issue in American history, you might Google orphan trains; Wikipedia; The National Orphan Train Museum in Concordia, Kansas (which maintains records and houses a research facility.) In addition, The Children's Aid Society in New York has an historical archive.

A number of authors have also written about the orphan trains; there again, if you Google, you will note the references.

All the characters in this novel are fictional, however the circumstances are not. Aisling O'Quinn was an unusually fortunate young lady.

# ABOUT THE AUTHOR

Karen Dean Benson gained a love of history from travels that took her into many different cultures around the world. A voracious reader from an early age, she loves research, history, and tales of complicated lives. Her stories, woven against the backdrop of a by-gone era, present numerous plot twists. Her *Ladies of Mischief* blunder through attempting to live within the social constraints of the 18th and 19th Centuries.

She and husband Charlie divide their time between golf courses in Michigan and Florida.

*Karen loves to hear from her readers!*
www.karendeanbenson.com

 facebook.com/karendeanbenson

ALSO BY KAREN DEAN BENSON

WITH SATIN ROMANCE

*Women of Mischief*
Devil's Grace: Renn Arelia's Story
Mission Song: Chenoa's Story
Mulberry Bend: Aisling's Story

*Short Stories*
From Florida With Love, Sunsets & Happy Endings
From Florida With Love, Sunrise & Story Skies